D0834947

"You would really die before letting my brother go, wouldn't you?" she asked in a wondering voice.

"It's my job."

"It's more than that. It's your damned religion," she said furiously.

He shrugged. "If I don't bring him in, a bounty hunter will kill him. Is that what you want?"

"It doesn't have to be you," she said, hating the tears that were suddenly welling up in her eyes.

"Why not me, Lori?" His voice had gentled, and his eyes were roiling with emotion. She didn't know whether he was baiting her, whether he was angry, or whether he was wanting her as badly now as she craved him. His head had lowered slightly, and somehow she had raised herself on her tiptoes. Their mouths were too close, much too close.

Heat was building inside her. And fear. How could desire and hate be such close traveling companions?

Then she didn't think at all, because their lips met, and she was lost in a flood of sensation that had no reason.

WANTED

Patricia Potter

BANTAM BOOKS
NEW YORK • TORONTO • LONDON • SYDNEY

WANTED

A Bantam Book/ November 1994

ISBN 0-553-56600-8

Published simultaneously in the United States and Canada

Bantam Books are published by Bantam Books, a division of Bantam Double-
day Dell Publishing Group, Inc. Its trademark, consisting of the words "Bantam
Books" and the portrayal of a rooster, is Registered in U.S. Patent and Trademark Office and in other countries. Marca Registrada. Bantam Books, 1540
Broadway, New York, New York 10036.

PRINTED IN THE UNITED STATES OF AMERICA

OPM   0 9 8 7 6 5 4 3 2 1

WANTED

PROLOGUE

West Texas, 1844

A scream of agony came from inside the adobe building.

John Davis felt the cry vibrate through him. Rivulets of sweat ran down his body and soaked the back of his rough cotton shirt.

He wasn't a praying man. But as he searched the hot, dry country outside the way-station compound, he prayed as he had never prayed before. A few hours, God. Only a few hours.

He looked at his friend, Ranger Callum Smith, who had galloped in on a horse now heaving with exhaustion.

"The Comanches are raiding this whole area," Cal said. "You have to get the hell out of here."

"Susan . . ."

John didn't have to say anything else. Another scream did it for him.

"Christ, John, but she picked a poor time for birthing."

John wiped his forehead with his bandanna. He had to do something; he didn't like feeling this helpless.

He had quit rangering because of Susan, because Susan had worried herself sick about him. Ten months ago the Overland Stage Company had offered him the job of managing this way station on the mail route. It was a chance to build a home and a future, and he had taken it because he could finally spend time with his wife, and the children who were at last on their way.

And now . . .

The Comanches hadn't come this way in over ten years,

not since the Ranger post had been established twenty miles away. But its manpower had been drained in the past months, most of the Rangers having been pulled down to the border, where Mexican bandits were laying waste to the new settlements there.

"I've got to go," Callum said. "I have to warn the settlers. But I'll get back as soon as I can."

John nodded. "I'll saddle you a fresh horse. You get some water from the well."

Callum nodded as another scream came from the house.

"How long . . . ?"

John shook his head. "Labor started late yesterday. Month early. Thank God some woman on the stage agreed to stay over."

He hurried to the barn, remembering how he had planned to take Susan to El Paso in three days, to the nearest doctor in a hundred miles. But then the pains had started just as the stage arrived. The lone woman passenger, a pretty but sad-looking woman dressed in black, offered to stay and help. Fleur Bailey, she'd said her name was, and she was returning home to Ohio after having lost her husband and two-day-old child.

Now she was in danger too. John cursed the Comanches, cursed himself for bringing Susan out here to this desolate place, as he finished saddling the pinto. He decided to get the wagon ready, too, so they could leave for the Ranger post as soon as the baby was born.

He watched as Callum mounted the pinto, gave him a brief salute, and spurred his horse into a gallop, disappearing quickly in the endless tall grass of the prairie. With any luck, John thought, by the time Callum returned from alerting the Kelly and Marshall families, he and Susan and the baby would be gone.

The baby. His child. He prayed again, then went back to the barn for two horses to hitch to the wagon. He set the other horses loose. He didn't want them trapped inside if there was an attack.

He heard the loud plaintive cry of a child.

Thank God, he thought gratefully. Perhaps prayers were answered after all.

He hurried to the cabin and opened the door. Fleur was holding a small bundle, a look of possessiveness on her face. He felt sudden apprehension, but then the woman smiled so sweetly at him, he immediately dismissed the momentary fear.

"A boy," she said as she cleaned the newborn with a wet cloth. Then she handed him to John, who stood awkwardly, feeling like a giant holding a baby bird.

When Susan screamed again, the woman stooped down over her and then looked up at John with a wondrous expression. "Dear heaven, there must be another."

Astonished at the unexpected news, John held his child as he listened worriedly to the continued groans and cries of his wife. Then there was one last scream, part agony, part triumph. Fleur, a stranger no longer in this most intimate of all dramas, straightened, holding a child. "Another boy. Twins."

John leaned down and kissed Susan, placing the first baby in her arms as Fleur cleaned the second one. She stopped in the middle of wiping one of the tiny feet. "Birthmarks," she said. "Almost like half hearts on their feet, one on the left, one on the right."

That observation meant little to John Davis. All that mattered was that his children were healthy despite the fact that they had come early. Now he had to make sure they stayed that way. He took Susan's hand in his. "Are you strong enough to move?"

Her blue eyes widened slightly in question.

"A small renegade bunch of Comanches," he said. "Probably nothing to worry about, but you and the babies would be safer at the Ranger post."

She swallowed. Her face was smudged from sweat and tears, and she looked tired, but she gave him a weak smile and nodded.

"I'll put a mattress in the buggy," he said, watching as her fingers ran over the older twin.

"Morgan," she whispered. They had already settled on that name if the baby was a boy. But the other? They hadn't expected him. Something to brag about at the Ranger post. Papa. At forty-three, he had become a papa twice over!

He knelt next to the bed and moved aside the brightly colored rug there to reveal a trapdoor. Below was a room he had made himself. Eight feet long, six feet wide, and five feet deep, it served several functions: a fruit and cheese cellar, a storage area for mattresses for those occasions when stagecoach passengers stayed overnight, and a hiding place in case of Indian or outlaw attack. The wood trapdoor was underlaid with layers of tin to protect the occupants from fire.

He carried two mattresses to the buggy, a double layer to make his wife more comfortable on the jolting ride.

When he returned, Fleur had diapered one of the babies. "You take the twins," John told her. "I'll bring my wife."

But Susan refused to relinquish the child in her arms. "I want to hold him," she insisted.

He turned to Fleur. "Can you take your valise and the other child?"

She nodded and quickly grabbed her valise. She had caught John's urgency. In the two days she had been there, she had learned that he was not a man who frightened easily. She had lost one husband and a baby. She didn't want to lose the one she held in her arms. The child felt so good. Just as her own son, Nicholas, had such a short time ago.

She nearly ran to the wagon, where she set the baby down and stowed the valise. She'd barely climbed in when the horses stamped nervously. She lost her balance and fell, just as she heard the sound of hoofbeats and a godforsaken yell.

She gathered the infant in her arms and ducked down

underneath the seat. The wagon moved as the horses tried to pull loose from where they were hitched. She thought about returning to the cabin and peered through a crack in the wagon. A dozen or more painted Indians were racing toward her. She would never have time. She could only hide here and hope they didn't find her.

"Don't cry," she whispered to the child. "Please don't cry."

There were shots then. So many shots. They seemed to surround her as she huddled deeper under the seat. And then she heard the snorting of the horses, felt the jerking of the wagon, back and forth at first, and then wildly. Somehow the horses had gotten loose.

With one hand she clutched the seat while with the other she held on to the baby. The wagon swayed and rocked as it hurtled across the prairie, and Fleur desperately tried to keep from rolling over on the infant. The shots faded behind her, and she concentrated her whole being on protecting the child, the little boy so much like her own.

She didn't know how long the wagon plunged across rocks and indentations. It seemed forever. And then there was another jolt and the wagon careened even more wildly. She knew the horses had broken free of the traces and that she and the child were passengers aboard a runaway vehicle.

The wagon hit a deep rut and stopped abruptly, and she was thrown against one of its sides, but the baby was pillowed by her body. Agonizing pain stabbed through her shoulder, but she managed to lift herself slightly to look up. The way station was no longer visible, but she saw smoke coming from its direction. So much smoke that the sky was dark with it.

She saw no savages, but they might be coming soon to look for the wagon, for the horses. That was what they wanted. She'd heard the Rangers talk about that.

She took the baby and crawled from the wagon. They

were in the middle of nowhere, but there was tall prairie grass here. She could hide. She and the baby.

He whimpered, and she pressed him to her. Nicholas. "I'll take care of you," she whispered, knowing that the others in the cabin must be dead. This baby was a gift, sent by God for her to protect, to take the place of her own boy.

John Davis knew he was going to die. His blood had turned cold when he heard the first Comanche yell. He ran to the door, estimating whether he could reach the wagon; more than likely, he would be caught in the open and Susan and Morgan would have no protection. He had to leave the woman and the other child in the wagon. Thank God she had moved out of sight.

He slammed the door and went for one of his two rifles. It was too late to hide in the cellar; the wagon and smoke from the chimney told only too well of someone's presence.

He broke the glass in the window, aimed, and fired. He hit one of the Comanches, then another. As they drew back, he looked over at Susan, who was now sitting up in the bed, clutching the baby. He laid the gun next to the window, moved swiftly to the trapdoor, and pulled it open. He reached for her.

"No," she said. "Put the baby in there, but I won't go. I can load for you."

He hesitated, then saw the determination in her eyes. He knew that look. If he forced her down, she would be back up immediately. He simply nodded, thinking how lucky he was, how lucky he had been, to be loved by her.

Maybe that luck would hold. If he could only hold out for an hour, if Callum could gather others . . . He put the small wrapped figure of his child in the cellar, holding him tightly for a moment first. Morgan. His firstborn. He rubbed the small dark fuzz at the top of the baby's head, and then shots intruded on that very short time of tenderness. He lifted himself up, closed the door, and replaced the colorful rug.

He turned around and saw that Susan had taken the other gun and was trying to aim it. But her hands trembled. John took it from her, his blue eyes holding hers for an instant before he looked out the window once more.

He saw the wagon horses pull free from where they were hitched and watched as the wagon went careening across the prairie. His distraction ended immediately when a bullet plowed into his chest. He heard Susan's cry, felt her arms go around him, and then there were more shots. He felt another pain, then the weight of Susan's body as it slumped on his, her blood mixing with his blood.

His last thought was of the babies. "God keep them safe," he prayed as his life emptied on the floorboards.

Callum Smith found the baby in the cellar. He had warned the two remaining families and accompanied them to the Ranger station, where one small unit of Rangers had returned from the border.

Five of them rode hell-bent for John Davis's place, only to find ashes—and two corpses burned beyond recognition. Disregarding the lingering heat from the fire, Callum went to the trapdoor, hoping against hope that he would find someone alive.

His glove protected his hand from the heat that remained in the tin. He and another Ranger pulled until it finally came off, and he heard a weak cry from within.

He lowered himself and found the tiny mewing bundle. The air was hot and stuffy, and he wondered at the newborn's will to live.

Callum picked the child up awkwardly. John had told him he intended to name the baby Morgan if it was a boy, after one of their old commanders in the Rangers. He swallowed. Neither John nor Susan had any family. What would happen to the little tyke? He handed the baby to one of the other Rangers, then climbed up.

If only they had arrived sooner, he thought as he took back the baby. If only . . .

He looked at the two embracing bodies. What had happened to the other woman? Probably taken by the Comanches. She had been pretty, blond. The kind the savages preferred in white women. The Rangers would look for her, but he didn't hold much hope. White women didn't last long with the Comanches, and he suspected this small group of renegades would head to Mexico now that the Rangers were back.

The baby. Callum felt responsible. He had let down his friend. His fellow Ranger. He couldn't let the child go to an orphanage. He owed John and Susan. He would take the baby and somehow raise it. Maria, his housekeeper of sorts, could take care of the child whenever he was gone. He would raise him as John would have liked.

As a Ranger.

Two days. Maybe three. Fleur Bailey stumbled along the rutted road. Her milk was drying, the milk that had remained in her after her baby died. The milk that kept Nicholas alive.

She was thirsty and hungry. Her left shoulder hurt like the devil, but she had to keep going. She had to find help.

She heard the sound of a wagon, and she dropped to the ground. She had become wary, afraid that the Comanches would come, or that someone would take her child from her. Her Nicholas.

She listened as the heavy wagon came closer and she could see the words on the gaudily decorated sides. DR. BRADEN'S MIRACLE MEDICINES.

A doctor. She crawled on the road, clutching the baby, and heard a shout, heard the sound of a team being pulled to a halt. She was tired, so tired. And safe.

Her eyes closed, her body finally succumbing to the

shock and exhaustion and fear of the last few days. She didn't even wake when a small man, less than four feet tall, scrambled over to her side. Nor did she feel the arms of the taller man, his dark eyes curious and compassionate, as he picked her up and carried her inside the wagon, while the small man followed with her son.

She wasn't aware of her mutterings, of her scrambled words about Comanches and a dead husband. All were dead, she said. All but her son, Nicholas.

CHAPTER ONE

Wyoming, 1876

A Texas Ranger's face had no place on a wanted poster!

Not for the first time, Morgan Davis pulled out of his pocket the wrinkled piece of paper, stared at the features sketched there, which were so like his own, then folded and replaced the poster. Every time he looked at it, his blood boiled.

He turned his gaze down toward the cabin that sat on the bank of a creek below. After eight weeks of trailing Nicholas Braden, he had finally tracked him here last night to Medicine Bow in southeast Wyoming. Braden *and* his sister, dammit. Morgan had been watching both of them move around outside the cabin since early morning.

When the two had first appeared, Morgan swore softly, reluctantly deciding to bide his time until exactly the right moment. It had taken him two months to locate Braden. A few more minutes didn't matter.

Morgan's hand went up to his face. After being mistaken for Braden several times, he'd decided to grow a mustache in pure self-defense. But he hated the damn thing. He hated being forced to change his own appearance because of a killer. Days of traveling had added even more bristle to his face, and he felt like one of the renegades he'd chased over the past fourteen years. He rubbed his cheeks, despising the feel of roughness, the dust that clung to him.

His outrage had grown when he'd observed that Braden had not felt it necessary to disguise himself. But it was that very carelessness that would be his quarry's downfall. Braden apparently believed he was out of the law's reach. He hadn't counted on Morgan's persistence.

Three months ago Morgan's life had suddenly changed radically from that of hunter to hunted. Three months ago the first bounty hunters had accosted Morgan.

He'd been returning to the El Paso Ranger station after spending four hard weeks tracking a group of cattle rustlers. He'd stopped for the night at a spring when two men rode up. Morgan had been suspicious. Hell, he'd been raised to be suspicious, and nothing in his fifteen years as a lawman had moderated that attitude. But with hand on his pistol butt, he'd extended prairie hospitality, offering to share his coffee. He hadn't liked the two strangers, but, then, he liked few people other than his fellow Rangers. He had a core-deep distrust of his fellow man, and there was a coldness in the newcomers' eyes that bespoke of an occupation Morgan despised. If they weren't gunfighters, he'd eat his well-soiled hat.

None of them talked much, except to discuss the hellishly hot weather. Morgan wasn't wearing his badge; he often didn't when he wasn't on duty. He didn't like attention. He didn't want people remembering his face. He worked undercover frequently, and he'd learned the value of anonymity. Only his eyes were memorable—a rare, deep indigo-blue—and he tried to hide them by wearing his wide-brimmed hat low on his forehead. He also often added an eye patch, which distracted attention from the distinctive color of his uncovered eye.

The three men had retired early, but something had nagged at Morgan, and he'd dozed lightly. In the late hours of the night the two strangers had made their move, and Morgan had heard the cock of a pistol. But Morgan had been faster.

Both were killed immediately. Morgan didn't make mistakes. He went through their pockets and immediately found the reason for the attack. The promise of a five-thousand-dollar bounty. A fortune! His eyes skimmed the drawing, visible in the bright light of a full moon. He stiffened. He might as well be looking at himself. He read the text slowly and carefully.

WANTED
NICHOLAS "NICK" BRADEN
For the murder of Wade Wardlaw of Harmony, Texas

There was a sketch, then a description:

Six feet tall, dark-brown hair, dark-blue eyes, 180 pounds
Rides bay horse
$5,000 Reward
DEAD OR ALIVE
Contact Lew Wardlaw or Sheriff Nat Sayers,
Harmony, Texas

Hell, Morgan thought, the description fit him. The face might as well have been his, and he too rode a bay horse. The five thousand dollar reward would have every bounty hunter in the west gunning for this Nicholas Braden. Few bounty hunters had scruples. They wouldn't give a damn if they had the real Nicholas Braden or not, as long as they had a dead body with that damned face. There was only one solution, he realized, and that was to find the real Nicholas Braden and return him to Harmony, Texas.

Morgan had heard that every man had a look-alike. But the likeness in this case was uncanny. Perhaps it was only the drawing. Perhaps in person the resemblance wasn't that close. He knew Braden couldn't be a blood kin. Morgan was an orphan, the only child of a couple who had been killed by Comanches immediately after his birth.

He had pocketed the drawing, buried the two bounty hunters, and returned to Ranger headquarters, where he'd requested the job of seeking out Nicholas Braden and bringing him to justice. It was the first favor Morgan had ever asked, and it was readily granted.

He had not left his troubles behind in Texas. The

poster had followed Morgan along his trail. He'd had encounters with two other bounty hunters. One he had wounded and left with a sheriff in a small mining town; the other, a man named Whitey Stark, had finally been convinced that he had the wrong man. At least he'd *acted* convinced at the wrong end of Morgan's rifle.

Morgan pinned on his Texas Ranger badge—not that it meant much in this territory. But he wanted no mistakes; he wanted Braden to know he was the law.

He wanted to take Nicholas Braden alive.

Usually Morgan wasn't that particular. A killer was a killer. Morgan had little remorse when he was forced to shoot one, and he never aimed to wound. A dead man couldn't shoot back. It was one of the first lessons he'd learned. But Morgan had no wish to carry a corpse hundreds of miles back to Texas, even though the alternative meant a long, hard journey with a live prisoner.

The only thing stopping him from cornering Braden now was the young woman. He didn't want a female involved in possible gunfire.

He surmised the woman was Braden's sister, even though they didn't look one bit alike. Lorilee Braden had honey-colored hair, and he imagined her eyes were that peculiar golden brown shared by her father and other brother, Andy.

Morgan had tracked the family first, hoping they would give him a lead as to Braden's whereabouts. And they had. He'd overheard them talk about Braden's ranch in Wyoming. He'd also learned from others that Braden had shot an unarmed kid in Harmony and that the entire Braden clan operated a small medicine show that traveled back and forth through Texas and Colorado. Con artists, that's what they were. Wherever they went, rumors followed of card cheating, shell games, selling little more than alcohol as medicine cure-alls.

Morgan loathed the fact that he was mistaken for one of them. It was a situation he intended to correct.

Soon.

Surprisingly, the sister stuck with Braden most of the morning, working alongside him as they completed a corral that they would probably never use. She had tied her long hair at the nape of her neck with a ribbon and wore men's trousers. He'd never seen a woman in trousers before, and he was surprised at the reaction of his own body at the sight of the slender body so neatly outlined.

He shouldn't be surprised, though. From what he'd learned of her, she could tempt angels down from heaven.

The sun was high in the sky when the woman went inside the cabin and Nicholas Braden rode off on a horse, a rifle in its scabbard on the saddle. Going hunting, Morgan surmised. There would be a lot of game here. Morgan had never been this far north, and the area looked like God's country. He'd never seen grass so plentiful. The hills were blanketed with it; nothing could have been so unlike the arid prairies of west Texas.

He waited fifteen minutes, then moved down the hill where he'd spent the night. He left his horse, Damien, tethered above, along with his rifle. The six-shooter should be enough. He had already fastened a pair of handcuffs to his belt; leg shackles and another set of wrist irons remained in his saddlebags. He'd learned the hard way to carry sufficient restraints for taking reluctant prisoners back to justice.

A wisp of smoke spiraled up from the chimney of the cabin as he snaked silently along the newly constructed fence. Additional timber lay in piles nearby.

Morgan reached the door, and his left hand went out to determine whether it was bolted from the inside. It wasn't. He pushed the door open abruptly, moving quickly to fill the doorway, his six-shooter leveled in front of him.

The woman spun around from where she was standing in front of a table, evidently cutting something. A knife in her hand caught the light from the sun suddenly flooding the cabin.

Morgan didn't move. He allowed her to take in his gun, the badge he wore on his shirt. His hat was pulled down and with the sun behind him, he knew she couldn't see him clearly. The new bristle covering his face would also hide the resemblance to her brother, temporarily at least.

To his surprise her eyes were fearless. And they *were* golden-brown, almost amber with flecks of gold. He saw that clearly enough.

He also saw that she was furious!

And she continued to hold the knife.

"Put it down," he said softly in his most intimidating tone.

She ignored the order. "What do you want?"

"Nicholas Braden," he said. "And I don't want trouble from you."

Her eyes went back to his badge. Morgan saw her swallow, watched a number of emotions move swiftly through her eyes. Then calculation. "Texas Ranger? Why . . . ?"

Morgan admired her composure—but, then, he should have expected it. He'd heard that she'd often played poker, that she was good at it. He'd also heard she cheated.

Obviously, she had learned to control her emotions, which he thought highly unique in a woman. She didn't scream or cry or plead, all the reactions he usually encountered when taking a fugitive.

He moved farther into the cabin and tipped his hat back so she could see him better. He wanted to startle her, so he could reach out and grab the knife.

He saw her eyes focusing on him, saw them widen suddenly. Her hand faltered for a moment, and he made his move, grabbing her wrist. The knife fell under the relentless pressure of his hand.

But just as he started to ease up, her booted foot stamped down on his and her knee jerked up to his crotch. Morgan felt an agonizing pain. He was barely aware of her moving toward the gun that had fallen from his hand with that blow.

He cursed himself for being careless, and, disregarding the agony that assaulted his lower body, he grabbed her waist just as her hands reached the six-shooter on the floor. The shot echoed in the cabin, and he realized that she'd meant to warn her brother. He wrested the gun from her and tugged her hands behind her; then he pulled her close to him, using his own legs to pin hers tightly together, to prevent another kick.

"Goddammit, lady," he said. "You might just have gotten Braden killed with that stunt."

Morgan felt a certain tension in her body, and he knew she was going to try something again. "Don't," he said. "Don't even think it."

"Or?" she taunted him. "Do Rangers kill women, or do they just hunt men for bounty?"

"You know about the bounty?"

"Why else would you come all this way?" she retorted. Those golden-brown eyes were pure fury. There was nothing soft about them.

"I have my reasons, and it's not bounty," he said, unexpectedly stung by her accusation, even as his hurting body made him wonder why he gave a damn about what this she-devil thought. What in the hell would he do with her? He couldn't stand here like this all day, holding her body trapped against his.

When she started twisting, trying to move away from him, he held both her wrists in one hand and took his bandanna from his neck. He quickly tied her hands behind her, then turned her around so her back was against his chest. She couldn't kick him again, not with any strength, in that position.

"Where did he go?" he demanded.

She was silent, though her body tensed into one furious package. Like a stick of dynamite, Morgan thought.

"You sure do want to get him killed, don't you, Lori?" he said, purposely using her name to throw her off balance.

Her back just stiffened even further. Her body was so tense, so seemingly brittle, that Morgan thought she would easily break into a dozen pieces if he made a sudden move. But her silence was maddening, her defiance purposely goading, as if he weren't worth a single word, a single glance.

Morgan sighed. He'd known this wasn't going to be easy. It was never easy to take someone with kin around, but he'd never encountered a woman like this, one who so readily defied a man so much larger and better armed than herself. He had hoped . . .

Hell, he didn't know what he'd hoped. He only knew what he had to do now.

He gazed around the cabin, looking for what he needed. There was a man's shirt hanging on a peg in the corner. That would have to do.

Holding on to her bound wrists, he moved over to the peg, forcing her to follow. He took the shirt and momentarily released her while he reached down swiftly and picked up the knife she had dropped.

She turned, watching him with those hostile golden eyes, as he cut the shirt into strips. She obviously sensed what was coming, because her jaw set stubbornly, and her wide mouth firmed into a straight, angry line.

She was tall, but the top of her head still came below his chin. She had to look up at him, and he felt the waves of enmity radiate from her. Strands of her honey-blond hair had come loose from the ribbon during their brief struggle and fell alongside her face.

"Open your mouth," he ordered, balling a piece of material in his hand.

She didn't say anything, refusing to give him the opportunity to stuff the gag into her mouth. She just stood there and looked at him, her lips firmly pressed together.

He shrugged. "We'll do it the hard way, then."

Just then her leg reached out again for his one still-aching vulnerability, but this time he was ready and stepped back. She was barely able to regain her balance, but she did so, and stood quietly.

Morgan didn't kid himself. If he tried to force her mouth open, she would bite. This woman was oblivious to the fact that she was bested, by strength if nothing else.

He was irritated by the admiration he was beginning to feel for her, and damned annoyed she was making things so confoundedly difficult.

How long before Braden returned? If he had heard the shot, he would probably be back by now. At least that was one thing that hadn't gone wrong.

"I want your brother alive," he said, "but if you make that impossible, I won't hesitate to kill him. Do you understand that?"

She nodded.

"Then open your mouth, Lori. Or so help me God, I'll leave you here hog-tied, and you can yell as much as you want. I'll just wait and ambush him as he rides in." He paused, allowing the words to echo in the room, in her mind, then added, "I don't miss, Lori, and I don't shoot to wound."

At the blatant threat to kill her brother, her eyes measured him and openly found him contemptible. But even as her gaze burned holes through him, there was a question in them. What would he do if she did as he ordered?

Did she really care for her brother that much?

"I want him alive," Morgan said again.

"And then what?" she asked suspiciously.

"I'm taking him back to Texas for trial."

"That's a long way."

Morgan didn't say anything. Texas *was* a long way. A lot of things could happen between Wyoming and Texas— but not if her brother was dead.

"He didn't murder anyone," she said suddenly, an unexpected plea in her face.

"That's not my affair. My job is taking him back."

"Lew Wardlaw owns that town. Nick won't have a chance."

Morgan shrugged. Everyone was innocent.

"You don't even care?"

"A judge and jury decide that."

"Not in Harmony."

He realized she was stalling for time and he forced himself to look away from her golden-amber eyes. God, a man could get lost in them. It would do him well to remember that this particular flower had sharp thorns. The pain in his crotch made remembering easy.

"Enough, Lori. Open your mouth."

"You won't . . . kill Nick?"

"Let's just say his chances will be a lot better if you cooperate."

Morgan saw acceptance settle in her eyes. But not surrender. She had simply weighed the odds and folded on this one hand, hoping she would have a stronger hand on the next go-around. He warned himself not to underestimate her. Not now, not in the future.

She opened her mouth, allowed him to place the ball of cloth in it, and then bind it with a strip of fabric from Nick's shirt. He took her arm, leading her out of the cabin into the woods behind it. He found a likely tree, strong but not too thick, and forced her to sit, first tying her ankles together and then her already bound wrists to the tree.

For the first time Morgan sensed fear in her—and it wasn't for herself. He couldn't guarantee that he would take her brother alive and he wouldn't make a promise he might not be able to keep.

It all depended on Braden now.

Lori frantically tried to undo the strip of cloth that tethered her to the tree. She'd already worked at the gag and given up, telling herself not to panic.

She hated the man who had forced this upon her, had made her obey him. But she hadn't doubted for a moment his threat to shoot Nick. One look at those cold blue eyes, and she had believed. Dear God, she had believed. The Ranger's eyes were hard and merciless in a way that she had seen before in lawmen.

She'd run into two kinds of lawmen: the corrupt ones and the ones who wore righteousness like a cloak. She detested both.

If only Nick survived the day, she could find a way to free him. No way could this bastard take her brother all the way to Texas, not with her on his trail, not if she could get word to Papa and Andy and Daniel Webster, her papa's best friend.

All that would be unnecessary, though, if she could free herself and warn Nick. But the knots that the Ranger had tied so easily wouldn't give. The more she tried, the more secure they became.

She leaned back against the tree, trying to think. Could her muffled attempts to warn her brother be heard? Or should she just wait until she could take the lawman unaware? Dr. Braden's Medicine Show had once employed a trick shooter as a prime attraction, and both she and Nick had practiced with him. Nick had been twenty, she only ten, but she'd had good eyes and a natural talent for it, and her budding skill had made her a prime attraction with the show. She had continued practicing over the years, for self-defense and simply because she enjoyed target shooting, doing something she excelled at.

The Ranger knew her name. She only hoped he didn't know some of the rather unusual talents she had, that both she and Nick had.

She thought only fleetingly of his similarities to Nick. They had startled her at first. She had tried to keep her surprise to herself, not wanting to give anything away to a man she instinctively knew would use any weakness. But the familiarity had been unsettling. The color of the deep-set eyes, the facial structure, the wide mouth. She wondered if the Ranger's beard hid the same indentation in the chin that Nick had.

She tried the bonds again, tensing her wrists, feeling the cloth cut into her flesh. The Ranger had handcuffs with him; when he hadn't put them on her, she'd immediately realized he was saving them for her brother.

She couldn't bear the thought of Nick going to jail, or worse, being hanged. The Braden family had never had much money—their father usually ended up giving away what little they brought in—but they'd always had one another, a deep affection and loyalty binding them firmly together. There had never been any neighbors or friends, because the Bradens constantly moved from one town to another. Only Daniel Webster, a dwarf who had a giant's heart, and an occasional entertainer often down on his luck, had been taken in and accepted as part of the family.

Nick had always been the conscience of the family. He had participated quite willingly as a boy and young man in their father's small cons, but lately he had been trying to get the family to settle down. The west was changing, he'd repeatedly said. Law and order were coming. The life they had lived was no longer feasible. People were now questioning the "miraculous medicine," and the Medicine Show was barely surviving.

But Jonathon Braden was reluctant to give up his gypsy ways, and his wife was totally devoted to him and supported him in all things.

Now Nick was paying the price. Nineteen-year-old Andy had fallen in love for the hundredth time, but this time he chose the daughter of the most important man in town where they had stopped for several weeks. The brother went after him with a whip, and Nick was forced to face him. The boy was killed in a fair fight, but Nick had known there would be trouble. Wade had been Lew Wardlaw's only son. His pride. Everyone in town knew that.

Nick had convinced Jonathon to head toward Denver, their home base, and Nick had planned to disappear. Then Lori learned that Nick had been charged with murder, and she went after him to warn him. She had stayed with him, much against his wishes. But there had been no use in forcing her to leave him. She would just follow.

They had made it safely to Wyoming and thought themselves safe there. No one knew about this land, except the Bradens. Nick had staked it out years earlier when the Medicine Show was in Wyoming, and he left the show each winter to work on a ranch house, which he hoped to use as a lure to the rest of the family.

He had loved the days spent there, the hard physical work of building something. So, to her surprise, had she. After years of living by wits, it had been paradise to accomplish something lasting. She was finally beginning to understand what had attracted Nick to this life.

But somehow the Ranger had tracked them.

Lori felt sick as she thought of the trap awaiting Nick.

She fought even harder against her bonds. And for one of the few times in her life, she prayed.

Nick Braden looked forward to a good rabbit stew. Lord, but he was hungry, and Lori was a good cook.

He'd been furious when Lori had followed him to Wyoming, but since they had arrived at the ranch three months ago, she had proved to be invaluable, first in helping him complete the cabin and now with the corral. And she was a cheerful companion, seldom complaining except good-naturedly.

It had always seemed a miracle to him that ten years after his own birth, his parents had had another child, Lori, and then a third, Andy. He'd wondered aloud once why Lori and Andy were so fair when he was dark. His mother had quickly explained that he must have taken after her father's side of the family, the dark Irish, while Lori and Andy resembled their father's Viking ancestors. Because Nick's question seemed to distress his mother so, Nick never mentioned it again.

The cabin came into view, smoke curling pleasantly from the chimney. He had already dressed the two rabbits caught in snares he'd set yesterday, and Lori would have baked fresh bread. This afternoon they would finish the small corral and start a makeshift stable. Winter wasn't far away. There was so much to do to prepare for it, but every time he viewed this land, he felt a new surge of optimism.

He'd yearned so long for a place to call home. He wanted to make it a home for the whole family. The gunfight a few months ago had made him realize how much. He had almost died then. If he'd been a second slower . . .

Regret rushed through him. Wade Wardlaw had been little more than a kid, but he'd given Nick no choice. Wade was going to kill Andy, who was no match for him, so Nick had stepped in, even though he'd never been in a gunfight before. He hadn't even known whether he could actually shoot another human being; he hadn't known until he had done it.

He tried to push the feeling away, though he knew it would always be with him. Nick had done a lot of things as a kid, conned and cheated and even stolen, but he'd never felt as if he'd really hurt someone, taken from someone who couldn't afford it. And now, feeling the responsibility for Andy and Lori, he was trying his damnedest to mend his ways.

The cabin looked peaceful, welcoming. He spurred his horse into a trot and rode up to it. As he tied the horse to one of the new fence railings, he felt its sturdiness with no little satisfaction.

He strode to the door, smiling. Lori would be pleased with his catch. She excelled at rabbit stew, using wild chives and potatoes and the spices she hoarded.

He opened the door and stopped suddenly. Instead of Lori, he found himself looking at a man sitting relaxed in one of his chairs, a six-shooter pointed straight at him.

The man's face was covered with a week's growth of beard, and a mustache sat above his lips. Nick had once grown a mustache, then shaved it off.

But he realized in that split second that if he had allowed it to grow, he might well have been looking at himself in a mirror.

And he saw that same, stunned knowledge in the cold, hard eyes of the man holding a gun on him.

CHAPTER TWO

Morgan studied the other man with wary interest. He had known from the poster, of course, that Nicholas Braden resembled him, but he hadn't expected a likeness this remarkable.

Braden was probably five pounds heavier, his hair a little longer. While more tidily cut than Morgan's, it curled slightly in the same unmanageable way.

Most startling was the color of Braden's eyes, almost the same dark indigo-blue under thick dark eyebrows. Morgan had more lines around his, engraved there by many hours in the sun, and his mouth had a harder look to it, a slight twist that reflected his own deep cynicism. Braden's eyes appeared a degree lighter, but that might have been the light in the room, and they were more curious than cynical. His skin wasn't as weathered, as sun darkened as Morgan's, and Morgan noted instantly that Braden wore his gun on the left rather than the right, as Morgan did.

But other than those slight differences, seeing Nicholas Braden was like looking in a mirror. An involuntary shiver snaked down Morgan's back as he registered all the details. He could almost believe kinship if he hadn't known it impossible. He had the odd feeling that he was about to arrest himself.

He shook the notion from his mind. "Drop those rabbits on the table," he said curtly, "then your gunbelt."

Braden didn't move. "Where's my sister?"

"The little hellion? Safe enough, Braden, if you do as you're told."

Anger flushed Braden's face. "If you've hurt her . . ."

"You're in no position to make threats," Morgan said, his gaze lowering for just a second to his Colt Peacemaker.

"Who in the hell are you?"

"Morgan Davis. Texas Ranger. And now you have five seconds to drop that gunbelt."

Morgan watched as Braden hesitated, obviously weighing his options and finding them wanting. Morgan half expected to find the rabbits thrown in his face, and he prepared himself for just such an attack.

Finally Braden carefully set down the rabbits and unbuckled his gunbelt, lowering it to the floor. "Lori?"

"Like I said, safe enough." Morgan stood. "Step away from the gun."

"What are you going to do?"

"Take you back to Texas."

Braden's face darkened, his body tensing. "I've dropped the gun," he said grimly. "Now where's my sister?"

"Safe," Morgan said. "Not far from here."

Braden moved a step toward him. "You haven't hurt her . . ."

"I think it's the other way around," Morgan said ruefully, moving the gun slightly in warning. He threw the pair of wrist irons over to Braden, who let them drop to the floor.

"Pick them up and put them on." Morgan's voice was like the handcuffs he'd thrown—hard, merciless.

Braden eyed them as a man might look at a rattlesnake.

"Do it, Braden. I don't have to take you back alive."

"I'm worth as much dead as alive, am I?" Braden said bitterly.

"Five thousand dollars, either way." Morgan watched Braden's face pale. Apparently the man hadn't known.

Braden's gaze didn't falter, though, didn't move away from his. Morgan realized Braden was no coward. Nor a fool. He was weighing Morgan, just as Morgan was weighing him.

Braden finally spoke after digesting news of his worth. "Why don't you just have done with it now?"

"I don't fancy traveling with a corpse for weeks," Morgan said, "but give me trouble, and I'll endure it right enough. Now lock those handcuffs on, and we'll go see how your sister is making out."

Something flickered in Braden's eyes. Then he picked up the irons and fastened them on himself. The chain between them was no more than twelve inches, having been made to Morgan's specifications.

Morgan rose slowly and holstered his own pistol, then picked up Braden's gunbelt and draped it over his shoulder. "First," he said, "we'll fetch my horse and then see to Miss Lori."

Morgan wasn't proud of using a woman as a weapon, but he soothed what reservations he had by assuring himself his plan was easier on everyone than killing Braden.

He prodded his captive again. "Up that hill."

Braden hung back. "What's a Texas Ranger doing in Wyoming?"

"In case you haven't noticed, Braden, it's my face on that poster as well as yours, and I've already had to kill because of it."

"My life for yours, is that it?" Braden said bitterly.

"*You* killed that boy, I didn't."

"That boy was a man aiming to murder my brother."

"So you murdered him instead." Morgan made his voice deliberately contemptuous. He saw no need in continuing this conversation. His only job was bringing the man in. "Get going, Braden."

Braden moved slowly, obviously testing him, his forbearance, his alertness.

"The longer you take," Morgan said, "the longer your sister is going to be very uncomfortable." He was learning what motivated his prisoner, what prods to use. What would he use tomorrow? Or the days after, when the sister was gone?

Braden picked up his pace, Morgan's hand guiding him toward his horse. He wished he could have left Braden in the cabin, but there was no lock on the outside of the door, and nothing in the cabin to which he could have handcuffed Braden. And it was possible this short trip might give him some measure of the man without the disturbing presence of his sister.

The thought of her was not welcome. What in the hell was he going to do with her?

He couldn't leave her out here in these hills alone, though she seemed capable enough of taking care of herself. Too damn capable, he thought.

Laramie was a day away. He would take her there, put her on a coach to Denver. The rest of the Braden clan had been heading in that direction.

When they reached Morgan's horse, Morgan took the reins in his hands and they started the downward trek. Braden was being cooperative, but Morgan had had a taste of Braden-family resistance, and he knew his prisoner was just waiting for an opportunity.

When they returned to the cabin, Morgan tied his horse next to Braden's similar-looking animal. A pretty little palomino mare was enclosed in the new corral. The sister's horse. Golden and graceful, the mount suited her. He wondered briefly whether it was as spirited as its owner, then chided himself for that moment of fancy. He would be rid of her tomorrow, and in any event, she hated him. He had no doubt that she would continue to hate him.

Morgan had little experience with women other than the soiled doves he and his fellow Rangers patronized. He was always on the move, never in any place long enough to develop any ties. He had none of the social graces decent women required. He had been raised in a rugged, dirty cow town by a succession of Rangers, and he'd received little formal education.

His practical education, though, was unparalleled. He could shoot the eye of a rabbit from two hundred yards, follow any trail of man or beast, live off the land for months at a time, and fight as dirty as any low-down horse thief. His sense of honor revolved totally around his fellow Rangers and duty. He was a Ranger through and through, never wanted to be anything else, couldn't even comprehend an alternative. He'd served as deputy, then sheriff, in lawless Texas towns during the years the Rangers had been disbanded after the war, but he'd just been waiting. He knew the Rangers would be reactivated. There had never been a force as close-knit, as effective, as the Rangers.

And arresting Braden was like any other job, except he had a personal interest. Seeing his face on a poster had been, by God, an insult to all he was. He had little sympathy for the man responsible for it.

And he damned well didn't like the way his attention kept going back to the little spitfire who was sure to make the next twenty-four hours hell.

As if his prisoner read his mind, Braden balked at moving again. "Where's my sister?"

"In back," Morgan said. He led the way to the tree several yards behind the cabin. The two prisoners saw each other at the same moment, and Morgan noticed her gaze resting briefly on the handcuffs before she glared at him.

Braden walked over to his sister, stooped down, and awkwardly pulled the gag from her mouth. "Are you all right?"

Morgan leaned back against a tree lazily and watched every movement, every exchange of silent messages between the sister and brother. He felt a stab of longing then, a regret that he'd never shared that kind of caring or communication with another human being.

Braden tried to untie his sister, but obviously he was

having trouble maneuvering with the handcuffs. Morgan heard a muffled curse and saw the woman's face tense with pain.

"Move away," Morgan said to Braden. Again Braden hesitated.

"Dammit, I'm not going to keep repeating myself." Irritation and impatience laced Morgan's words.

Braden stood, took a few steps away.

"Farther," Morgan ordered. "Unless you want her to stay there all night."

Braden backed up about ten feet, and Morgan took his place beside Lorilee Braden. Using a knife from his belt, he quickly cut the strips of cloth binding her. Unfamiliar guilt rushed through him as he saw blood around her wrists. He hadn't tied her that tightly, but apparently the cloth had cut into her skin as she struggled to free herself.

He put out his hand to help her up, but she refused it and tried to gain footing by herself. But her muscles had apparently stiffened, and she started to fall.

Instinctively reaching out to help her, Morgan dropped the knife, and he saw her go for it. His foot slammed down on it, and her hand went for the gun in Braden's gunbelt.

"Dammit," Morgan swore as he spun her around, his hand going around her neck to subdue her. From the corner of his eye he saw Braden move toward him. "Don't," Morgan said. "I might just make a mistake and hurt her."

All rage and determination, she was quivering against him, defying him with every ounce of her being.

Braden had stopped in midstride, anger darkening his eyes. "You do real well against women, don't you?" he taunted.

Morgan had always had a temper—he felt ready to explode now—but his voice was even and cold when he spoke. "You'd better tell your sister to behave herself if she wants you to live beyond this day." When his arms tightened around her, she wriggled to escape his hold, and his body reacted to the feel of her against him. It puzzled him. It infuriated him. He didn't like what he didn't understand, and he couldn't understand his reaction to this she-cat. She was trouble, pure trouble, but a part of him admired her, and he despised that admiration as a weakness in himself. "Tell her!"

"Lori."

Braden's voice was low but authoritative, and Morgan felt her relax slightly, then jerk away from his hold and run to Braden. He watched as Braden's handcuffed hands went over her head and around her, holding her as she leaned against him. A criminal. A killer.

A rare wave of loneliness swept over Morgan, and for the first time in his life, he felt intense jealousy and a longing that nearly turned him inside out.

"Touching scene," he observed sarcastically, his voice rough as he tried to establish control—of his prisoners and of himself.

He tried to discipline his own body, to dismiss the lingering, flowery scent of Lori, the remembered softness of her body against his. She was a hellion, he warned himself, not soft at all, except in body. He'd already underestimated her twice. He wouldn't do it again. He would get rid of her in Laramie.

But still his eyes couldn't move from the brother and sister. He couldn't remember ever having affection or softness in his life. There had been curt nods when he'd done something right, but never a gentle touch. And now he recognized a hunger for tenderness, one he'd never acknowledged before, and it angered him.

"That's enough," he said. "I want to get going."

"What about my sister?" Braden asked. "She can't stay here alone."

"We'll ride to Laramie. I can put your sister on a stage there to Denver. I believe that's where your family was headed."

"How in the Sam hill did you . . . ?" Braden stopped. The Ranger had found him. He had known Lori's name. He obviously was good—very good—at hunting men. It was something to remember.

Morgan shrugged. "Move," he said. "I want to be on the trail in an hour."

Lori had slipped from under her brother's handcuffed wrists and faced Morgan. "I'm not getting on any stage. I'm going with you."

"The hell you are."

"You can't stop me."

"Oh, yes I can, Miss Lorilee," he said curtly. "There's bounty hunters on my trail, and it's a damn long way. I don't need any added complications."

Her chin went up, her legs braced stubbornly. Her eyes, all amber fire raked him. She was daring him to defy her, and Nicholas Braden was looking on with amusement, an amusement that did not improve Morgan's temper.

"We've wasted enough time," he said. He turned to Lori. "You can get his bedroll together. Two blankets. One change of clothes. Rain slicker. Coat. Tin plate. Cup."

"And what can I take?" she said acidly.

He raised an eyebrow. "A dress, perhaps?" His tone was purposely insulting. He didn't want to feel what she was already stirring in him. He never felt emotions where his job was concerned, had never allowed them. That had been schooled into him since he was a tadpole, more thoroughly than his letters.

Her gaze turned to her brother, and there was another silent exchange that Morgan didn't understand. Then she turned back to him and gave him a blinding smile he sure as hell didn't trust. "Perhaps I will take a dress," she said.

Morgan remembered the tales he had heard of her. The charmer. The come-on for fake medicine. For card cheating. The smile had a powerful effect as heat surged through him, lingering where it shouldn't.

He stood there, feeling like a fool, rooted to the ground as he tried to control the uncontrollable. It was an unfamiliar experience, and he sensed Braden's amusement grow stronger. There was a reckless streak in Nicholas Braden that irritated Morgan. He sensed that Braden took few things seriously, whereas he, Morgan, had always taken everything seriously. He wondered which way was the wisest, but only for the briefest of moments.

He was what he was, and he felt no need for change. "Ten minutes," he said. "And we'll be riding out of here, with or without supplies for him." He nodded his head at Braden.

The Bradens moved then. Morgan followed them into the cabin and ordered Braden to sit. Morgan didn't want both prisoners moving around a cabin that might contain some kind of usable weapon.

Morgan watched intently as Lori packed a bedroll, then took a small metal object from a shelf and moved toward her brother.

He intercepted her, confiscating the object in her hand. A harmonica.

"Surely you can't object to that?" Her voice was disdainful.

Morgan looked over to Braden. "Do you always let her do all your talking for you?"

Braden smiled and winked at his sister. "She does pretty well."

Morgan shrugged, tossed the harmonica to Braden, who caught it easily in his manacled hands. He tucked it into his shirt pocket without comment.

"And you, Miss Braden," Morgan said, turning toward Lorilee. "A violin? Guitar?"

"Oh I just sing, Ranger . . . ?"

"Davis, Morgan Davis," Morgan responded grimly, aware of the challenge in the room. They were both testing him. He didn't like it one bit. "And, Miss Lori," he said with some sarcasm of his own, "I think you have five minutes to gather your belongings, or you'll go just as you are if I have to tie you over a saddle."

"Whatever you say, Ranger," she said sweetly, leaving him with the exact knowledge of what arsenic-laced sugar must taste like.

     •   •   •

They didn't stop until well past nightfall. Even then Morgan was reluctant to bring a halt to their journey. He knew he would get no sleep tonight with the she-cat along.

He had placed her with her brother on the same horse, and had strung that horse and the pretty little mare on leads. Using the second pair of handcuffs, Morgan had fastened Braden to his saddle horn, giving his hands little room for movement. Lori was seated behind Braden's saddle, and Morgan knew she must be sore from riding the horse's backbone. Her head had drooped to the back of her brother's shoulder.

The arrangements were not the best, but Morgan feared that if Lori rode her own mare, she would try to get the reins of her brother's horse and make a run for it. He didn't plan to give her that opportunity, or any other.

Morgan found a stream and called a halt. He dismounted and tied his horse to a tree, then took the leg irons from his saddle bags. He went over to Braden's horse and offered Lorilee a hand, but she refused it, slipping gracefully from the back of the horse.

"Stay where I can see you," he told her curtly. With a movement of his head Morgan ordered Braden down, his hands still locked to the saddle horn. When his prisoner was on his feet, Morgan quickly attached the leg irons before releasing Braden from the saddle.

Nick Braden said nothing, his face revealing little, but Morgan sensed the anger and tension in him as strongly as if it were his own. He didn't understand the bitter frustration that pounded at him, the frustration Braden must be feeling. It was almost as if he were in Braden's mind rather than in his own, and *he* was feeling a sense of outrage, of helpless fury . . . when he should be feeling satisfaction.

He had no use for con men, for killers, and Braden was both of those. Morgan had never been purposely cruel to a prisoner, but neither had he ever been concerned about one's comfort.

But now . . .

Damn Braden and his sister.

Morgan's voice was harsh when he finally spoke. "Get accustomed to it, Braden. It's routine."

Braden's eyes flashed his anger, the blandness gone. "You don't give a damn whether I'm guilty or not, do you?"

"No," Morgan said flatly. "That's not my job."

"Neither is leaving Texas. You have no jurisdiction here. You're just as bad as those bounty hunters you mentioned."

Morgan shrugged, not acknowledging the thrust that hit its target. "Think what you want." He went back to his horse and started unsaddling it, ignoring his two prisoners. When he was through, he turned back to them.

Lorilee had moved over to her brother and was studying his handcuffed wrists in the moonlight. "He's bleeding," she accused.

Morgan unlocked the cuff on Braden's bloody right wrist. "You can use your bandanna to wrap it," he said.

He unsaddled Braden's horse and gave his prisoner the reins to both the Bradens' horses. "Water them," he ordered, knowing that the man wasn't going anywhere with the leg irons and that he probably could use a few moments for his private needs. He watched as Braden shuffled awkwardly toward the stream; then Morgan turned his attention to Lorilee, who was also watching her brother, dismay and concern making her face even more expressive, more striking. "You can gather some wood for a fire," he said.

"Go to hell," she said; and the bite was not in the words themselves, but in the almost broken way she said them. Her eyes were bright, too bright, almost shimmering in the moonlight, and he knew she was holding back tears. The glimpse of her silent pain hurt even more than that kick she'd given him earlier.

Even killers have family . . . people who care about them. It doesn't change what they are, Morgan thought. And he knew he was right. He was a lawman. Lawmen didn't allow emotions to interfere with duty.

Hell, he didn't even have any emotions, he told himself. He was just tired. And it was going to be a sleepless night. His eyes studied her, and he saw her straighten, her back stiffen with pride. Her eyes still glistened, but she made no attempt to wipe them. She simply radiated mutiny.

"It's going to be cold," Morgan said mildly. "I'll be staying awake, so I don't care that much, but Nick . . ." He used the shortened name on purpose, just as he had used hers. It showed his control and authority. He could do anything, say anything, and the Bradens could do nothing about it.

He watched her swallow hard to keep from retorting, her fingers fisting at her sides. He sensed the content of her internal debate. Was it worth fighting him now when he was alert? Or should she wait? She didn't want to wait. She would have happily killed him at the moment, and he knew it.

"You enjoy this, don't you?" she finally said through clenched teeth.

"No," he said softly, surprising himself with the admission. It lost him some of that control, but despite his better judgment, he didn't want her thinking him an unfeeling monster. "No, I don't enjoy it, but that doesn't make any difference."

"What would make a difference?" Her voice had softened. It was an offer, pure and simple, and Morgan felt his gut tighten. She hated him. He could see it in her eyes, yet for her brother's sake she was offering herself to him. He felt as if a knife had been thrust into him and twisted. He turned away.

"Nothing, Miss Lori, and I don't think your brother would have liked hearing that last question."

"What do you care?"

Morgan faced her. "Is there anything you wouldn't do to free him?"

"Do you have a sister?"

He shook his head.

"A brother? Anyone?"

He didn't answer this time, just stood there, a bleakness washing around him, a loneliness so strong he couldn't move, couldn't think, couldn't reply. The silence answered for him, and a flicker of understanding crossed her face, then disappeared. She turned away from him and started picking up twigs, branches. She didn't look at him again, merely gathered up the makings of a fire.

In an hour a fire was going, and Morgan had spitted the rabbits Braden had trapped earlier. A pot of coffee sat on the edge of the fire, and the flames hissed and sizzled with the juices of the cooking meat. Lori had bandaged both of her brother's wrists, and they sat together, the two of them united against Morgan.

Nick took the harmonica from his pocket and started to play. He was good, and the mournful ballad that permeated the night air with sorrow increased Morgan's own sense of isolation. Occasionally the two men's eyes would meet, would question, would duel. And Morgan felt that odd kinship again. It was only that Nick Braden resembled him, he told himself. And then Morgan would find Lorilee's gaze on him, studying, weighing, judging.

After a silent dinner Morgan tethered Braden to a tree. He knew he should tie the girl, too, and he walked over to her, taking his bandanna from his neck, intending to use it. But when he took one of her wrists, he saw the dried blood from earlier, and he sighed. His eyes met hers, and her chin lifted, almost daring him to bind her again. She even put her two wrists together in front of her.

"Go ahead," she said, "if you're afraid of me."

Morgan felt like a damn fool for the second time that day. "Not likely, Miss Lori," he said grimly. "Children don't frighten. They're just damn nuisances."

Her eyes glittered, but she managed a smile. "Do you still hurt, Ranger?" she said with feigned concern.

He did. But he sure as hell wasn't going to let her know it. "Hell, I've been hurt more by a mosquito," he said.

Her smile broadened wickedly, and Morgan realized she didn't believe him. She had known exactly how much she had hurt him. That realization did not improve his temper. And he wasn't going to give her the satisfaction of feeling important enough to be trussed up.

"Go to sleep," he said flatly.

"You're not going to tie me?"

"Don't test me, Miss Lori. You weren't tied up long enough today to know exactly how uncomfortable it can be."

"As my brother knows?"

He didn't answer. Nick Braden was going to be very uncomfortable before this journey was over, but that wasn't Morgan's concern.

"Damn you," she said quietly, and turned away from him.

"Miss Braden," Morgan said, and this time there was no mockery in his tone. She turned around. "I'll be awake tonight, so don't do anything you or your brother might regret."

"I wouldn't dream of it," she retorted.

He watched as she undid both her and her brother's bedrolls and helped Braden wrap himself in the blankets. She leaned down and whispered something to him, and in the moonlight Morgan saw a slight smile come to his face. Morgan's gut knotted, and he felt like the outsider he'd always been. He realized Lorilee Braden thought she had gotten the better of him, and perhaps she had, but only because he had allowed it. He simply didn't have the heart to bind her tonight merely because she was loyal to her brother. She had committed no crime, done nothing wrong, and he appreciated loyalty, even when it was misplaced. And Christ knew he had gone without sleep before for lesser reasons.

He continued to watch as she lay down on her own bedroll several feet from Nick and a noticeably long way from Morgan. She was still almost immediately, but Morgan sensed a feigned sleep. She would wait, hoping he would fall asleep.

Morgan tucked his rifle next to him and leaned against

the tree, watching fragile clouds scurry across the sky, sometimes eclipsing the moon, throwing the camp into darkness. He had stayed awake many a night when tracking outlaws or Indians, or as a scout during the war. He enjoyed the stillness and innocence of a night sky. He thought of it as innocence—a pure, pristine beauty unsullied by man's greed or anger or hate.

He had tried to explain the feeling once to Callum, his father's friend who had been his principal instructor. Callum had only laughed. Night, he said, is a breeding ground for evil.

But Morgan never thought of it that way. It was one of the few disagreements he'd had with Callum.

Morgan's eyes returned to Lorilee. He wondered what Callum would have thought of her. But Callum, the closest thing he'd had to a father, was dead, and the night, brilliant and beautiful as it was, was going to be damnably long.

CHAPTER THREE

Impatience nibbled at Lori. Then it began to gnaw in earnest.

He had to go to sleep!

Huddled underneath the blanket in the cold night air, she slowly opened her eyes, allowing them to adjust to the darkness before turning ever so slightly to where the Ranger had settled.

He was still sitting, the rifle resting on the ground near his right hand. His head was leaning against the tree, but she sensed an alertness about him. Lori gritted her teeth.

"Can't sleep, Lori?"

She sat up, knowing it was foolish to feign sleep any longer. She stared at him . . . hard. In the moonlight his face looked even darker. Everything about Morgan Davis was severe and harsh. Lori wondered if he even knew how to smile, and then she recalled the bleakness in his eyes when she had asked about a family.

He hadn't understood. He would never understand how she felt about her family, how Nick felt, and that gave her one advantage over him.

"No," she finally replied. She moved close enough to him to talk without raising her voice. Perhaps she could make him understand that Nick was innocent, that he didn't have to be chained. She looked over at Nick, and she sensed he was listening. He wouldn't be sleeping, not trussed up as he was. "Can't you at least take off those leg irons?"

The Ranger shook his head. "No," he replied flatly.

"Why? He can't go anyplace with his wrist chained to that tree."

He peered at her, and his eyes seemed almost black now, dark holes she couldn't penetrate. Yet she felt an odd, irritating familiarity. Because he resembled Nick? She didn't want to think about that. She didn't want to believe he and her brother had anything in common, other than a few facial features that meant nothing at all.

He just shrugged. "He seems to be doing all right."

"You don't know him."

"You're right, Miss Lori. I don't know him. I don't want to know him. I don't need to know him. Now, I would advise you to get some sleep. We have a long ride tomorrow, and I won't be slowed down."

"What about you? Don't you need sleep?"

His lips twisted in a mirthless smile. "I've gone as long as three days without sleep, Miss Lori, when I'm tracking someone. And I plan to get some in Laramie, since you're so concerned over my well-being."

Lori shifted slightly at his sarcasm but made no move to return to her bedroll. He raised an eyebrow, then allowed it to settle slowly back into place with lazy indifference. She saw his body tense, though, and she knew he wasn't as indifferent to her as he tried to appear. But, then, neither was she.

Something was happening. She didn't know what. She didn't know why. But she felt little knots of heat flame in odd places and move along her blood, like prairie grass in a fire, tumbling across the plains, igniting everything in its path.

She struggled to speak, to ease the sudden stiffness in her throat. She'd always been able to charm. She knew she wasn't beautiful, but laughter and smiles came easily, just as they did to Nick, and she'd discovered they more than made up for any physical lack. But the few smiles she'd directed his way hadn't seemed to work on the Ranger. Even now his expression was wary, suspicious. It had to be five hundred miles or more back to Harmony. Five hundred miles of rough terrain, of mountains, valleys, and rivers. Indians. Outlaws. The rest of the Braden family, if she could locate them and send word.

And sleep. Eventually there had to be sleep. The Ranger might consider himself an iron man, but no one could go weeks without sleep, without lowering his guard. He had made a mistake in not tying her. He didn't know that, but she did. If he couldn't do it tonight, he wouldn't be able to do it tomorrow night, or the next, and then . . .

He might think he was going to leave her in Laramie, or put her on a stage, but she knew otherwise.

"I'm not concerned about your well-being at all," she said honestly. "I'm just curious. Have you tracked so many men?"

He shrugged. It seemed to be his usual response.

"How many?" she insisted.

"Why do you want to know?"

"Know thine enemy," she responded quickly with a whimsical smile that usually softened the most difficult of men. She had found that honesty disarmed much more swiftly than subtle methods.

"Smart," he said. "Is Nicholas that wise?"

"Know thine enemy?" Lori's retort was quick, and she saw a hint of appreciation in his eyes before it disappeared just as quickly. "He *is* your enemy," she said softly, "just as I am. You'll never bring him back to Texas." She hesitated, then tried reason once more. "He really is innocent. That was a fair fight in Texas. Don't make him—or me—do something we don't want to do."

"And what would you do, Lori? How far would you go? Would you kill? Or do you just maim?"

"What do you think?"

His dark, hard gaze seemed to impale her. "I think you'd better get some sleep."

"You didn't answer me before," she said. "How many men have you hunted?"

"Enough," he said flatly.

"Do you have trophies?" she taunted. "Locks of hair? Notches on a gun? Do you enjoy being a hunter?"

Lines tightened at the edge of his mouth, and the glow from the fire gave his eyes a dangerous glint. "Go to sleep, Lori."

Lori felt her heart skitter oddly. It was a new feeling and she didn't understand it, not at all. It spurred her anger. "Don't call me Lori. Only people I like call me that."

"I didn't ask you to come sit here. I assumed that indicated . . . a brief cessation in hostilities," he replied dryly, letting her know he thought no such thing. His words irritated Lori, as did everything about him. The way he looked like Nick. The way he sat with Indian stoicism. The way he created strange, hot sensations in her. The latter most of all. He had no right.

"You aren't really going to try to leave me in Laramie?" she asked.

"I'm not going to try anything," he said stiffly. "I'm going to do it."

"What about my horse?"

"I'll make arrangements."

"There are laws against horse stealing in Wyoming."

"There are also laws against attacking lawmen."

"You're not here as a lawman," she accused. "You just want the bounty."

"I don't give a damn about the bounty," he said, something more than irritation in his voice. Lori sensed she had hit a nerve. She wondered exactly how sensitive it was.

"Then why . . . ?" Nick had said nothing to her this afternoon—not about the Ranger's reasons, or motives, or Nick's own intentions. The Ranger had always been too close, always listening. She studied his every feature now, particularly the eyes. "You look like him," she said, "but you're nothing like him. You don't have his heart."

A muscle tensed in his jaw, and he looked away. And then she saw the dimple, that same ridge in his chin that Nick had. It had been hidden before by the new beard, but it was visible when he turned his head at a certain angle. "Dear God, but you do look like him," she whispered.

"Enough that three men tried to kill me, and several others are on my trail," he said roughly.

She frowned. "Is that why you came all this way . . . ?"

His silence answered for him.

"You could almost be brothers. . . ." Lori stopped. It was impossible. She knew it was impossible. Nick was *her* brother, just as Andy was. It was impossible and unfair. Morgan Davis had tracked down her brother simply because they looked alike.

"More than a few bounty hunters would be glad to substitute me for your brother and bring me in dead," the Ranger said. "But he's not my brother, and I'll be damned if I want to look over my shoulder the rest of my life because of something he did."

Lori was silent for a moment, digesting his words. "You'll sacrifice him to save yourself," she accused bluntly.

The Ranger's lips thinned. "He murdered a man, Miss Braden. And then he ran."

"Because he had no choice. They would have lynched him. And it was a fair fight."

"Then half of Harmony's lying. I've already been there."

"And you've tried and convicted him," Lori said heatedly.

"I told you that's not my job."

"But that's what you'll be doing. You'll be the killer then."

"I've never arrested a guilty man yet," he said wearily. "There isn't one who didn't swear he was innocent."

"You never believed them?"

"Once I did," the Ranger said bitterly. "He was like your brother. Had a pretty young thing with him, said she was his wife and was pregnant. She pretended to have a miscarriage, and he grabbed my gun when I was trying to help her. He put three bullets in me. Probably would have put three more if he hadn't heard riders coming and lit out. Left his wife there. I found out later she wasn't his wife, wasn't even pregnant. She was just some saloon girl he took up with several days earlier."

"Did he get away?"

"Then he did," the Ranger said shortly.

"Then?"

"I got him eventually."

"Where is he now?"

"Do you really want to know, Miss Lori?" His voice was almost gentle. Almost but not quite. That one moment of gallantry years ago apparently had robbed him of any compassion or trust he might once have had, Lori thought. Or had there been other moments of betrayal as well?

"How long have you been a Ranger?"

He looked surprised at her abrupt question. "I joined the Rangers in sixty-one."

Lori was startled. "You must have been very young." He looked several years older than Nick. The very harshness of his expression made him seem a decade older, and there were lines in his face that Nick didn't have. Still, the hard leanness of his body, the restrained energy in him, told her he couldn't be that much older.

She waited for an answer.

But Morgan Davis's face closed completely. "Know thine enemy," he observed, a curious half smile on his face.

That hadn't been the reason for her comment. She had simply become intrigued by him during their conversation. She'd always been able to draw people out, with her keen ability to listen. Listening was the key, her father had always told her. But this time listening had trapped her, too. There was an intensity in him that somehow spoke to her in a way nothing else ever had. Equally as interesting was that quality of aloofness about him, a sense of isolation that touched something inside her, even as she told herself she had to hate this man. Trick him. Use him. Even shoot him if necessary.

She tried not to let her own feelings show, her sudden reluctance to leave. "Know thine enemy," she confirmed as she stood and went back to where her bedroll lay. She felt her brother's eyes on her, even though he lay in the shadows. He had been still. Too still.

Lori covered herself with the blanket, wrapping it tight against her. She felt chilled. Chilled and alone. She would no longer try to keep from sleep. *He* wouldn't sleep. She knew it now. But he would be tired tomorrow.

Very tired.

Nick clenched his teeth as the Ranger unlocked the cuff chaining him to the tree. The lawman's eyes were weary, but he seemed just as cautious as he had been the day before. He had lost none of that sharp edge that seemed a primary part of him.

Nick fought the urge to swing a fist at Morgan Davis for those brief seconds his hands were free, but he was still sitting, and he knew he couldn't move fast with the leg irons. Still, he itched to wipe every feature of his own face from the Ranger's. His fists clenched into balls as he recalled the way Lori had sat with the man last night, at the way they had talked for so long. He knew exactly what Lori was doing, and he was helpless to do anything about it.

He could damn well fight his own battles. He didn't want her involved in this, nor did he want her to think she could charm someone like Davis. Nick had met few men like him before, but he recognized the breed: hard, unbending, and so damn sure they were right.

Nick kept his face empty as the handcuffs were again locked around both wrists, now protected, thanks to Lori, with scraps of his bandanna. He rose awkwardly, unable to do much more than shuffle along in a humiliating gait.

The Ranger already had a fire going, a coffeepot on the coals. Lori had brought some freshly baked bread with her, and she broke off a piece for Nick and herself, ignoring the Ranger. She was clearly challenging the Ranger with every move. Nick damn well wished he knew what she thought she was accomplishing. Morgan Davis wasn't like all the other men who swarmed around her, and Nick already sensed her fascination with someone who wasn't taken in by that damned breathtaking smile of hers.

But now the Ranger ignored her, taking some jerky from a saddlebag and eating it without comment. He poured himself a cup of coffee and then two more, handing one carefully to Nick, who took it with both hands, and one to Lori. Then he rose and went to lean against a tree, watching silently as he had since the first moment he had encountered Nick.

Watching. Waiting. Nick understood that. He understood a great deal about the man apparently committed to taking him back to hang. From the first moment he'd faced the Ranger, an eerie recognition had flashed between them. It was more than their physical resemblance; it was an internal familiarity, a sense that they had met before, though he knew well they had not. Nick hadn't had time to explore those mental ramblings; his concern for Lori and his own well-honed sense of self-preservation had shoved them aside, but now as he watched Davis watch him, the thoughts returned, and he realized he knew exactly what Davis was thinking.

Davis was the kind of man, Nick knew with certainty, who never swerved from the path he chose, who didn't know how to bend, who never allowed emotion to influence him. Nick, on the other hand, had learned to bend a long time ago. Perhaps he'd been born that way, or just taught. His father had no rules. There was no black and white in Dr. Jonathon Braden's world. He lived every moment to the fullest, believing the Lord—or fate—would provide the next day's meals. He was a con man, plain and simple, with a con man's incurable optimism. He was, in many ways, like an ageless child, excited by travel and people and new places.

Growing up with him had always been an adventure.

Nick had been well loved, not only by Jonathon and Fleur, but by the various flotsam—performers, itinerant peddlers, hobos, and stragglers—who stayed with the Medicine Show a day, a week or a month, or, like Daniel Webster, years. Nick had grown up pleasing crowds, conducting small cons, and like his father, he saw no wrong in bringing excitement to people who had little of it. If there was a little stretching of truth, a bit of sleight of hand in the shell game, an occasional crooked gambit when money was low, Jonathon had justified it as entertainment for those who could afford it. He never conned a poor man and often gave money to those in need, even when his own family went with less.

He was one of a kind, and Nick loved him, though as he grew older, he longed for more stability, a bit of security, for those he loved. Jonathon was in his mid-sixties now, Nick's mother fifty, and Nick wondered how much longer they could live the wandering life Jonathon loved. And there were Lori, who had never had any kind of normal life, and Andy, who was as wild now as a Texas longhorn. They'd all had love in abundance, love and a fierce loyalty to each other, but Nick knew Lori, in particular, needed more. She was twenty-two and knew more about poker than courting. She'd had admirers. Dear God, how she had had admirers. But the Bradens were never in one place long enough to develop any attachments, and Lori shuddered at the thought of becoming a farm wife. She was used to being free in her dress and in her actions; Jonathon had always encouraged her to be so, and Fleur had thought the moon rose and set on her daughter, who was pretty and clever and nigh on irresistible when she set her mind to it.

Nick sipped the last dregs of the coffee as Morgan Davis moved from where he'd been standing and kicked dust into the fire, quickly extinguishing it. "You have a few minutes while I saddle the horses if you want to wash," he said, directing his words to Nick.

Nick stood, grateful for the boon of a few moments'

privacy even though he knew the Ranger was risking little. Nick could barely walk with the leg irons, much less run or mount a horse. Lori rose too.

"You stay here," the Ranger said, "until your brother returns."

"I'm not your prisoner," she retorted.

Davis had already put a blanket on one of the horses and was lifting a saddle. Very deliberately he set it back down, his gaze clashing with Lori's as Nick watched, disquiet flooding him at the battle of wills enacted before him. She had no chance, none at all, against someone like Morgan Davis.

"No," Davis said softly. "Not at the moment." His gaze flickered over to Nick. "But he is, and you're only making things more difficult. He doesn't go if you don't stay."

As Nick watched Lori's face change from defiance to angry acceptance, he realized that if there was one thing he and the Ranger agreed on, it was the need to leave Lori in Laramie. It would take Morgan at least five weeks to get Nick back to Texas, and no one goes five weeks without making a mistake. That's all Nick needed: one small mistake. And then what? Nick couldn't leave him alive, or Davis would chase Nick the rest of his life; he was that kind of man.

Nick knew he was no killer. He had killed once to save his brother. He wondered whether he could kill to save himself. He wasn't sure.

Either way, he didn't want Lori involved.

His eyes met Morgan Davis's, and a curious understanding passed between them. Davis frowned, his face grim. And then the lawman turned away and started to saddle the horse again.

Hampered by the leg irons, Nick shuffled toward the stream. His momentary relief at the prospect of fresh water and privacy was gone. Soon there would be just the two of them, this Ranger and himself. Life for one meant death for the other, and they both had just silently acknowledged that fact.

Nick swore he wouldn't be the one to go down, but the notion gave him damn little peace of mind. That old, peculiar sense of being incomplete flooded over him now. He stumbled, the chain between his legs tripping him, and fell to the ground. He lay there for a moment, filled with despair so strong, he couldn't move.

If anything happened to him . . .

Jonathon and Fleur needed him. Andy. And, dear God, Lori! He understood that now more than ever. She was so competent in so many ways that he often forgot she was a woman who had yet to discover what being a woman meant. She had looked up to him and imitated him for so long, he had come to think of her almost as a younger brother rather than sister. But he was not oblivious to the electricity that passed between her and the Ranger, and that scared the devil out of him. She had no idea what kind of man Morgan Davis was. He would be disaster for a free soul like Lori.

Nick's life or the Ranger's?

For his family's sake, Nick knew which it had to be.

CHAPTER FOUR

They stopped at a stream in early afternoon, though they were close to Laramie.

Lori had changed clothes before they had left the camp-site that morning, switching to a modest blouse and a split skirt that, except when she sat astride a horse, seemed to be the real thing. Women, she knew, had more freedom in Wyoming than in other places. They sat on juries and had obtained the right to vote. Wearing pants, however, was certainly not acceptable—and she didn't know when or how she might have to use her womanly wiles.

The Ranger had viewed her attire with something like bemusement. She had tied her hair behind with a ribbon, and she knew her brown blouse brought out the amber in her eyes. She'd tipped her hat back rakishly on her head. Though she knew she was no beauty, she was attractive enough, particularly in a part of the country with few women.

Nick's wrists had again been cuffed to the saddle horn, and he had moved restlessly in the saddle throughout the morning. His eyes had been dark and guarded, his shirt soiled, when he'd returned from the stream this morning, and Lori had had to restrain herself to keep from going to him. She knew that look, that warning, which kept every-one, even those close to him, at arm's length. The moody silence was rare, and Lori bit back words of concern. He wouldn't appreciate them, especially in front of the Ranger.

But for a moment his glower reminded her of the Ranger's—and then she dismissed the thought. Nick was nothing like the humorless, laconic lawman. The only thing they had in common outside of looks, she thought bitterly, was that they both wanted to get rid of her. But she wasn't that easily discarded.

Nick had said she would only get in the way. That he couldn't concentrate if he worried about her. The Ranger just wanted her out of the way, period. But Lori knew Nick couldn't so easily escape the man intent on taking him back. She had noted the Ranger's caution. How could Nick ever escape as long as he was shackled so thoroughly?

At the stream Morgan allowed Nick off his horse—only, the Ranger made it clear, because he felt the horses needed a short rest. Nick had stretched his arms, rubbed his sore wrists, and walked. Morgan had not insisted on the cursed leg irons, though the handcuffs stayed in place.

Lori stifled a small groan as she tried to walk. She was accustomed to riding long distances, but she was not used to doing it on the rear end of a horse. As always, the Ranger watched them both with the single-minded intensity of a cat watching mice it intended to devour. He gave the horses a handful of oats and allowed them to drink slowly, and Lori knew he had more regard for them than he did for her brother, whom he treated with a practiced but wary indifference.

The Ranger showed no sign of exhaustion, no lessening of the caution he'd practiced since the first time she'd seen him. Lori wondered whether he had one feeling bone in his body. Her eyes met his, held for an instant, and he turned from her. Nick was several feet away, his face a mask Lori couldn't read. She sensed he wanted to spring at the Ranger, that he needed desperately to do something just to alleviate the tension in his body; but then his gaze found hers, and she watched him forcibly restrain himself.

The Ranger saw it, too. Lori knew from the way his own muscles had tensed under the dark-blue cotton shirt he wore. "Time to go," he said, his shadowed eyes a warning to them both.

Nick shrugged. "Whatever you say."

The Ranger raised an eyebrow, but said nothing, merely followed Nick to his horse. The Ranger locked Nick's wrists to the saddle horn again and then watched him mount before offering his finger-locked hands to Lori as a step up.

And then Lori wondered whether he had made his first mistake. The reins to Nick's horse were free. If only she could scoop them up, then Nick could make a dash for it. The Ranger's horse was tied securely several feet away, her mare, Clementine, also secured on the lead to the Ranger's bay. If only Nick's hands weren't chained to the saddle horn.

Her gaze went down to the Ranger's holster. She had to get his gun. She offered her left foot to him, prepared to throw herself on him and grab for the gun, but he was obviously ready for her.

Morgan expected it. As her body moved toward his, he quickly twisted and she landed in his arms, her face just inches from his, his hands tight around her back and hips. This was the third time Morgan had found her unwillingly in his arms, and each time seemed to increase the heat that built inside a body he was usually so able to control.

He held her just a trifle longer than necessary, and then he set her on her feet, his lips twisting into that half smile that suggested so little amusement. "An accident, Miss Lori?"

She straightened and looked him straight in the eyes. "What do you think, after forcing me to ride on that horse's backbone for a day and a half? Every part of me is stiff."

"That so? Didn't feel like it to me," he drawled with his soft, slow Texas accent.

Lori glared at him. "Are you going to help me or not?"

"I don't think so," he said with the patient tone one uses with a child.

He left her and tied the reins of Nick's horse to the lead, then mounted his own horse. He turned back. "You think you can get up on your own, or do you want to walk awhile?"

Lori turned to her brother, put her hand on his arm, which he stiffened, and used it to vault her left foot into the stirrup he relinquished. She settled down behind him.

"I thought you could manage," the Ranger said, then kicked his mount into a trot without waiting for an answer.

Three hours later they rode into Laramie. Morgan still felt that damn internal fire that had bedeviled him those few seconds Lori Braden had twisted in his arms. Her face had been so close, her eyes wide and surprised and shadowed by dark lashes that contrasted with the honey-colored hair.

He'd wanted to kiss her, dammit. He'd wanted it in the worst hellish way. He hadn't wanted to let her go. She'd felt good in his arms, soft and supple and not stiff at all. But she'd been soft, he knew, because he'd startled her. There was nothing soft about her feelings where he was concerned. She would as soon stick a knife into his heart, and he didn't fool himself about that, either.

He wished that she wasn't a part of this. Outside of the Rangers, he'd seen damn little loyalty in his life, even less selflessness. Too bad—Nick Braden didn't deserve it. There were altogether too many witnesses in Harmony who'd seen Braden draw on an unarmed man.

As they rode into Laramie, the streets were busy, filled with wagons and soldiers. Fort Laramie, he knew, was north of there, and he wondered if something had happened. General Custer and his men had been massacred just months ago, and he'd heard there were punitive expeditions being readied to confront the Cheyennes and Sioux in northern Wyoming. He wished them luck. He'd had his share of Indian fighting in Texas.

He looked back. Braden sat stiff and proud, even as

men and women on the street stared at the three riders moving over the dusty road. Morgan found the sheriff's office in the center of town, asked a loiterer if the sheriff was in, and dismounted when the man nodded. He again offered his hand to Lori, knowing she would refuse it, then unlocked Braden from the saddle horn, taking his arm and ushering him into the sheriff's office.

The heavyset man sitting behind a desk glanced up as they entered, then stood as his gaze went from man to man and back again. He immediately assessed the handcuffs and the Ranger's badge. His eyes rested briefly on Lori, widening with appreciation; but he quickly turned back to Morgan, staring pointedly at the badge.

"Texas Ranger?"

Morgan nodded.

"Long way from home, aren't you?" His eyes still flickered from man to man, considering them both. "Brothers?" he asked.

"Hell, no!" Morgan's reply was more explosive than he'd intended, but he was damned tired of this. And he knew he probably looked more like an outlaw than his prisoner did. He had taken no time to shave that morning, and he wore several weeks' growth of beard. He took the folded poster and a Texas arrest warrant from his pocket and handed them to the sheriff.

"I'm Morgan Davis. Braden's wanted in Texas for murder."

"Len Castle," the sheriff said, identifying himself. "What do you want from me?"

"Keep him in custody until I can get his sister on a stage to Denver. Couldn't leave her alone out there. I think there's some bounty hunters on the look for him."

"You think right," the lawman said. "Two men through here two days ago, asking about your man. I told them to get the hell out of my town."

Morgan's gut tightened. "Man with blond, almost white hair?"

The sheriff nodded. "Said his name was Stark."

Stark. Whitey Stark. The man who had trailed him weeks ago. Morgan knew he should have killed him then, but he'd been tired of killing over a damned look-alike. It was a mistake he wouldn't repeat. "Which way did he go?"

"He headed toward Cheyenne."

Which meant, Morgan realized, that Stark was about three days behind him. Morgan had also stopped in Cheyenne, the territorial capital, to search for Braden's land deed. Stark would find it, just as Morgan had.

"When's the next stage to Denver?"

"Two days. It runs twice a week."

"Can you keep Braden that long?"

The sheriff looked regretful. "Court's next week. I have a full house. But you might try the territorial prison, half a mile down."

"Hotel?"

"Best one's down the street. Bill Hickok's there. So is Bill Cody. Getting ready for one hell of a fight up north."

"Sioux?"

"And Cheyenne. Got them trapped, I hear. Hope they wipe out every one. I had friends with Custer."

"We shouldn't run into any trouble?"

"Not if you're headed south. There might be a few small bands cut off, but ain't much to worry about."

Morgan nodded.

"Wish I could help you," the sheriff said, "but the jail ain't safe now with so many in it." He shook his head. "Damn railroad brought every sort of riffraff here."

"If you see those bounty hunters . . . ?"

The sheriff grinned. "I'll send them north." He nodded at the girl. "Miss."

Lori gave him a sweet smile that made Morgan's muscles tense. He wished to hell he knew what she was thinking. "Sheriff," she acknowledged, and the lawman's expression became downright simpering.

Morgan decided not to give her a chance to try something. "Braden," he said curtly, guiding him toward the door.

They had reached it when the sheriff's voice stopped him. "You sure you ain't brothers?"

"Quite sure," he said, turning around, "since my parents were killed when I was born, and there wasn't any before me." He didn't know why he felt compelled to explain, but then he didn't care for the sheriff's slightly accusing voice. He was goddamn tired of being put in the wrong. The injury was done to him, by God, not Nicholas Braden. His life hadn't been his own since Braden had murdered young Wardlaw.

The warden at the territorial prison agreed to keep Braden for two days. He had space, and Morgan gave him a voucher that guaranteed Texas would pay expenses. He then found the hotel and rented the remaining two rooms, one for himself and one for Lori.

As he left her at the door, she turned and faced him, her face tight with anger. "I'm surprised you didn't try to keep me there too."

"I thought about it," he said mildly. "They do have some women incarcerated there. But I don't think you can do much with him locked up in there. And you *are* going to be on that stage Wednesday."

He had considered handcuffing her to the bed—but, then, where would she go? And she was a woman, after all, a woman who really hadn't committed a crime.

Lori glared at him with those golden eyes, then opened the door, went in, and closed it without comment. That worried Morgan more than words did. Hellfire, but he would be glad when this was over. He stood in front of the closed door for several minutes, then walked to his own, wishing it were closer. And then he dismissed the thought. There was nothing she could do now. Braden was safely lodged.

He went down to the street and sought the name of the most reliable stabler, then took the three horses there. He gave the owner ten dollars. "No one," he said, "especially not a young lady, is to be allowed near the horses."

The man nodded, his eyes on Morgan's badge.

Morgan found a bathhouse and then a barber. It felt good being clean again. But he cursed under his breath as he looked in the mirror. Even with the mustache remaining, his likeness to his prisoner was stronger than ever.

He tried to think instead of a good meal—a steak—and some sleep.

Lori Braden came immediately to his mind. He supposed he would have to buy her dinner. He didn't think she had any money, and he'd planned to pay the stage fare, anyway, providing the driver with some extra money for her expenses.

No expense would be too great to rid himself of her. Still . . . he suffered a moment's regret. She had been an intriguing challenge, and she had made him feel alive for the first time in years. He hadn't realized until now how completely he had buried feelings, any feelings at all.

Since the war? Since Callum had died? Or had Callum simply trained them out of him from boyhood? He couldn't remember ever feeling much. Not even fear, as a child. Danger and death had been too much a part of his life since he'd started walking. He'd grown accustomed to them, as accustomed as rising in the morning.

He sighed heavily. Goddamn Braden for awakening devils better left at rest.

Lori stared out the window to the street below. At any other time she would have been down there, making herself part of the crowd, eager to become one with it. She had heard of Bill Hickok and Buffalo Bill for so many years, she would have liked to see them in person.

But not now. Nothing mattered now except Nick. And besting Ranger Morgan Davis. *He* wasn't going to give up. And after seeing the Ranger's quiet, unflustered efficiency for the last two days, she figured he might just well succeed.

And Nick would die.

Her gaze wandered over the street; then she noticed the Ranger. The way he walked, that easy pantherlike gait, made him seem always on the prowl.

A manhunter.

A shiver ran down her back and through her extremities. It amazed her that the very sight of him created such havoc inside. Hate. That was what it was, she assured herself. Just plain hatred. He'd treated Nick like a criminal, her like a nuisance to be tolerated. He was wrong on both counts. And too much the righteous fool to see it.

But God help her, he was thorough. She would give him that. He knew his business, and he didn't take chances.

Lori left the window and went to the small carpetbag she had packed. She had few things with her: the shirt and trousers she had worn yesterday, the skirt and blouse she was wearing now, and one dress. There were also a few coins she had managed to slip underneath the dress. There wasn't much. Nick had left most of what he had with the family, and the rest had been spent on timber and supplies.

Lori changed into her dress made from an attractive light brown-and-white-checked material that highlighted her eyes and molded her slender body. The high neck and puffed sleeves gave her an air of innocence.

She studied herself critically in the mirror, brushing her hair until it fairly glowed in the late-afternoon sun filtering through the window. She then twisted it into a French knot. Perhaps a dress and pretty hair arrangement could do what trousers couldn't, a smile obtain what anger hadn't.

Lori would send a telegram telling Papa what had happened, look for her horse, and charm the Ranger.

If the latter didn't work, she would have to go to the alternate plan.

For that she needed a gun.

For that she needed backbone she wasn't sure she had.

For that she would have to kill the Ranger.

A sudden tightness squeezed Morgan Davis' chest as he stared at Lori Braden. He didn't remember ever seeing a woman quite as pretty, as enchanting, as she looked the moment she opened her door to him. Those golden eyes glowed, and he knew instinctively that they must do that a lot, that she had a zest for life she'd buried yesterday in her anger. He knew he liked those eyes this way a hell of a lot better than when they shot sparks at him.

He warned himself that she was treacherous. But she didn't look treacherous at the moment. She just looked . . . pretty.

And vulnerable. So goddamn vulnerable. Her mouth smiled, not wholly, but with a wryness aimed to disarm, where a sweet one would have aroused only suspicion.

She was good. She was very good.

She was so good, in fact, that he almost forgot she wanted something from him very, very badly, and it certainly wasn't his charm or good looks.

Still, he would play along and see where this led. Her nose wrinkled slightly, and he knew he still smelled pungently of some kind of aftershave lotion, though he had tried to wash most of it away.

She tipped her head slightly and studied him.

"Don't say it," he warned her, knowing that the resemblance to Nick Braden was stronger than ever now that his cheeks were cleared of dark bristle.

She nodded. "You're nothing alike, anyway."

She had already told him as much in not very flattering terms: Nick Braden had a heart; he didn't.

"You don't talk alike. You don't walk alike. You don't think alike."

"I hope like hell not."

"You have nothing to worry about," she said, a touch of

vinegar in the cordiality she was obviously trying so hard
to convey. But it was nigh on killing her, and he sensed it.

"I thought you might want something to eat," he said,
his mouth twisting in its own wry smile. He was finding, to
his deep dismay, he liked her in several ways. There was
an innate honesty to her—at least in her resentment of
him—that kept surfacing despite her attempts at charming him. And that damnable loyalty. He respected that
most of all.

"How gallant," she answered with the slightest touch of
sarcasm, and he led her down to the crowded hotel dining
room.

They both ordered steak, and he was amused at that,
too. She ate with the enthusiasm of a cow hand, though he
wondered at times whether her concentration on the meal
wasn't partly to avoid conversation with him. When she
had no more reason not to look at him, she glanced up,
those amber eyes as beguiling as any he'd seen. He expected more defense of Nick Braden, but as usual she
surprised him. Cupping her chin in her hands, she focused all her considerable feminine attention on him.

"You . . . said your parents died when you were
born."

He nodded warily.

"How?"

He put down his knife. "Another one of your ploys,
Miss Lori?"

"Maybe," she admitted with that appealing forthright-
ness. "But I'm also interested," she said. And she was. She
wished she wasn't. She wished she didn't want to know
anything about him at all. She *shouldn't* want to know anything about him. But she *had* to know. Some demon inside
her was making her ask questions she shouldn't want answers for.

He studied her closely for a moment, then shrugged.
"It's no secret. They were killed by Indians hours after I
was born. They put me in a fruit cellar when the attack
started. Rangers found me there later."

"Is that why you became a Ranger?"

He frowned, as if puzzled by the intrusion into his past, then decided it made little difference whether he answered or not. "My father was a Ranger. The man who found me was his best friend. There were no relatives. No one stepped up to claim me. So Callum decided to raise me rather than send me to an orphanage."

"Rangers raised you?" It was worse than she imagined.

"Yep. And a series of . . . sporting ladies." He waited for her reaction with an amused glint in his eye. It was the first real humor she had seen in him. Yet there was something else too. Not vulnerability—there was nothing vulnerable about this man. But there was the smallest flicker of . . . a kind of loneliness she had sensed in him before.

Her eyes sparkled for a moment, and he sensed again that vibrancy in her, a passion for life that was totally unfamiliar to him . . . and intoxicating. And he was even more intrigued. The fact that he'd been raised by whores apparently bothered her not at all.

"What else would you like to know?" he said, his lips twitching now with rare amusement.

"I'm not sure I should ask," she said, mischief in her voice. "I think you're trying to shock me."

"Why would I do that?"

"I don't know," she said, leaning her elbows on the table and planting her head on folded hands so she could study him better. "But I think I like it."

He chuckled. She was the most unpredictable woman he'd ever met. And, at the moment, the most desirable. Yet . . .

"You said you joined the Rangers in 1861?" she prompted after a moment's silence.

"Miss Lori, I was a Ranger from nigh on the time I first walked. I curried and fed the horses, I swept the headquarters building, I shined the badges and cleaned the rifles. I never wanted anything else."

"Never?"

"Never. Rangering was as natural as learning to put pants on, one leg at a time."

Lori found herself leaning forward. "And during the war?"

"My company was pulled into the regular Confederate Army in sixty-two. After the surrender the Rangers were disbanded for nine years. But I still worked with a number of them, marshaling one cow town after another."

"Waiting?"

"That's right." There was a curious look in his eyes now. Skeptical and a bit abashed. Lori knew he had said a great deal more than he intended. "You're a good listener, Miss Lori."

"Like you, I learned certain skills when I was young."

"I wouldn't think listening would be one of them."

Sparks were there between them now, live and biting. Intense. Frightening. Lori felt as though she were losing control, floundering in waters she didn't really understand. Her gaze met his, dueled, and unfamiliar warm currents flooded her body, so very aware of his lean, straight one across from her.

"What would you think would be one of them?"

"I studied the Braden family, Miss Lori. Cardsharping. Selling whiskey as medicine. A swindle here and there. You're right there in the middle."

"Are you always so judgmental?" Lori hated the slight tremor in her voice, that edge of hurt.

His gaze met hers, the already deep blue darkening with thoughts only he knew, which he kept to himself. "I try not to be judgmental at all," he said.

"You just do your job?" she replied, the sarcasm back. "Yes."

"But you are judgmental, Ranger," she said, the tremor gone now. "You'd made up your mind about us long before you came here. You don't know anything about us."

"The evidence . . ." Christ, he was doing it again. Defending himself for doing his job. Yet he regretted his words about her family. He abruptly summoned the waiter, paid the bill, and rose. "It's been . . . interesting, Miss Lori."

"It has, hasn't it?" she agreed, her eyes flaring with anger, and Morgan wondered what she was planning now. A prison break wouldn't surprise him, even hopeless as it was.

She wended her way through the crowded room, ignoring him as she reached the main reception area, then went up the stairs. At her door she stopped, turned, and faced him. "Thank you," she said simply. He had expected a taunt of some kind, another challenge delivered, and the lack of one worried him. He looked at her suspiciously. "What are you planning?"

"A good night's sleep, Mr. Davis."

"Why do I doubt that?"

"Because you're a suspicious man," she said with that charming smile of hers. "Would it help if I swore that's all I had in mind tonight?"

He believed her. For once he believed her, even as he weighed every word.

"Then good night," he said, realizing he'd damn well better sleep tonight since hell might break loose the next one.

She hesitated, looking up at him as if searching for something. Morgan found himself pierced by those striking golden eyes, eyes unexpectedly vulnerable again with a plea he knew he couldn't grant. The heat that had danced between them since the first moment he'd seen her, the sparks kindled during their probing at dinner, roared into flames.

Morgan had been acquainted often enough with a woman's desire to recognize it now, even though he knew it was all mixed up with other more dangerous emotions. He told himself it was exactly that combination that excited and tantalized him in a way he'd never experienced before. It couldn't be anything else.

Her face was inches from him, her scent of wildflowers hovering in the air, teasing his senses. A fever he'd never known for a woman rushed through him, consuming what good sense he had, making mockery of his vaunted self-control. He felt a stirring deep inside, a hunger that was both familiar and new.

Still, he could have walked away, if her own face hadn't been creased in a kind of wondering confusion, if her own eyes hadn't suddenly glowed with the same fervor that was burning him.

Her lips suddenly seemed to beckon him, and he lowered his own to hers with a desperate need that astounded him with its intensity. Giving in to that need made him angry, and his mouth was anything but gentle. It sought, it took. He suddenly wanted to be the conqueror, but her mouth was as hungry as his, as demanding, and the air between them exploded into a firestorm. Anger and raw need crackled between them, fueling emotions too complicated to understand, much less to control.

He was taking her brother to hang. She was trying to stop him. The rational part of him knew that, but irrationality reigned. For some godforsaken reason, desire—irresistible desire—was taking possession of two people who distrusted each other with every ounce of their being. But that knowledge only served to deepen the fierce, elemental hunger that seized them both. Like forbidden fruit.

Except Morgan had never wanted forbidden fruit before, had never succumbed to whatever devil there was that made usually sensible people want what they couldn't have.

Their mouths crushed together, and some part of Morgan's mind knew she was as helpless as he—and as angry about it. He knew it in the desperation of the kiss and the fierceness of hands that crawled up around his neck. They were reckless and demanding, the fingertips biting into his skin.

His tongue sought its way into her mouth, and he was surprised at her gasp, as if she had never been so invaded before. But she responded with renewed fire, her own tongue exploring his, fighting even while responding. He heard a moan issue from his throat as their bodies pressed together and he felt his arousal against her—and for the briefest moment her body moved even closer to him. Then, suddenly, she wrenched away, her eyes huge with bewilderment, glazed with a mist that had nothing to do with tears.

She stared at him for a moment, and he saw her tremble, her lips quiver with a denial that was like a blade through his soul.

"No," she whispered. She spun around, opened the door to the room, and disappeared inside, leaving him to stare at a dirty wall, his body in tight, painful knots and his thoughts in a confused disarray he never thought possible.

CHAPTER FIVE

Lori spent the next morning avoiding the Ranger. She kept telling herself she had to think of him that way. Not as Morgan Davis. Not as an individual, not as a man she'd kissed. Dear Mary and Joseph, how they had kissed. She flushed every time she remembered it, which was altogether too often.

She had to think of him as the man taking Nick to hang, not a man who had aroused such remarkable sensations within her, that deep, wanting need that had pulsed inside her all night long, keeping her from sleep, from being able to think. She had never felt such things before, had never experienced the irresistible lure to explore them farther.

Even less did she want to think of dinner, of those few moments when he had lowered his guard and she had sensed that wistfulness, that wry acceptance of a lonely childhood that almost made him likable. Almost.

She hated her body for betraying her, her mind for allowing any emotion other than fierce anger.

Over and over again, during the long night, she reminded herself of exactly what he was. A Ranger who could, and would, without compunction, destroy her brother—and with him, her family. If anything happened to Nick, it would break all their hearts, especially her mother's.

Lori suffered through the night, through dawn, the torment of both her physical and emotional reactions to Morgan Davis. She finally rose and sat at the window, watching the street below fill with people. She sat unmoving until she saw the Ranger leave the hotel, heading for the stage office. Probably checking on the stage again, she thought balefully. And then she left her room—to send a telegram to her friend in Denver.

She next went by the stables to visit Clementine and was told by the owner that she was not allowed near the horse. Tears did nothing to bend the man's resolve, and she guessed that the Ranger had slipped him a few extra dollars. Full of simmering anger, along with grudging appreciation for his foresight, she visited the mercantile to see what she could find that might be helpful. Unfortunately, she didn't have sufficient money for a gun, but she was good at improvising and soon found something useful.

She kept looking around to see if the Ranger was following her, but she saw nothing. He was either very good at following discreetly, or he felt confident enough in his own plans that he disregarded her as a threat. He would pay for that piece of male arrogance, she told herself. Over and over again she told herself that—to keep from remembering last night.

She fingered the bottle of laudanum she had just purchased and considered her plan. Lori knew the Ranger would probably keep tabs on both the mercantile and the gunsmith's shop. He was too careful not to. At least she hoped as much. It was important that he know about her little purchase.

She had pondered all night over how to outfox him, after reaching the conclusion that charm wasn't going to work—not with a man who had practically been born a lawman. The alternative made her physically ill. Her stomach constricted, and she knew she was committing herself to something that would forever haunt her. But she saw no choice, none at all. She couldn't let Nick down; she represented his best opportunity, no matter what either man thought. She couldn't take a chance that Nick would escape on his own—not with the singularly careful way the Ranger handled him.

But she had to have a gun, and she had to have wits. Her cunning could be of much more value than violence. She searched every alternative open to her. She was depending on the Ranger's caution, that he would discover her purchase, think she planned to drug him and steal the weapons, and would be waiting for her tonight.

Two men through here two days ago, looking for your man. The sheriff's words. Bounty hunters. The Ranger had been speaking the truth—but, then, he would, she thought somewhat bitterly.

So they hadn't been safe at all. Lori wondered whether Nick would ever be safe again. Certainly not as long as Morgan Davis was alive.

She forced her thoughts back to the immediate problem—freeing Nick *now*. Then they could worry about the future. She looked at the bottle of laudanum she had bought. Considering the Ranger's extreme distrust of her, he would probably be checking on her movements as well as items in her room. In fact, she was depending on it.

Lori knew there was no way to free Nick from the territorial prison. Nor could she harm Morgan Davis before he left with her brother. If a Ranger was killed, another would be sent to retrieve Nick. They would, in fact, probably send an army. Morgan was very much one of theirs, she had discovered from her conversation with him last night.

No, she would let the Ranger take Nick back into custody—then she would ambush them someplace along the way. But she had to have a gun, and she had to slip away from the Ranger before he put her on the stage in the morning and she lost her chance to follow them. The Ranger knew there were bounty hunters on the trail, and he wouldn't tarry long in Laramie to look for her. Nor would he take the route across open plains. She figured, instead, he would try to slip through the mountains.

She needed a gun and her horse. And she thought she knew exactly where and how she could get them.

The sheriff!

When she was in his office, she hadn't missed seeing the number of gunbelts hanging from the wall, probably those of the unfortunates locked in his jail. She just might be able to liberate a gun, one that wouldn't be missed for a while. She doubted the sheriff counted them each time a visitor entered his office. And she could appeal to him for the return of Clementine. She tried to remember every word the Ranger had said to the sheriff. Nothing damaging about her, nothing that would create suspicion. And Lori hadn't missed the admiration in the Laramie lawman's eyes.

She brushed her hair now until it literally shot off sparks. She had fashioned it into a French knot last night to look older; today she let it hang loose to look younger. Young and innocent—and in need of help to escape a heartless Texan.

Lori tucked the bottle of laudanum into the small carpet bag, tore a piece of sheet from the end of the bed, and tied two strips around the upper calf of her leg, three inches apart. She then pinched her cheeks to bring color into them. After checking the streets, she hurried to the sheriff's office.

He was sitting exactly where he had been before, and he stood slowly as she entered, nodding to her, the gleam of admiration obvious in his eyes. Lori bit her lips nervously and gave him a wide-eyed, pleading look.

"Sheriff Castle . . ."

He looked pleased that she had remembered his name.

"I . . . I was hoping you could help me."

He smiled. "If I can."

"Can he . . . can that Ranger really take my brother back to Texas? He's innocent. He shot to protect me when that . . . man he's accused of murdering tried to . . . tried to rape me."

The sheriff's eyes narrowed. "That so?"

She nodded. "But his family was influential, and his father put up that reward money. That's all the Ranger cares about . . . and the fact that someone mistook him for my brother. He doesn't care about justice at all."

The sheriff eyed her shrewdly for a moment, then relaxed. "I wish there was something I could do, miss, but he has that Texas warrant."

"That doesn't give him any say over me, does it?" she asked.

He shook his head. "None I can see."

"He's taken my horse, told the stableman I can't even see it." She blinked tears back. "Clementine's the only thing I have left."

"No other family, miss?"

"My father in Denver," she said, her eyes filling with tears again. "He's getting on in years—this is going to kill him. I have to get to him, but the stage takes too long . . . and there's Clementine. I've had her since I was . . ." She looked away, her voice trembling.

He looked at her in horror. "You can't ride alone, miss. Not in this country."

"I thought you might know . . . some trustworthy person I could hire to accompany me." Now that, she thought, should relieve his conscience.

There was a noise in the back, where she guessed the cells were. He looked impatient, but the noise grew louder as if there was a fight back there. More like a gift from God, she thought. She had been praying for a disruption of some kind.

"I'll be back in a moment, miss," he said, and went through a door to the back of the building. Lori moved quickly to where the gunbelts were hanging and removed a weapon from one of the holsters in the back, covering it with another. She returned to the front of the desk, sat, and swiftly pulled up her dress, fitting the gun into the strips of cloth tied to her leg. She had just smoothed her skirt over her legs when the lawman returned. Lori was dabbing her cheeks with a handkerchief.

"Sorry, miss," he said, sitting back down and regarding her sympathetically. "Just offhand, I don't know of anyone, but I'll make inquiries, and I'll tell Jim Evans at the stable to let you see your horse anytime you want."

"Do you think . . . I can ride Clementine out to see my brother before . . ." Tears started to trickle down her face again.

"Doggarn, I don't know why not," he said. "I'll just give you a note for Jim. And for the warden out there." He hurriedly wrote out the notes, muttering about Texas Rangers who thought they were God.

Lori told herself not to overdo it as she gratefully took the notes, but she gave the sheriff a blinding smile. "It's nice to know someone cares about justice," she said, "not just rewards."

"I'll be on the lookout for someone to accompany you," he said, "but I don't hold out much hope."

"You've already been so good and helpful," she whispered brokenly. "I won't forget it."

He flushed with pleasure, ready by now to go to war with the Ranger, who had no business in Wyoming anyway, by his reckoning. People around there didn't treat a lady so poorly, practically stealing her horse and all.

"I'll walk you back to the hotel, miss," he said.

The last thing she needed was to be seen in his company. She hoped the sheriff was also the last person the Ranger would expect she might go to for a gun. She shook her head. "Thank you," she said, "but . . . I . . ."

Another tear dribbled down as she made a creditable show of trying to compose herself. "You've been so kind. Please . . . understand, but I need to be alone . . . I had so hoped you might be able to help Nick."

He shook his head. "It's out of my hands."

"I don't want anyone to see me like this," Lori said with a sudden burst of inspiration. "Is there . . . a back way?"

He nodded, his eyes full of sympathy. "I have rooms upstairs. There's a side entrance."

Again she smiled, a sad, grateful smile that she knew was difficult to resist. Smiles came naturally to her, and she'd learned long ago how effective they could be. "After that horrible Ranger, I never thought I could admire a lawman again." She held out her wrists to him, and the marks on them were evident. "He even tied me up because I said he didn't have any right to take in Nick."

The sheriff swore softly, then said, "Begging your pardon, miss. He needs to be taught some manners."

Lori shook her head. "He'd just take it out on my brother. Please don't say anything."

"I'll let him know he'd better show up in Texas with a live prisoner," the sheriff said. "A good lawman has that duty."

She looked at him with her eyes wide. "You would do that?"

"Yes, miss. Don't like that kind of lawman any more than I do lawbreakers."

Lori reached up on her tiptoes and spontaneously gave him a kiss on a cheek. "You've restored my faith in the law," she said shyly.

His face went red again, and he abruptly moved to the door he'd disappeared through earlier. Beyond that there were stairs to the right; to the left there was another door, the top part barred. She followed the sheriff up the stairs to a landing. There were two doors in the hall and one on the end, which he approached. He took out a set of keys, unlocked the door, and held it open for her.

She looked out on a small porch, with steps leading down to an alley that ran beside the building. She turned back to the sheriff. "I can never thank you enough."

"No need, miss. You need anything, you come see me."

She nodded.

So far, so good.

She tried to be happy about her success, but she kept seeing the Ranger's face the night before, that quick flash of humor, those moments when she'd glimpsed a deep loneliness within him. The gun felt very heavy against her leg.

Tears burned her eyes. Success had a very bitter taste.

.   .   .

Morgan listened intently to the owner of the mercantile as he packaged the supplies the Ranger had just purchased.

"Oh, yes, she was in here," the man said to Morgan's question. "Pretty little thing. But why would she want a gun?"

Morgan sighed. So he was right, after all.

"Hope she's feeling better," the man said.

Morgan raised an eyebrow. "Feeling better?"

"Terrible headache, she said. I suggested a few drops of laudanum. Sure hope it helps. Doc's out of town, or I would have sent her to him."

"Laudanum?" Morgan repeated.

The man nodded, pleased with himself for his helpfulness.

Thoughtfully, Morgan left. So that was what she intended. Another . . . friendly dinner. Drugged coffee. And then only God knew what she had planned—he sure as hell didn't. He'd never met anyone like her. Christ, just thinking about her last night, that kiss. Part of him went rigid at the recollection, even as he warned himself against her. He'd tried to tell himself all night that the kiss had been just another confidence game, another act. A swindle.

Still, she couldn't have faked her response to him. She had been too angry at herself. He had seen that fury in her eyes, had recognized it because he'd felt the same damn disgust at himself.

At least he didn't have to worry about her the rest of the day. He would ask her to dinner again, pretend to drink whatever she would drug, and then wait for her next move. There was really damn little he could do until then. The jail was filled. He couldn't ask the territorial prison to confine her when there was no warrant for her, and he had no legal reason to hold her. He would feel one hell of a lot better when she was on the Denver stage tomorrow. One Braden was enough to worry about.

He didn't like the nagging voice inside that whispered he might miss that intriguing challenge she represented.

He had a feeling that the brother might represent an equally challenging one, once his sister was safely out of the way. Still . . . there was something about Lorilee Braden that made him feel very much alive, made his body rumble with pleasure and his mind smile. He didn't know when last it was that he had bantered as he had last night, when he'd smiled and even teased a little. And when she smiled . . . it was like the brilliant first glimpse of the sun after a fortnight of storms.

He decided he would get some sleep that afternoon. He sure as hell didn't think he would get any that night, and he knew he had to leave in the morning. The warden had said he could keep Braden no longer, and Morgan knew the bounty hunters wouldn't be far behind now.

Yep. Sleep was what he needed now. If only he could keep her from haunting his dreams, if only his body could relax, numb itself against its own primal reactions.

Lori heard him come down the hall, heard his footfalls stop at her door, then continue on to his own room. She knew they were his, the way they hesitated outside her room. She also knew it simply because she *felt* it.

She changed clothes, slipping into her split skirt and shirt. She didn't dare take the carpetbag, which meant she would have to leave her dress, but she very carefully wrapped her pants and shirt and tucked them, along with her coat, into her bedroll. She slipped into the corridor after making sure no one was there. The stairs led down into a main lobby, and she couldn't take her bedroll that way. At the end of the hall, however, was a window and a fire escape, which led to the back of the building and an empty lot.

She dropped the bedroll out the hall window, then leisurely strolled down the corridor, walked down the stairs, and out the door. The stable was just a few doors away. She handed the sheriff's note to the stubborn stable owner, whose attitude changed abruptly. He saddled Clementine for her.

"I'll be back soon," she said, dispensing another smile. "I'm just going to see my brother."

She had to restrain herself from urging Clementine into a gallop. Instead, she very sedately walked the mare down the street as the stableman went back inside the barn, and then she doubled back, turning down a road to the back of the buildings. She retrieved the bedroll, quickly buckling it to the back of the saddle. The pistol she had stolen from the sheriff remained well anchored on her leg. Once she was out of sight of town, she would place it in the saddlebags. It was rather uncomfortable, despite the small sense of security it gave her.

She should have several hours before the Ranger discovered her missing. With luck it would be dark. By then her tracks would be mixed with so many others leading out of town, he would never find her.

But she would find him. She had a very good idea where he would head once he left Laramie with Nick. And because the Medicine Show had traveled the towns of north Colorado, she suspected she was far more familiar with the area than he. Lori knew just where to watch for him. If he didn't show by noon tomorrow, she would know he had decided to take the direct route across the plains, and she could easily catch up with him. He couldn't travel very fast, not with Nick, who would slow him as much as he could.

Morgan knocked on her door, then tried the doorknob. It was locked, and there was no sound inside. He went down to the desk and asked the clerk for a key. Since he had paid for the rooms, he received no argument. Morgan was beginning to have a very bad feeling about all this. Night had fallen; the stores were closed. She should have been in her room.

He unlocked the door and lit the gas lamp. The carpetbag, partially open, lay on the bureau; the brown-checked dress was carelessly thrown on the bed. Other than those two items, the room was empty. He went to the carpetbag. There were a few personal female items within, including a corset. He located the bottle of laudanum and balanced it in his hands as he tried to think.

She had left enough of her belongings that she could still be in town, but he had the uncomfortable feeling he'd been outsmarted. That feeling was growing more acute by the minute.

Where would she have gone?

He ran down the steps and strode quickly to the stable. Lorilee Braden's mare was gone. He confronted the stable owner, who showed him the note from the sheriff. She'd said she would be back shortly.

How long ago?

The man shrugged. "Four . . . five hours."

"What direction?"

"I didn't watch."

Morgan swore to himself. The man had been charmed by Lori. That much was obvious. He wasn't going to offer one bit of information. Morgan was tempted to confront the sheriff, but there was no telling what tales Lori had spun to convince the lawman to interfere. Morgan doubted he would get much cooperation from him now.

It was too dark to trail her. At least Braden should be safe enough in the territorial prison.

Or was he?

Morgan was beginning to wonder if anything was beyond the wily Miss Lori. He just hoped to hell she hadn't somehow got her pretty hands on a gun. He doubted, though, that even if she had, she was capable of killing anyone. Her weapons, he believed, were her charm and wits.

He saddled his bay, rode to the territorial prison, and found his prisoner still there. No young lady had asked to see him. Morgan almost decided to take Braden then and there, but his supplies were still in his hotel room, Braden's bay still at the stable. He might as well wait until morning.

What in the hell was Miss Lorilee planning?

Morgan only knew he preferred bounty hunters to Miss Lori any day. But now it seemed he might have both of them on his trail. He knew how to handle the hunters, but he was beginning to realize he didn't know how to handle the woman.

It was a humiliating discovery.

Nick never thought he would be glad to see a lawman's face, but he was damned grateful to see Morgan Davis's, even if it did look so irritatingly like his own.

The last two nights had been hell. He knew now that he would rather hang than spend time in a place like the Wyoming Territorial Prison. His cell had been little more than a tomb, four feet by seven feet, containing a hammock and a slop bucket. He had never realized before that he hated and feared small places, though he had always preferred sleeping outside, even as a small lad, to spending nights in the cramped, crowded interior of the Medicine Show Wagon.

Apparently because he was a temporary resident, he had been left his own clothes, rather than forced to wear the black-and-white-striped uniforms of the other inmates, and his hair had been left unshorn. But there was a stench that remained on his clothes, even as he held out his hands for the handcuffs and followed the taciturn Ranger outside to the horses. He felt as if he could breathe for the first time since he was locked in the small cell. The panic, the constriction in his chest, the fast, painful beating of his heart dissipated in the bright light of day. He took full swallows of sweet air, felt the morning sun bathe him with freshness.

He waited patiently as the Ranger once more used the second set of handcuffs to lock his wrists to the saddle horn. He noted there were only the two horses and wondered about Clementine.

"Lori?" he said.

The Ranger's jaw set.

"She's on the Denver stage?"

The Ranger didn't answer as he finished his task and mounted his own horse. Nick's horse was already on a lead.

"Damn you, Davis. What about Lori?"

Morgan looked back, his face expressionless, but Nick sensed—no, he felt—a cold, simmering anger. For a moment he thought the man wouldn't answer, but then he appeared to change his mind. "She left on her own last night."

"What do you mean, on her own?" Nick's hands tightened around the saddle horn as he kicked his bay to move up even with the Ranger.

"Just what I said. She took off yesterday afternoon on her horse."

"And you let her? A woman alone?"

"Would you prefer I had her locked up with you?" Davis said, his voice rough with anger.

If Nick hadn't been so worried, he would have smiled at Davis's obvious discomfort. So Lori had outsmarted him in some way. That was a good sign. If Lori could do it, it meant the Ranger wasn't as good as he appeared to be.

But Nick *was* worried about Lori. There was no telling what she might do now. He had wanted her out of this, on her way back to Jonathon. Only when he believed Lori was safe could he plan his own moves. Now . . .

Lori had always been reckless, perhaps because she had always been so good at everything she tried. Or perhaps because she had been so enchanting as a child, everyone forgave her everything.

"What will she do, Braden?" Nick was surprised at the question. Surprised it was asked. Surprised that Davis expected an answer.

He shrugged. "I don't know. I never know what she's going to do next."

"There's a bounty hunter named Whitey Stark on our trail, probably no more than a day behind. He and at least two others. They won't be gentlemanly if they meet up with her."

"Is that what you are, Davis? A gentleman?" Nick asked mockingly. "Somehow I find that hard to believe."

The Ranger turned and stared at him through eyes that were colder, harder than Nick thought his own had ever been. "Don't worry about it, Braden. Your sister is very good at playing men for fools."

Nick felt an icy chill go down his back. He wasn't sure what Lori had done, but he knew he wouldn't want to be in her shoes if she met the Ranger again.

He just prayed that she was making her way to Jonathon to enlist help, even as he feared it was a fruitless hope.

CHAPTER SIX

Hunkered down low on the edge of a ridge, Lori watched the two distant figures and knew she had guessed right.

Although they must have been more than half a mile away, her eyesight was excellent. She couldn't see faces at this distance, but she could identify two bay horses, one slightly trailing the other, and two figures that looked astoundingly alike in the way they sat their horses.

She didn't know why she had been so sure the Ranger would take this route. She knew it was the one Nick would have chosen, if only he could. He loved the mountains and knew them well. There was something of the loner in Nick, though he rarely allowed it to show with his family. Lori knew, because she knew him better than any of the others, because she had watched him look longingly at the mountains and take rides or long walks when he thought everyone else was asleep.

Despite his quick smile, there was a part of him he didn't share with anyone, not even her. There were times the smile was swallowed in some vast darkness she didn't understand. She often had wondered whether he regretted the ever so frequent occasions when everyone in the family relied on him so completely.

She watched the small figures grow even smaller, then disappear. Lori knew the Ranger must be a good tracker. He was, after all, a professional hunter of men, and she knew she had to be extremely careful. He would be looking not only for her, but for the bounty hunters the sheriff had mentioned. But he also had Nick to watch, which meant he couldn't backtrack or circle. He would just make the best possible speed on a route he hoped no one would suspect.

Lori still didn't know why or how she knew he would choose the mountains. Because Nick would have? Or because, in the several days she had spent with him, she had learned a little about how he thought. Both answers bothered her. They ate at her conscience and even a little at her heart. The Ranger *had* tried to be considerate in his own rough, suspicious way. He could have locked her up. Handcuffed her to a bed. She suspected he'd thought of each of those possibilities.

She refused to think about that kiss, that attraction, which ran between them like bolts of lightning. She'd always heard that love and hate were two sides of the same coin. Strong, violent emotions turned inside out. Love tied to hate meant nothing—nothing at all. As an exploding backfire drains the air of oxygen, it would die of its own intensity.

She viciously shoved away thoughts of the Ranger. Nick's life was at risk. The brother who had taught her to ride, who had teased and loved her, who had been her only friend, only confidant, for so many years. The Bradens had long ago learned to rely solely on each other, to protect each other fiercely, and Nick had no one but her at the moment.

She returned to Clementine, who was munching happily on prairie grass. The two men were headed toward a pass below the Colorado border, and then they would most likely follow Trail Creek, the same route she and Nick had previously taken. The Ranger probably hoped any pursuers would assume he had followed the more direct route through Fort Collins.

She mounted, grateful that Clementine was much faster and stronger than either her appearance or her name indicated. If she rode hard, she could reach the pass before the two men. Nick would slow the Ranger down—he vould be in no hurry to reach Texas, even if he wasn't aware Lori might be close.

She bit her lip, knowing she was setting into motion events that could never be undone. She had never shot a man, had never purposely hurt a living creature—she had even refused to fish. As she pondered the consequences of what she was planning to do, Lori looked down at her hands and saw them tremble. She tried frantically to reason with herself. She didn't owe the Ranger anything. It was just that he bore a surface resemblance to Nick, a resemblance that made him a dangerous enemy, and she couldn't forget that. If she wasn't strong, Nick might well die for something he didn't do.

And she wasn't planning on killing the Ranger. Just wounding him. Leaving him a horse to get help. Buying some time for Nick. Still, her stomach churned, revolted at the very thought of shooting someone. Confused, and angry that she was, Lori tightened her thighs around Clementine, gave her a slight slap on the rump, and raced toward Colorado.

Morgan looked toward his prisoner with exasperation as Nick Braden massaged his ankle with a handcuffed hand.

Another damn delay! Nick Braden had been slowing him in small, almost imperceptible ways since the moment they had left Laramie two days ago. Several times Braden's horse had balked, apparently almost throwing him, yet Morgan believed the animal better trained than that. Each time Morgan had had to dismount and calm the bay, losing valuable time. On the morning after leaving Laramie, Morgan had allowed his prisoner to wash at a nearby stream. He had removed one of the handcuffs so Braden could change clothes. In minutes a shirt was floating down the stream and Braden was splashing after it, thoroughly dousing his second shirt. Since the morning was cold, Morgan had agreed to let the shirts dry by a fire, delaying them nearly an hour.

Morgan had pushed hard the rest of the day. They had stopped to water the horses in late afternoon, and Braden had asked to stretch his legs after the eight-hour ride. Morgan had agreed, taking his usual precaution of affixing the leg irons. After shuffling a few steps, Braden had stumbled over a rock, falling and grabbing his right ankle. Morgan reluctantly unlocked the leg iron and watched as Braden pulled off his boot and then a wool sock, his face grimacing with pain. The ankle *was* swollen, goddammit.

Morgan pulled out the map he had discussed with the prison warden. He and Braden had been climbing upward the last few hours and had reached a narrow pass formed by a swiftly moving creek. The riding was already rough. It would get rougher, he knew, once they were through the pass. He had wanted to get through there tonight.

Nick Braden's face was expressionless as he looked up at Morgan. He was waiting, apparently docile, but Morgan sensed the man's watchfulness. He always sensed it—but now every one of his *own* warning signals was blasting like a series of dynamite explosions vibrating within him. His hand automatically went to his gunbelt. The touch was reassuring. He looked out at the aspen-and-evergreen-forested hillsides. Nothing moved, and he had been damnably careful during the two days, backtracking last night after he had secured Braden to a tree. He would have sworn no one was behind him. He wondered at his own skittishness.

Morgan knelt down, his hands running over Braden's ankle. It wasn't broken, but neither was it right. It was swelling rapidly and had turned reddish purple in color. At the least it was badly twisted. "We'll camp here," he said curtly. Braden's gaze never wavered from his but waited for Morgan's next instruction. If Braden was acting, Morgan thought, he was damned good at it.

He remembered Braden and his sister whispering, but they had no way of knowing which route he would follow. And if Lorilee had been following without Morgan's noticing, he'd eat his own sweat-stained hat.

Still, he didn't plan to take chances.

"Move over to that tree," he said, indicating a slender but strong aspen.

Braden hesitated.

"Don't forget what I told you in Medicine Bow. The minute you're more trouble alive than dead, that situation is going to change." He knew his voice was cold, hard, as biting now as the wind that was beginning to stir the golden trees.

Braden looked at the tree a few feet away and then, using his one good leg and his handcuffed hands, slid over to it. Morgan quickly took the empty band of the leg irons, twisted it around the tree, and locked it back around the chain, effectively securing Braden. He tossed the man his sock and boot.

"I'm going to water the horses," he said, wondering why he was explaining anything. "Then I'll start a fire and heat some water for that ankle."

"I'm surprised you care."

"I don't," Morgan said grimly. "But I don't want you slowing me down anymore."

Braden gave him a crooked grin, and Morgan knew as a certainty that the stumble had been planned in some way. The injury was real, but it had been no accident. Just an attempt to delay, to test him. Morgan was getting damn tired of it.

He kept reminding himself of that as he watered the horses, then hobbled them for the night. Morgan quickly gathered sufficient wood for a small fire. He would heat water, make a poultice for Braden's ankle, then extinguish the fire, though it promised to be a cold night. He didn't particularly want to be silhouetted against flames, nor did he want the glare of flames to signal their presence.

He looked toward the horizon as he tended the fire. Another hour before nightfall. He balanced his rifle against a tree, well out of Braden's range. Morgan felt more than one kind of chill as he tore up one of his own few shirts, and soaked it in the water he'd heated. He handed the cloth to Braden and watched as the man carefully wrapped it around his ankle, wincing at the heat. "My thanks," he said.

"Think nothing of it," Morgan replied with the same mockery he'd heard only too often from his prisoner. "Because tomorrow you're riding all day, no matter what that ankle looks like."

"I never thought differently."

"No? All that pain for nothing?"

"I don't know what you mean."

"Oh, I think you do," Morgan drawled. "And we'll make up every damn minute."

Braden shrugged. "Whatever you say."

Morgan snuffed out the fire. Night was falling rapidly now, and clouds were blotting out the moon. It was just as well they had stopped. Dark would be complete tonight.

"Get some sleep, Braden. We leave at sunrise."

There was no answer, but through the last glimmers of light Morgan saw the gleam of Nick's white teeth. He gritted his own. He knew, and Braden knew, he would be getting damn little sleep himself.

Lori had watched the two men approach from where she'd waited among some rocks overlooking the only pass in fifty miles. She willed them to come to her, but they stopped short of her pistol range, and then she saw Nick fall and clutch his ankle.

She thought about trying to move down, within pistol range, but the Ranger kept glancing around. Any movement of a bush, a rock, would alert him, and she couldn't afford that. Not now.

She would inch down during the night, when darkness might cover that tiny movement. And then at dawn . . .

At dawn, what?

Lori chewed some jerky, as much to soothe the jitters in her stomach as to take nourishment. When she touched the pistol she had stolen, her hands shook. Ordinarily, she had complete faith she could hit any target, still or moving. In fact, she used to shoot apples off her brothers' heads, and off those of any spectator brave enough to volunteer. She was a crack shot.

She still wasn't sure she could purposely wound or kill a person, least of all one who looked so like her brother that she was startled anew every time she saw them together. One whom she had kissed with such angry intensity, who had stirred such unfamiliar wants within her, who had made her smile, who had even stirred her heart with that lonely directness.

But she had to try. The Ranger would not surrender his guns, especially to her. She knew that as well as she knew her brother was innocent of murder.

She shivered in the cold night air. She wore a coat over her shirt and pants, but she'd left her bedroll on Clementine a fair distance away. She didn't dare leave this spot to go find it. Lori stretched out on her back and stared up at the sky, so black tonight without its usual trinkets. It was as if someone had laid a blanket across it, quenching every light. She felt the same about her soul.

Nick watched the dawn come. He had been too uncomfortable to get much sleep, just a few moments now and then. He felt more drugged than rested.

It was, he thought with perverse humor, hellishly cold. September weather was unpredictable in these mountains. He wouldn't be surprised to see a snowstorm, what with those spinning dark clouds rushing across the sky.

But it wasn't the cold that kept him from sleep. He was used to sleeping outside in all kinds of weather. The ankle hurt like hell. He just might have outsmarted himself this time. He had purposely fallen, not that he had to try very hard with the damnable leg irons. He had wanted to fake a minor injury, enough to slow them down again. Instead the irons had caused him to pitch down harder than he'd intended, throwing all his weight against that right ankle.

He reached down and felt it again. The ankle was even more swollen this morning. He would never get the boot back on, but neither did he think Davis would attach the leg iron to it. At least he hoped not. Hell, it wasn't necessary now. He would be lucky if he could even get up on his feet.

Nick looked around at the forest. The aspens were changing color. Yesterday, in the sun, they had been bright gold, but now, under the heavy clouds, they looked drab. Or perhaps it was his mood.

He saw only one bright spot. Lori had not appeared and must have done what he had told her for the first time in her life. Otherwise she would have shown up by now; she just plain didn't have the patience to wait this long, and he also doubted whether she could have trailed them without being spotted. So he reasoned she had gone to Denver for help, taking Clementine; the mare would be a great deal faster than a stage. Now it was just Nick and the Ranger, a situation Nick much preferred.

He sat up, losing his two blankets. It was damned difficult keeping them wrapped around him with the handcuffs curtailing his movements. It was like having one hand instead of two. And the leg iron didn't help. His good leg was stiff from lack of movement— stiff and cold.

Frustrated, he looked toward the man responsible for his difficulties. The Ranger had already started saddling the horses. Nick wondered whether he ever slept. As if he felt Nick's gaze, Davis turned around even as his hands continued to buckle the saddle straps. "Your ankle?" The question was as curt as it had been the night before.

Nick tried to stand, using the aspen, to which he was still chained, for support. He had a pressing private need, which was beginning to compete with the ankle pain in discomfort. "Still hurts like hell," he admitted.

"Can you walk?"

Nick was standing now, balancing his weight on his left leg. Agony shot through him as he displaced some of that weight on the injured ankle, then a little more. The pain increased, but it was bearable. Anything was bearable if he could get free, and perhaps he could use the injured ankle to further that cause. He looked laconically down at his good foot, the iron band still ringing it. "Not chained to this damn tree, I can't," he said, grimacing with the pain still coursing through him.

Davis gave one last pull on the saddle, then took a key from his pocket and walked cautiously over to Nick. The Ranger was wearing a gunbelt, but his rifle still lay next to his bedroll. He saw Nick's glance, followed it, and seemed to hesitate; then he dismissed it. Nick certainly wasn't going to be able to sprint for the rifle, not with his injured ankle. Davis handed the leg-iron key to Nick, who realized the Ranger had no intention of kneeling in front of him to unlock the cuff. Nick had hoped . . .

Nick leaned down unsteadily and unlocked the metal around his ankle, not bothering with the other band still locked to the chain that had kept him tethered. He took a tentative step, wincing at the new billow of pain that rocked him. He set his jaw, concentrating. He moved several steps away, each one pure torture as he realized he might as well still be hobbled for all the freedom of movement he had. He stopped and leaned against a tree, aware of the Ranger watching every movement. The ground was freezing to his unbooted foot, enhancing the pain of the wrenched ankle.

He rested a moment against the tree, then took care of his necessities, still mindful of the Ranger's scrutiny. When he took several steps back, the ankle gave way. He started to fall, grabbed what seemed to be a heavy branch. It broke off, and he felt an arm going around him, lowering him to the ground. He also heard a low round of curses as Davis inspected the ankle. With surprisingly sensitive fingers the Ranger rebound the ankle, drawing the bandage tighter for more support. He then made a woolen boot out of the end of one of the blankets. When he was finished, he dug some jerky and hardtack from his supplies and gave a portion to Nick, as well as a canteen. "Five minutes and we leave."

Nick watched as the Ranger turned suddenly, starting toward his bedroll. A shot rang, and Nick saw a look of pain and surprise cross Davis's face as red stained his left shoulder. He spun around, starting to fall, but as he did, Nick saw him twist toward the rifle. In a blinding succession of movements, Davis had the rifle in his hands and found a tree for protection against more shots.

Lori's hand shook on the gun. She thought she heard the shot echo over and over again in the canyon, but perhaps the sound was only in her mind.

She had aimed for the shoulder. For the gun shoulder. But which was it? For a split second she just couldn't remember. Nick was left-handed, and she had automatically shifted her aim to the left.

She closed her eyes for a moment. She had hit him, she knew that. She had seen him reel with the impact before falling, grabbing the rifle and rolling out of sight. How badly was he hurt? She knew she was a good enough shot to hit what she aimed for. But she had never shot to wound before. This had been far different from shooting off a hat or an apple or aiming at a paper target.

She searched the area below. She had waited so long for the perfect shot. She had wanted Nick free of the tree, free of the leg irons, before she fired, in case anything went wrong, in the possible event both she and the Ranger were killed. And then her brother had been in the line of fire. There had been just that moment of opportunity when the Ranger was in clear view.

Where was he now? She felt sick about what she had done. Ambushed a man. She didn't know whether she could shoot again, but she might well have to. She had hoped that the one shot would disable him sufficiently that she could release Nick. They could bandage the Ranger's wound, leave him on a horse a short distance away, and make a run for it. But she had seen him grab the rifle, and in that moment she knew she had probably hit the wrong shoulder. She also realized she had wounded a very dangerous tiger.

She didn't know whether she should stay up there or move cautiously down. And Nick? She didn't see him, either, though he had been in partial view just before the shot. She had to find out! She had nothing to lose at this point by identifying herself. And she still had the high ground, still had the cover of rocks.

"Nick?" she yelled out.

"Get out of here," she heard him call back, his voice uncustomarily shaken.

And then another voice. "Get down here, Miss Braden, or so help me God, I'll kill your brother."

"No!" Her brother's voice. "Leave, Lori."

A rifle shot rang out, and Lori felt herself shake all over. "Nick?"

"The next one goes in his heart." The Ranger's voice was as cold as a sudden blizzard sweeping over the Rockies. She knew he meant it. Dear God, what had she done?

She stood up slowly, the pistol dropping to her side.

"Drop the gun," the Ranger ordered. There was no "Miss Lori" now. No "Lori." Just a cold iciness that promised death. She wished now for that mockery, for anything other than the frozen fury she heard in his voice, fury that she knew included her brother as well as herself.

The gun dropped from her now numb fingers.

"Now, slowly, climb down. I want to see both of your hands," he said.

She had taken several steps when there was an exclamation of some kind below, and then she heard another shot. Nick. Nick had tried something. Disregarding the Ranger's order to go slow, she scrambled down. "Nick?" she screamed as she ran toward the place she had last seen him.

Lori saw him then. He was lying crumpled on the ground, his face in pine straw, his body perfectly still. She paid no attention to the Ranger standing two feet away as she knelt beside her brother. There was blood on the side of his head, but he was breathing.

Thank God, he was breathing.

"He's still alive," the Ranger said. "For now." He emphasized the last two words, and Lori turned to look up at him. He was leaning against a tree, the left side of his shirt a damp bright red. He cradled a rifle in his right arm.

She wanted to say something. She wanted to ask about him, even to offer to help, but she knew she couldn't. She knew he would refuse. Contempt blazed in his eyes, and his jaw was set against the pain she knew he must feel. She was feeling a pain of her own as she looked into his face; the lines there seemed deeper than two days before.

"What happened?"

The Ranger shook his head. "The damn fool came after me. Even in handcuffs and a bad leg. We fought over the rifle. I won." He said it as if there had never been any doubt over the outcome.

Her eyes went to his shoulder. He hadn't mentioned his own wound. It had been very nearly an equal fight.

His gaze met hers. "You don't aim so good."

She wanted to tell him she had, that she had hit exactly where she'd tried to hit. But she knew he wouldn't believe her. And why should he? Why shouldn't he think she'd tried to kill him?

Nick moved then, a soft groan coming from deep in his throat.

Lori looked back down at him. Nick moved slightly; then his eyes opened, widening as they saw her. His hand started to go out to her, then stopped. His face was lined, and it had never looked as much like the Ranger's as it did then. There seemed to be no difference in years now as pain etched furrows around his eyes.

"Lori," he whispered, a quiet despair in his voice that struck through her like a sword. His gaze went to the Ranger. "Don't . . . hurt her. She was just . . ."

"Trying to kill me," the Ranger finished for him in a

voice so impersonal that it frightened Lori more than his anger ever had.

Nick shook his head, but the Ranger paid no attention. "I've had enough of the pair of you," he said.

Lori's hand dug into the pine needles, into the earth. She half expected a bullet to plow into Nick. Into herself. Her hand reached for Nick's handcuffed ones, but she avoided his eyes. He slowly tried to sit up. She knew it was pride forcing him. She hurt for that pride, for him. She hurt that she had cost him more than pride. She might have caused his death. She turned her head toward the Ranger. His face was paling, his jaw squared with determination. A puddle of blood was widening at his feet, dripping from a shirt now soaked.

"Nick didn't know . . ."

"I don't give a damn whether he knew or not. I wouldn't believe either of you if you sprouted wings and . . ." His voice faltered for a moment, then regained in strength.

"Braden, move back over to that tree where you spent last night."

Nick stared at him.

"Goddammit, do it. Now!"

Nick tried to stand. Lori rose with him, letting him use her as a crutch. They made the few steps to the aspen, and Nick sank to the ground. Lori breathed a sigh of relief. At least the Ranger wasn't going to shoot him—or he would have done it minutes ago.

"Lock the leg iron around his ankle." He was talking to her, his voice still impersonal, though Lori sensed he was barely holding his anger at bay. A chill that had nothing to do with the cool mountain weather seeped through her. She hesitated, and Nick, apparently sensing her reluctance, leaned over to do it himself.

"No. *She* does it." His voice was strained but emphatic. There was no reprieve, and Lori knew he was at the limit of whatever patience he had. She leaned over and picked up the iron band. The key was still in the lock. She tight-

ened the band around Nick's good ankle, and then she
saw the swollen right one. "Oh, Nick," she said.

"Throw me the key."

Lori didn't hesitate this time. There was no advantage
in further angering the Ranger.

He left the key where it dropped, took out another one,
and tossed it to her. "Unlock the cuff on his right wrist."

Lori obeyed silently.

"Now lock it onto your own wrist."

Lori stared at him in dismay. "He needs help. You . . .
need help."

"You really believe I would trust you now, or your goddamn help?" He said bitterly. "And something tells me
your brother will survive a bump on the head and a
twisted ankle. Lock it, Lori, or I'll do what I should have
done back at the cabin. Kill him, and save myself one hell
of a lot of trouble."

She closed the cuff around her wrist.

"Tighter, Lori."

She tightened it as far as it would go. It was still a little
loose but not enough to enable her to slip from it.

"Now that key."

She held on to it a moment, then tossed it to him.

He turned then, leaning against the tree, averting his
face from them. He was still a moment, his slumped shoulders reflecting weariness that he had refused to show until
now. Lori bit down on her lip to keep from exclaiming, to
keep from offering help. She needed to help him.

He could have killed her, and he hadn't. Not even when
she had ambushed him. Not even when he thought she
had tried to kill him.

He could have killed Nick.

The Ranger stayed still for several minutes, as if to
gather strength; then he removed his shirt and tore part
of it off, tying a bandage around his shoulder to slow the
bleeding. Without saying anything he walked to where he
had placed their gear. He picked up two canteens and
threw them to Nick. Then he walked away again, disap-

pearing from sight. For a moment she was terrified he might leave them like that, but he returned, his left arm bent stiffly, his right arm holding a pile of firewood. He dropped the wood, added kindling, then ignited it with a match. She watched with growing horror as he placed his knife in the fire.

The Ranger ignored both of them, as if they didn't exist. He undid the bandage, inspected the edge of the wound with his fingers. Even from the twenty feet or more that separated them, Lori winced at the raw, jagged wound still leaking blood.

"Is the bullet still inside?" It was her brother who spoke, his voice soft and serious.

The Ranger didn't acknowledge the question.

"Dammit, man, you can't probe for it yourself."

"Shut up," the Ranger said.

"What about Lori?" Nick said with desperation in his voice. "What if . . . ?"

"What if I die?" The question was curiously impersonal. "I expect those bounty hunters will be here in a few days." He gave Nick a mirthless smile. "Of course, if I had any compassion, I probably should leave them a warning."

Nick's fist clenched. Lori just felt sick. She was sick over what she had done, sick about the trouble she had brought Nick. Most of all, she was sick thinking about what the Ranger was going to do to himself.

The Ranger took the knife from the fire and allowed it to cool for a few moments. He leaned against a tree for support, and then she saw him put the blade to the wound and move it. His grim lips clenched together so tightly, they formed an almost invisible line, but he didn't stop and he didn't utter a sound. Then she couldn't watch anymore. She turned her face to Nick's jacket, closing her eyes, knowing her body was as tense as his. She wanted him to do something, but there was nothing he could do.

No matter what, even if he lost his own life, the Ranger wasn't going to risk losing them. He was going to take Nick in.

And now she was his prisoner too. The Ranger would never forget or forgive what she had done. She remembered his telling her about another prisoner, another woman. The chill in her turned to ice. Ice so cold it burned.

She felt Nick's body relax slightly, and she turned back. The Ranger's bare chest was covered in blood now, as were his pants. But he held a bullet in his hand. She didn't have time to be relieved. The Ranger placed the knife back in the fire, waited until it glowed with heat, and then placed it against his wound, holding it there for several seconds before dropping it at his side, his body straining so hard it seemed to draw into the tree. She saw both his hands bunch into agonized fists as he fought off the pain.

And then she felt Nick's body react, as if it too had been brutally invaded. He seemed to be flinching from something, his breath coming in rapid rushes. "Dear God," he whispered in broken syllables.

Lori felt a dampness on her cheeks, and she brushed it with her free hand. She felt sick, nauseous, at what she watched, because she knew she was responsible. She wanted to go to the Ranger, to touch him and somehow make his suffering more tolerable. But she couldn't, and she knew it, and she knew she would never forget this day, this hour, these terrible minutes.

She tried to fight back the tears, the sense of helplessness, the rage at herself. Her brother had dug his heel into the ground several inches deep, and he was oblivious now to her. She knew that he was feeling terrible pain. She didn't know why, but she felt the trembling in him.

Her gaze went back to the Ranger. The knife beside him was no longer glowing; the stench of burning flesh filled the air. But his eyes were closed, and his body was relaxed. Thank God he had lost consciousness. She didn't even think what would happen to her if he didn't wake up.

CHAPTER SEVEN

Sudden, searing, inexplicable pain shot through Nick's shoulder, and he dug the heel of his boot into the ground. His shoulder had already been aching, and he'd attributed it to the several falls he had taken. But this, which had grown with steady intensity as Morgan Davis probed with the knife, was something else altogether. He could barely keep from groaning.

Like Morgan, he found his fingers balling up in tight knots, fighting the pain, fighting the confusion in his mind. And then Morgan lost consciousness, and the pain seemed to slide away from Nick. He didn't understand it. There had been rare occasions in the past when he'd had sudden pain or discomfort for no apparent reason. But this was too damn coincidental.

It couldn't be sympathy. While he didn't condone what Lori had done, he had no liking for the Texas Ranger. He did, however, have a certain admiration—it took guts to do what Morgan Davis had just done.

Nick moved slightly. He was still aching from that piercing pain in his shoulder, and from the blow to his head inflicted by the butt of the Ranger's rifle when Nick had jumped him. Nick had been so afraid he might shoot Lori. But he couldn't blame Davis for his anger at being ambushed. The Ranger couldn't know that Lori, pretty little Lori, was a sharpshooter—that Davis would have been dead if that was what Lori intended.

Nick was angry at Lori at the moment—now he had her

to worry about, too. And God help them if the Ranger died. He suspected that Davis wanted them to appreciate just that possibility. There would be no more allowances made for Lori. No more small considerations—such as the first night, when he'd left her untied.

The cold was filtering through Nick's sheepskin coat, and he found himself worrying about the Ranger, lying with the upper part of his body exposed to the cold air, the lower part covered by blood-damp trousers. He worried, he told himself, only because at the moment both he and Lori were dependent on the man. There wasn't a damn thing he could do, though, but feel the cold himself and sense Lori's own despair. He knew that she had watched miserably, and with real self-condemnation, as the Ranger doctored himself.

Despite her fierce loyalty and recklessness, Lori had a compassionate heart. He knew it hadn't been easy for her to fire that gun, that she had done it only for love of him.

He studied her now. She looked far younger than her years, with her face smudged, her hair falling over her eyes. Her handcuffed hand had been digging into his arm while Davis had cut into himself. "It'll be all right," he told her, soothing her as he had when she'd been a child.

"No," she disagreed. "It will never be all right. I thought . . ." She stopped, her voice breaking. "I didn't think at all. I couldn't think of anything but getting you away. . . ."

"No faith," he said with a wry smile. "I've always handled everything in the past."

"He's . . . different."

Nick looked over at the still-silent figure. "Yes. But somewhere along the way . . . he would have become careless."

"He won't now," she said morosely.

Nick wished that weren't true. But he had seen the expression on Morgan Davis's face after he'd been shot. If this job had been personal to the Ranger before, now it had become very personal indeed—now that Lori had taken that shot. Nick had not missed the spark of interest the Ranger had tried to hide during the last few days—an interest in Lori that was something more than wariness. And now he suspected the Ranger's anger toward his sister would be deep.

"There was a lot of bleeding," Lori said, disrupting his thoughts after a moment's silence. "What if . . ."

"He won't die," Nick said with certainty. "He's too damn stubborn. And," he added with a wry smile, "I don't think he would have left you here like this if he even considered the possibility."

Lori wasn't so sure. She could only imagine how the Ranger felt toward her now. He had revealed a little of himself several nights ago at dinner; she knew he probably bitterly regretted that now, believing she had exacted the information to use against him. But she hadn't. She had been truly intrigued by him, touched by a life he described so casually, but that had had to be hard and lonely. He would never trust her again.

She tried to turn away from Nick, away from the sight of the Ranger, but the handcuff restraining her hand wouldn't allow her even that relief.

"Lori?" Her brother's query was soft, worried.

Lori's eyes returned to the still figure of the Ranger, his body exposed to the cold. "What have I done, Nick?" she asked in a voice ragged with guilt.

Nick wished he knew. He wished like hell he could do something, anything. The wind was cold, blowing hard now, and the Ranger would be damn lucky if he survived the loss of blood. He knew the Ranger wouldn't release him, not even to get help. Nick had studied his captor intently the past few days, and he knew the man would die before giving up, before surrendering his prisoner.

Nick only partially understood such dedication to an ideal. He knew he would die for his family, perhaps even for a very good friend, but never for a cause, or for something as nebulous, and often unjust, as the law. He would even probably kill the Ranger to save his own skin, though killing would never come easily to him. The Ranger apparently had no such compunction.

Or did he? Nick knew he was damn lucky to be alive now. Other men would have killed him with a hell of a lot less reason—and done worse to Lori. Damn it to hell, he wished his shoulder would stop aching. He must have hit it far worse than he'd thought. He moved his hand to rub it, only to be reminded that Lori was attached to his wrist, and that made him realize again the seriousness of their situation.

What if the Ranger didn't make it?

They would starve to death . . . if they didn't freeze first. He picked up the canteens with his free hand. Both were full. The Ranger must have filled them earlier that morning. Even in pain Davis had thought of them, had apparently realized he might well lose consciousness, or worse.

His mouth felt dry, like cotton, but he was afraid to drink. He had no idea how long they might be like this.

Wake up, dammit, he willed the Ranger.

Wake up!

Fire and ice consumed him, each heightening the pain caused by the other. Morgan tried to sink back into the darkness, the oblivion, but something kept calling him. His left side flamed as he tried to move. He felt heavy, so very heavy. He had to fight to open his eyes. It was as if someone had fastened them with padlocks. Christ, how could he be so hot and so cold at the same time? And so tired.

He finally forced his eyes open and tried to focus them. His body was shaking. So cold, so very cold, except for that vicious, rampaging fire in his shoulder.

And then he remembered. The shot. The pain. And eyes. Treacherous amber eyes.

He wiped his face with his right hand, then slowly tried to sit. He was so damned cold, and he felt the freezing wind against his naked upper body. Shirt. He'd taken off his shirt after the shot. Had to get something. Had to get warm. He tried to move, and the pain in his shoulder intensified. He held back a groan and looked around.

The shirt was beside him, but it was cold, stiff, and still a bit damp with blood. His leather coat lay a few feet away. It too had a bullet hole and was splotchy with blood. He pulled it around him, but he knew he needed to tie a bandage around his shoulder to stop the leak from the wound. And another shirt. A blanket. It was cold. And he was tired. Tired and weak. So damn tired and weak. And cold.

He thought of his prisoners. His half-open swollen eyes found them twenty feet away. Both of them had coats, and the blankets Braden had used last night. He looked away from them. He didn't want to see the girl, didn't want her to have the satisfaction of seeing how well she had succeeded. She'd almost killed him. A few more inches . . .

Why hadn't he guessed? Why hadn't he thought her capable of this? That softness . . . in her eyes at dinner that night. What a fool he'd been. He rose to his knees, then, through sheer force of will, to his feet.

Waves of dizziness attacked him. He leaned against a tree, willing them away, willing strength to creep back into frozen limbs. Ignoring the Bradens, he located his knife on the ground and ripped into strips what remained of his bloody shirt. Painstakingly and awkwardly, he bandaged his shoulder, wincing as cloth hit the open suppurating wound. When he finished, he rested a few moments, closing his eyes while summoning another small burst of strength. Then he stood again, unsteadily, and, carrying his gunbelt, stumbled to his horse. He had already saddled the animal, tied his bedroll to it. Using the knife again, he cut it loose. He didn't think he could untie it with the one shaking good hand.

The bedroll fell to the ground, and Morgan fell next to

it, jerking it open. He'd had two extra shirts, one of which he'd given to Braden for his injured leg. He took his last one, tried to pull it on over the crusted, black raw burn on his shoulder. Christ, it hurt. His whole body now was shivering from cold, the fingers of his left hand virtually useless with pain, the ones on his right shaking. He forced them to work, to drag the sleeve over his left arm, then over his good arm, and he buttoned the shirt only with the most willful concentration. Then, with the same painstaking procedure, he buttoned the coat that had rested on his shoulders and had fallen when he had. One arm, then the other. Buttons. Then the gunbelt. Christ, but it hurt to fasten the buckle. And he was still so damn cold. He rested next to his bay.

Fire. He needed a fire. Not only for himself but for the other two. Milling clouds darkened the day sky. He'd been warned about these mountain storms. He closed his eyes. He knew he couldn't travel far, not like this. Not with two prisoners ready and eager to take him.Kill him. So eager to do exactly that.

Shudders shook his body, whether from outside cold or from the hard freeze inside him, he didn't know. Whatever was soft in him, whatever had ignored the warning signs he usually heeded, now hardened into stone. But that didn't warm the chill he felt, a chill more painful than that blowing across the canyon.

For a few moments the other night in Laramie, he hadn't been alone.

But he had. He just hadn't realized it. And now he had to decide what to do with Lorilee Braden—if he, and the Bradens, lived through the next few days. Two cripples. A treacherous woman. Bounty hunters on their trail. And now possible snow. Christ, what else could go wrong?

Still, the Bradens were his responsibility. He wasn't going to let Nick Braden go, nor could he leave them to the storm or to bounty hunters, who would show damn little mercy. He forced himself to move again, up on his feet. A fire. He needed the warmth of a fire. They all did. Then he could decide what to do.

Morgan felt in his pocket for the keys to the leg irons and handcuffs. He had to let one of them fetch wood, and since Nick had injured his leg, it had to be the woman. Morgan knew he didn't have the strength left to gather enough wood to last through the day and night, and he doubted he could travel before then.

If only the storm would hold off.

He tried to think. Concentrate. Lorilee's horse. Her pistol. It must be back there at the rocks. He had to get both before he sent her after wood.

He walked slowly back to the Bradens. Nick had straightened, his back stiff, his eyes wary. Lori had drawn up her legs, resting her head on her knees, and she gazed at him under long dark-brown lashes. He couldn't read them, but maybe he didn't want to. He sure as hell wouldn't trust what he thought he saw in her eyes.

At least they had the horse sense not to ask him how he was.

He glowered at Lori. "Where's your horse?"

"About a half mile from here."

"Which direction?"

"North."

Her answers were as flat as his questions.

"Give me a landmark."

Lori looked toward the rocks from which she had shot him. "That group of aspens standing among the pines."

He nodded and turned, noting the way her free hand was knotted into a fist. Because she had failed to kill him?

Morgan was starting to leave when Nick's voice stopped him. "There's going to be a blizzard before long."

Morgan turned back. "There's nothing I can do about that."

Braden's jaw worked. "I know of a cabin not far from here."

"We're staying here. Thanks to your sister, I'm not in any condition to ride."

"It's not more than two miles."

"We stay here," Morgan repeated, trying not to stumble as he moved toward his horse, thanking God as he did so that it was already saddled. He didn't think he could lift a saddle now. It was going to be damned hard to lift himself.

He used his right hand to clutch the saddle horn, giving him the balance he needed to lift his battered body into the saddle.

"Davis!" Morgan ignored Braden's last plea and, trying not to betray how very weak he was, he pushed his horse into a trot.

Nick yanked the chain linking his ankle to the tree. He bent over, forcing Lori to move with him, and for yet another time his hands inspected the iron ring around his ankle. How many times had his hands probed for a weakness, a way to slip his foot from the ring? He'd never felt so helpless, so unable to protect Lori, let alone himself.

Davis was a Texan. He had no knowledge of the mountains or how fast the snow could fall and envelop everything. They could freeze to death in a matter of hours without shelter from the coming snow and ice and wind. The Ranger would succumb first, with his wounds. But that was damnably little comfort, chained as Nick and Lori were. They would simply take longer to die.

There was one slim chance, a last resort. The iron cuff around her small wrist was loose. She had tried unsuccessfully to slip from it, but if the skin was slippery from blood . . . Perhaps a chance. A damn slim one.

Nick looked at his sister, ached for her. Something vital had drained from her in the past few hours. No spit and vinegar. No defiance. Her back had been even stiffer than his own, her face like a mask. And he knew she was hurting in a way she'd never hurt before.

He would wait for now. Perhaps he could still convince Davis to make for the cabin. He looked up at the sky again. They had only a few hours. He felt it.

. . .

Morgan found the palomino after picking up Lori's pistol from the ground where she'd dropped it. The horse was standing patiently, its reins tied to a tree. The welcoming neigh made it clear the animal was pleased to see someone approaching. The mare stamped nervously on the ground, stretching its long golden neck as if to look for its mistress.

Morgan leaned down and untied the reins. He barely managed to sit back up in the saddle. How much longer could he go before he rested again? It had probably been foolish coming here, but he couldn't leave a horse tied alone, not with the wild animals in the mountains and especially with a storm coming, nor could he allow Miss Lori to go after the horse. No telling what she would do, how she would try to finish what she had started. Or what surprise she had hidden in the saddlebags.

He clenched his jaw, more against that thought than against the waves of pain that kept rolling through him. Why did the fact that she had shot him in ambush bother him so much? Why had it hurt so damn badly in ways other than physical? Braden was just another job. An outlaw like so many others he had brought in. Lorilee Braden was a complication, a problem to be dealt with, just as he would deal with anyone interfering with his duty.

He was disturbed, he told himself, because of his lack of judgment, not because of the feeling that had come to life in places he thought dead. He had been played for a fool, and he was paying a fool's price; the only thing to do now was learn from it. He obviously had not learned years ago when he'd been taken in by a woman's tears. It was a mistake he wouldn't make again. His fingers tightened around the mare's reins as he turned his own horse and started back.

Snow started to fall as he reached the campsite. He dismounted and tied the horses, knowing he couldn't avoid Lori any longer. There were tasks he couldn't manage by himself, and they had to be done before he succumbed to exhaustion and weakness.

Wearily, he approached Braden and his sister, his fingers retrieving the key to the handcuffs. He tossed it to Lori, keeping a safe distance from them both. "Gather some wood," he ordered abruptly as he unholstered his Colt and pointed it at Nick. "Remember, I'll have the gun aimed at him every moment you're gone. The slightest unexpected sound or movement, I'll shoot."

She unlocked the handcuff and started to move, but her brother's hand held her back. "Go ahead and shoot. Get it over with, damn you," Braden said, "and let Lori go."

"Heroics, Braden? They won't work."

"No heroics, Davis," Braden said, his voice flat. "I've never been one for heroics, not like you. Hunting men has never appealed to me, but I *am* practical. If we stay here, we'll die. You'll be the first. Right now that wouldn't trouble me at all, but your death means ours. A long, slow painful death. I'd rather die here now and give Lori a chance."

"No!" Lori's agonized denial pierced the frigid air.

Morgan's finger tightened on the trigger, but Braden's gaze never faltered, never blinked. Merely invited. Dared. Willed. Part of Morgan wanted to shoot, to have this done and over. Slowly, he lowered the Colt to his side.

Braden's voice became persuasive. "I'll do whatever you want. Give you my word, my oath. My parole. Whatever. Just get us to that cabin."

Morgan's gaze left his and moved to Lori. She was holding her breath, her eyes full of fear, but he knew it wasn't for herself. "And you, Lori," he drawled, "would you do the same?"

She nodded, her eyes searching his face for some sign of softening, some tempering of the white-hot anger she'd ignited. "Anything," she whispered.

"Anything?" His voice was rough with bitterness, with cruel mockery, with pain.

She closed her eyes for a moment, her mouth trembling, and he felt a momentary sympathy; but it was gone almost as fast as it came. These two would kill him as soon as look at him. But he knew Braden was right: he *would* be the first to die. He was too weak to fight the cold and exposure of a winter storm. And he knew he couldn't leave these two to die after him.

Still, he hated to give Braden even this kind of victory. The man would damn well pay for it, he pledged to himself. Morgan couldn't remember when he'd felt this kind of vengeful anger, and he didn't much like it in himself. But it was undeniably there, fierce and needing.

"How far did you say the cabin was?"

"Two miles or so. It belonged to a trapper who moved on last year after the beaver were trapped out. It's solid, a roof and fireplace.

Morgan hesitated, looking around. The flakes were thicker now, dusting the ground with white. The wind was blowing harder, filtering through his coat. God, he needed rest. He was fighting to keep on his feet, from slumping against a tree and closing his eyes. He knew Braden was right. If he went to sleep now, he would probably never wake up.

"Davis?"

Morgan's attention went back to Braden.

"I've never broken my word." He hesitated. "I've never begged before, either. At least let Lori go."

Morgan looked at him with contempt. "So she can ambush me again? Or maybe she has more of that laudanum she bought in Laramie?"

"What do you want from me?" Braden said in a pleading voice. "Dear God, I'll do anything."

Morgan hesitated. He would never trust Nick Braden or his sister. But he had damn little choice. "All right," he said. "Your word. Your word that neither you nor . . . your sister will make any attempt to escape."

Braden looked at Lori. She nodded.

"I want to hear it," Morgan said.

"I swear," Lori said, her voice beginning to break. "Now you, Braden."

"I swear it," Braden said. "Until the storm is over."

"Already making exceptions, Braden?"

Braden's jaw set.

A wave of defeat washed over Morgan. These two were willing to die for each other, and just as willing to kill him. He never felt so damn alone in his life. He tried to shake that feeling of desolation, and his eyes raked over them as he finally spoke. "I wonder how much your word is worth." His voice revealed how little he trusted them. "You and I already have a debt between us," he warned, turning to Lori.

She swallowed hard. "I . . . I'm really . . . sorry. But you won't believe that either, will you?"

"Oh, yes," he said flatly. "I believe you're sorry. Sorry that you missed anything vital."

The snow was coming faster now. Still free of the handcuffs, Lori was sitting, waiting for his decision.

"Get the bedrolls together," he said abruptly.

She didn't say anything but quietly took Nick's blankets, rolled them up, then looked back to Morgan for additional instructions. "I assume you can saddle a horse," Morgan said, and she nodded. "Then saddle your brother's horse."

Lori made no comment but wrestled with the saddle, finally getting it over the big horse's back. The second pair of handcuffs were still attached to the saddle horn. Morgan watched as she buckled the saddle under the big bay and moved away. He then directed his attention to Braden. "Put the cuff on your other wrist," he ordered.

Braden's jaw worked. "I gave you my word."

"Oh, I accept it," Morgan said wryly. "And I expect you to keep it. Still, I'd hate to see temptation get in your way. I don't think ethics is the strong suit of your family."

Morgan followed Braden's glance over to Lori. She'd heard the comment, and her face flushed. Braden fastened the cuff to his free wrist and threw the key to Morgan, who exchanged it for the key to the leg irons.

"Unlock the one around the tree," Morgan said. "The other stays on."

Braden did as he was told and stood, balancing on his good ankle. Lori was still waiting for his next directive. Christ, he had to get all three of them on horses now.

He nodded his head toward Braden's horse. "Lori, you mount first, and tighten that cuff around your right wrist. Now, Braden, your turn. Mount behind her."

The snow was coming fast. Braden limped over to his bay, dragging the other end of the leg iron. He paused, set his jaw as he put his leg in the stirrup, and, clasping what he could of Lori's slim waist, swung up behind her. Morgan watched every move like a hawk watching its prey. It was awkward as hell, both for Braden to get up and then for him to settle in the saddle with Lori in front. There was no place for his handcuffed hands, even as she tried to inch up as much as possible to give him room.

While both his charges were busy arranging themselves, Morgan slipped the keys to the handcuffs and leg irons into a tiny pocket sewn into the lining of his hat. Then he picked up his hat and rifle and tied his bedroll to the end of the saddle. He paused a moment, fighting to stay conscious. He leaned his head against the horse, steadying himself. Then he untied Braden's and Lori's horses from a tree and fastened their reins to a lead rope.

He mounted slowly, fighting to keep from falling. He looked over to Braden. "Which way is the cabin?"

"Down this canyon," Braden said. "About halfway through there's a break in the rocks on the left. A rough path upward."

Snow was covering the ground now. Morgan couldn't even see the sky. How in the hell was he going to find a path? But Braden was right, he knew that now. This was a different kind of snow from what he knew. He instinctively felt the danger in it.

His wide-brimmed hat couldn't keep the snow from his

eyes as they rode. The wind penetrated his jacket, and his gloved hands felt brittle after just a few moments. He bent, partly against the wind, partly because he no longer had the strength to stay upright.

Ice and fire. Like this morning. They licked at his insides, sapping what strength he had. It seemed like hours before he heard a shout behind him and looked up. A break in the rocks.

He turned his horse, found the path, and clutched the saddle horn in desperate determination as the horse moved on, seeming to sense a destination ahead. He couldn't see anything, just a wall of white, and he realized he was blinded by the snow.

White. That was all he saw. And then black.

And then there was nothing.

CHAPTER EIGHT

Lori shivered as she watched the man riding in front slump over the neck of his horse. She was freezing, and *she* had her brother's warmth against her. He had lifted his handcuffed hands over and around her, pulling her body against his, sharing body heat. The Ranger had none of that.

She couldn't tear her gaze from the man, no matter how much she wanted to. She should be feeling a measure of triumph, she thought. Instead she felt shame and a hollow grief she only partially understood. Her brother's survival depended on another man's destruction; she hadn't expected the dilemma to be so personally agonizing.

There was something inexpressibly poignant about a man trying to do the impossible. Especially this man. So stubborn, so unbending. She'd never met a man before who was so completely incorruptible. He didn't give an inch, not to himself, not to others.

She told herself it was because he looked so much like Nick that her heart had somehow become affected. But the deep, trusting family love she had for Nick was nothing like the kind of leapfrogging, heart-jabbing, conflicting emotions she couldn't contain when she looked at the Ranger. They were feelings too new and strange and deep to puzzle out.

The Ranger's horse went slogging on through the snow, following the opening between trees despite the lack of guidance. She wondered how he managed to remain on the horse. But even as she wondered, his body started to lean, then fell to the ground, the horse stopping with him, its head dropping to its master's body, nuzzling him in question.

Lori felt the tug of Nick's arms. They were leaving her, going up over her head again, his body warmth leaving her. She felt him slip from the saddle behind her. Half-frozen, she watched him limp to the Ranger's side. She wanted to go to Morgan Davis, but she was locked to the saddle horn. She watched Nick check the Ranger's pulse, then his pockets. He swore as he apparently came up empty and walked back to her.

"He's still alive," he said with a grim expression. "I'd hate to think what it would take to kill him."

Lori swallowed. "What are we going to do?"

"The cabin's just above us. Problem is, I can't carry him, not with these damn handcuffs, and I can't find the key." They both looked at Lori's hand, still handcuffed to the saddle. She wouldn't be of any help.

"We can't leave him here to die."

There was the smallest bit of hesitation on Nick's part, and for a moment Lori felt sick that he might even consider the possibility. But his jaw worked as it did when he was concentrating.

"No," he finally said, "I just don't know how we're going to move him. I hope to hell those keys didn't fall out of his pocket." He straightened. "I can't put him back on the horse, not with these irons. Goddammit."

"How far is the cabin?"

"A hundred yards or so. No more than that."

So close and yet so far. Every part of her was shaking with cold. The day that had been all white, was now gray, washed in a deepening darkness that proclaimed the onset of night. Had it been only one day since she had lain in ambush for the Ranger? It seemed a lifetime.

Nick moved then, untying his bay's reins from the Ranger's lead and handing them to her. "Go on up," he said. "The trail dead-ends at the cabin."

"I'll wait for you," she insisted.

He raised an eyebrow. "Don't trust me with him?" There was a bite in the words. "I gave my word, Lori."

"I . . . I just don't want to be alone," she said. "And you might . . . need me. Encouragement at least." She tried a small smile as she looked down at her handcuffed wrist again.

His expression softened. He turned around and went back. If only he could revive the Ranger for a few moments, get a little help from him. If not, he would have to rig a sling of some kind. He knelt next to the man who was so damned determined to see him hang. Despite his words to Lori, it would be so simple to leave him there to die. An easy choice, really: his life or the Ranger's.

Easy but for Lori, who would never forgive either him or herself.

Easy but for his own rather tarnished honor. He knew the Ranger could have left them both to die.

Nick looked longingly at the Colt in the Ranger's holster. He had sworn he wouldn't try to escape, not until after the storm. Still, it wouldn't hurt to take the man's gun. Wouldn't saving his damned life be enough? He could save the moral dilemma for later.

He slipped the gun out of the holster and into his belt, then tried to bring the Ranger back to consciousness. "Davis," he said. "Damn you, Davis, wake up."

He slapped the Ranger's face once, then again. "Davis!"

Still nothing. He sat next to the man and did as he had done earlier—tried to will him back to consciousness. He felt a curious bond with the Ranger, perhaps because they so resembled each other, but he couldn't help thinking it was more than that. He knew the Ranger, and how he thought, better than he'd known any other man, even on much longer acquaintance and surely in much better circumstances.

When willing didn't work, he used instinct to try another tack. "Davis," he said in a low but penetrating voice. "That's right, Davis. Just give up. Give up and die. I'll go free. I'll win, Davis, just like I knew I would, given time. Just like Lori knew."

Nick smiled grimly when he heard a low growl from deep inside the man next to him. His eyes slowly opened and blinked against the faint gray light; his body shuddered, a deep, heaving movement of immense effort. A gloved hand went to the holster instinctively and found it empty. The Ranger glared at him, and Nick knew he'd won. Morgan Davis would somehow find the strength to make it to the cabin. Nick held out his handcuffed hands. "What did you do with the keys?"

Davis ignored the question and struggled to sit up.

Nick shrugged. "I'll find them. In the meantime, it's going to be damn hard getting you to the cabin."

"You . . . gave your word."

"So I did," Nick said. "I didn't say a damn thing about saving your ornery life." He held out his hands again. "Take them. See if you can stand. We've got to get inside before we all freeze to death."

Davis did so, his two hands clasping Nick's as he struggled to his feet. The grip was surprisingly strong.

"Lean on me," Nick said. "The cabin is just yards away." Leading the Ranger along, Nick took several steps, his blanket-wrapped bad foot nearly numb with cold, the leg irons dragging from his good foot and catching in brush. They made several steps before stumbling, Davis catching himself on Nick's shoulder. Nick righted himself, turning angrily to the Ranger. "This would be a hell of a lot easier if you would give me those damn keys."

Davis shook his head, and Nick swore a long, colorful oath.

They slowly made progress, each step more difficult with the deepening of the snow. Nick looked around and saw Lori following, guiding the horse with her free hand. Davis's horse was following on his own. It seemed hours before he saw the outline of the cabin.

As they reached the door, Nick pushed it open and felt Davis stumble again. As Nick braced himself, a hand went

his side in a movement so unexpected, it took him a
oment to realize what had happened.

Davis had his Colt back and had braced himself against
e wall, leveling it straight at Nick. Nick permitted a wry
mile. At least there was no longer a moral dilemma.

"Lori?" Nick asked softly.

"You can unbuckle the saddle. Help her in with it."

"You aren't going to . . . keep her chained to it?"

Davis ignored the question. He moved inside the cabin,
esitating until his eyes adjusted to the dim light. Then he
umbled painfully to a cot along the wall and sat down.
You can also get some wood," he said in a voice strained
y effort.

Nick's jaw worked. He looked down to his bootless
oot, the ice forming on the blanket material that had been
ut to cover it. He'd been so intent on getting the Ranger
nside that he'd ignored it. Now the pain was incredible.
ut he just nodded. He didn't think complaints about pain
ould hold much weight at the moment.

The Ranger's gaze, though, had followed Nick's down
o his leg, and he swore. Morgan frowned, his eyes nar-
owing as he studied the wet cloth legging. "Your boot?"

"Lori put it in the bedroll."

Morgan Davis hesitated, and Nick realized how ex-
austed the man was. The Ranger rarely hesitated. Or for-
ot anything. His strength must be depleted. Nick didn't
now how he had made it this far.

The Ranger finally spoke. "Get your sister, I'll fetch
ome wood inside."

Nick shook his head. "I don't think you can. I'll do it.
here's some cut on the side. I was here last spring. The
ottom logs should be dry." He limped to the door, then
aused. "I can be more help if you take off these hand-
uffs."

The Ranger shook his head. "She must be getting
old," he prodded.

"I saved your damned life," Nick exploded.

"After you took my gun. Your word is worth about as

much as I expected," Davis said. "And it was your sist
who nearly killed me. I don't owe you a damn thing."

Davis started to slump. He closed his eyes for a m
ment, and Nick thought about trying to jump him, but th
eyes opened again, studying Nick coolly. Nick shook o
the tempting thought. Lori would be going crazy outsid
And Morgan Davis surely couldn't last much longer lil
this—even though he appeared to have more than th
cat's fabled nine lives.

Nick moved out the door. Lori had dismounted, waitin
for rescue. It was nearly black out now, the only col
provided by the white snow, which continued to fall
thick flakes. Nick limped out to her.

"Nick?"

"I don't think you need to worry about the Ranger," h
said bitterly. He unbuckled the saddle slowly, hindered b
the handcuffs. He grabbed part of it as it started to fal
keeping it from jerking Lori off her feet. She looked
him, and he managed what he hoped was a reassurin
smile. "He still doesn't trust us," he said with dry unde
statement.

He helped her into the cabin. The saddle was heavy bu
usually wouldn't have been a problem for her; nov
though, she was exhausted and cold, her fingers near
frozen. He helped her lower the saddle as she, by nece
sity, sat on the floor. "I'll get some wood," Nick said.

The dark figure in the corner made no commen
merely watched every movement. Nick made his wa
back out again. He could barely move now; every step wa
agonizing. There were a few logs outside the cabin, woo
he'd cut months ago when he had stayed there. He gath
ered some twigs and branches for kindling, then scoope
up several logs in his arms, balancing them precariousl
with his manacled hands. He had to get a fire going, t
bring some heat for Lori and himself.

He could care less about the goddamn Ranger. Th
more he thought about it, the more he wished he had le
the man in the snow to die, as slowly as possible.

Nick carried several armloads of wood inside, slammed the door closed, and set several logs in the hearth of the fireplace. He stacked them. "I don't have magic fire," he said sarcastically to the figure in the corner.

The Ranger tossed a match at him, and Nick struck it against the hearth. The flame struggled at first, then flared toward the logs. None of the three in the cabin moved until the logs glowed, and heat radiated, and all of them moved toward the warmth together—reluctantly, but without choice. They needed that warmth to live.

Nick sprawled in front, taking off his gloves, then unpeeling the wrapping around his leg. His bedroll was buckled to the saddle he'd just brought in, and Lori was already unrolling it with her free hand, silently handing him a blanket to rub and dry the leg. She drew the other one around her, moving as close to the fire as she could get, reveling in its warmth, almost forgetting for a moment the man who sat on the one cot in the room. He was as apart, as detached, as ever. A chasm yawned between them, and tension crackled more furiously than the new fire a few feet away.

Morgan knew he was hanging on by a thin thread. Only that part of him that was sheer tenacity had responded to Nick Braden outside in the snow. The sound of Braden's voice kept echoing in Morgan's consciousness. As did the nagging question of why the man had bothered. Because he'd needed the keys to the handcuffs? That was the only thing that made sense. Morgan said thanks to whatever part of him had decided to hide those keys. The hat was next to him now, saved by the leather thongs that he'd knotted under his chin during the storm.

He looked around him. They were all on the edge of exhaustion, the girl and Braden as much as he. Braden had been right. They wouldn't have survived out there. *He* wouldn't have survived out there. And even now they needed food, and he knew something had to be done for the horses. So much to do, and he was so tired, not to mention the constant, burning agony of his shoulder.

But first he let the warmth seep through his wet clothes, fill the cabin, which was unexpectedly well built. The sparsely furnished room was small, and it retained the heat radiated by the fire. He was on the only bed, and that was nothing more than a rough wood platform anchored on four wood stumps. It was obviously fashioned to keep the occupant off the cold floor, and nothing more. Everything else was gone, stolen or burned for firewood.

Rough as the bed was, it was inviting. Anything was inviting. So tempting just to lay his head down.

Food first. And then secure his prisoners. But how? There was not a damn thing to use. And he knew how badly he needed sleep. Rest.

As warmth replaced some of the cold in his body, he started to feel a corresponding strength. He regarded his companions. Nick Braden was sprawled lengthwise in front of the fire. Lori was huddled next to him, her hat gone, lost someplace in the snow, and her hair still damp. Her head had dropped to the saddle, and her form looked fragile, defenseless. Only the pain in Morgan's shoulder reminded him how deadly she could be.

His gaze met Braden's in the firelight, the only light now in the cabin. Christ, there was so much that needed to be done. Two exhausted cripples and an even more exhausted woman. "The horses need shelter, and there's coffee in my supplies." Morgan said. "And some food."

Braden sat still for a moment, then pulled his boot from the bedroll. He'd laid his sock on the hearth, and he felt it now—still damp but warm. He pulled it on and then tried the boot on his swollen ankle. It hurt like hell, but he finally forced it on. "There's a lean-to in back where the horses will have some protection." Anger had drained from his voice, replaced by flat practicality.

"How long will this storm last?" Morgan disliked asking the question, betraying his own unfamiliarity with this part of the country. Braden, he knew, had been there frequently.

Braden shrugged. "Two days, maybe three. It's early for a prolonged bad storm here."

Morgan sighed. With his luck on this job, the storm would last for weeks. He rose and nodded for Braden to go out ahead of him. Braden braced himself, then opened the door, and the cabin was filled with a roaring wind. Morgan stepped out behind him and closed the door.

He headed for his horse, took the rifle from the scabbard, along with saddlebags he tossed over his good shoulder. He held on to those but dropped his bedroll next to the cabin door. With unspoken understanding Braden unbuckled Morgan's saddle, dragging it and a sack of the supplies to the door of the cabin and leaving them there. The two of them then led the three horses to the lean-to and tethered them there.

Morgan followed Nick back into the cabin. He put the rifle and his saddlebags holding Nick's and Lori's guns at the back of the cot. Then he sat, fighting pain that kept trying to pull him back again into the luxury of unconsciousness.

As Braden made coffee, Morgan took off his jacket and shirt. The bandage was soaked with blood. Braden took one of the cups they'd been using, wordlessly heated some water from a canteen, and passed it to him. Morgan carefully took off the bandage, setting his jaw to keep from uttering a groan.

But Lori wasn't as contained. "Dear God," she whispered. Then pleaded, "Let me help."

He grimaced. "No," he said abruptly. "I've had worse."

"Please."

"So you can finish what you started?" he said in what sounded like a low growl, even for him. "No thanks."

She sat up, and her face glowed with concern in the flames. Part of him wanted to believe in her, but he couldn't. He wished she didn't look so damn pleading and vulnerable . . . and pretty. She had no right to look like that after what they'd been through. He thought of those hands on him, what they would feel like if they were gentle and soothing. But nothing about her, he reminded himself, was gentle. That kiss had been a lie. A trap.

He busied himself trying to clean the wound, catching the smothered groans in his throat. He couldn't afford infection now. He needed this snowbound time to regain his strength. Then they could resume the journey, and he could prefer charges against Lorilee in the first town they came to. He would drop them later, when he knew she could be no more trouble. In the meantime, he had to be on guard. . . .

He finally finished and bandaged his shoulder again, pulled on his shirt and jacket for warmth, and sat back, watching Braden, limping badly, pour coffee and distribute some hardtack and jerky he'd dug from the supply bag. His prisoner then collapsed in front of the fire. Lori said very little, just took the small offerings and ate and drank silently. Occasionally her gaze found him, and she would stare intently at his shoulder. Then she would turn away. She was, no doubt, wishing she had been more accurate. Still, Morgan found himself missing her sass and defiance.

When they had finished the sparse meal, the room was warmer and the coffee heated their insides. They were all near collapse—he more than the others, he suspected. He took the handcuff key he'd slipped from his hat while Braden was busy and threw it to her. "Do you need to get some exercise?"

Her face reddened slightly, but she nodded and unlocked her hand from the saddle horn, even as Braden looked at Morgan with chagrin. Morgan knew he was wondering how he had missed the keys.

"Do I get some exercise, too?" Braden asked mockingly.

"When she returns," Morgan said with equanimity. "You can bring in some more wood with you."

"And then what?" Braden asked.

Morgan knew exactly what he was asking. This was a very small room. There were weapons in it. There was a wounded man and two prisoners who would like nothing better than to subdue that wounded man. And they both knew Morgan had to get some sleep.

Braden lifted his manacled wrists. "Don't do this to her," he said. "I've asked damned little of anyone until . . ." He hesitated, then continued slowly, "But I'm asking this." It was the first time Braden had shown any feeling, and Morgan's gut tightened. He sensed how much it had cost the man to make that request of him. Braden and he were alike in that way; they abhorred asking favors and were very good at hiding what they thought.

But Morgan didn't feel he had a choice. He simply didn't trust either of the Bradens, promise or not. Not after the kiss. Not after the ambush.

"No," he said simply.

Braden's jaw worked. "Your damn pride, Davis? A woman shot you?"

"Ambushed, Braden. Let's be precise. I don't give ambushers a second chance."

"She could have killed you. She's that good."

Morgan merely lifted an eyebrow in disbelief.

Braden swore under his breath, then looked directly at Morgan. "I'll kill you someday, Davis."

"You'll try," Morgan said, wishing he understood that nagging ache that remained in his gut.

CHAPTER NINE

Lori squirmed miserably between the blankets. She was head to Nick's feet, her right wrist handcuffed to his leg irons. Nick's hands were bound behind his back with the second pair of handcuffs. The infernal Ranger had found the one way to keep them both helpless while he slept. There was no way they could move more than a few inches.

As the fire had waned and the floor had grown colder, even under the four blankets she and Nick shared, her guilt and sympathy for the Ranger faded rapidly. She was beginning to regret not aiming for the heart, after all. She tried not to remember that as uncomfortable as she and Nick were, the Ranger had to be even more so.

Lori heard the Ranger's slow, labored movements as he rose from the cot. She didn't want to give him the satisfaction of seeing her turn toward him, so she just listened as he picked up several logs and put them on the fire, then retreated back to the cot. It creaked as he settled down again with a slight groan.

Nick moved restlessly next to her. He had to be hurting with his hands pinned behind him and his injured leg still encased in that boot. The Ranger had hesitated briefly, but then had ordered Nick to fasten the leg iron around his swollen ankle. . . .

Still, Nick had slept for a while. She had heard his regular breathing, felt his stillness. And she must have dozed.

They had all been so tired, fighting the storm. Fighting each other. "Nick?" she whispered.

"I'm all right," he said, moving now that he knew she was awake. He shifted his weight again. "Try to get some sleep."

She listened for the soft snore of the Ranger. She wanted to say more, but she was afraid she would wake the man a few feet away. There was no way she could lean toward Nick, or Nick toward her, or they would lose the blankets, and then there would be no way of replacing them. She silently repeated every one of the curses she'd ever heard Nick utter. She'd never run into anyone like Morgan Davis before. He was pure heartless iron, and eyes that had mellowed in Laramie had turned as cold as the wind outside.

Lori tried not to think of the kiss in the hotel hallway, of that momentary warmth that was now gone forever. He wouldn't forgive what she had done, that was clear enough, and though she didn't believe he purposely exacted revenge on Nick, his increased caution meant even more trouble for her brother.

She wished she could sleep. She was stiff with remaining so still, because she hadn't wanted to disturb what little sleep Nick was able to get, what little respite from his misery he could manage. She wondered whether it was still snowing, and whether they would be forced to stay together like this much longer. The tension between them had been so thick last night, she'd thought the cabin would explode with it.

"Don't worry," she heard Nick whisper. "It will be all right."

But Lori had the terrible feeling that nothing would be right now, not ever again. Nothing would ever be as it once was. After that kiss, with her conscious decision to shoot Morgan Davis, she had lost an innocence she knew she would never regain, a belief in herself that was gone forever. And she knew she would never again see in his eyes what she had seen those few nights ago.

She wondered whether the overwhelming sense of loss would ever go away.

On the third day in the cabin, Morgan thought he would go crazy if they couldn't leave soon. Physically he felt better, and he knew his shoulder was mending faster than he had any right to expect after the punishment he had given it that first day of the storm.

But another day in the cabin with Lori and Nick Braden, and he would be likely to go out and shoot himself and be finished with the misery.

He wished like hell they would at least complain about their treatment, but Nick had said nothing more about Lori, obviously feeling it would do no good and unwilling to abase himself again. He'd never complained for himself, though Morgan knew from his tired eyes he was unable to sleep at night and that the leg iron bit painfully into his ankle. Still, Morgan saw no remedy for it. He needed rest. He had to have it. And the reason he needed it was the Bradens.

And Lori, he knew, was too damn proud to complain. He saw it in the way she lifted that charming little chin every time he bedded them down for the night, almost daring him to relent. During the day he gave them some freedom. He allowed Lori to move around at will, though he kept the handcuffs and leg irons on Nick Braden. Nick, he knew, was the danger now, especially since Morgan had regained only a portion of his original strength.

Morgan allowed Lori to go out alone, but he always took Nick with him when either of the men had to attend to personal needs, bring in wood or snow to melt for water, or tend the horses. The snow was still falling heavily, sometimes so hard it was difficult to keep sight of his prisoner. And drifts made walking precarious for both of them. And so the three were forced to tolerate each other in the cabin. Nick spent much of the time playing the harmonica until Morgan wanted to throw it into the fire. But he also understood it was the only thing the man had right now, and so Morgan simply gritted his teeth and suffered it.

But Lori drove him especially crazy. She would sing as Braden played in the evening, both of them hunched on the floor before the fireplace, their faces silhouetted by the flames. Braden's face was too hauntingly like his, and Lori's, so bewitching as she sang of love gained and lost, made his damned loins ache with such intensity, the pain in his shoulder paled by comparison. He wanted to reach out and grab her, to kiss her again, even knowing how dangerous she was. And he loathed himself for that weakness.

Despite his contemptuous words about treachery, he respected her. He admired loyalty more than any other quality. He had fought three long years for a cause he didn't believe in, simply because of his oath to the Rangers. When his company was transferred to the Confederate Army, he believed he had no choice but to fight, and fight he did, with all the skill he had. He understood doing things one normally wouldn't do, out of a greater loyalty. He had battled his own conscience often enough, but a man was nothing if not faithful to a set of rules he believed in.

He had never believed that philosophy applied to women, too, or maybe he just hadn't thought about it. Morgan had seen the regret, even pain, in her eyes whenever her gaze had lingered on his shoulder. Still, he would never trust her. He knew that she, like him, would do what was necessary to accomplish her purpose—freeing her brother.

That knowledge didn't make the proximity to her any easier.

Restlessly, he strode to the door and opened it, preparing himself for the blast of air. It came, but the snow was lighter, and he said a rare prayer that tomorrow they might be able to leave. The storm, however, had had several benefits. It had obliterated their trail, and it had given him time to recuperate.

But now he had cabin fever. He didn't want to think it might be a different kind of fever—for Lori.

They would leave tomorrow. Make for Georgetown, where he would ask the sheriff to hold Lorilee for him until he had time to get Braden back to Texas.

"It's almost stopped snowing." Lori's voice came from behind him. They were the first voluntary words she had spoken to him in three days. Everything else had been short answers to questions or orders.

He turned. "Yes," he said flatly.

"Does that mean we'll be leaving?"

He nodded. "In the morning."

Her gaze went to his shoulder.

"It'll be all right," he said.

She averted her eyes. "Can I go out?"

"Five minutes, no longer," he said. "And don't go far. I saw cougar tracks this morning."

She got her coat. He stopped her. "Take my hat. It's cold out there."

She gave him a steady stare. "Do you care?"

"I don't want anything else slowing us down," he replied.

"Of course," she said, her lips quivering slightly. "How stupid of me."

He gave her a partial smile then. His smiles, Lori thought, were attractive, perhaps because of their very rarity. Perhaps because there was that odd self-consciousness about them, as if he were unfamiliar with the smallest pleasantry. "I don't think I would call you that, Miss Lori," he drawled.

She wanted to ask him what he would call her, but she also feared asking. Instead she moved on outside, leaving him leaning against the doorjamb.

Lori went to the side of the cabin where Clementine was tethered. She needed to take care of the horse. She didn't really want to think why. She just needed to *do* something, to take care of something. Neither the Ranger nor Nick would allow her to do anything, and she felt ready to explode with just that need. To do something, anything. She'd never had Nick's patience.

She rubbed her face against Clementine's head, the Ranger's hat tipping slightly as she did so. It was oversized for her, and it smelled of him. Leather and sweat. She had never thought the combination attractive before now, but it was tantalizing in this cold, lonely wilderness.

Clementine neighed and tossed her head, as if to assure her mistress that one thing, at least, was right. But nothing was right, and Lori couldn't see how it ever would be again. She buried her head in the horse's mane, tempted to leap on Clementine's back as she had years ago and just gallop away. But she had no weapons, no supplies, and she had already been foolish once. She would do as Nick was doing. Wait for the right time. And then what?

"Thinking about running?"

He was there, leaning against the log wall of the cabin, his dark hair blowing in the wind.

"I wish I could," she said wistfully, hoping he didn't see the sheen of mist in her eyes.

He moved closer. She turned away from him, so he wouldn't see the weakness that was there now. But she had something to say, and she knew she was going to say it.

"When I was twelve," she began slowly, "I used to shoot apples off my brothers' heads. It was part of the show, just like the magicians and the Indians. I would shoot apples off Nick's head, and he would shoot out the flame of a candle I held between my fingers."

His face was like granite, but she watched a muscle move in his cheek. "You must trust each other a great deal."

"Yes," she said simply, although she had never really thought of it that way. She turned and gazed upward at him. "I just want you to know that if I really wanted to kill you, I could have. Easily."

Something flickered in his eyes, but she didn't know what it was. He was still too hard to read, too secretive now that she had breached his defenses once. He was determined not to let it happen again. She could feel that determination.

"Then you should have, Miss Lori," he drawled, but even with the soft spoken words, there was an implacable quality that turned Lori cold. "Because you won't have another chance."

"You would really die before letting him go, wouldn't you?" she asked in a wondering voice.

"It's my job."

"It's more than that. It's your damned religion," she said furiously.

He shrugged. "If I don't bring him in, a bounty hunter will kill him. Is that what you want? He'll be running the rest of a very short life, and anyone around him will be in danger."

"It doesn't have to be you," she said, hating the tears that were suddenly welling up in her eyes.

"Why not me, Lori?" His voice had suddenly gentled. It was honestly curious. She turned away, but his hand caught hers. "Why not me?"

The command in his voice forced her to look back up at him. His eyes were dark, not blank now, but roiling with some kind of emotion. She didn't know whether he was baiting her, whether he was angry, or whether he was wanting her as badly now as something deep inside her craved him. His head had lowered slightly, and somehow she had raised herself on her tiptoes. Their mouths were close, too close, much too close.

She heard a noise coming from deep in his throat, a groan of private protest, but he, like her, seemed unable at the moment to heed it. A tear trickled down her cheek, freezing there. She barely noticed because heat was building inside her, a kind of volcanic heat that fought desperately for release. And need. Need just as strong as the heat.

And fear. Fear that she would be consumed by the explosion that was building between them. How could desire and hate be such close traveling companions?

But she didn't hate him. She wanted to. She wanted to as badly as she had wanted anything in her life. But she didn't. She couldn't. She looked at him, at that hard, unyielding face, and she saw something else, a flicker of life trying to emerge.

Then she didn't think at all, because their lips met, and she was lost in a flood of sensations that had no reason. They were like gluttons, soaking up the essence of each other, each driven by a furious desperation that was irresistible even while it should have warned. She felt his mouth drive hard against hers, felt the invasion of his tongue, and she welcomed it, seduced it, marveled at how it could awaken so many senses in her. He had been carrying his rifle, and now it fell to the ground, and his arm went around her, his hand burying itself in her hair.

He brought her body closer to his, as close as they could come with two coats between them. She wanted even closer. She wanted his warmth and his strength even while she feared it. She felt herself tremble, one shock wave after another flowing through her, causing her heart to beat faster and harder than it ever had before.

Forbidden fruit. It had always appealed to her. It had become legend in the family. Tell Lori she couldn't have something, and she *had* to have it. Like the time they told her she couldn't shoot. She was too young. She was a girl. And she had charmed the Medicine Show's sharpshooter to teach her in secret. She became so good that Jonathon relented, and she became part of the show. Against Nick's advice.

Forbidden fruit. The one man in the world she couldn't care about.

Fear squeezed her heart.

Pull away! But she couldn't. She melted instead, melted

against that strength that was so potent, so alluring. She knew suddenly she had been waiting all her life for this kind of power, for this feeling of wanting . . . to merge with another human being. To lose part of herself but to gain part of another. Heat licked around the core of her as he pulled her tighter to him.

All thought disappeared then, swamped in overwhelming sensations. She heard another soft groan and his lips gentled, became exploratory, inviting, wheedling as if he too were trying to find his way in this unknown thicket of tangled emotions. Anger was at the edge of them, but the core was pure, raw desire.

"Goddamn you." Lori heard the voice. Her brother's voice. And then felt the impact as Nick threw himself at the Ranger. She went down as well as the two men, and she twisted to avoid their bodies as they went rolling over the snow.

In stunned silence she watched them. Nick was hampered by the handcuffs and leg irons, but assisted by anger. The Ranger was hampered by his wound and surprise. But even then she knew Nick had no chance, not with the irons. He'd balled up his fists and now struck a strong blow against the Ranger's face, but the Ranger had been able to duck the next one, his good right hand grabbing the chain between the wrists and jerking them cruelly, throwing Nick off balance.

Nick managed to pull away, rolling a few feet and then lifting his legs together and kicking them into the Ranger's stomach. Lori heard a grunt, and then Nick sprawled his body over the Ranger's, his hands trying to get behind the Ranger's head as the lawman twisted to avoid the maneuver. His own fists went up, pummeling the side of Nick's head.

The Ranger's leg caught Nick and he twisted, rolling them both over until Nick was now under him, and one knee pinned the chain of the handcuffs while his good hand slammed into Nick's chin.

Lori moved, reaching for the rifle the Ranger had

dropped, and rested it in her arms. "Get off him," she ordered, her voice loud in the white, frozen world.

The Ranger stilled, but his body and hands still held Nick down. "Are you going to shoot me again, Lori?" His voice was rough, the words coming in pants as he struggled for breath. His body was heaving with exertion.

The words were like rifle pellets shot through her body, tearing through her heart and other vital places. "If I have to," she whispered.

"Your kisses are deadly, Miss Lori," he said dryly.

Nick had been still until that moment. Now he tried to buck the Ranger off him, but his captor merely shifted his weight, brutally twisting the chain of the handcuffs until Nick stilled again.

"I said let him go," Lori said, her voice stronger.

"I don't think I will, Lori," the Ranger said, his voice purposely drawing out her name with a kind of intimacy designed to infuriate. She heard the menace in it, and an anger he was barely restraining. They were edging every word.

Lori felt her hands shake. He was testing her. But he was wrong. She *would* shoot.

"Go ahead, Lori," the Ranger invited. "Of course you might hit Braden here. Unless you're as good as you say you are." He was mocking her now, daring her. Her finger closed around the trigger, but she couldn't force herself to pull it. Not at this moment. She held on to it.

"Can't use it when I'm this close, Lori?" the Ranger said. "It's easier from ambush, isn't it? When you can't really see a face?" She knew he was pushing her, wanting to know whether she would really fire or not.

And then she knew. She knew, damn him. Holy Mary and Joseph, but she knew. She lifted the barrel and aimed into the woods and fired. It clicked. The chamber was empty. He'd emptied the shells.

"Put it down," the Ranger said.

But it was her turn to taunt now. "You still don't know, do you, Ranger?" she asked. "You don't know whether I would have fired or not? That was the whole purpose of this game, wasn't it?"

He glared back. Desire still burned in his eyes, but so did blue-hot anger. "No," he said. "I'm not quite that smart. I didn't anticipate . . ." He stopped, then continued in a more controlled voice. "I emptied the rifle the first night in the cabin. It seemed wise under the circumstances."

Lori knew a fury she'd never felt before. It was mixed up with all those other incomprehensible feelings. How could she have ever felt anything for a man who would almost beg her to shoot, knowing that the gun was empty?

"You're detestable."

"You didn't think so moments ago."

"I just wanted the rifle," she lied.

He slowly lifted himself from Nick, taking the several steps toward Lori and forcing the rifle from her. He then watched as Nick rose slowly and painfully to his feet. His wrists were red with blood from where the iron bracelets had dug into the flesh during the fight.

"Take care of him," he told Lori wearily.

Nick turned toward him. "Isn't one Braden enough on this trip, Davis? Do you have to destroy both of us?"

Morgan Davis didn't answer.

"Stay away from my sister," Braden said, his teeth clenched, his hands balled in tight fists.

"I think she can take care of herself, Braden," the Ranger said, and Lori wondered whether she really heard a note of defeat in his voice.

And as the ache inside her returned, as her heart reacted to the wistful tone of his voice, she knew he was wrong. She couldn't take care of herself at all when she was around him.

CHAPTER TEN

They left the cabin the next morning.

Morgan's face was swollen, his left eye black, but Nick looked even worse. Morgan received no satisfaction from that fact. Braden had been chained; Morgan had not. He liked a fair fight, and theirs had not been a fair fight, even with Morgan's wound.

And damn, but he hungered for a chance to expel the explosive frustration he felt. Just plain fists. A no-holds-barred match between him and Nick Braden.

But it wasn't Braden who made him feel like a stumbling fool. Christ, how could he have been so reckless? There had been something about Lori's upturned face, the shimmering desire that flickered there. And he had been helpless to do anything but move closer to her.

Helpless, hell! Just damned weak. He'd never been weak before. He would not make excuses now, would not blame her. She had been just as helpless as he against that flash fire of desire—he could see that in her eyes as well.

Still, she hadn't been above trying to take advantage of it. He just didn't know whether she would have pulled that trigger if she hadn't realized the rifle wasn't loaded. He would probably never know now.

And the sizzle between them, that damnable attraction that was always present, had never been so evident as it had when they had found their way back to the cabin. The meal of bacon and beans had been entirely in silence, and there was no playing of a harmonica as Braden nursed his torn wrists. The silence was as deadly as Morgan had ever endured, and he had welcomed the first light of dawn after a restless night.

Now the sun sparkled on the snow. Snow was melting from the remaining golden leaves of the aspen, and drops of water sparkled like diamonds from them. It was a day of glory in the mountains, the kind Morgan had never experienced before, and ordinarily he would have quietly absorbed the beauty of it, allowed himself the rare luxury of contentment.

But instead, it only served to deepen the suffocating feeling of loneliness. He was standing alone against the world, doing what he had to do because it was right— because he had been doing it all his life, upholding the law.

It *was* right, dammit. He tried to dismiss the doubts that were beginning to nag at him. Doubts that were like pinpricks to his conscience, doubts that hadn't allowed him to rest last night, and which continued throughout the day.

Doubts he'd never had before.

Nicholas Braden wasn't his normal prisoner. Loyalty and selflessness were not usually qualities Morgan found in his prey. Yet Braden had flung himself on Morgan yesterday, knowing he couldn't possibly best him wearing irons. He'd not done it to escape, but because of his sister. Morgan had never before seen such affection between brother and sister, and he just couldn't liken Braden's actions to a man who would shoot an unarmed boy. Nor did he believe Lori could have such loyalty to a man who would murder in cold blood.

Of course, he had been fooled before. And it had cost him dearly.

He looked back. Nick Braden was again handcuffed to his saddle. Lori rode her own horse, but he had tied her hands with the last remnants of the shirt he'd been wearing when she'd shot him. It wouldn't bite into the skin as rope would, and he knew she was more comfortable in her own saddle than riding behind Braden. Both of their backs were straight, their bodies betraying a pride and defiance that continued to haunt him.

Beth Andrews knelt at the year-old grave, her head bowed before the simple wood cross. "I tried, Joshua. I tried to hang on to your land . . . but I can't. Not any longer." She buried her head in her hands, letting the tears flow free for the first time since Joshua had died of blood poisoning.

A careless moment with the ax. A rare, careless moment, a deep cut he had not taken seriously. "It's nothing, sweetheart," he had said. "Nothing for you to worry about." He'd never wanted to worry her, had always treated her like a princess, since the day he'd first come into her father's store in Independence. He'd been a big man, and her small stature seemed to frighten him. If so, it was the only thing that had ever frightened him.

He had also been the kindest man she'd ever met, his large size belying a heart that opened to everyone. Unlike so many westerners, he had no prejudice against the Indians, and when they'd settled in a Colorado valley, he had immediately befriended the Utes who grazed their horses here. And they had been left in peace as Joshua carved out a farm, growing wheat, vegetables, and breeding livestock, crossbreeding mustangs with the stallion that had been his pride and joy.

He'd taken such pleasure in the farm, rising before daylight and grinning as he watched the sunrise. "God has already given me paradise," he used to say. "You and our daughter and this land."

She'd always felt so safe with him, from the first moment he'd shyly taken his hat from his head and so hesitantly asked her to take dinner with him. He'd been so unlike others who'd tried to court her: the smooth-talking drummers or the rough cowboys. For him she'd tried to cling to the land. For him and for their Maggie.

But she didn't have his strength. She didn't have the strength to plow the often rock-hard ground, nor control the stallion enough to breed it to the mountain mares, nor the skill to break the mustangs that Joshua had rounded up. The fences were in disrepair. There wasn't enough firewood for winter. She didn't have money for a hired man, not enough to compete with the promise of silver and gold in these mountains. The few drifters that passed through seemed more interested in her person than the few coins she could offer, and she'd chased several off with a rifle.

There was another concern. Joshua's accident had made her only too aware of the scarcity of doctors. She lived in fear that something would happen to Maggie.

The final straw had been the visit of a group of Utes yesterday. They had decided she needed a man. She could have her choice of four braves, they told her. And they expected to hear her choice before the next full moon. One week.

She heard a noise behind her. Maggie—six-year-old Margaret Ann—stood there silently. All the joy had seemed to drain from her daughter when Joshua died. Her laughter had faded, the bright, eager smile so very rare.

"You're crying, Mama," she said with a wondering voice.

"I miss your daddy," Beth said.

Maggie's eyes opened wide, and Beth suddenly realized that by holding everything inside, she had failed Maggie. By not grieving with her, her daughter had somehow believed she hadn't grieved at all. Beth had thought she had to be strong for her child; instead, her daughter assumed she hadn't cared.

"We have to leave here," Beth said gently.

"I don't want to."

"I know, love," Beth said. "But I can't take care of it any longer."

Maggie's lip stuck out. "I don't want to leave. Papa's here."

"He would want us to go," Beth said. "He would want us safe."

Maggie thought about it. "What about Caroline? Can she go with us?"

Beth sighed. A pig. How would they take a pig with them? But Caroline was Joshua's last gift to Maggie. As a piglet, Caroline had immediately started following Maggie around. Her daughter's tears had prevented Caroline's destined slaughter, and Joshua had given Carolina to Maggie for her very own. Maggie had clung to her pet in the past year.

"We'll try," Beth said. She wasn't sure whether the Utes were keeping a watch on the homestead, or whether they had just expected she would accede to their demands in a week's time. She would have to chance a wagon in any event; she couldn't leave everything. And a pig wouldn't slow them more than a wagon. They could always cut Caroline loose, if necessary.

They would leave at night. Tomorrow night. Five days before the Utes returned for their answer. She and Maggie would head for Denver.

Maggie continued to regard her solemnly, big blue eyes begging a promise.

"Yes," Beth said with more surety. "We'll take Caroline with us." She took Maggie's hand. "We'll bring some flowers here tomorrow." She gave the small hand a squeeze. "And you can give Caroline a bath so she'll be ready to go."

Beth knew what a disaster that would be. Maggie would end up twice as muddy as Caroline had ever been. But it would keep her daughter's mind off leaving. She'd never known anything but this homestead.

Beth swallowed. It would be hard for her to leave, too. There were so many rich memories here. Maggie was born here four months after they'd arrived. They'd had neighbors then, William and Carolyn Greene, and Carolyn had helped with the delivery. But then William got silver fever and they moved away, leaving Joshua and Beth alone in the rich valley.

It had been lonely at times. But the very beauty of the valley, of the mountains that ringed it, had more than compensated. There had been Joshua and Maggie, and the hot springs where they'd loved to swim, and until recently they'd had the friendship of the Utes. Beth realized now the friendship had been a dangerous one. The Utes felt responsible for her, and that, to them, meant marriage.

Beth took one last look at the grave before turning back to the cabin. There were decisions to be made. What to take, and what to leave. What do you save from seven years of marriage? What do you discard?

And how do you start to live again?

The days had blurred for Lori. Had it been four or five since they had left the cabin?

She slumped in the saddle, wishing that the Ranger's wound wasn't healing so quickly. Each day he kept them longer in the saddle, and now it was nearly dusk, and they hadn't come to a halt yet. She was hungry and tired and dirty. They all were. They had so few changes of clothing. She had one—a shirt and the divided skirt—but both men had gone through their extra shirts, and thus far the Ranger hadn't allowed them time to wash what they had. He seemed possessed with moving.

He was possessed, period. He rode grim-faced, mindless to his pain, to any discomfort.

At least the weather had moderated, as it did so often in these fall months in the mountains. They had left the snow, and the sun shone bright. At noon the Ranger had unlocked Nick's handcuffs long enough for both men to discard their coats. Then they had stopped at a stream in late afternoon to water the horses, but he'd allowed neither of them down.

The sun should have been healing, but it wasn't. If anything, the wounds between them were festering. They no longer had the storm to fight. They had only themselves. She was beginning to feel the edges of panic. She had promised another telegram to Jonathon. Her family would be waiting in Denver for word. If only she knew where the Ranger was heading; she saw him occasionally take a map from his saddlebags and study it, then refold carefully, as he did everything.

Lori was aware he was skirting the main trails, following less traveled ones, but doing it cautiously. Natural wariness, or did he suspect trouble? She remembered in Laramie he had tried to find out whether anyone had been asking for them. And each morning as they broke camp, he buried the ashes from the fire. There were still traces of riders, of course. There was no way of totally eliminating them, but he was obviously trying to keep them to a minimum.

She tried not to think now. Not about the Ranger. Not about her discomfort, her empty stomach. She wanted to stop, then as soon as they did, she wished they were back on the trail. Whenever they did stop, her proximity to the Ranger was even more uncomfortable than being handcuffed to the saddle. After she'd rebuffed several attempts, he had stopped offering his hand to help her down. She couldn't bear the touch of it, the heat it always seemed to generate inside her, the recollection it summoned of those two kisses.

She would look at the dark, shadowed coldness in his eyes and remember that too-brief warmth. And the pain would be more than she could bear.

Lori closed her eyes, trying to think of good times, carefree times, when the Medicine Show had done particularly well in a town, and the family was together. Laughing, teasing, except for her mother, who was the quiet one, the fey one. She always watched the exuberance of the others with an uneasiness that Lori had never understood.

The horses stopped, and she opened her eyes. The Ranger was finally dismounting near what appeared to be a spring of some kind. He tied his own horse securely;

then, as had been his practice since the first, he told Nick to dismount and locked the leg irons around his ankles before releasing his wrist from the saddlehorn. He offered her brother his coat back and then closed the handcuffs on both wrists. He always left Lori's hands free until it was time to bed down, obviously assuming he could handle anything she might try while he was awake. It annoyed her, even though she knew he was right. She had as much chance against him as a snowball had of lasting ten seconds in hell.

With the lowering of the sun behind the peaks, the temperature was dropping again. She had become responsible for gathering the firewood while the Ranger unsaddled the horses, and she started her search, stopping for a moment at the spring. She kneeled and tested it.

Hot. It was one of the warm springs that had so delighted her on the journey up to Wyoming. She put both hands in and rinsed her face with the slightly aromatic water. How she longed for a bath. To wash her clothes, and Nick's.

She left the spring and gathered up the firewood. It had evidently not snowed there. The wood was dry, and ignited into fire almost immediately. Nick had wandered over to the spring and had followed her lead in washing his face, then looked longingly at the spring. Lori knew how much he too wanted a bath. While not a dandy by any means, Nick had always had a certain fastidiousness about himself. He was usually clean shaven, always first to find a bathhouse in the towns they'd visited. Now his face was covered with bristle, as was the Ranger's, making their appearance even more strikingly similar.

But Nick would die before asking the Ranger a favor for himself. Lori knew that. She approached the Ranger. She still couldn't allow herself to think of him in any other way. Not as Morgan Davis. Not as a man she was irresistibly drawn to. Just the Ranger. That reminded her he was an enemy.

He looked up at her approach, a question in his eyes.

Words had been sparse between them since that evening at the cabin.

"Lori?" His voice was curious. Not warm. Not cold. Just curious.

She stood awkwardly, then blurted out words. "That spring . . . it's a warm spring. It would be good for Nick's ankle."

He hesitated.

"I'll wash your clothes," she offered in exchange, not wanting to beg, but to make a simple bargain.

The blue in his eyes darkened, but his facial expression didn't change. "That's not necessary," he said.

He rose, dug in his pocket for a key, and went over to where Nick was sitting. He leaned down and unlocked the leg irons, ignoring Nick's surprise. He then unlocked one of the handcuffs, allowing Nick to discard his coat and shirt.

"Don't make me regret this," he said roughly, then moved back, standing against a tree, his hand resting easily on his pistol.

Nick grinned for the first time in four days. "I wouldn't think of it," he said, pulling off his boots and rolling up his trouser legs as far they would go. His ankle was still slightly swollen, and he lowered both legs into the spring and stretched out his arms, sighing with relief as he did so.

Lori decided to dare more. "There's soap in my saddlebags," she said.

The Ranger nodded.

Lori smiled. "Thank you," she said, and she nearly danced over to the saddlebags, extracted the soap, and joined her brother at the end of the spring. She took off her own boots and dangled her legs in the water. Nick looked up at her, the old devil in his eyes, the devil that had been missing ever since the Ranger had appeared in the cabin, and he grinned with real pleasure as he took the soap and started scrubbing.

He bent over to wash his hair, and Lori pushed him in.

His hand reached out to grab her for balance, and she went in beside him, her head going under. She resurfaced, laughing. For a moment she forgot where she was. She and Nick were together, teasing like old times. The water was warm and buoyant and felt wonderful, even with all her clothes on.

Then she saw the Ranger. He was frowning, and the momentary joy drained from her. But she was in the water now, and she wasn't going to get out until she'd washed her hair. Nick's grin was gone too as he lifted himself out of the spring, his trousers dripping wet. His body shivered slightly as the cold air hit it. But he waited until she was done and then gave her a hand to help her out, the infernal handcuffs dangling from his left wrist. Lori started shivering and headed to the fire, only too well aware of the Ranger's eyes on her.

He said nothing, however, as she hunched next to it. Nick had pulled on his dry shirt and was hunting in his bedroll for his other pair of trousers. Lori turned her head, allowing him that small piece of privacy, as she sensed the Ranger would give him none. Even from a distance of twelve feet she felt the alertness in the Ranger, like a rattlesnake ready to strike.

She heard several clicks and knew that Nick had finished dressing, that the Ranger had replaced the leg irons and handcuffs. She hated him then. For a moment she and Nick had been free, and now that loss of freedom was more poignant than before.

What had she thought? That the Ranger would relent, would let Nick go? That one soft moment had changed his mind? What a fool she was.

She bit her lip, trying to restrain the tremors she felt, hoping they were from the cold air now brushing her wet clothes, but knowing they were something else altogether.

And then he was next to her, her bedroll with her other set of clothes in his hand. His voice was as cold as her thoughts. "You'd better change," he said, handing her things to her, "before you get pneumonia. I don't want any more delays."

Morgan turned over in his blankets again. He'd been doing that all night. Christ, would he ever have another tranquil moment?

Not until he got rid of the Bradens.

He kept seeing her, first that glorious smile when he'd agreed to her request and then her laughing face as she surfaced from the water. He had seen her smile before, but he'd never seen joy on her face. It had struck him like a lightning bolt, how her face transformed from pretty to beautiful, the eyes so alive and the mouth creased with pleasure. He had not been able to take his eyes from her, and he had wished he could always see her this way.

And then she had climbed from the water, the clothes clinging to her, outlining a figure that was nothing less than perfect, and he felt his body stiffen with reaction. She had looked at him, and the joy had faded from her face, faded because of him, and caution replaced pleasure. He'd felt something vital drain from his body, even while his loins continued to blaze.

It had taken every bit of his considerable will to turn away as she changed clothes, to sit across from her as she prepared beans and bacon for their dinner. And then he had watched her comb her hair, drying it by the fire. It was splendid in the firelight, gold and red silk. Braden had played his harmonica again, something he had not done in days, but Lori didn't sing.

Instead, her golden eyes silently accused. He knew he would carry the image of them forever.

Whitey Stark smiled as he noted the recent ashes in the fireplace of the mountain cabin. So he had been right. He had argued the point with Curt. They had wasted several days in Denver before Whitey had convinced his companions that the Texas Ranger would choose a mountain route.

The ashes hadn't yet mixed with dust. The storm had ended three days ago. They had probably left then. A three-day head start. But Morgan Davis had a prisoner with him. And probably a woman. He'd found traces of three horses, not two, and he knew a woman had been with them in Laramie. The damned sheriff had tried to mislead him, but others in the town had been more informative. A few coins had brought forth a great deal of interesting information, including the fact that the Ranger had dined with the woman, and that there had been an obvious attraction between them.

It was the kind of information Whitey fancied. The woman could be a weapon.

And now he had found something else among the ashes. A bloodstained piece of cloth. One of the occupants of this cabin had been hurt, which would slow them down even further. He and the Nesbitt brothers should catch up with Morgan Davis and his prisoner in no more than three days. Their quarry had to follow the stream to get through the mountains, and then he and Curt could pick up the tracks. If Whitey pushed hard enough, they should track them down within the next week. This time the Ranger wouldn't get a drop on him. This time they would get the drop on Morgan Davis.

Whitey knew he would have to kill both men. He would have no choice. He had run into Morgan Davis before and knew he wouldn't relinquish a prisoner, even if it cost him his life.

And then there would be the woman. The waiter at the hotel had said she was very pretty.

He would find out for himself. Soon.

CHAPTER ELEVEN

Morgan rose before dawn the next morning and used the hot spring to bathe. Both the Bradens appeared to be sleeping. He wished he still was. He wondered whether he would ever sleep well again, or whether his nights would always be haunted by Lori and Nick Braden.

The water, though, was pleasant, and he understood the Bradens' delight with it last night. He let the heat of the springs wash over him, reduce some of the tension in his muscles. And he felt clean for the first time since his bath in Laramie.

Because the springs were in sight of Lori, he bathed with his trousers on, although he shed his shirt.

The first light was visible in the east, a pale stream layering the night sky. A few defiant stars remained, but he knew they would soon be eclipsed, blocked out by a power greater than their own.

The water soothed him, the hot, fragrant spring easing his physical weariness as well as blocking the renegade thoughts in his mind. His wound was much better. He wouldn't bandage it this morning. God knew, he had little left to bandage it with. They needed additional clothes, all three of them.

He had looked at the map last night, aware that Lori was watching him. Georgetown was the town closest to them. With hard riding they could reach it by late afternoon. To avoid Whitey Stark and others of his ilk, Morgan had hoped to skirt all towns, to live off the land, but Lori's presence had made that all but impossible. He couldn't leave the two Bradens alone while he went hunting. If something happened to him . . .

Perhaps he would leave her at Georgetown if he could find a sympathetic sheriff. As a lawman, though, he knew there might be problems. They wouldn't hold her without charges, without a witness willing to stay long enough for trial. And he didn't want that. He probably should. She had waited in ambush for him. Morgan would have easily shot a man who had done so, and without compunction.

Hell, what a mess. He could try to put her on a stage-coach again, but he suspected the same thing would happen that had happened before. She would charm someone into letting her go. He understood that now. He also understood the lengths to which she would go to free Braden. And that, by God, was not going to happen.

Morgan washed his hair, all the time seeking a solution to his problems and finding none. He sure as hell didn't want to take Lori all the way to Texas. Neither did he fancy the alternative, looking for her behind every tree, worrying whether she was safe, or whether Whitey Stark, who was probably also on the trail, might find her first.

The very idea made him sick. But so did tying her to the saddle, and chaining her at night. It grew increasingly difficult as she stared at him with those wide, vulnerable eyes, even when he knew it was an act. Damn her. She was as vulnerable as a rattlesnake. Still, he felt as if he were caught in a whirlwind, a storm of need and desire so strong, it was all he could do to keep his hands off her.

He had never been indecisive before in his life, not that he could remember. There was right and there was wrong. There was black and white, and he'd never believed in shades between them. That belief had made his life easy. He'd seldom questioned his own actions. But now he found himself questioning all of them. And he didn't like it. Not one damn bit.

Disgusted with himself, he finished washing his hair

and shook his head, throwing drops of water in every direction.

Georgetown. They would head for there today. He could purchase a couple of new shirts for himself and Braden, along with additional supplies. Perhaps he could find an answer there. He hoped to God he would.

The sweet trilling of a bird woke Lori. She moved cautiously so she wouldn't wake Nick. He had been restless throughout the night, chafing, she knew, at his enforced idleness. Besides the likeness of their faces, the Ranger and her brother had that barely suppressed energy and restlessness in common. Nick liked to prowl at night; he could never stay still.

Daybreak. Ordinarily one of her favorite times. She loved the first stirrings of life, the soft songs of the birds calling to one another, heralding another day. But now there was no joy in it. Each day brought Nick closer to a noose. Each day found her warring with herself, her almost unbearable attraction to the Ranger, her fear for her brother.

Her gaze went to where the Ranger had been sleeping. Only his blankets remained, uncustomarily messed. A map lay nearby, and she wished for a very long arm to reach out and grab it. She would sell her soul to know exactly where they were going.

She might even have to do it. Sell her soul.

She heard a splashing over at the pool and looked in that direction. The Ranger was emerging from it, his chest beaded with drops of water. He was magnificent. He looked like some God of war with the various scars on his chest, which was hard and muscled, though his body was lean—leaner than Nick's. He hadn't shaved yet, and he looked much as he had the day he first appeared at the cabin. Hard and ruthless and utterly self-sufficient. Unforgiving and unfeeling.

Yet she knew he wasn't the latter. His kisses said otherwise, even as he'd tried to hide it. She burned inside at the thought of those kisses and how she had responded to them, how she was responding even now.

He approached, his wet denim trousers clinging to his legs, to other parts that drew her attention. She had to force her gaze away—to the sun rising in the east, to the trees, to anything but the man who so intrigued and infuriated her.

The Ranger didn't glance her way. He went directly to his bedroll, grabbed another pair of trousers, and disappeared into the woods. In a minute he reappeared, the bare upper part of his body still glistening with water, but the lower part clad in dry clothes. Without words he strode to where she sat, leaned down, and quickly unlocked the handcuff binding her to Nick.

She moved quietly away from Nick, who, as far as she could tell, still slept. She quickly gathered wood for a fire as she had during the other mornings, while the Ranger slipped on a shirt and ran a comb through his hair. He ran a hand across his cheek, obviously feeling for the growth of beard, and he frowned at what he discovered. He buckled on his gunbelt, which lay next to him, then rubbed his cheeks again. With a wary eye toward Lori, he opened his saddlebags, took out soap and a mirror, and moved to the spring again.

Lori's eyes immediately went to the map that still lay on the bedroll, along with the saddlebags he left there after extracting what he wanted. She moved faster, quickly finding sufficient dry wood to start a breakfast fire.

"I need matches," she told the Ranger, who had just lathered his face and had made the first smooth movement with his straight razor as he balanced the mirror on his knees.

He hesitated. "Bring me the saddlebags," he said.

Lori stooped at his bedroll, her back to him, though she made sure he could see exactly what her hand was doing with the saddlebags. With her other hand, hidden from his view, she scooped up the map and tucked it into her shirt.

She stood and walked over to him, the saddlebags in her hand. He made her wait while he took several more strokes with the razor; then he searched in one of the bags for a box of matches and silently handed it to her.

"May I have some privacy first?" she asked with mock politeness.

He stared up at her, part of his face still rough, part covered with soap. "Five minutes, no longer," he said curtly. "And you know the rules. Don't even think about approaching the horses."

"Yes, sir," she said sarcastically.

If his eyes were fire, they would have burned right through her.

She wanted to say more, but she didn't want to make him more suspicious than he already was. She had to get into the woods, study the map, and get it back. All before he finished shaving.

Lori moved with what she hoped was leisurely defiance, no different from any other morning. Just out of sight, she pulled out the map, and her gaze raked it. He hadn't drawn a line, but the town of Pueblo was circled, and the way the map was folded indicated they would be traveling through the middle of Colorado, through the mountain trails rather than the easier but much more public trail that skirted the plains. She would have to get a message to Jonathon and Andy. If the Ranger changed routes, at least they wouldn't be too far, and she could notify them by telegraph of a change.

She tucked the map into her shirt and hurried back. The Ranger was drying his face with his bandanna, and Lori moved quickly to his bedroll, pretended to trip, allowing the map to fall where it had been.

The Ranger was next to her in seconds. "Are you hurt?" he said with a concern that shamed her. She shook her head. He held out his hand to help her up. She hesitated, knowing what always happened when she touched him. But then she took it, feeling his warm, strong grip. She smelled the lingering scent of soap on him, and her hand involuntarily tightened on his as she came to her feet. His hand held on, a second more than necessary; then he released her, his eyes suddenly bleak.

"You should be more careful, Lori," he said. "Two casualties on this trip are enough."

Her eyes went to the wound on his chest. It was unbandaged, and it still looked raw and ugly. She studied his other scars. "How did you get those?" she asked.

He shrugged. "Two during the war. The other one . . . that woman I told you about. The pregnant one." His mouth quirked up at the side, so unexpectedly that she found herself responding. His smile was so deprecating, so . . . like a small boy discovered playing in the mud.

Perhaps the spring had mellowed him. Or the quiet dawn. She just knew she liked him this way. Very much. So much that her heart pounded with curious little lurches. And that was dangerous, so very dangerous.

How could she plot against someone she liked? She forced her gaze away from him, toward Nick, who was now stirring. The Ranger's eyes followed hers, and the smile disappeared.

"If you want breakfast," he said, "you'd better start the fire. I want to move soon."

"Where are we going, or am I not allowed to ask?" she said, unexpectedly wounded by the sudden chill in his voice.

"Georgetown," he said. "To see if I can find a stage for you."

"I won't go," she said. "I won't leave Nick."

"Would you prefer a jail cell?" His voice was cold, and she wondered whether she had imagined that smile seconds earlier.

"Is that my choice?"

"It could be." His eyes narrowed. "Attempted murder of a peace officer."

"Then you would have both Bradens, wouldn't you?" she taunted bitterly. "Two trophies for the manhunter. Two heads for the price of one."

He gritted his teeth. "Dammit, I didn't want it this way. I don't want it this way, but you leave me little choice."

"You have lots of choices," she retorted. "You just won't acknowledge them."

"What about you, Miss Lori?" he asked in a deadly calm, answering her question with one of his own. "Did you feel you had a choice other than to ambush me?"

"Yes," she said flatly. "I could have killed you, instead."

"Then you should have done it when you had the chance, because you won't get another one," he said in a voice that came close to being a growl. Disbelief burned in his eyes. He was still convinced she'd tried to kill him. He would always believe that.

He *wanted* to believe that, she realized with sudden insight, because it put distance between them.

"I wish I had," she said, turning her back on him. She wanted to hide the tears in her eyes—tears of frustration, she told herself, tears for Nick. But also, she knew, she grieved for that lost, brief moment of warmth that had snaked between them.

She started the fire, hunching down in front of it as the Ranger unlocked Nick from the tree. Lori saw the strain on her brother's face as he stretched sore muscles. She looked back toward the Ranger's bedroll. The map was gone.

The two men disappeared into the trees. Lori looked toward the Ranger's saddle, at the rifle there, but now she knew it was unloaded, and the bullets were probably in his saddlebags, which he had thrown over his shoulder.

She waited for the flames to die and then sorted through the stock of supplies. Limited amounts of coffee. Bacon. Cornmeal. Some hardtack and jerky. She was sick of the latter, which had been mostly their diet for the last week. Well, she would be generous with the bacon and cornmeal since they were headed for civilization. She didn't mind at all making the Ranger spend his own money. Georgetown. It was a sizable city. The Medicine Show had gone through several times but had never stopped to perform, not since she could remember. Jonathon preferred smaller towns, towns without doctors or sheriffs.

There would also be stagecoaches to Denver. Frequent ones. And definitely a telegraph office. She had to find a way of sending a telegram, though she knew he would be watching her every minute this time . . . if he didn't make good his threat to put her in jail. She didn't worry so much about a stagecoach. She could find her way free of that, easily enough. A few miles down the road, a sudden illness, something nice and contagious like cholera.

Jail might present another problem. But with the single exception of the Ranger, she'd never met a lawman she couldn't charm when she set her mind to it.

She put a generous portion of bacon in the frying pan, and it had almost finished cooking when the Ranger and Nick reappeared. Nick sat, graceful despite the irons on both his wrists and ankles, and sniffed hungrily. Lori took the bacon from the pan and set it aside, then mixed corn-meal with water and a tablespoon of the bacon drippings and put the mixture back in the skillet to cook.

Nick grinned. "Hoecake."

She nodded, ignoring the Ranger, who stood and watched. It was the first time Lori had cooked anything for them. The Ranger had taken care of what little cooking he'd allowed; mostly they had survived on hardtack and jerky and, in the cabin, beans the Ranger had boiled until they were almost paste. He'd been worried, she supposed, that she would throw hot grease on him or do something equally destructive when he'd been so weak.

Now she simply acted on her own, and he watched her without comment but with caution, as if afraid she was making dynamite instead of simple food. He frowned as the cornmeal mixture bubbled and browned, and she expected a rebuke for doing something he'd not specifically permitted.

But he said nothing. He left the fire and saddled the horses, buckling the bedrolls in place before joining them at the fire again. She'd turned over the hoecake and poured coffee into the two tin cups that the Ranger carried in the supply sacks, along with tin plates. She divided the bacon, then took the hoecake from the pan and cut off three slices. The Ranger looked startled when she handed him a plate and put both hers and Nick's on the second plate, as she'd left her own utensils behind in Laramie.

Nick glanced up at the Ranger. "Lori's a good cook," he said with a slight, wry smile. "Hell of a lot better than you."

The Ranger merely grunted and sat down, cross-legged, staring at the hoe bread as if it might poison him. His gaze rested on Lori skeptically, as if trying to figure her motives, then went back to the plate. He tentatively took a bite, chewed slowly, then nodded at Lori. It was, she suspected, as close to approval as he would ever give her.

When they were finished, the Ranger used the remainder of the coffee to quench the fire. When he was sure all the embers were out, he scattered the remains, trying to disperse any sign of a campfire. Nick stood, lounging against a tree. Lori stole a glance at him. An onlooker would have taken his stance for nonchalance. She was only too well aware that it was something else entirely. Lori knew he was a volcano ready to erupt—just as he had at the cabin, and he would have as little chance this time.

She shook her head at Nick, cautioning him to wait. He sent her a scathing look of defiance. Lori knew he was losing his patience, tired of the Ranger's orders, gut-sick at being chained like a vicious animal. She walked over to him and lowered her voice so the Ranger, who was packing the last of the supplies, couldn't hear. "I saw his map. He's heading to Georgetown and then to Pueblo. I can send a telegram, alert Jonathon and Andy."

"No," he said. "I don't want them involved, any more than I want you involved. He's too good for Andy, and Jonathon . . ."

Nick didn't have to continue. Jonathon was a natural

confidence man, but he didn't have a violent bone in his body.

"They can get help," she insisted, then shut her mouth as the Ranger looked over toward them suspiciously.

Nick just shook his head. "This is my problem."

Lori bit her lip. "No," she disagreed as the Ranger stalked over to them, obviously aware they were discussing him.

"Let's go," he said in that curt, impersonal manner of his, those deep-blue eyes full of suspicion. She turned back to Nick and found identical eyes glaring back. Until that moment the expressions in both sets of eyes had been so different—Nick's usually light and untroubled, even after his capture, the Ranger's brooding and contained. Lori caught her breath as the similarity between the two men struck her forcefully. Nick's face rooted her to the ground. How could two people be so alike and not be related? Even their expressions at this moment were identical. The Ranger was a fraction taller, leaner, but everything else . . .

But Nick was her blood brother. The Ranger was from Texas, an orphan, he'd said, whose mother and father had died in an Indian attack.

"Lori?"

It was Nick's voice, worried, and she stared down at her hands, knotted in tight fists, the skin pale from the pressure. She felt as if the blood had just faded from her face as well, though she didn't know why it would—why . . . all of a sudden, she would have such a strange feeling, an odd premonition of tragedy.

"Lori!" Now it was the Ranger's voice. Commanding.

She shook her head, trying to rid it of cobwebs constructed of half-formed thoughts—and of sudden, inexplicable fear.

Lori felt hands on her. Nick's familiar ones. Familiar and dear. Safe. Not as hard and callused as the Ranger's but just as competent and sure. His hands, still linked by the handcuffs, were touching her chin, forcing her face up to meet his eyes. "What is it, Lori?" he asked softly.

She couldn't tell him. She didn't know herself. She just felt death. Emptiness. A terrible loneliness filled with dark shadows.

"You're as pale as a ghost," he said worriedly. "Are you ill?"

She managed to shake her head. "Just . . . tired, I think. I was dizzy for a minute." She let herself lean against him, her head on his shoulder, as she had so many times as a child, soaking up his confidence, his strength.

Lori felt him relax slowly, and she suddenly realized that, at least for now, some of his impatient anger had faded in his worry over her. He wouldn't go after the Ranger now, wouldn't go after him and get killed.

After a minute she straightened and took a step backward. "I'm all right now. I don't know what happened." She looked toward the Ranger, whose expression was as inscrutable as ever. "I'm ready," she said, and walked over to Clementine. The Ranger, in his efficient way, had already tied her horse's reins to the lead, along with Nick's horse. Lori mounted by herself and then submitted to her hands being tied to the saddle horn. He hesitated a moment, as if reluctant, then quickly bound them with the strip of cloth as she caught just the whisper of an oath from his lips.

Lori watched as he went through the usual ritual with Nick, handcuffing him to the saddle horn before unlocking the leg irons. She saw Nick's shoulders heave slightly as if barely restraining himself from doing something reckless, and then he mounted gracefully, trying so bravely not to show how much his pride was battered. Nick's rage had returned, and he held it barely in control —for her sake, she knew. He was reaching the point where he would risk everything, including his life, to free himself, no matter how slim the chance.

Lori knew then she had to find a way to stay with them. Otherwise, she knew, one of them would die before reaching Harmony, Texas. Nick had been biding his time, but he'd nearly reached the end of his endurance.

She watched the Ranger untie the reins of his own horse and mount. He looked infinitely tired, his mouth set, the lines around his eyes even more pronounced. But as completely in charge as he had always been, as quietly competent as the first moment she'd seen him.

Nick turned in his saddle and looked at her, apparently reassuring himself she was all right. She tried to smile, but the last hour had drained her of optimism. Those feelings had run too deep, too real. Her brother turned back slowly, his gaze still questioning. She knew he was still worried about that moment back at the campsite.

And so was she. She couldn't stop those beads of apprehension that had now settled in her stomach, the knot of fear that was growing inside her.

Morgan felt as tightly drawn as the military drum that had once tattooed him into battle. He had just watched ghosts flit across Lorilee Braden's face—nothing else could quite describe that look, that sudden moment of fear as she had stared at her brother, her golden, expressive eyes widening with apprehension. The emotion was palpable, her raw fear making jagged cuts in him.

And then he had watched Nick Braden soothe her, her head resting against his shoulder with such trust. Morgan had wanted to stand in his place, comforting her. God, how he had wanted to do that, and instead he had to watch, like the outsider, and the enemy, he was.

He turned and looked at Braden. His prisoner's face seemed carved in stone now, the ease gone from it. Their eyes met for a moment, and Morgan realized he had over-estimated Nick Braden's apparent acceptance of his captivity, his facade of good nature. Enmity gleamed in those eyes now. Enmity and challenge and promise.

You or me, Nick Braden was pledging silently.

Morgan understood for the first time that it was likely

only one of them would survive this journey. Morgan also knew suddenly that despite his disadvantage, Nick Braden would be a formidable foe.

And Lori? Lori with the honey-brown hair and golden eyes and the passion simmering beneath those boy's clothes. Lori, who obviously loved so deeply, if not wisely. What would happen to Lori?

If he killed Nick Braden, Lori would hate him.

He *could* allow Braden to escape.

He could, and he could never live with himself again. Nick Braden was a wanted murderer. Morgan was a servant of the law. If he bent now to personal feelings, his whole life would have been a lie. And Braden would be no better off. Not with a five-thousand-dollar reward on his head.

If only he could be sure that what he was doing was right.

CHAPTER TWELVE

Georgetown, one of Colorado's largest towns, was brimming with activity. Its very size, Morgan hoped, would allow the three to fade into its busy streets. As Morgan and the Bradens saw the first buildings ahead, the Ranger stopped the horses and untied Lori's hands. He was going to be conspicuous enough with one prisoner. He sure as hell didn't want word getting out that he was also holding a woman prisoner. Word traveled fast out there, running from mining town to mining town.

He thought a warning in order, though. "You're going to behave yourself, Miss Lori," he said. "You are going to stay at my side every minute and do exactly as I tell you."

"Why?" she asked defiantly.

"I want to attract as little attention as possible. You may want every goddamn bounty hunter in this state after your brother, but I don't," Morgan said impatiently.

She shrugged. "I don't see any difference between you and a bounty hunter," she said.

Morgan's gut twisted. "He may make it alive to Texas with me."

"And he might prefer a bullet to a noose," she retorted.

"He might also prefer to keep you out of jail," Morgan said, looking over at the object of their conversation.

Nick shifted in his saddle, his gaze going from Lori to Morgan. Unlike Morgan, Braden seldom wore his hat, and a lock of dark hair had fallen over his forehead. He looked amused. "You haven't seemed interested in my 'preferences' to this point, Ranger."

Morgan glared at the two. He didn't like being baited, and they were both very good at that. The girl, in particular, seemed to sense his weakness: his repugnance at being lumped with bounty hunters, his reluctance to cause her real harm. He gritted his teeth. "I meant what I said about preferring charges."

"Given the choice between you and jail, I'll take jail," she said cuttingly.

"Then I'll arrange it," he said coldly, squashing the sudden ache that ran through him. "Unwanted attention or not."

"Lori." Braden's voice had hardened, and something indefinable flickered through his eyes as he turned in his saddle toward her. A warning? Morgan couldn't tell.

Lori's angry gaze left Morgan's face.

"Do as he says. For me. Please." Nick's voice was suddenly cajoling.

"He's a self-righteous, officious . . ." She paused, and Morgan knew she was searching for precisely the most insulting term.

"Bastard?" he offered helpfully. He kept remembering the way she had looked last night when she'd pushed Braden into the pool, the way her face had lit with laughter. Now her eyes were narrowed with pure malice.

"Snake," she said. "A bastard can't help being what he is."

Morgan shrugged, surprised again at how well she aimed her arrows, and started to turn his horse back toward the road.

"Wait," Braden said.

Morgan hesitated.

"Can I talk to my sister a moment?"

"Go ahead."

"Privately," Braden said, gritting out the word between his teeth.

Morgan debated a moment, then nodded. Hell, they

could have whipped up a dozen plans last night while he slept. He couldn't stay awake every moment or listen to their every word. He moved several feet ahead, as far as the lead allowed, and sank down into his saddle, allowing some of his attention to focus on the golden hills. Another part of him, though, was alert to any unexpected movement. He was aware again of being the outsider, of being made to feel the villain.

And then Nick spoke. "She'll do what you say, Morgan."

For how long?

But Morgan didn't express that thought. Christ, if only there was a stage to Denver. He spurred his horse into a trot, only too well aware that a stage probably still wouldn't solve his problem. She would find a way to return to Braden. In some ways he knew it would be best to take her with them, so he could keep an eye on her. He *could* justify that, now that she had shot him.

But he quickly dismissed the idea. It would be sheer torture. He already felt like a horse with burrs planted under the saddle. He reacted to her as he'd never reacted to a woman before. Morgan had always been content with his solitary life, needing little more from a woman than a purchased night. He preferred to pay so there wouldn't be any recriminations or attachments or expectations that he would give more than one night's pleasure.

But Lorilee Braden was something else altogether. She was like a lovely wildcat. Beautiful and golden and elusive. She challenged him, taunted him as no one else had ever dared to do. She made him feel alive, by God, even when he knew she would probably kill him, given the opportunity. What kind of a fool did that make him?

He didn't want to answer that. Instead he thought of what they needed. He wanted to stay there as short a time as possible. First, the stage office. Then supplies. Shirts. A change of clothes for Lori.

Morgan ignored the curious stares directed at him and his prisoner as they passed some fine homes, a bank, a telegraph office. He stopped at the stage office, dismounted, and tied their horses to a hitching post, before approaching Lori and offering her a hand down. Surprisingly, she took it.

He wondered what in the hell Braden had said to her.

He took her arm and entered the office, leaving Braden still in the saddle, his hands cuffed to his saddle horn, the horse secured to the hitching post.

The clerk inside looked up. "When is the next coach to Denver?"

"Nine in the morning."

Morgan had hoped against hope there would be one tonight. Or had he? He wasn't sure, and that was the hell of it. "One ticket for the lady."

Lori's eyes burned through him, but she said nothing.

"Can you suggest a hotel?"

"The best one is the Hotel de Paris. Even has bathtubs. Expensive, though," he said, eyeing their dusty clothes with sudden doubt. "And then there's the Nugget," he added with less enthusiasm.

Morgan hesitated as Lori's golden eyes watched him. He finally nodded. "Where's the sheriff's office?"

"In the courthouse. He ain't there, though. Gone up to Denver to some lawman's meeting."

"Deputy?"

The clerk shrugged. "Don't know about him."

"Where's the jail?"

"Behind the courthouse, down the street."

Morgan pulled a pouch from his pocket and paid for the stage ticket, then took her arm again. Braden was slumped in his saddle, his eyes half-closed. Morgan helped Lori back on her horse, then mounted his own and turned the horses toward the courthouse. He needed to get Braden bedded down in the jail for the night. Then Lori would be his only worry.

The courthouse was closed. He rode around to the stone jail behind it, the other two trailing him on the lead. Morgan swore in frustration as he read the rough writing on a note pinned to the solid wooden door. "Gone after hoss thieves. Deputy Smythe." He hoped the man was a better lawman than speller. He turned around to where the others waited and mounted again.

"No one home?" Braden said with a taunting grin.

Morgan ignored the question. He could take them to a hotel or get the hell out of town, bed down in the woods as they had been. But he'd still not regained his full strength, and he was tired, so damnably tired. Even after the plunge in the hot spring this morning, an honest-to-God bath sounded real fine. But looking after two Bradens, particularly Lori, in a hotel?

They would be there for just a few hours. Until tomorrow morning.

The Nugget or the Hotel de Paris?

They had ridden by both. His usual choice would be the unpretentious Nugget. He'd never cared much for fancy. But from the clerk's disdain he could assume there would be no baths. And probably no locks on the doors.

He didn't want to admit it, but something else weighed his decision: the way Lori's eyes had lit at the mention of the Hotel de Paris. He had been damned rough on her the past ten days. Red ridges circled her right wrist where he had handcuffed her nightly. She hadn't complained, and that made him feel guilty.

He wondered whether the hotel would even accept him and his prisoners. He had the money. He spent damn little. His needs were few.

The Bradens were waiting on his decision. How many times had they done that? He knew how galling it was to Nick, and to independent Lori. He shifted in his saddle and eyed Braden speculatively, his gaze lowering to the handcuffed wrists. They seemed to freeze under his scrutiny. He took the key out of his pocket and leaned over, unlocking both sets of handcuffs and tucking them into his saddlebags, where he also kept the leg irons.

"You'll stay in front of me," he said, "and your sister alongside me. When we get to the hotel, you will dismount and go inside, again in front of me. Remember, I'm damn fast with a gun, and I'll have my arm on Lori. You make a break for it, and I'll make sure your sister goes to prison for that ambush."

Without immediate comment Braden rubbed his wrists, first one and then the other. Then he stretched, slowly and deliberately. He finally acknowledged Morgan's order with a slight smile. "You don't want my word?"

Morgan looked at Lori. "I have something better."

"You really are a bastard, Davis," Braden said.

Morgan shrugged. "Get moving."

"To the Nugget?"

Morgan smiled without humor. "I think we'll go to the Paris."

The hotel was as fine inside as it had looked from the exterior. Carrying his saddlebags over his shoulder, Morgan asked for two connecting rooms that fronted the street, ordered two baths immediately, and three steak dinners to be delivered to his room in an hour. He also asked whether someone was available to stable the horses and run a few errands.

Nothing seemed to fluster the clerk, not even their dusty clothes or Lori's unconventional dress. He just kept nodding his head and repeating the words, "Yes, sir," as if he were a parrot. A porter directed them to the second floor and grandly opened one door, then another, and unlocked a door connecting the two. Told which horses were theirs, he said he would bring the bedrolls "directly."

Morgan tipped him generously, then asked if he could find a store open to buy two shirts and a ready-made dress. The porter sized up the three, nodded. Morgan gave him several bills, and the man grinned and left.

He turned around. Nick Braden was striding back and forth, obviously relieved to be free of restraints. He was staying a distance from Morgan, apparently trying not to give him reason to reattach them, and Morgan felt strangely reluctant to do so. Lori had disappeared into the other room, but Morgan could hear her moving around.

The Ranger went to the window, though he never turned his back on Braden. As he'd requested, the room fronted the main street. Dusk had fallen. There was still activity, but now most of it consisted of men going into the saloons on the street. He leaned against the window frame, where he could see both the street below and his still-prowling prisoner across the room. "Sit down," he finally said.

Nick Braden hesitated a moment, obviously reluctant. His right hand rubbed his left wrist again. His gun hand, Morgan remembered. Braden was itching to use it, judging the distance, the wisdom of going for Morgan's gun. Morgan's own hand flexed suddenly, in that same odd way so like Nick Braden's.

"Don't even think about it," he warned Braden. Their eyes dueled, and he knew the man was considering risking all. Morgan's hand went to the butt of his Colt.

Lori walked in from the other room. She stopped, her gaze going from one man to the other. She blinked a moment, as if in surprise, and then she looked at Nick. "No," she said softly, and Morgan watched him slowly relax. That was the second time today she'd managed to defuse him.

After tomorrow she would be gone. And Morgan knew there would be a reckoning between them. He knew with growing certainty that Nick Braden had obeyed him until now because of his sister. That was one reason Morgan risked bringing them there. Braden wouldn't do anything to hurt Lorilee. He had to admire the man for that.

A knock came on the door, and Lori opened it. Four men came in, each holding deep buckets of water for the bathtubs that sat in each room. All four went into the other room and poured the steaming contents into the bathtub. They disappeared back into the hall and returned with another load for the second bathtub.

Morgan watched Lori's expression. She was guileless

in her astonishment. He would have bet anything he had that she'd never been in a good hotel before. The one in Laramie had been satisfactory at best. No porters there. No baths. Lodgers had to go to the bathhouse if they wanted more than a bowl of wash water. He hadn't been in too many fine ones himself, but enough to know you could get whatever you wanted. She was such a bewitching combination of deadly determination and innocence. He remembered her laughter last night. He wanted to hear it again before she left them.

He bowed and turned toward the other room, holding out his hand in invitation. "Miss Lori," he said.

She hesitated, her eyes narrowing.

"A good-bye present," he said lightly.

She stiffened. "I don't accept presents from . . ."

"Snakes?" he reminded her, a sharp ache reaching into his abdomen.

She agreed by letting the word hang between them.

"Go ahead, Lori," Braden said, stepping toward her and smiling. He, too, disturbed Morgan by his contradictions. The man was a murderer, Morgan knew. Yet Nick Braden was so damned considerate, so gentle, toward his sister. He'd never once used her to try to escape—and he could have many times.

He locked the door to his own room and then walked into Lori's, securing the door there that led to the outside hall. He returned to his room through the connecting door, leaving it partly open, and walked to the window to look out. The street was lighted by the windows of the open saloons. He was used to looking for people, at people. He was used to memorizing faces, and he did so now.

He heard the connecting door close, and he strode over, opening it slightly, not enough to see but sufficient to hear. He wondered whether he had been wise to permit her even that liberty, but he heard the creak of boards, then the splash of water, and more splashes.

Braden looked at him. "I want her on that stage too," he said in a low voice.

"So you can come after me?"

"That's one reason."

"I don't want to kill you, Braden."

"That's where we differ, then," the other man said, staring directly at him.

"I thought you weren't a killer," Morgan taunted him this time, his doubts spurring him to say things he usually wouldn't trouble to voice.

"Anyone can be made into one," Braden said, his voice still low—but now it had a harsh bite to it. "You seem to be expert at that."

"You have one of two choices, Braden," Morgan said, tired of the fencing, weary of the whole damned misbegotten situation. "You can use that bathtub or you can handcuff yourself to that bed while I take one. Either way, shut up."

Nick Braden stared at him for a long moment, then began to discard his clothes as Morgan turned away and again stared into the street below.

The Ranger was in a strange mood, Nick thought as he closed his eyes and sank deep into the bath. The Texan had been as edgy as a trapped cougar all day. Until now Nick had thought the man had no weak points. He appeared to have little or no emotions at all, not even when Lori had ambushed him. He'd just continued to go about his business in the same efficient, impersonal way. In the ten days he'd been with him, this evening was the first time Morgan Davis had shown even the slightest inclination toward humanity, though Nick had to admit he'd never been purposely cruel. Just very, very cautious.

And he was still being cautious. Nick didn't fool himself about that. Davis didn't miss a damn thing, not the slightest movement. His hand was never far from his pistol, and despite the wound, Nick knew he was now probably as fast as he ever was. The fight at the cabin proved that. He'd thought with the Ranger's wound he'd have a chance, even with the handcuffs. But the man didn't appear to feel pain. Nor did he seem to tire as ordinary men did.

Even Lori had not had her usual devastating effect, though Nick hadn't missed those fleeting glances the Ranger threw her. Nor had he missed Lori's reluctant interest in the man. He had never seen that glow in her eyes before—the glow she tried, but never quite managed, to hide when she looked at Davis.

And then there was that damned kiss. Nick had hoped, perhaps wistfully, that it had simply been one of Lori's tricks, albeit an unwise one, and the Ranger had taken only what had been offered. But now he wondered.

Which was why he wanted her on that stage in the morning. As far as he knew, the Ranger was the first man she hadn't been able to wind around her pretty little finger. That was surely her fascination with him. Lori needed a strong man to match her own stubborn nature, but the Ranger was a joyless, soulless man who would drain her dry.

He rubbed his wrists again. They were sore, as were his ankles where the leg irons had been clamped at night. The hot springs had helped, but he'd been hampered by his clothes and the handcuffs the Ranger had kept on his one wrist. This was the first time in ten days he wore no iron, and it felt damn good.

The Ranger was still leaning against the windowsill, staring out. He looked like the predator he was, wary and alert, and ready to spring. Nick wondered fleetingly what had made him that way, this man with his face.

Even sometimes with his thoughts and feelings. He remembered again feeling that strange, sudden agony when the Ranger had burned his own wound closed. If the idea hadn't been totally impossible, he would have believed that there was some blood tie. Perhaps a common ancestor, sometime back in history. But even that was unlikely. Nick's birth was registered in Denver, the son of Jonathon and Fleur Braden. The Ranger was Texan, through and through.

No, there was no connection, only an unholy coincidence.

Time was running out. Nick leaned over and took up the soap and towels the porters had brought, and started washing. Because of Lori's playfulness at the pool, he hadn't had time to wash thoroughly, and he did so now. Christ, it felt good after the way they'd been traveling. He began scrubbing his left foot, and the birthmark became visible again through the dust and dirt that had accumulated—the half heart Lori used to tease him about. "Only half a heart," she used to say. "Where's the other half?"

"You stole it a long time ago," he used to retort in a gentle ritual. And she had, with her whimsy and curiosity and passionate loyalty. A loyalty he now feared could destroy her.

A knock on the door interrupted his train of thought. The Ranger walked swiftly across the room and unlocked it. A rolling table loaded with food appeared first, then two waiters, and finally the porter to whom the Ranger had given shopping instructions. The latter carried several packages.

Nick felt oddly vulnerable in the bathtub, but the smells made his nose twitch. He hadn't realized how damned hungry he was. He started to rise, a towel in his hand, but the Ranger scowled at him, and Nick sank back into the cooling water, realizing once more how much a prisoner he remained. One more order from Morgan Davis, and he would explode, goddammit.

He watched as the Ranger tipped the men, and they withdrew, leaving the food and packages. Davis nodded to him. "You can get out now."

Nick did so, sullenly, and pulled on the trousers. The Ranger had ripped opened the packages and threw him a fresh shirt, which Nick put on without comment. Davis opened another and pulled out a blue cotton dress. He threw it to Nick. "Give it to your sister."

Nick stood at the nearly closed connecting door. "Lori?"

She opened it, dressed again in the divided skirt and blouse she'd worn into town. She looked at the dress in Nick's hands, then at the Ranger. "I don't want it," she said.

"You'll need it for the stage tomorrow," the Ranger said matter-of-factly.

Her chin set stubbornly. The Ranger ignored it, and Nick felt the tension radiating between the two of them as their wills clashed. In the air hung a near-palpable sensuality, a raw, connecting power that held Morgan and his sister tightly in its grasp. Even the Ranger's usually guarded eyes had depths Nick hadn't seen before, and Lori's body was rigid—but Nick saw her hand trembling.

Nick moved, dropping the dress, and the Ranger spun around, his hand going to his gun. His attention had been fixed on Lori—a rare mistake. A muscle moved in the Ranger's face as he realized how vulnerable he had been. For a brief moment he seemed puzzled as to why Nick had not taken advantage of the opportunity, but then his gaze returned to Lori, and he gave a brief nod.

The stakes had just gone up, and they both understood that. The Ranger had betrayed his interest in Lori, and Lori—well, Lori was not exactly oblivious to the Ranger. Nick didn't like it one damn bit. But he still wasn't going to risk his sister's life or freedom, and now perhaps something even more fragile—her heart. Yet Nick inwardly vowed retribution. Something as important as his life had just been violated.

Nick felt a muscle in his own jaw flex, his hands knot at his side. The Ranger's gaze went to them, and Nick expected him to order the handcuffs back on. He stood stiffly, waiting. He knew, in fact, that he needed the restraint, or he would attack the Ranger now, whether Lori watched or not. If his sister's spirit was to be broken, he did not want to be a part of it. And he sensed now he would be. Whether he or the Ranger was killed, Lori would be destroyed. He swallowed hard and forced his

2

hands to relax. The Ranger's eyes remained on him, reading his thoughts with that inscrutable gaze.

"Miss Lori," Morgan eventually drawled, only a hint of tension edging his voice, "would you do the honor of cutting the meat for yourself and your brother? I think I trust you a mite more."

Lori moved to the table and picked up a knife, carefully cutting the meat under the Ranger's level gaze. She looked up only once, and again Nick felt the jagged electricity between the two, like the conflicting winds that stirred the most violent of storms.

Thank God she would be gone tomorrow. But he feared that the inevitable showdown between him and Morgan Davis would always haunt her, would take something away from the joy that had always been a part of her.

She was quite obviously discovering what it meant to be a woman. Nick had always known that this time would come. But not with a man like Morgan Davis.

And Nick's hatred for him spun into a hot, burning, consuming thing.

CHAPTER THIRTEEN

Lori twisted in the fine feather bed. Her right wrist was handcuffed to one of the bedposts, held in place by a ridge in the carving. She suspected the proprietor would be horrified that his furniture was being used in such a fashion.

She had never been in so fine a bed. She wished that was the reason she couldn't sleep, but it wasn't. Morgan Davis was. Her brother was. The very real prospect of her departure from both was.

And her betrayal was.

All were reasons for her inability to sleep. The steak, at least what she could eat of it, had settled miserably in the pit of her stomach. Why did she feel so terrible about doing something that might save Nick? She squirmed again, trying to rid herself of guilt.

In the room where she had taken her bath, Lori had found pen, ink, and paper in a desk and had scribbled a telegram to her father while she made splashing noises. Lori had hidden the telegram, together with a note, in her clothes, and when she'd had the opportunity, she tucked them under one of the empty dishes for the porter, along with the last coin she had. She could only hope that the porter who fetched it would do as she asked. She had given him her most heart-affecting smile, a tear hovering artfully in the corner of her eye.

She had composed the note carefully. She hadn't wanted to put off the man she hoped would send the telegram for her. *Traveling through mountains, heading for*

Pueblo. Meet us there. Will try to move slowly. Lori. Together with the earlier telegram sent from Laramie, Jonathon would know what to do.

And Lori knew that meant ambush. Jonathon and Andy and Daniel Webster would be no match for Morgan Davis. They would have to lie in wait for him, just as she had done. She doubted whether Andy and Jonathon would be as scrupulous as she about where their bullets might go.

She shouldn't care.

But she did. Dreadfully.

All of Morgan's instincts were firing cannon balls. He lived by those instincts. He always heeded them. And now they wouldn't let him rest, though he needed it.

He worried, too, that it might not be instinct at all, but just Lori Braden. She always managed to send off another kind of rumbling, the kind located in his lower regions.

Yet he haunted the window. He'd given Braden the bed, he told himself, because he needed to keep watch, because it was easier to handcuff Braden to the poster than to hog-tie him so completely he couldn't be a threat. But truth be told, he was feeling increasingly uncomfortable with what he was doing. He was even beginning to question his own motives. Was he transporting Nick Braden because he was wanted, or because the similarity of their faces had made Morgan's life awkward?

Braden was sleeping as peacefully as the innocent. If he had a guilty conscience, it sure as hell didn't show. But Braden's hatred did show. It had all the way through dinner. What Morgan didn't understand was why it bothered him. God knew he didn't expect prisoners to like him, particularly when they were charged with murder. But the enmity went so much deeper than the usual hostility and defiance. It went gut-deep.

And Morgan knew it had hardened tonight. Braden didn't want Morgan touching his sister. And Morgan *had* touched her. He and Lori had touched each other—hell, seared each other—with glances alone. He still felt the heat, like a furnace in his loins.

He looked back down to the street—one more time, he decided, before retiring to the chair for several hours of sleep.

And then he saw them. Three men riding into town. One man wasn't wearing a hat, and his hair was white in the moonlight. Three of them now. Where had they picked up a third? He followed their progress to the Nugget down the street. They dismounted and went inside. Morgan waited. One of the men soon came out and led the three horses toward a livery stable.

They were bedding down for the night. Their questions would come in the morning. Morgan didn't want to be there in the morning.

He thought about their entrance into town. He had shaved this morning; his prisoner had not, which meant the resemblance was not as striking as it might otherwise be. He had left no indications that a prisoner was being held at the hotel, fearing the reluctance of a good hotel to harbor a wanted murderer. He hoped Stark wouldn't inquire about his presence at the Hotel de Paris, never considering Morgan would bring Braden to such a place.

How did Whitey Stark know they would head to Georgetown? Had they been followed? Or had Stark already checked out Denver, recruiting other bounty hunters to stake out other towns along possible routes? With the reward so high, he could easily have found more hands. Morgan only knew he didn't want Stark on his tail. He didn't want another ambush. He didn't doubt Stark's aim, nor his ruthlessness. Morgan knew they had to get lost in the mountains soon, before Stark realized they had stopped there.

Morgan lit the oil lamp and shook Braden. He woke immediately, his eyes holding none of the drowsiness of deep sleep. Morgan wondered if he had been sleeping at all.

"Bounty hunters," he said. "We're leaving."

Braden sat up abruptly. "What about Lori? The stage?"

"We can't chance that now." Morgan's jaw set. "You don't want Whitey Stark any place around her, and if he thought he could use her to get to you or . . ." His mouth clamped tightly together.

"Hell, you already have me," Braden said.

"That won't make any difference to Stark. He'll try to kill us both."

"That's supposed to bother me? I'm a dead man, anyway. I wouldn't mind taking you along to hell with me."

"You don't want a chance to do it yourself?" Morgan taunted, antipathy gleaming in his usually hooded eyes.

Braden smiled. "You have a point, Ranger."

"I don't want trouble with you. No disturbance."

"I've been the soul of cooperation, Davis," Braden said.

"Because of Lori."

"Because of Lori," Braden confirmed, though he didn't have to. Morgan's remark hadn't been a question.

"Remember that," Morgan warned him.

"I don't want her with us."

"You think I do?"

"Yes, dammit," Braden retorted angrily. "Convenient, isn't it, Morgan? You know she would do almost anything to help me. You didn't mind taking advantage of that fact at the cabin." He hesitated, then added very deliberately, "You sure you saw bounty hunters?"

Morgan barely kept himself from going after his throat. "If it wasn't for her," he said, "I'd turn you over to them now."

"No, you wouldn't, Ranger. You wouldn't admit defeat that way. You'd rather take your trophy in yourself."

These were almost the same words Lori had used, and Morgan didn't feel one whit better when they came from Braden's mouth. Christ, they were good at goading him. Morgan decided it was stupid to continue in this vein. They were wasting valuable time. He went to the connecting door, which was partially open, and with the light from his own room, he looked down at Lori Braden.

She was sleeping. Her hair was spread out over the pillow, and her face was relaxed. Her arm looked awkward handcuffed to the bedpost, and he felt that peculiar mixture of guilt and something stronger, something that stirred a part of him never disturbed before. He didn't want to think it was his heart.

He had sometimes wondered whether he even had one. He'd never really had anyone to love, unless he counted various Rangers who had tossed around the role of piecemeal fathering. But they kept dying on him, and he'd steeled himself against caring too much, against counting on anyone.

The war had made him even more of a loner. Too many of his friends had been killed. You couldn't hurt if you didn't care. He'd tried desperately not to care; he'd tried so hard that he thought he'd succeeded until the day he'd learned Callum had been killed. Rough and demanding Callum, who had never once touched him with affection, but who had been his one constant. For the first time that he could remember, he'd cried. He'd gone into the prairie like a wounded animal and cried like a baby. He had never done it again. He'd never allowed himself to care again.

And now he did. But he cared for a woman who'd tried to kill him, and who would probably do it again—who would always hate him for doing what he had to do.

God help him, he cared. The sudden understanding was so strong, it nearly gutted him. He'd denied it until now, had convinced himself it was only lust. But his heart had never stilled before just by looking at a face. He'd never felt so damn weak in the knees, so awkward when he was around her. He'd tried to cover it with abruptness, with indifference, by banishing her. He couldn't do that now. Not without putting all three of them, including her, in more danger than she'd ever considered.

He knew Whitey. Unfortunately, he'd never been able to prove anything against the man, not in Texas, but Whitey Stark always left bodies behind him. And not always just those who were wanted.

His fist tightened around the doorknob. More days with her. And nothing was going to improve. If anything, the hostility between him and her brother had festered into a powerfully malignant thing.

He started to walk in, to wake her, and then decided to let her sleep while he went down to pay the bill and offer a small bribe to the night clerk to forget he ever saw them. Thank God he hadn't stabled the horses in the public livery. The decision to stay there had been the right one, he realized, even though he admitted now to himself that his motive had been as much to give Lori some comfort before shipping her off to Denver as to throw off any pursuit.

Morgan hadn't taken off his gunbelt. His hand went to it now, almost automatically, reassuring himself it was there. He gave Braden a fast, warning glance. His prisoner was sitting up, his feet on the floor, his eyes alert and watchful.

Morgan slipped from the room. It must be around two, he thought. The saloon down the street had just closed.

The clerk looked up, obviously surprised.

"Bob Dale," Morgan identified himself. "We'll be leaving early in the morning," he said. "I'd like to settle now."

The clerk nodded, gave a sum, and Morgan paid it without comment; then he added several bills. "My wife . . . well, we just got married, and her pa isn't too happy about it. I'd appreciate it if you just forget about us."

The clerk's eyes widened. "Of course, sir."

"He sent some men after her. No telling what he might say. He's tried every trick known to mankind," Morgan added confidentially. "You see he wanted . . . Elizabeth to marry his business partner. An old man . . . and . . ."

The clerk nodded with understanding.

Morgan smiled his gratitude. "Do you have a back door?" He already knew they did. He always checked such matters. He also knew it was locked.

The clerk nodded. "It's locked, though."

"Can you unlock it?"

The clerk hesitated. Morgan added another bill to the pile. At the rate he was going, he would be broke before long.

The clerk grinned. "I'll unlock it now. Good luck to you and your missus."

Morgan gave him a rare smile.

Lori woke reluctantly. It had taken her a very long time to fall asleep. Now she didn't want to leave that state of oblivion.

"Lori." The voice was insistent. "Lori."

The voice was deep, like Nick's, but the intonation was different. Harsher. She moved. Something had changed. And then she knew what. Her right wrist was free.

She kept her eyes shut another minute, knowing what she would see before she saw him. She felt weighed down with sleep, or lack of it. She didn't know which. Surely, it couldn't be dawn yet. It couldn't be time for the stage.

Dread filled her at the thought of leaving Nick.

"Lori!"

She opened her eyes. The Ranger was standing there, fully dressed, the gunbelt in place as always. Why did he always have to look so confident, so powerful?

Lori stretched in the comfortable bed. Wallowed in it, actually. She kept her gaze away from him. Yet instinctively, she knew she was provoking him. Or something else. Sweet Mary and Joseph, she wanted a reaction from him. Some kind of reaction—*any* kind.

"Lori." This time his voice was lower. Even harsher. Rather strangled, in fact.

"Do you always walk into ladies' bedrooms?" she asked sleepily.

He grunted an unintelligible reply.

Lori looked toward the window. Only darkness came from behind the curtains, not the first rays of sun.

"We're leaving," he said abruptly. "Get ready."

"What time is it?"

"Early morning."

"Very early," she guessed.

He shrugged, as he did so many times when he didn't want to answer a question. Her gaze fixed itself on his, and she sat up, hugging the quilt to her. She didn't need to. She was still clothed in the shirt she'd been wearing for the last few days. "What's wrong . . . Nick . . . ?"

His gut tightened again. Nick. Always Nick, goddammit. Why did she care about the murdering bastard? It didn't make him feel one damn bit better that he was jealous of her blood relative. "Bounty hunters," he said. "Rode in an hour ago."

She stiffened. Despite what she'd said a day ago about Morgan not being any better, she knew her brother stood little chance with any bounty hunter.

"Where are we going?"

"South. Along the river. Too many tracks out of town for them to follow, and the creek bed will keep our signs to a minimum."

"How did they find us?" She felt fear for the first time. She hadn't felt it in Laramie. She'd been too angry, too determined to free Nick—too sure of her ability to do that.

"I don't know," he answered honestly. "They might just be checking all the mining towns. We lost time during the snowstorm."

And because she had shot him. She was grateful he didn't remind her. She merely nodded. She'd learned by now that there was no arguing with him. Once he'd decided on something, there was no reprieve. She wondered briefly if he ever bent and decided he didn't. He'd crack wide-open first. If, she thought bitterly, there was anything inside him to crack.

He abruptly left, leaving her to pack what few things she had. She hesitated as she looked at the dress, then rolled it up in the bedroll. She didn't want anything from him . . . but it *was* something else to wear, and she didn't doubt she might need it. Despite the bath she felt dirty and grungy in the clothes she had been wearing. She had kept them on last night, purely in self-defense. The Ranger gave her privacy only up to a point.

She wondered now whether he'd had any sleep at all, wondered if there was a way to take advantage of that possibility. And then she warned herself against underestimating him again. As long as he had the gun and the irons, he had the upper hand.

Until Pueblo.

In just a few minutes she joined the two men in the other room. Nick had a days-old beard; the Ranger still had not permitted him to shave. Her brother was wearing his coat, but his hands were cuffed in front of him, though his ankles were free. The Ranger gave him one pair of saddlebags to place over the handcuffs in case they ran into anyone. Then Morgan Davis eyed her warily for a moment. "I hope you know what's at stake," he said.

Lori nodded, her hands loaded down with her bedroll. The Ranger also gave her Nick's, and he took his own in his left arm, leaving his gun hand free, Lori noticed.

"We'll go out the back to the hotel stable," he said. "You two go first. To the right and down the back stairs."

Lori felt the weight of too little sleep. Her mind was muddled with the lack of it. So was Nick's, she noticed; his steps lagged, the usual energy drained from him. She wondered how the Ranger could be so decisive, his eyes so alert, and she silently cursed him for it.

She and Nick exchanged glances. He gave her a wry smile, and her heart ached. There was defeat in that smile, something she rarely saw in him. She knew it was partly because of her. He'd wanted her on that stage as much as the Ranger did. She hadn't told him she'd had no intention of going all the way to Denver. She wasn't going to leave the two men alone, not after seeing the anger between them nearly explode last night.

Lori knew now that the Ranger would not shoot her brother in cold blood. She also knew, though, that Nick was reaching the point of doing something reckless, of not giving the Ranger a choice, or what the Ranger saw as a choice. She reached the stairs and started down them. All three of them were silent, careful in their steps. Doing as the Ranger ordered. Resentment boiled up in her, and she measured the steps. Perhaps if she stumbled . . . Nick could back into the Ranger, and the two of them, she and Nick, could . . .

"Don't even think about it, Lori." His voice was low, almost inaudible, and Lori swallowed. Had she hesitated a moment? Or did he already know her that well? She didn't bother to deny it, just kept moving, balancing her load to open the door.

In minutes they were riding out of town at a gallop. An opportunity lost, but at least, Lori thought, she wasn't on the stage.

And there was Pueblo.

Whitey Stark swore. He stared at the note at the telegraph office. He had missed them again, and this time only by hours. Still, he had what he needed.

"Pueblo," the copy of the telegram said.

He was surprised the Ranger had permitted the girl to send the telegram. But, then, in Whitey's opinion Morgan Davis was often a fool. The Ranger had a code of honor Whitey didn't understand, would never understand, and because he didn't, he held it in contempt. A weakness. Whitey distrusted weakness.

And he hated Morgan Davis. Davis had foiled several of his intended captures. Whitey had been close three times to nabbing a wanted man, spending months in tracking, only to find that Davis had beat him to it.

Now five thousand dollars was at stake. So was his pride.

He had been tailing Morgan a month earlier, knowing that the man was after Nicholas Braden. An acquaintance had told him a Ranger had been asking questions in Harmony. Whitey had thought he would trail Morgan, save himself time and trouble. He'd even played with the thought of shooting Davis and taking him back as Braden, but he didn't dare do that in Texas. He didn't want the Rangers on his back the rest of his life. He wanted it to look as if Braden had shot the Ranger, and then he, Whitey, had killed Braden. He had to kill them both.

Everything had gone well enough, until the Ranger had backtracked once and found him. He'd disarmed Whitey, taken his rifle and his treasured pistol with the pearl handle, and thrown them into a river. Whitey hadn't been able to find them, even after days of searching. That pistol had been important to him. He'd taken it off a gunfighter he'd killed, and it represented his prowess, his power. Davis had not only humiliated him but had taken his most prized possession.

He'd had just enough money to purchase a new pistol and rifle, neither near as fine as the ones he'd had. And he'd recruited Curt Nesbitt, whom he'd worked with before, and Curt's brother, Ford. Curt and he had the same philosophy. No value in taking a wanted man alive. Whitey had made it clear, however, that he would have the pleasure of shooting the Ranger, and that he would take two thirds of the bounty. The woman would be a bonus, and then they would have to kill her, too.

Whitey turned away from the telegraph office, where he had bribed the operator. A clerk from the Hotel de Paris, the man had said, brought in the telegram.

The Hotel de Paris! He never would have suspected Morgan Davis would stay there. He hadn't even checked there, by God, though he had checked the other hotels, the sheriff's office, which was empty, and the town doctor, who reported no callers. Morgan Davis was a hell of a lot smarter than Whitey had thought. Still, the Ranger had made a mistake. The telegram was a big mistake.

Whitey studied his own map, every town anywhere close to the mountain trails that led to Pueblo. He and the Nesbitt brothers would separate, cover each of those trails. The woman would slow the Ranger down. So would his prisoner. The telegram had promised as much.

.   .   .

Daniel Webster visited the Denver telegraph office as he had done every day since that telegram arrived more than a week ago. He ignored the stares that always accompanied him. He had learned long ago not to care.

Andy was in the saloon, getting knee-walking drunk again. He'd been consumed by guilt ever since his brother was almost hanged for saving his hide. Daniel had some sympathy but not a lot. It was time that Andy grew up.

Daniel approached the counter, which came to just about the top of his head. He stood on tiptoes. "Any messages for Jonathon Braden?"

The operator handed him a telegram with a smile. Daniel smiled back. The telegraph operator had stared at him years ago when he'd first come in, but now, again like so many others, he had discovered that Daniel was like everyone else and treated him that way. He'd even interfered several times when another customer had cruelly teased Daniel about his tiny size. Some people never accepted Daniel. Some took great pleasure in taunting him, calling him a freak, to make themselves feel superior.

Daniel took the telegram and opened it. He was a part of the Braden family: There were no secrets, and he was as worried as all of them about Nick and Lori. He remembered the previous telegram word for word. He had gone cold when he read it. Nick Braden had been his protector since Nick had been ten and started towering over Daniel, though Daniel had then been around twenty-five. Anyone, even adults, who teased or taunted Daniel had Nick to contend with, and Nick, when he was angry, could be dangerous.

Daniel loved Nick and Lori as if they were his own brother and sister. And they were. Jonathon had found Daniel when he was eight, little more than a starved animal. He had been sold to a circus by his family, who was ashamed of giving life to a dwarf. He'd been displayed in a cage for several years.

Jonathon had bought him from the circus owner,

though it had gone against his grain to buy and sell human beings, and had patiently taught him to read and write, had even raised him as his own. Daniel had been fifteen when Jonathon had come across Fleur and the baby so many years ago.

It was Daniel who had helped care for them, particularly the boy, after they found the mother and child in Texas. And then Jonathon and Fleur had fallen in love, and they'd seen no reason that the child shouldn't think of both of them as his real parents. After Fleur and Jonathon were married, they had registered the father of the boy as Jonathon. And Jonathon had always considered Nick his, even after the other two children came.

Daniel had kept that secret all his life. He would carry it to the grave with him if that was what Jonathon wanted.

And now Nick was in grave danger. The first telegram from Lori had been sent from Laramie. It had simply said that Nick had been taken prisoner by a Texas Ranger who planned to return him to Texas. She would send another telegram as soon as she could.

Daniel had known exactly what that meant. She would try to rescue Nick on her own. Lori had always been full of confidence, and she had reason. She was unusually bright and intuitive, quick to master a variety of skills, particularly anything involving coordination and concentration, and used to getting her own way. And she did it so charmingly, flashing that bright, open smile, that no one would gainsay her.

But a Texas Ranger? Daniel Webster was an observer. He had to be. And the Medicine Show had traveled Texas enough that he knew the breed. Hard and relentless. It took a particular kind of man to withstand the loneliness and isolation of that kind of life. A sheriff was different. He lived in a town and had good times as well as bad. The Rangers had few good times. They had only each other.

He read the telegram again. Lori had been unusually brief, which meant she was being watched. *Traveling through mountains. Headed for Pueblo. Will try to move slowly.*

"Try." Which meant she was with them.

Daniel walked over to the saloon and found Andy. He ignored the usual jocular commentary on his size and simply handed the telegram to Andy, who read it quickly. He jerked upright, knocking over the chair, spilling the beer on the table. "Come on, Daniel," he said as he threw several coins onto the table, which had righted itself.

Daniel ran to keep up with the long-strided Andy, uncaring of the comical sight he presented, and didn't voice his usual protest when Andy tossed him up into the saddle of Andy's pinto and mounted behind him. Andy spurred the horse, and they raced the mile to the cabin where the family was wintering.

Three hours later Andy was heading for Pueblo on the pinto, and Jonathon, Fleur, and Daniel were behind him in the Medicine Wagon. Fleur wouldn't even think of being left behind. She couldn't shoot, but Nick was her baby, her firstborn. And Lori . . . Lori was everything any parent could want. So passionate about life. She embraced it as few others did.

Traveling through mountains. Daniel snapped the whip over the head of the horses harnessed to the wagon. They would have to move fast, but they were taking the faster plains route. They should make good time. If only Lori succeeded in moving "slowly."

If anyone could accomplish that, Daniel knew, it was Lori.

CHAPTER FOURTEEN

Morgan ruthlessly kept them moving. They were all dozing in the saddle by the time he considered calling a halt in late afternoon. Even he had nodded off several times, jerking full awake at a sudden sound. But, then, he'd slept in the saddle on other occasions. His bay was well-trained, and he trusted it not to misstep or shy at an unexpected noise; his prisoners were once more tied to their saddles.

He had hesitated before binding Lori's hands, but he had no time for her tricks, and he was too damn tired to be as alert as he should be. He had known instantly on the stairs at the hotel that she was thinking about making some kind of move; her back had tensed as she'd hesitated. She just damn well wasn't going to give up. So when he'd saddled the horses, he'd used his bandanna to tie her hands to the saddle horn and had handcuffed Braden as he always did.

He had followed a streambed until late morning, walking the horses through the shallow water, then had made for the high country, where he hoped the rocks would make a trail even more difficult to follow. Once he'd secured the Bradens, he would backtrack, make sure they weren't followed. He wished he could think more clearly. He should have done something about Whitey a month ago, but the bounty hunter wasn't wanted, and no sheriff would hold him. Morgan could have killed him, probably should have, but he was still too much a Ranger to kill an unarmed man in cold blood, even an animal like Whitey

Stark. Now there were three of them, normally not that much of a threat—except now Morgan had his hands full with Nick and Lori Braden.

His back stiffened just thinking about her. He had taken the lead, had tried to keep his eyes from the slender girl, whose hair now fell halfway down her back in an untidy braid. Anyone else would look like hell after what she'd gone through, but weariness had only seemed to magnify those golden eyes that cut through him each time their gazes met. He didn't know which was more agonizing: the hostile defiance that so often gleamed in her eyes or those rare moments when they blazed with a passion that had little to do with anger.

Or maybe that forbidden passion had everything to do with anger. Remember that, he warned himself. Remember that before you find a knife in your back. Either way, she radiated life. That was one thing that so intrigued him about her. All that life.

Just before they left the stream, he watered the horses and filled the canteens. They would have a dry camp this afternoon. No fire, no smoke. Jerky and hardtack would have to do for food. He knew he needed sleep. They all did. And they would be safer without a fire and then moving again when nightfall came. There was a full moon that night, and he might as well take advantage of it.

He found a small, protected clearing, well shielded by trees, and stopped. He took off his gloves and untied Lori's hands, dismounted, and then offered his hand to her. To his surprise she took it, sliding off the saddle. She stumbled as her feet hit the ground, and Morgan found himself catching her, his arms automatically going around her. He wondered only fleetingly whether the stumble was accidental or on purpose, because his body immediately responded to hers, to the softness, to the way it leaned into his for the briefest of moments.

But any idea he might have had that the stumble was deliberate was immediately put to rest. She stiffened and backed away as if burned. Automatically, his hand reached out to steady her arm, and she jerked away at his touch. There was no doubt that she detested even that touch, and his hand fell away awkwardly as if he were a small boy reaching for a forbidden pie and caught at it.

He turned away, wishing the rejection of his very touch didn't hurt so goddamn much. He had been wrong surmising, even for a second, that she might have welcomed his nearness, that those kisses had been anything but a lure, and she couldn't even bear to play that game now. He stalked over to his horse, took the leg irons from his saddlebags as Braden dismounted, and waited for the inevitable. He locked them onto Braden, and then freed him from the saddle horn. Braden stretched his arms and stared at Morgan. "Don't you ever sleep?"

"I'm about to do just that," Morgan said.

"That means I'm going to be real uncomfortable again."

Morgan didn't reply. He turned back to Lori. "You have a few minutes." He didn't have to say anything more. She glared at him but then turned and disappeared into the woods. Morgan leaned against the tree. Damn, he hated this. He wished he could ask for her word. He wished she would give it. He wished he could accept it. But he just plain didn't trust her. "You too," he said to Braden. "But *you* keep in sight."

"Bit edgy, aren't you, Ranger?"

"Don't goad me, Braden."

"Or what? What else can you do?"

Morgan spun on him, almost swinging, but stopped himself at the last minute. He wouldn't be tempted into hitting a chained man.

"Three minutes, Braden. Then you get attached to a tree. You can use that time any way you want."

Braden didn't move. "What about food? Coffee?"

"You'll get water and jerky."

Braden's jaw set. "And Lori?"

"The same. I didn't ask her to come after you in Laramie."

"You could have left her in Georgetown."

Morgan felt a sick helplessness. "Let's get one thing straight. I don't want her here any more than you do. But I know those goddamn bounty hunters. If they even thought she knew the direction we'd be taking, they'd grab her. And they wouldn't be as gentle as I've been. You can be damned sure they know about her, know she was in Laramie with us."

Nick weighed the information. The telegram. Lori had told him about the telegram she'd sent. Would the bounty hunters check the telegraph office? He hadn't wanted her to do that, hadn't wanted to drag Jonathon and Andy into this, but Lori hadn't listened to him since this whole mess started in Texas months ago. He realized it was more urgent than ever that he escape.

"Can't you stop them?"

"Not until they try something."

"The law," Nick said contemptuously. "You'd let them kill Lori before you'd do anything. I'm innocent, goddamn you, and you drag me to hell and back. But you ignore someone you think would hurt a woman. Run from him. What kind of twisted justice is that?"

"Your time is up, Braden. Over to one of those aspens."

Nick's lips curled. "That's it, Davis? Another order instead of an answer. Or don't you have one? Just mindless, stupid obedience to what you call duty. Well, you can take your damn duty and stuff it down your throat. I'll be damned before I let you chain me to that tree." His cuffed hands balled into fists. He was too tired now to be careful, too frustrated, too worried about his family. He almost welcomed a bullet before suffering any more humiliation from this ass of a Ranger, before further endangering everyone he cared about.

"And Lori?" the Ranger said softly. "You want her to see you die?"

"It looks like she will one way or another. I'd rather she see me die by a bullet than a noose. Besides, you won't shoot me. Not like this."

"Don't bet on it. As far as I'm concerned, you're still a murderer."

"Then do it!"

The challenge was thrown at the Ranger, and Nick saw muscles move in the Ranger's weary face. Then the Ranger removed his gunbelt and let it drop as he moved closer to Nick. Hindered by the handcuffs, Nick locked his hands together. He had learned exactly how much he could move with the leg irons, and he took the one possible step before throwing his locked fists into the Ranger's jaw, putting all his strength into the blow.

Damn, but it was pure pleasure.

Nick's mind registered the sound of his hands against the man's jaw, but the Ranger didn't go down, though he stumbled backward. Nick fastened his eyes on the gun in the holster just feet away. But the leg irons so limited his movement, the distance might as well have been miles. He drew his fists back again, knowing that the Ranger had allowed that first blow. Nick didn't know why. He just hoped he would have a second chance.

He didn't.

The Ranger stepped back, and Nick stumbled. He righted himself, but he lost the power behind his move, and he stood there furiously, knowing that he was impotent. He wondered why the Ranger didn't strike back, instead of watching him with that infuriating impassivity that seemed to mock him. Nick knew it was hopeless, that he was nothing more than a bothersome fly buzzing about the man, and that made him angrier, thrusting aside the momentary frustration. He put all his strength behind one great all-or-nothing effort. He lifted his hands as he propelled his body toward the Ranger in one great lunge, seeking to get the chain between his wrists around the man's neck.

The movement threw them both to the ground, but the Ranger managed to catch the chain before it went over his head and jerked it down. The two men rolled over and over, much as they had at the cabin, Nick trying to use the only thing he had, his weight, to pinion his tormentor and then somehow get the handcuffs around his neck.

He had a few pounds and desperation on his side. The Ranger had free hands and legs. Nick was able to roll over and for a moment pin the Ranger down. Then he saw the Ranger's gunbelt inches away. Nick reached for it, giving the Ranger a moment to regain his balance and bring his knee up, kicking Nick in the groin. The pain was paralyzing, and the Ranger pushed Nick all the way off and grabbed the gun.

Nick doubled over, lay there, trying to get his breath as the Ranger buckled the belt back on, then reached down and grabbed Nick's shoulders, dragging him to a slender tree. The Ranger quickly chained him to the tree. Then he stood, and Nick knew he was waiting for him to look up. Pain and defeat ran deep inside Nick. For a moment he'd almost thought he had a chance. He finally looked up at Davis, not wanting to appear to be avoiding his gaze.

Nick was surprised to find emotion on the man's face. There was regret, even a kind of compassion, that Nick immediately rejected. A growl came from between his teeth, the pain in his groin still too strong, too incapacitating, to do anything more.

Whatever the Ranger had intended to say evidently died in his throat. He turned away abruptly, and then Nick saw Lori, her face pale, her body seemingly frozen in shock. He wondered how much she had seen.

The Ranger saw her apparently at the same time. Nick saw his whole body go stiff, and then Lori whirled on him, her hand going back, and Nick could hear the impact of her palm against the Ranger's cheek.

Lori had taken more than her five minutes. Let him come after her, she thought. She had gone beyond the small clearing, to where she felt all alone. She needed to stretch all those sore and cramped muscles. She needed the quiet of the forest to think, to put all her rollicking emotions to some kind of rest. Something had happened when her body had slid down to his and she had almost fallen. She'd been so tired, so stiff from being tied to that saddle, unable to shift into different positions as she usually did when riding a long way.

But then her body leaned into his, and all the weariness vanished, replaced by a rapacious fire that pushed her body even closer to his. She felt his hardness against her, and her own need for him had grown irresistibly strong. She'd looked up and seen the sudden hunger in his eyes, but it was the unexpected gentleness in his hands that completely undid her. She'd had to jerk away before she succumbed to that mixture of pure masculine sexuality and those rare but so compelling seconds of kindness. She was so tired, so susceptible to the Ranger's overpowering presence. She felt, in that moment, that she was betraying both herself and Nick.

Then she had jerked away. She felt like disappearing through the woods, catching herself a sunbeam filtering through the trees, and riding it to some faraway, uncomplicated place.

She kept astounding herself by the attraction she felt for Ranger Morgan Davis. The fact that he looked so much like her brother should put her off, should repel her. How could she be so fascinated by a man who looked just like the boy and man she'd grown up with? But, then, the similarities were only skin-deep. The Ranger had none of Nick's warmth and compassion, none of his quick humor.

So why did she give a fig? Because she thought some of those qualities might lie hidden deep inside him; she couldn't quite accept the fact that he was as cold and uncaring as he appeared to be. Emboldened by the thought, she quickly took care of her personal needs and started back. She had reached the clearing just in time to see the Ranger knee Nick and watch her brother double up in agony. She didn't care that Nick would have done the same given the chance, that the two men had been in a life-and-death struggle in which there were no rules. She saw only her brother's pain.

And she wanted to kill the Ranger herself. At least do the same to him as he'd done to a man handcuffed and leg-ironed. The Ranger turned at that second, and their eyes met. She glimpsed a sudden bleakness in them before they emptied, became that unfathomable blue, shades darker now than Nick's. And then they became wary as if he read her anger, the violence boiling inside her.

She reached him, her eyes filled with contempt, and then her hand went back and she hit him as hard as she could, not noticing until the moment of impact the already swollen bruise on his cheek. Her hand hurt from the force of the blow, yet he made no move to retaliate. That made her even angrier, and she drew back her other hand.

This time he caught it, and then caught her knee with his leg, just as she went for his crotch. His left hand locked both of her wrists behind her, and he pulled her close, so close she felt the tension of his body, the swelling again of his manhood. She tried to pull away, to buck against him, but he only held her tighter. He looked down, and for a second she had the wild thought he was going to kiss her. Then she looked at his eyes, and some of the wild fury in her calmed. She had never seen such loneliness in a man's eyes, such utter bleakness. She felt as if she'd just uncovered a raw wound. Her body stilled and she just stared up at him.

Every part of her was vibrantly aware of his nearness. Lori felt herself shivering, not only in reaction to the way his proximity made her hot and tingling, but at the unexpected pain in his eyes. She knew then that he hadn't wanted to harm Nick. He had taken her blow to prove that.

When she looked up at him, when she knew she should hate him, she felt a compassion of her own, an overwhelming need to bring a little softness and laughter into a life she sensed had little, to a man who substituted duty for every human emotion.

He suddenly let her go, as if he'd intuited the swing from fury to pity. He detested the latter. She knew it from the red that suddenly flooded his face. The lines around his eyes seemed to deepen. He sighed, a shudder visibly rocking his body, whether from the physical punishment he'd just received, or from something else, she didn't know.

"Go over and sit next to your brother," he said wearily. He followed, kneeling between them to rearrange the handcuffs so that Nick and Lori were chained together. His gaze moved from one to the other.

"I don't want to go through this every day," he said harshly, "but I will if I have to." He turned to Nick, and Lori saw him studying every feature of her brother before speaking again. "You're going back to Texas, Braden, if I have to carry you hog-tied on my back. I'm not going to ask you to make it easy, 'cause I know you won't. But be warned, I won't pull punches because of your sister. You start something, and I'll damn well finish it."

He stalked over to the horses, unsaddled them, and pulled off the bedrolls, carrying them over to his two prisoners. He gave them a canteen full of water and a measure of jerky and then retreated to a spot twenty feet away, where he rolled a blanket around himself and turned away from them.

Morgan woke slowly. He hurt. His wounded shoulder ached from the fight he'd had with Braden. His face felt battered and his mouth swollen. He felt like hell.

His mood was no better as he thought briefly of the last few days. He knew the situation could only worsen. Braden had been cooperative till now because of his sister. He had been biding his time, waiting for the moment Lori was on a stagecoach and safe. But now Braden knew that was unlikely, and Morgan knew he could expect more attacks, more trouble, more defiance. Christ, he hadn't wanted to hit Braden yesterday, not the way he did, but Braden was after the gun. The kick had been the fastest, most efficient way of disabling him before Lori returned and joined in the fray.

He turned over and looked at the sky, which was afire with sunset. Violent and passionate, although he'd never thought of the sky in those terms before. His whole world, in fact, was shifting, and he wasn't sure he would ever quite find the solid foothold he once thought he had.

Morgan had never felt guilt before in taking a prisoner back. He'd never had the slightest hesitation in shooting one who tried to escape. He'd never spared more than a passing thought as to their ultimate fate. This time was different. He had a grudging respect for Nick Braden, the way he continued to try to protect his sister and, at the same time, defy what Morgan knew were insurmountable odds. He himself had stacked them that way.

Dammit, Nick Braden was getting to him.

Morgan slowly sat up. Thirty minutes and the sun would be down. Another hour or two and the moon would be bright enough to ride again. He looked over at the Bradens. Both were asleep, the girl's head resting on her brother's shoulder. Morgan wondered briefly how it would feel if she were to rest against his shoulder, that silky honey-blond hair draped over his chest. He tried to banish the thought as soon as it formed. But he grew hard at the thought of her body against his. Damn, he was like a stallion sniffing a mare in heat.

Morgan saddled his horse. He would do some back-tracking while dusk lasted, make sure no one was behind them. He carefully led his horse away from where the others were sleeping before he mounted. God only knew how much sleep they had gotten after the violence of this afternoon, and he intended to travel again until noon tomorrow. Those few hours of sleep were all that he needed.

It was full dark when he returned. He'd circled around and found no trace of man or animal. He did find an old mining road heading in the direction he planned to take. They would follow that tonight, make up some time. There shouldn't be anyone on it tonight. At dawn they would go back up along the ridge of the mountains.

Beth pulled up the team when she saw a rutted trail angling from the road. An old mining road, she thought. They could drive about half a mile, out of sight, and stay there. They would rest the horses, and she needed some sleep. Maggie was already sleeping in the bed of the buckboard, her tiny form resting on a pile of blankets next to a trunk. Caroline and their stallion, Joshua's pride and joy, trailed behind, tied to the wagon with a rope.

It had been two days since the night they had left the cabin. Another two days before the Utes said they would return for her answer. She just hoped they wouldn't come sooner. She particularly feared one of the chosen men, Chorito, the son of a chief, who always looked at her with hungry, greedy eyes. He wore army trousers Beth suspected he hadn't traded for, and at times his face was painted. He was usually surrounded by six other young braves, all of their faces sullen.

She'd had the sick feeling from the beginning that no matter whom she chose, she would end up with Chorito. He would threaten or kill or trade for her. Although most of the Utes were peaceful, there had been sporadic attacks on settlements and increasing resentment against the growing number of farmers claiming what Utes considered their grazing lands. She'd always suspected Chorito was one of the raiders.

She unhitched the horses and tethered them, then gave them water from the barrel she carried with her, and a hatful of oats. Then she watered and fed Caroline. Maggie was still sleeping when Beth squeezed between the trunk and Maggie. Beth put her arm around Maggie, felt the child snuggle into her for warmth and comfort. She had to keep her safe. She had to. Three days to Georgetown. Several more to Denver. And then she would sell the stallion. Perhaps start a small restaurant with the proceeds.

Just three more days, and they should be safe. With that reassuring thought, Beth finally slept.

CHAPTER FIFTEEN

As the sun peaked through the eastern hills, Morgan paused on the rough, rutted road that led downward. It twisted and turned along the side of the mountain. The other two horses kept moving until they were abreast of him, but he didn't spare them a glance, just as he hadn't since they'd left the clearing. He was doing his damnedest to distance himself from them, although it was growing more and more difficult.

Somewhere along the way Nick Braden had become a person to him, not just an object to deliver to justice. And Lori? He couldn't even think of her without hurting, and the ache wasn't confined to his lower regions. That was precisely the crux of his difficulty. If what he felt had been merely lust, he could have disciplined his body. But she'd made him want something more. She'd exposed a raw emptiness in his life, an emptiness she had filled so fleetingly during that second kiss at the cabin, when her lips had gentled and her hand had touched him with something close to tenderness. He kept remembering that instant, so much that he started wondering if perhaps he imagined it, giving it substance where there was none.

Now she hated him, with ample reason. She had flinched every time he neared her last evening as they prepared to go. She had refused his help in mounting. She hadn't glared at him as she usually did, but rather turned her head as if even the sight of him was more than she could bear. . . .

A scream shattered the uneasy silence. Then gunshots. Another scream, then the loud, terrified wail of a child or animal. A war cry.

Morgan's blood went cold. He'd heard that sound before. He'd heard it in Texas, and he'd heard it in his nightmares. The scream came again. He looked over toward Nick and Lori. Their faces were intent on him, waiting. He moved to the edge of the road, looking down to its bend. A buckboard sat at the bottom where the road evened out. He saw a woman in the back clutching a child, one of her hands holding a pistol helplessly as seven painted warriors circled the wagon.

Braden had moved up, too, his horse responding to the pressure from his knees. His face went white. He turned to Morgan. "You're going to need help."

Automatically, Morgan hesitated.

"Goddamn you," Nick said. "I'll give you my word I won't try to escape, not until . . ."

"Until you're back in my custody," Morgan said softly, knowing he'd already made his decision. He did trust Braden that much.

Braden nodded. Morgan took Nick's holster and gun from his saddlebags, loading it with bullets from his own gunbelt, thanking a higher being that they used the same caliber. He took the key to Nick's handcuffs from his pocket and leaned over, unlocking them, leaving them to dangle from the cuff connecting them to the saddle horn. Morgan's voice was low as he warned him. "I have your word, Braden. Don't forget it." He handed him the gunbelt and then he took a knife and cut Lori's bonds. "Stay here," he said curtly.

Braden was already riding ahead of him, his body low on the neck of the horse as he raced down the road. Morgan took his Colt from the holster and followed his prisoner. As they reached where the road leveled off, he saw that two of the Indians were in the wagon, one swinging up the child to a mounted warrior as the second held the struggling, screaming woman around her waist. Braden fired his gun into the air, apparently trying to frighten them off, but Morgan saw one of the mounted warriors take aim at Braden and fire. The bullet missed, but Braden whirled around and fired. He didn't miss, and the Indian fell from the horse.

Others turned toward Braden, swinging their rifles in his direction. Morgan shot one, and the remaining two rifles turned back toward him. As Morgan fired at one, he saw Braden aim at the other, hitting him, and then Morgan was too busy to see anything else. He heard a noise behind, and he whirled just as an arrow whizzed past him by a fraction of an inch. He fired his Colt and another Indian went down. He heard shots in front of him where Braden had been, then a grunt of pain.

He turned. Two of the Indians were racing off to the trees, the riderless ponies between them. Four other warriors lay on the ground, and Braden had apparently jumped the one holding the child. They were wrestling on the ground, and the child lay screaming nearby. Morgan and the woman reached the little girl at the same time, the woman sweeping her up with a small cry. Morgan turned back to Braden and the Indian, who were rolling around in the dirt, the Indian clutching a knife and trying desperately to reach Braden with it.

Morgan followed the movements, trying to get a shot, but he was afraid he would hit Braden. The knife sliced down, and Morgan heard a grunt of pain; then Braden stilled, and the Indian raised his hand to strike again. Just as Morgan was about to fire, Braden suddenly bucked the Indian off him, his hand reaching for the knife in a movement that apparently surprised his opponent. Braden twisted the knife and pushed it into the Indian, then rolled over on top of him, making sure he was dying.

When the Indian's last movement stilled, Braden wearily stood. His coat was bloodstained, and he took it off. There was a rip in his shirt, and blood pouring out of a long slash. He looked at the carnage around them, then at Morgan, and finally at the woman kneeling next to the child. He walked over to her. "Is she all right? I . . ." His voice broke. "He was going to ride off. I didn't know what to do but jump him, and I . . . I couldn't catch her."

Lori was there then. Morgan didn't know when she'd arrived, how much she'd seen. But she knelt next to the child with the woman and Nick, then, apparently satisfied the child was all right, turned her attention to her brother. "Nick," she exclaimed, her hand going to the rip in his shirt.

The child whimpered as Morgan approached, making him feel once more achingly out of place, once more the outsider.

The woman looked up. She wore a bonnet, but strands of long brown hair had escaped from it, and she had clear sky-blue eyes. They were misty as they looked from one man to another and then to Lori. "Thank you," she said as she hugged the child again. "Thank you." Her hands went tenderly over the child, making sure that little was wrong but fear and bruises. Then she looked up again at Nick, her gaze resting on the blood darkening Braden's shirt. Her eyes grew larger as she realized he was still waiting for an answer. "She's fine . . . but you . . ."

Morgan broke in. "We need to get the hell out of here. Two of them got away. There might be more out there."

Lori stood. "Not unless you want him to bleed to death. That would solve your problems, wouldn't it?"

Morgan refused to turn away under the blazing anger in her eyes. "Then fix him," he said curtly, not wanting to remember the way Braden had shot the Indian who had been aiming straight at him. Not wanting to consider the fact that Braden could have mounted one of the Indian ponies, or even his own, and ridden off during the melee. Morgan didn't even want to think about the fact that he had trusted Braden.

The woman on the ground looked from one to the other, obviously trying to understand the tension. "I'm good at nursing. Please let me help."

Lori stooped down next to her. "Then let me take the

girl." She held out her hands and gathered the child to her. Morgan watched as the child's initial resistance yielded to Lori's natural warmth, warmth the little girl had shown to everyone but him. Nick grinned up at him, recognizing Morgan's dilemma, and Morgan wanted to hit him, wound or not. His prisoner was obviously making him the villain. And, dammit, he was beginning to feel like one.

Morgan approached the woman. "Do you know why they attacked? If there might be more?" He'd been told the Utes were peaceful.

The woman blushed, and she looked even prettier. She looked at one of the men lying on the ground. "He . . . he wanted to marry me after my husband died. And he's the son of one of their chiefs."

Braden had been staring at her as if mesmerized. Now he looked up at Morgan. "If he's the son of a chief, you're right. We better get out of here. The Utes are basically peaceful, but more and more they're being forced from their land, and there's a lot of tension. All they need is something like this."

The woman spoke up again. "Their camp is two days from here. They offered me . . . the choice of four of their warriors after my husband died. They weren't supposed to come for an answer for several more days, but Chorito . . . he . . ." Red color deepened the natural rose of her cheek, and she looked away, obviously ashamed.

Morgan changed the subject to spare the woman further embarrassment. "Then we have a little time." He walked over to where Nick stood, now leaning against the wagon, and pulled up his shirt, looking at the slash. "It needs to be sewn," he observed calmly as he reached down and took the pistol that lay nearby. He checked it for bullets, found there were none left, and tucked it into his belt.

"No fire?" Braden said laconically.

"*I* didn't have anyone I could trust," Morgan retorted.

He turned to the woman. "Morgan Davis, ma'am. This is Nick Braden and his sister, Lorilee."

The woman smiled shyly, but her gaze shifted from the Ranger to Braden, trying to understand the antagonism between the two men who looked very much alike. "You aren't brothers?"

It was Braden who answered first. "Hell, no," he said, then caught himself. "Begging your pardon, ma'am."

The woman looked startled, but then manners apparently took over. "I'm Beth Andrews. My daughter, Maggie."

"Well, Mrs. Andrews," Morgan said, "if you think you can take care of his wound, you better do it. We need to get out of here. Where were you heading?"

"Georgetown, then Denver."

Georgetown.

Christ. He couldn't leave them alone, nor could he take them back to Georgetown and chance running into Whitey Stark. He'd been at a disadvantage before with two prisoners. Now he would have a woman and a child as well. He walked a few feet away, watching as the woman retreated to the wagon and returned with a small bag. Lori was whispering into the child's hair, tucking her head away from the dead bodies that lay on the ground.

Beth Andrews's soft voice reached Morgan. "Can you get us some water? We have a little in the wagon."

Morgan untied his canteen from his saddle and took it to her, watching as she washed the wound.

"Any alcohol?"

Morgan shook his head.

She took some powder from the bag and sprinkled it into the wound. "After my husband died, I made sure I had sufficient medical supplies. This should prevent an infection." Her face clouded for a moment, as if reliving bad memories. She shook her head, trying to dismiss them, and took a needle and thread from the bag and leaned over. "This is going to hurt," she said. Braden nodded, his body tensing as the needle worked its way in and out of the skin. He saw Lori flinch at each stitch, but Braden didn't utter a sound. When the woman finished, she took a bandage from the bag and wrapped it tightly around his chest.

"Thank you, ma'am," Braden said, his gaze following her as she rose and went over to her daughter, taking her in her arms.

"Thank *you*, Mr. Braden. They would have taken Maggie . . ." She held the girl tighter.

"What happened to your husband, Mrs. Andrews?" Morgan asked, wanting to know more.

Her arms tightened around the child. "He died a year ago. Blood poisoning."

Morgan looked at her with new compassion. Blood poisoning was an ugly way to die. "You've been out here this long? Alone?"

"I tried to keep our farm going, it was my husband's dream, but I just couldn't do it alone, and then a few days ago the Utes came by. They admired my husband, everyone did, and they apparently thought it was their responsibility to . . . take care of us."

"Even against your will?" Lori asked, horrified.

"I think they thought they were honoring me by offering me their warriors. I knew they wouldn't accept no for an answer, especially . . ." Her voice trailed off, but Morgan noticed her quick, fearful glance at the now dead warrior who had been manhandling her in the wagon bed just minutes earlier. She looked at Braden and seemed to strengthen. "I thought, hoped, we could reach Georgetown before they discovered I'd left." She looked at Braden hopefully. "Can you help us get there?"

A muscle knotted in Nick Braden's cheek as he shifted uncomfortably.

"I'm afraid not, Mrs. Andrews," Morgan broke in. "We're headed south."

Beth Andrews glanced again at one man, then the other. "Mr. Braden?"

Nick Braden met her pleading gaze steadily. "If it was

up to me, I would take you," he said. "But I don't have any say in the matter. He's in charge," Braden said, then added softly, "at the moment." He didn't elaborate.

Morgan swore softly to himself. "He's wanted for murder," he said flatly. "I'm taking him back to Texas. There's some bounty hunters behind us who wouldn't mind taking him back dead."

She looked stunned, disbelieving. Her gaze went to Nick, asking him to disagree, to deny the charge.

He gave her that crooked smile that was so disarming. "It's true, ma'am," he said softly. "I *am* wanted. But it was self-defense. The Ranger here doesn't want to acknowledge that fact."

"But you had a gun," she protested, still obviously reluctant to believe one of her rescuers was less than a hero.

"A temporary truce in defense of a fair damsel," Nick replied. "A truce very limited in nature." His eyes went to his gun now tucked into Morgan's belt.

"I'll take your word again," Morgan said softly. "No more irons if you give it to me."

"And go back to Harmony willingly? You're loco," Nick Braden said.

Morgan shrugged. "We'll do it any way you want." He turned to Beth Andrews. "Ma'am, the best we can do for you is take you along. You'll have to leave the wagon here. If those Utes return, they'll come in numbers, and we can't outrun them with that wagon. We'll find you a stage or train as soon as possible. I'll send someone back for your belongings. It doesn't look like this road is used any longer, and we can cover it with undergrowth. But we have to hurry."

She nodded. "Can we take Wind Dancer, our stallion, and . . ." She hesitated. "Caroline."

Morgan's puzzlement obviously showed, because she hurried on. "Caroline is our pig," she said, and for the first time Morgan noticed the pig tethered to a tree.

Braden chortled. Lori smiled.

"She's Maggie's pet," Beth pleaded. "She's the last

present her father gave her. It would break her heart . . ."

A pig. A damned pig. Morgan was about to say no, and then he looked at the small girl, who was staring at him with fearful eyes. Her face was streaked with tears, and he saw bruises coloring her arms.

"Caroline," he said in a choked voice, wondering how everything had gotten so out of control. He'd had a simple task: bring back a fugitive. And then Lori had complicated what should have been routine. Now another woman, and a child, by God. And a pig.

"She's not any trouble. She's used to following Maggie," Beth said quickly.

"Hell, why not?" Morgan finally said. It would just be a few days. They might well have lost the bounty hunters by now, and even if they hadn't, perhaps the additional tracks would confuse them. It sure as hell confused him. In minutes he and Braden had unhitched the horses from the wagon and used them as pack horses for as many of the Andrewses' belongings as possible. Nick had looked at the stallion with something close to awe.

"My husband brought him all the way from Kentucky," Beth said softly. "He was breeding him to some of the Indian ponies."

Braden whistled. "The toughness and endurance of the mountain horses with that blood. They would be fine animals."

"They were," Beth said with pride, her gaze resting on Braden's face, obviously looking for the murderer that the Ranger said was there. "I had to sell what we had when he died, but I kept Wind Dancer."

Morgan saw her examine Braden's face, saw her face soften as she obviously decided on her own that he was not the murderer Morgan had pronounced him to be. More trouble, he sensed immediately. He stepped between them. "We only have three saddles," he said. "Do you ride, Mrs. Andrews?"

She nodded. "My husband taught me."

"Without a saddle?" Morgan disliked the choices being given him. He had to have his saddle, because of the rifle scabbard, the saddlebags with the weapons and ammunition in them. Nick also needed a saddle. The irons were the only way to keep him under control, and Morgan knew it. He'd half hoped Braden would give him his parole; Morgan would accept it now. But he should have known better. Nothing had changed. Braden's eyes had told him as much.

He moved his right arm slightly. His right side hurt. He must have twisted it in some way, though the pain was burning, not the dull ache that came from a strained muscle. It made him irritable. More irritable than usual.

The woman hesitated, then nodded, but Lori broke in. "She and Maggie can use my saddle."

Morgan turned his glare on her.

"*I'll* give you my word," she said bitterly.

Morgan swallowed the chunk of bile rising in his throat. Lori's golden eyes were all fire again. She knew he had been thinking only of how to get her brother back to Texas. Mrs. Andrews was looking tired and vulnerable and scared. The child looked at him with terrified eyes, and he realized his voice had been harsh. Nick Braden was looking at him with that damned amusement that so often lurked in his eyes.

Morgan nearly choked on the chunk of bile rising in his throat. Christ, *he* was the lawman, and he felt like the devil incarnate.

But he merely nodded. "Mrs. Andrews and the child will have the saddle, then." He made makeshift reins for Lori and offered his hands to help her mount. As usual, she refused and led the horse over to a stump, where she mounted on her own.

Braden started to help Mrs. Andrews, but then Morgan saw him wince with pain, and he went to give her a hand and lift up the child. The youngster shied away from his touch, and he felt a deep, stabbing pain of his own, deeper than the one that still plagued his side. He looked up at Mrs. Andrews. "I'm sorry," he said.

She tried a smile, but it didn't quite work. She had already obviously allied herself with Braden. The hell with it, Morgan thought. *He* was right. He was doing his job as he always did it. He stalked over to Braden's horse and motioned for his prisoner to join him. To his surprise Braden didn't balk when Morgan attached the handcuffs to his wrists. Morgan didn't know whether it was because of the woman and child, or because the wound had sapped his strength. He told himself he didn't care.

But that doubt inside him was growing. When he and Braden had approached the Utes, Braden had first fired into the air, obviously reluctant to kill. That was not the act of a man who would kill an unarmed man. The gnawing question deepened: was he really taking an innocent man to his death?

And what did that make him?

Morgan clenched his jaw together as he rigged a lead, tying Braden's horse and the stallion to it. Mrs. Andrews said the pig would follow, but he'd found some rope in her wagon, and he rigged another line from her saddle to the animal. All he needed now was to lose the damn animal and have a heartbroken kid on his hands as well as three hostile adults.

When he finally finished, he mounted. He didn't like leaving the dead Indians in the clearing, but if the Utes were anything like the Texas tribes he knew, they would return for their dead. Neither he nor Braden were in any condition to dig graves in this hard, rocky country.

He touched his heels to the sides of his bay, and they started down the canyon.

CHAPTER SIXTEEN

Nick struggled to keep upright in the saddle. The toll of the last two weeks had already drained him of his usual energy. Sleep had been sporadic at best, the restrictive irons compounded by Lori's own restlessness. And now the loss of blood and the throbbing pain from the knife wound had weakened him further.

He wasn't going to ask for rest, though. The Ranger had allowed himself none when Lori had shot him. Nick wasn't going to show himself less a man. But, God, when was Davis going to stop? It was as if all the demons in hell were nipping at his heels, the way he drove them all.

What time was it? The sun had hit its zenith some time ago. It was midafternoon, he guessed. Except for that brief battle, they'd been riding since just after midnight. Even the horses were exhausted.

He kept his gaze off Beth Andrews, who had the bluest eyes he'd ever seen and the gentlest hands. He closed his eyes and felt those hands again on his bare skin. It had almost been worth being cut. As she had sewn her stitches, he'd fixed his gaze on her eyes as a way to keep from groaning. Those eyes had hurt for him, had so obviously admired him. And they'd been so grateful.

For a few moments he'd felt like a man again, not a wild animal in chains, not a posted murderer without a future. But the respite had been brief, and when the Ranger had locked the handcuffs on him in front of the woman and child, Nick had wanted to crawl under a rock. He couldn't

even manage *that* now, he thought bitterly, not without the
Ranger's permission. His only satisfaction was that the
Ranger's problems were growing progressively more serious. Yet, just as Nick hadn't been able to use his sister to
free himself, he knew he wouldn't use the two newcomers.
Like the Ranger, he had to wait, to bide his time, until
there were only the two of them, a prospect growing dim-
mer.

His hands tightened around the saddle horn. His head
was getting heavier. His side burned like the devil's
abode. He tightened his legs around his mount, urging it
to catch up to the Ranger's.

"Davis," he said.

The Ranger turned to look at him. His eyes narrowed
and then he stopped. "Christ, why didn't you say something sooner?" He quickly dismounted, just in time to
catch Nick as he swayed in the saddle and started to drop,
his hands still bound to the saddle horn.

Nick was only barely aware of the Ranger catching his
horse's halter, stopping its movement before Nick was
dragged. He tried to catch the saddle horn with his hands,
ashamed at the sight he must present. Then his hands
were free, and the Ranger helped lower him to the ground.

Nick wanted to shrug him off, but he couldn't. He had
no strength. He just lay there, his breath difficult to dispel,
and then Lori was next to him . . . and . . . Beth.

Pretty . . . pretty Beth.

Lori fell in love with Caroline as well as with little, solemn
Maggie.

The pig, once released from its tether, followed Maggie
wherever she went, occasionally giving her a bump to get
attention. The animal and Maggie took Lori's mind from
the two men who were dominating her thoughts.

The Ranger had already started a fire. She was surprised when he suggested it, and even more surprised
when he'd gathered the wood for it. He had been adamant

the night before about not having one. He had always been a man of few words, but he had even fewer now. The mouth was a tight line, his eyes dark and enigmatic. The lines around his eyes were more pronounced, the two-day beard darkening his hard jaw.

Beth Andrews was tending Nick. She'd wanted to, and Lori had sensed that Nick would like that. She hadn't seen that genuine smile of his since the killing in Harmony. But he had given it to Beth Andrews back at the road, even through his pain from the knife cut. And she'd quickly realized that Mrs. Andrews had more experience in nursing than she did. So Lori had backed away and had reassured little Maggie, who had asked if the man was going to die like her daddy had.

Lori had hugged her, trying to hide the mist in her own eyes. "Of course not, darlin'."

Not now.

Maggie had gone over to the pig and given it a big hug, which the pig accepted rather graciously, Lori thought with what amusement she could summon, and then Maggie had crept back, watching her mother and Nick solemnly. As Mrs. Andrews bathed and rebandaged Nick's wound, she frequently glanced around, obviously reassuring herself that her daughter was all right.

Lori couldn't resist Maggie. Her dark hair was bound in two pigtails and her eyes were much like her mother's, a pure blue that were filled with more sadness than a child should know. Even now she was watching more pain, more misery, and Lori wanted suddenly to take her away from it.

Nick was in good hands, she knew that. She approached Mrs. Andrews. "Is it all right if I take Beth to the stream we just passed? We can fetch some more water."

The woman looked up at her, studied her for a moment, then smiled. "I think she would like that."

Lori glanced toward the Ranger, who was watching the fire, and silently asked his consent. She hated to, and he knew it. He gave her a curt nod.

"Would you like to go and help me?" she asked Maggie, instinctively knowing the child would respond to a request for help rather than a decision made without her approval.

"Can we take Caroline?"

"Of course," Lori said.

Maggie nodded in that solemn way of hers, and Lori wished she could hear her laugh. She decided she would do her best to make her laugh. They *both* needed laughter.

With the silent help of the Ranger, she gathered up all their canteens. She took four and the child took two, and they started through the pines. It was a beautiful fall day. Although the night had been cold, the sun was warm this afternoon, and the sky clear. The snow had not reached this area yet, and the remaining leaves were still golden, though every time a breeze rustled through the branches, more blew down, drifting like tiny kites to the ground. Nick had made her a kite once and had taught her to fly it to the clouds. She shook the poignant memory away.

She looked down at Maggie and the pig following behind. Her dark mood, plaguing her since the usual confrontation with the Ranger, started to dissipate. There was something about a beautiful day, a bright sun, and a child's innocence that made it seem as if, somehow, everything would turn out all right. She had to believe that! She went upstream, where they found a sloping bank, and they filled the canteens as Caroline rooted around the trees for whatever pigs rooted for.

And then, when they finished, Lori skipped a stone through the water, and Maggie immediately wanted to learn how. She caught on swiftly and stood in awe as one of her stones finally skipped just once, creating a series of expanding circles in the water. Maggie's eyes lit, and Lori grinned, feeling happy and carefree for the first time in weeks. She started humming a song, which she often did when she felt that way—"Sweet Betsy from Pike."

"Sing it," Maggie demanded, looking up at her with fascination.

Lori did. She used to sing it frequently to attract crowds

to the Medicine Show. She sang it through once for Maggie, and then again slower.

"We'll try it together," she said, pleased when the girl's sweet but pure voice blended with hers, hesitating every once in a while, but then joining in again. They tried it a third time, and Maggie was almost perfect in remembering the words, giving Lori a shy smile when they finished.

Lori tried to think of another song, one not so sad, one that would bring laughter to Maggie's usually all too serious eyes. Caroline snorted suddenly, and Lori wished she could think of a song about a pig, and finally she did. At least it mentioned a pig. She gave Maggie a conspiratorial grin. "How would you like to learn a song just special for your mother?"

Maggie nodded, her gaze now intent on Lori.

"It's called 'Cat Went Fiddle-de-dee,'" Lori said, and she started slow, punctuating each word with glee.

> *"Had me a cat; the cat pleased me.*
> *Fed my cat under yonder tree;*
> *The cat went fiddle-de-dee.*
>
> *"Had me a dog; the dog pleased me.*
> *Fed my dog under yonder tree;*
> *The dog went bow-wow-wow,*
> *And the cat went fiddle-de-dee.*
>
> *"Had me a hen; the hen pleased me.*
> *Fed my hen under yonder tree;*
> *The hen went cluck-cluck*
> *The dog went bow-wow-wow*
> *And the cat went fiddle-de-dee.*
>
> *"Had me a pig; and Caroline pleased me.*
> *Fed Caroline under yonder tree;*
> *Caroline went krusi-krusi*
> *The hen went cluck-cluck*

The dog went bow-wow-wow,
and the cat went fiddle-de-dee."

By then Maggie was joining in on the refrains. Lori
added a cow and then suggested Maggie make up a verse.
She chose a horse and a lion, making a roaring sound, and
then they were both laughing, trying to remember all the
animals. Lori's heart twisted as she heard the laughter,
watched the delight in the girl's eyes. Maggie's father had
died a year ago, Beth had said, and apparently life had
been difficult since then, too hard for a sensitive little soul
like Maggie.

Instinctively, she leaned over and gave Maggie a big
hug, and then yelped as a small movement of the water
washed over one of the canteens, and it started drifting
down the creek. She grabbed for it, losing her footing. She
fell partly into the water, one leg getting completely
doused. Maggie giggled as Lori regained her balance and
returned to dry earth. Lori sat down and took off her
boots, shaking the water from them and regarding her wet
trousers with no little disgust. Holy Mary and Joseph, but
the water was cold.

Then she shrugged. She would have to wear the dress,
after all. The Ranger's dress. Her other clothes were too
disgusting even to think about until they were washed.
She grinned at Maggie. "We'd better go back before I
drown myself," she said. "And I think it's time to eat under
yonder tree."

Maggie giggled again, putting her hand in Lori's. "Do
you know any other songs?"

"Well," Lori said, "have you heard the one about Frog-
gie and his courtship?"

Maggie shook her head. Lori started the song, picked
up her boots with her free hand, and, hands linked together, the two started back to the fire.

.   .   .

Drawn by the sound of Lori's voice, the lilt of "Sweet Betsy from Pike," Morgan Davis watched the woman and child from the safe haven of the trees. He had come to check on them, to make sure they were safe. They had been gone much longer than it should have taken to fill canteens.

He listened and watched, contemplating a Lori he hadn't seen before—a gentle, carefree Lori, whose laughter was more enchanting than the song of birds. He heard the child's giggle for the first time, saw her delighted face, and the way she so trustfully put her hand in Lori's. His heart, the one so many said he didn't have, twisted with emotions he didn't entirely understand. He had realized, of course, that he was very strongly attracted to her, that he wanted her physically. What man wouldn't? He'd tried to explain his feelings as normal masculine need. He knew he admired her dogged loyalty and stubbornness even as it so thoroughly made his life miserable.

But now . . .

He felt like a small boy peering into a shop window, seeing magic and riches he hadn't known existed. He found himself hurting, just watching, and he didn't know whether it was because the picture was so innocently charming, or because he'd seen so little of this side of Lori. This simple joy of life, and the ability to share it. He had robbed her of that, had almost crushed it from her during this journey.

Almost. Her head was tilted with delight, not defiance, her mouth smiled beguilingly as she charmed the child into laughter. He wanted her to laugh with him. Christ, he didn't even know when he had last laughed. Or when he had sung. He knew he had never skipped a stone or had a pet. Animals, according to Callum, were to be used. They were beasts of burden, or potential food. A pig as a pet was preposterous.

But then, he had watched the affection between the child and the animal, and he'd be damned before he would say it should be a pork chop.

Christ, what in the hell was happening to him?

He didn't know. He just knew he was beginning to see things in a different way, was beginning to feel emotions he thought he'd blocked off years ago, when he was a child and there was no outlet for them. There had never been anyone to hug or share secrets with. There had been chores, expectations. *Be like your father. He was the best Ranger there was. If he hadn't quit, he would probably still be alive. Marriage weakened him.*

He tried to banish the voices. Most of them gone now, stilled by the war or fights with Mexican bandits, Indians, or yanqui renegades. His hand went to his pocket, where he'd placed the badge. It was who and what he was, dammit, and he couldn't change that. Not now.

He heard another giggle, and his attention went back to Lori and Maggie. Lori's trousers were plastered against her legs, outlining their fine shape, and she was carrying her boots, her bare toes digging happily into the pine straw. That fine golden hair was loosely braided, and several tendrils had escaped and fallen down her back. One of her hands brushed it aside carelessly, totally oblivious to appearances.

She was lovely that way. Like a laughing wood sprite who could steal the heart of the most hardened of woodsmen. She had, in the past few days, stolen his. He hadn't been able to admit it until this moment, but as he watched her now, he knew something inside him had changed, was changing. He was recognizing a hunger inside, a longing to touch and be touched with something other than lust or anger.

He wanted to bask in her laughter. He wanted that fierce loyalty for his own. And he had not the slightest idea of how to obtain it.

As the woman and child turned his way, he moved in the opposite direction, out of sight. He didn't want to be caught spying like some lovesick schoolboy. Or even like a Ranger checking up on his prisoner. If only this mess had some solution. But it didn't. If he didn't take Nick Braden back, neither Braden nor he—nor anyone around them—would ever be safe. If he did, Lori would never forgive him. And he might well be responsible for an innocent man being hanged.

Neither prospect was acceptable. But damn if he didn't want a touch of that smile, that laughter. He wanted more than that damnable physical attraction between them. He wanted her. All of her, including pieces of her heart. The last thought was astounding to him, but once he recognized it, he understood what had been causing all the upheaval within him these last days, the gradual softening toward Nick.

Or was it Braden himself?

He didn't know; he seemed not to know anything anymore. Every belief he'd ever had was spinning like a top, and he didn't know how to right them again, to stack them in proper order as he'd always done before.

Because there had been nothing else before. He didn't want to go back to that nothingness. As confusing as this was, he was intrigued, challenged. He'd discovered holes in himself he hadn't realized existed. He felt alive for the first time in his life. A breathing, feeling human being. Not just a hunter.

He had not the slightest idea what to do with someone's heart. Not that he would get much of a chance to find out.

He remembered the feel of her hand against his cheek two days ago, the look on her face when she'd seen him knee Braden in the crotch. She hadn't seen Braden's bitter attack, nor would she care that Braden had started it. But Morgan wondered now whether he hadn't baited Braden just to rid himself of the frustration fuming inside him. Frustration because of his reluctant attraction to Lori. Frustration because of his growing doubts about Braden's guilt, which had been reinforced by the man's actions this morning. Nick Braden, he knew now with certainty, was no murderer.

If only Braden would return voluntarily to Texas with him, Morgan knew he could help him; he could enlist the assistance of his captain, and a judge he knew, to investigate further. But he doubted whether Braden, or his sister, would ever trust him now. He swore to himself and veered off back toward camp and his horse. Braden needed hot food. Morgan needed to get the hell away from everyone before he made a total fool of himself.

Nick was sleeping when Lori returned. The Ranger was nowhere to be seen. She felt a momentary disappointment, though she didn't understand why. She should be glad to have him out of her way. At least he hadn't chained Nick this time. Nor her. He might as well have, though, she realized immediately. Nick was too weak to go anywhere. And the Ranger's horse and all the weapons were gone.

She went over to Beth Andrews, who was sitting beside Nick. She put her fingers to her mouth, warning Lori to be quiet, and then stood, moving some distance from her patient.

"How is he?" Lori said.

"I think he just needs some rest. He's awfully weak from loss of blood and exhaustion."

"The Ranger?"

"He left just seconds ago with his rifle." She hesitated, "Does he always glower like that?"

Lori smiled dryly at the apt observation. "Unfortunately."

"My husband would say he looks like a bear shinning up a thorn tree."

"I think I would have liked your husband," Lori said. "I certainly like your daughter."

Beth Andrews's face softened. "I heard her laugh. Thank you. She hasn't done much of that lately."

"I haven't either," Lori said. "I needed it, too."

The other woman studied her for a moment. "I wish I could help."

"You already have," Lori said. "It's also been a long time since I've seen Nick smile."

Beth's eyes clouded. "He's really innocent? Then why . . . ?"

"Why is the Ranger taking him in?" Lori completed the question, seeing the hesitation in the woman's eyes, the reluctance to offend. "Because," she said bitterly, "they look alike. The Ranger doesn't want his picture on wanted posters. It's . . . inconvenient."

Beth was horrified. "But if . . ."

Lori's voice broke slightly as she answered. "He doesn't care. He just doesn't care. . . ."

The other woman cocked her head. "I don't think . . . that's really true. He was concerned about . . ."

Lori shook her head. "He's concerned about Nick dying before he gets him back. He told me he doesn't want to take a dead man back." Her voice was bitter. She couldn't forget that unfair fight yesterday, the way Morgan had driven them relentlessly today.

She saw the disbelief in the woman's eyes, but just then Nick turned restlessly, and Beth returned to his side. Lori watched, to make sure Nick hadn't worsened, but the woman gave her a reassuring look and settled quietly next to him.

Lori changed clothes, to the only clean, dry ones she had: the damnable dress. Then she sat down next to Maggie and Caroline and started a story about a little girl with a medicine show, and some of the adventures she'd had.

CHAPTER SEVENTEEN

The sun was setting, only part of it visible, the other part tucked among the mountains, when Morgan returned. He had two rabbits with him. Not wanting to risk gunfire, he had set snares, then gone backtracking, making sure they weren't being followed. God knew they were leaving enough tracks with six horses and the damn pig. On his way back two of the four snares yielded a catch, and he had quickly cleaned them.

There would be broth tonight for Braden. Perhaps some stew for the rest of them.

He paused at the clearing. Beth Andrews was huddled next to Braden. Lori's hands were moving gracefully as she sat in front of the fire with Maggie, who was listening intently to her. Lori was wearing a dress. His dress. It was the first time she'd worn one since Laramie, and he had forgotten how pretty she looked in one. The porter had done well. The dress fit perfectly, molding her fine breasts and slender waist. In the first dusk, framed by the fire, she looked totally charming. His body reacted, from the fire in his lower region to the softening of a heart that was now involved.

Lori looked up, sensing his approach. She gave him a tentative smile, then seemed to catch herself, and her lips turned down in a small frown. Her gaze went to the rabbits.

"For your brother," he said roughly.

The brightness returned to her face, and a lump

formed in his throat. It took so little to bring back that smile. She whispered something to the child, then stood up and went over to him, reaching out to take the rabbits. Her eyes met his briefly. "Thank you," she said in a slightly husky voice, then turned abruptly away. He watched as Beth joined her and together they put the meat in a pot with water and set it over the fire.

"How is Braden?" he asked Beth.

"Sleeping," she said in that soft voice of hers. "I don't think there's an infection. He's just lost a lot of blood." There was censure in her voice, and guilt gnawed at Morgan again.

He just nodded and turned toward Lori. Her golden eyes were watching him intently. He returned the look steadily. He had decided during the afternoon that he would talk to her, find out more about Nick, try to discover what, if anything, he could do to help the man. Try now to get her to trust him.

He might as well try to push the sun around.

"Help me water the horses," he said suddenly, his voice harsher than he intended.

"Is that an order or a request?" she said, obviously bristling that he had kept them going today when Braden was so ill. But Braden had hidden his pain well, until he'd nearly fallen from his horse. Morgan hadn't expected that, had thought the wound wasn't that severe, that Braden would tell him if he needed to stop. His prisoner hadn't been reluctant to slow them before.

"Please," he said, startling her, startling himself. Her gaze met his, and she felt she was plummeting into uncharted depths. His eyes weren't shadowed now, but neither could she identify the emotions in them. She only knew that despite everything between them, she was more drawn to him than she'd ever been drawn to another man, that she wanted to move into those arms, to feel his lips again. The want radiated between them, a live thing that twisted and curled, connecting them in intimately physical ways even though their bodies didn't touch. She shivered with the unwanted desire that flooded her. She saw his hand clench with the same reflexive movement, a defense against something he couldn't control.

She finally nodded, feeling a little like a puppet, moving as if someone else were pulling the strings. She watched as he took the reins of the three stallions, his and Nick's bay and Beth Andrews's horse, and she took Clementine and the two pack horses. She noticed that he had unstrapped the bedrolls, though he had not unsaddled the horses. His rifle still sat in its scabbard. He was still being careful.

He would always be careful, she warned herself.

She'd noticed he hadn't replaced the handcuffs on Nick, nor had he used the leg irons. That told her he thought Nick was too sick to run. So sick that the Ranger didn't take his usual precautions. Still, he was keeping his eye on the weapons. He stopped at the stream, well out of sight and hearing of the others. He didn't speak as he allowed the horses to drink, and she did the same as dusk fell gently around them, the brilliant reds of the sky fading away until the sky was dark blue and the first star twinkled down at them.

Lori wondered if she had just imagined the undercurrent in the Ranger's voice, if he had really just wanted help with the horses. Then why the "please"? Why not just the usual order? But he stood there patiently, letting the horses drink their fill; then he took them up the creek bank and tied them to trees. He returned and took the reins and ropes to the two pack horses and tied them just as deliberately as he had the others.

He turned back to her, his darkly stubbled face rough in the dim light, his eyes impossible to read now as he studied her. Then he held out a gloved hand. She surprised herself by taking it.

He led her to where the bank of the stream rose, making a natural seat, and he helped her down with a gracefulness she hadn't expected of him. Then he sat next to her, directing his eyes away from her, toward the stream, where he appeared to study some unknown object.

"Tell me what happened in Harmony, Texas," he said.

Lori didn't know what she'd expected, but it wasn't that. She also knew it wasn't an idle question. He never indulged in idle conversation. She looked at him, searching for the reason behind the sudden interest in Harmony.

"Why?" she asked bluntly.

He didn't answer, but he turned and looked at her. His eyes were troubled, the lines around them even deeper than before. "I want to know," he said simply.

Her anger, always bubbling just beneath the surface, and made stronger by her raw attraction to him, cracked open. "Why?" she asked again. "You haven't cared before." She heard her own voice break, and she hated it. She hated showing him that she gave a fig about what he thought. She hated that she cared.

"I want to know, Lori." The uncertainty was gone now. The demanding Ranger was back in place. An order, plain and simple.

"All right," she said. "I saw it all. Will you believe me?"

He studied her, evidently debating the question in his mind, and she started to get up. His hand stopped her, pulled her back down. "Just tell me," he demanded.

Lori felt her chin quiver. She had wanted this. She had wanted him to listen. "We have a younger brother, Andy. He made the mistake of trying to court Lew Wardlaw's daughter."

The Ranger nodded. He'd seen Andy Braden, a big, good-looking kid with an obvious streak of recklessness.

"Lew and his son, Wade, didn't want him anywhere near their princess," she said bitterly. "We were gypsies to them, dirt, just like you think," she added with anger. "Well, the Princess didn't feel the same, and one night she sneaked out of the house to meet Andy in town. Wade followed them, caught up with Andy behind the livery stable and found them kissing. He pulled his sister away and then took a whip to Andy."

She paused, remembering it, remembering the starlit night when everything had changed. "Nick and I"—she looked toward the stream—"we were playing poker in the saloon when we heard someone come in and say a man was being whipped outside by Wade Wardlaw.

"We knew it was Andy. We had tried to warn him about Wardlaw, but he wouldn't listen. We ran out, and Andy was on the ground, bloody, and Wardlaw was hitting him over and over again. One of the Wardlaw hands was standing nearby with his gun drawn. When Andy tried to get the whip, the man would spray the area around him with bullets. Andy didn't have a gun with him that night; he wouldn't have been a match for Wardlaw in any case.

"Nick went for the whip, and Wardlaw swung it at him, then went for his gun. So did the hired hand. Nick was just a fraction faster. He wounded the gunhand and fell to the ground, trying to avoid Wardlaw's bullets. Wade Wardlaw didn't stop firing, and Nick rolled behind a water trough and fired. He didn't want to kill Wardlaw, any more than he wanted to kill the gunhand. But Wardlaw was furious, jerking the gun around, shooting at anything that moved, and Nick's bullet hit his heart."

She stopped, the memory still vivid. She hadn't had a gun; only Nick had. She'd been afraid to move, afraid that she would ruin Nick's aim, and then Wardlaw was dead.

For a moment Lori forgot that the Ranger was next to her. She saw that street, the horror unfolding. But when she felt a hand closing around her straight, rigid fingers, she went on tonelessly. "Someone scooped up Wade Wardlaw's gun, and his sister claimed Andy had attacked her, that Nick had killed her brother in cold blood when he'd come to her assistance." Lori looked up at the Ranger. "Two of the men watching were Wardlaw hands, the few others worked in businesses owned by Wardlaw— everyone but the town drunk, and he was too scared to disagree."

"What happened then?"

"My father and Daniel came, and the three of them

were able to hold off the onlookers until they got Andy to the wagon and drove off. Nick knew what would happen, that he wouldn't stand a chance in court, so he headed in another direction, trying to draw the posse away from the others."

"And you?"

"I knew where Nick would go. I followed him. Andy had Papa and Daniel."

She fell silent. She didn't want to look at his face and see doubt. "Nick," she finally said, "has always been the strong one in the family, ever since I can remember. I love Papa, but he's not . . . always practical. He just thinks everything will turn out for the best. He's always for the underdog, sometimes foolishly. He just likes lost causes, I suppose." She looked up at him. "His family were slave owners in Virginia. He hated slavery and apparently said so to the extent he was disowned. He'd spent two years at a university, and he loved books, he taught all of us to love them. But he wasn't very good at any one thing, or perhaps he didn't have the patience or temperament to learn a trade. He joined a medicine show and eventually inherited it when the owner died. He . . . loves that life. He has a lot of curiosity about places and people, and he can go where he wants to go. That's how he met Mama."

She stopped, stared at him defiantly. "I know what you think about my family, but you're wrong. Papa is . . . well, he never meets a stranger. He never sees anyone in need without trying to help. He doesn't see anything wrong in what we do. The tonic and Herbs of Life don't hurt anyone, and we provide entertainment for people who don't get any."

Lori glanced up at Morgan, a sudden glint of mischief in her eyes, "Of course, we have been known to 'sucker' marks, but only those who were greedy and could afford it." She bit her lip and then continued, obviously determined to tell the whole truth. "Nick and I have even cheated some at cards, but only when we needed the money really badly. We're both very good without cheating, and we've been accused of it even when . . . we didn't."

Morgan wanted to smile. That damn, appealing honesty again. That convoluted logic that fascinated him. But he forced himself to remain still, not wanting to stop the words, the chance to learn more about her. About her family.

After a quick glance to determine censure, Lori continued. "We were never lonely because we had . . . each other." There was just a trace of wistfulness in her eyes, and Morgan understood more of the close relationship between Lori and Braden. *We had each other.* Regardless of what she said, it must have been a lonely life for a child. No roots, no friends outside of family. But if there was any regret, she didn't reveal it. "There was something new all the time. Papa was always finding some itinerant entertainer who would teach Nick and me and Andy all sorts of things."

"Including how to shoot," he inserted wryly.

She looked up at him and nodded. "And to perform tricks with horses, to sing and to play various instruments. In addition to the harmonica, Nick can play the guitar and banjo." Lori hesitated a moment before continuing slowly. "I think I always liked it better than Nick. I like people, and I . . . like singing for them. I used to love the sharpshooting shows." She looked up at Morgan. "I'm very good." She was telling him again that she could well have killed him if she'd wanted to.

"Nick . . . he was good at performing too," she continued after a moment's pause. "But his heart wasn't always in it. Nick wanted to enlist during the war, but he felt we needed him. I was only ten and Andy six, and Nick, well, he worried about us. And lately . . . he's been wanting to ranch."

Lori looked straight into the Ranger's eyes. She had told her story, had pleaded her case as best she could. Now she tried to gauge his reaction, trying to decipher whether or not he understood anything she was saying, that Nick was innocent, that he was a good man.

Her heart froze. His face was still stone. "He has to go back, Lori," he said slowly, making each word clear. "But I'll help him."

Lori heard only the first part. The second sentence meant little. Nothing could help Nick in Harmony. Nothing. The five-thousand-dollar reward said as much. He didn't believe her. Nothing had changed. She started to rise again, but his hand, as before, wouldn't let her.

"Let go of me," she said bitterly.

"Lori, listen to me," he said in a low, insistent voice. "There's a big bounty on his head. Someone will claim it."

"It doesn't have to be you."

"Dammit, I have no intention of collecting the bounty. I told you that before."

"I don't believe you," she lied. She did believe him, but she wanted to hurt him, as he kept hurting her.

He stiffened. "I've never hunted a man for money."

"Then why . . . ? Because you look alike? Because you're afraid they'll come after you?"

He sighed. "That was part of it," he admitted. "I've been a lawman all my life. Having my face on a poster was like . . . an insult to everything I've believed."

"You obviously don't believe in justice," she retorted, so furious she could barely speak. He always did that to her, made her angrier than anyone ever had before. Because he was so blind . . . and because even then he raised these wanting feelings in her.

"I believe in the law," he said. "It usually works pretty well."

"And when it doesn't?"

"I try to see that it does," he said quietly.

"You said you were in Harmony," she accused, "and you were convinced Nick was guilty."

He nodded. "I had no reason not to be. Everyone told the same story."

"But you have reason now?" she said, holding her breath. Maybe she *could* convince him to let Nick go.

He hesitated. "Maybe."

"Then release him."

"You aren't listening, Lori. You know how many killers out there are hunting him?"

"We'll go far away."

"Goddammit, you can't go far enough."

Lori stared at him, stunned. He wasn't going to release Nick, no matter what he thought, or what she said. "Why did you ask, then? Why did you want to know what happened in Harmony?" Her voice broke.

"I can't let him go, Lori, or you'll both end up dead, perhaps your whole family, but once we're in Texas, I *can* help."

"Assuage your conscience before he dies, you mean," she said. She hated the tears that were beginning to burn behind her eyes. His hand caught her chin and drew her face up to meet his eyes.

"I don't want anything to happen to you," he said in a low, harsh voice. His eyes were intense, the blue so dark that now they appeared black in the evening dusk. She had never seen them like that before. He'd always so surrounded himself by a wall of solitude that she'd often wondered if anything penetrated it, whether he ever let anything or anyone intrude into that private world he hoarded to himself. He'd always struck her as a lonely man, one who made an art out of aloneness, even attempted to make a virtue out of it.

A muscle moved in his throat, and she felt the tension in him, the struggle inside him to keep from doing exactly what she knew he was going to do.

Morgan fought himself, but it did no damn good. He had watched her every expression, the earnestness as she struggled with words to defend someone she loved. The anger. The sadness. The pleading. He sensed how much she'd hated pleading. And something exploded inside the places he'd always guarded. That trapdoor sprang, exposing the raw loneliness, the emptiness that had always been so much a part of him.

He wanted her to trust him. To believe in him as she believed in Braden. And he didn't know how to make that happen. He didn't know how to force it. And then he just reacted. Out of need. Out of desire. Out of some kind of hope that he could *make* her believe in him.

His head lowered. His lips met hers. Roughly at first, because of that fierce need he didn't know how to harness. Her lips, at first resistant, gave under the persistent onslaught and responded as hungrily as his. He didn't feel victory, though. He sensed her reluctance, her anger at herself for yielding to him. And he wanted to drive away that anger. He wanted it more than he ever wanted anything in his life.

Morgan had never been gentle with a woman. He'd never been rough, either. He'd just been . . . efficient. Taking care of needs. He looked at Lori's face, so full of conflicting emotions, and he wanted to be gentle, to be trusted. He wanted so much more than he'd ever given or been given.

He wanted to explore everything. He wanted to see her smile, her eyes light with that spontaneous pleasure he'd seen earlier that day. He wanted those eyes to light for him. His kiss gentled, deepened, invited. His arms went around her, and he felt pleased when her body relaxed against him and she opened her mouth to him. A little bit of trust. A very small bit, but he would take what he could, he thought with a sudden burst of elation.

She didn't want to respond to him. She wanted to push him away, to call him a murderer. She could do neither. She found herself betraying all she loved and held dear as her mouth responded to his, and the kiss became a desperate, needy thing, a conflagration that should have been damped by anger and loneliness, by uncertainty and her own sense of betrayal to herself. Instead it seemed to feed on those very emotions.

Dear Mary and Joseph, but she needed him. She didn't hold any more illusions that he might help her, yet she was attracted by that unyielding integrity of his. He could have lied, but he hadn't. He was her enemy. He had just told her he would continue to be her enemy, and yet . . .

He filled her heart and body and soul and mind with a completeness that astonished her. She had no will when he was near, when he touched her. And, dear God, he was touching her. Every place. His mouth was hard against hers, his tongue insistent as it reached inside her mouth and explored, hungrily at first, and then seducingly gentle. Surprisingly gentle for a man like him, a hard man who didn't know how to bend.

His long fingers ran around the back of her neck, massaging her tired muscles until the tension faded from them and her body relaxed against his even while shock waves of desire shot through her. Hot, searing need was building within her, settling in the core of her, sending tingling sensations along her every nerve ending. Every resolve she had, every reservation, melted under his touch. She needed his strength, even while she feared it. He took his mouth from hers, feathered her neck with kisses as he guided her down until she was flat on a cushion of soft, weathered pine needles. His hands were touching her with such tenderness, barely moving along her neck, then her shoulders. He leaned down, and his tongue ran lightly along her cheek.

Her body shivered with reaction, with the pure delight of that extraordinary giving she'd never believed possible from a man so obviously unused to it. "Ah, Lori," he whispered hoarsely, "I . . ."

But words were impossible between them. Lori couldn't bear words. She couldn't bear promises or lack of them. She couldn't bear regret. She couldn't bear awakening to the reality of her situation, or what he was. She could only feel. He captured her mouth again in a long, smothering kiss, his body taut, and she knew he was experiencing the same tormenting need that rocked her body. The need was so painful . . . yet so exquisitely new and strange and wonderful.

"Lori?" The question was mouthed by him so quietly she barely heard it. His eyes, intense and brooding, also asked. Her hand went up to his rough face, the dark bristle making it so formidable. But the eyes reflected wonder, a bright-blue flame burning deep within them.

She didn't know what to call him. He'd always been the Ranger. An impersonal name for an enemy.

"Morgan," he said, as if reading her mind, his fingers tangling in her hair, undoing the loose braid.

"Morgan," she tried, feeling it strange on her tongue.

"Not so hard to say, is it?" he said, a touch of wistfulness in his voice.

"Everything about you is hard," she whispered.

His mouth quirked in a small smile. "You're very perceptive, Miss Lori," he said.

The heat inside her intensified. She felt his hardness against her, felt his manhood straining against his trousers. She blushed that he had so misunderstood, and yet . . .

He was still waiting for an answer to his earlier question, the unspoken question that hovered in the air. Her hand went up and tangled in his thick dark hair. He leaned down and kissed her again, this time with tender violence. Every slight movement of his body or his hands made her body hum with feeling. It was awakening, twisting with each new sensation, quaking slightly under the unbearable need building inside her.

She felt his hands begin to unbutton her dress, felt them move under the chemise she was wearing and caress her breast, teasing the nipples with his fingers. When he moved his lips from her mouth down to her breasts, she felt as if warm honey were running through her veins.

"Morgan," she whispered, and she felt his body stiffen with the recognition she'd just given him.

Her hands went around his neck, and she lifted her head slightly to lean it against his dark hair as his mouth explored and tempted and teased. She felt as if she were caught in an exquisite whirlpool, drawn more and more into turbulent, twisting currents of feelings. Drowning in them. Drowning in her need for him, for that mixture of tenderness and barely restrained violence she always sensed in him. His hands were at her waist, tugging at her underdrawers. She felt them roll down over her hips, the chill of the air against skin.

And then she found herself helping him unbutton his shirt, and her hands played along his chest, lightly over the new wound, more curiously over the old ones. His chest was so hard, like a board except for the muscles that shaped it so handsomely. Her fingers hesitated at his nipples, and she played with them as he had with hers, then she traced a line down to where his trousers were buttoned. He stiffened, then his hands went to them and he quickly unbuttoned them, pulling his boots off and then his pants. He was sitting, wearing only long underdrawers that molded against hard muscles and lean legs.

Lori thought she had never seen anything so sensual, so gloriously primal. So perfect. She held out a hand to him, and it was all the response he needed. He took it, his large hand making hers seem so small as he turned it over and traced lines in it with his other hand. She had to keep reminding herself he was right-handed. She was so used to Nick. . . .

The thought was like a storm cloud descending over her, ominous and warning. Her hand jerked back in sudden protest, and he went still for a moment. Then he lowered his body to lie next to her, and he kissed her, long and hard and demanding, seeking, she knew, to exorcise that ghost that hovered between them. The kiss ignited an explosion inside her, a series of detonations that exposed a raw craving so strong, she knew it had to be satisfied or she would explode. She knew her eyes must be saying as much, they seemed enormous in her face as she watched him. Loving him. Hating him. Wanting him.

With a groan his body moved above and down on hers. She felt his throbbing manhood against her, only thin cloth between the two bodies, a slight abrasive barrier, which, if anything, exacerbated the burning need inside her.

And then it was gone, that cloth, and she felt his smooth skin against the now incredibly sensitive crevice at the juncture of her legs . . . and an insistent throbbing of her own deep inside. It was a clutching, wanting throbbing she'd never known before, and she was frightened by its intensity. Frightened and fascinated that such a thing existed, and she hadn't been aware until this very moment.

She felt his fingers then, gentle but insistent as they teased the entrance to her womanhood. Waves of sensation washed over her as she felt that part of her grow warm and wet. Her arms went around him, drawing him closer, frantic now for what was being promised. His hands moved, and she saw his face. So much intensity. He hesitated as his gaze met hers. "Lori," he said roughly, like a man in extreme pain, and then his tense, stiff body moved, his manhood touching and teasing that most intimate part of her. She felt him enter, slowly, and she was astonished at the feeling of the tentative invasion. So strange, so foreign . . . and yet so oddly exquisite. And then he probed deeper and she felt him strain against something and there was a sudden pain, so unexpected that she couldn't stop a small cry.

The movement stopped, and she felt so many things, the strangeness of him in her, the pain that was now receding even as the core of her seemed to close around him, to react in a greedy way of its own. She felt the stiffness of his body as he hesitated, the sound of his expelled breath and a curse. She felt the throbbing in her grab and hold him, and that craving she hadn't understood grew like Jack's beanstalk, wild and uncontrollable.

"Morgan," she whispered, unaware until the word came that she had uttered it.

His breathing was ragged against her hair, and then his lips touched hers, so lightly they felt like butterfly wings. Her own body moved then, hungry, so hungry. Instinctively she lifted her body to him, seeking more of him, and she felt him fill her, move inside with a rhythmic dance that made her explode with sensation, one after another, as that passage came alive with wonderful, tingling feelings too fine, too exquisite to even try to understand. Even as wondrous as they were, though, she knew they were but a prelude, that they were climbing toward some nirvana, toward some place she'd never even imagined.

Her arms tightened around him, her mouth kissing, nibbling as her legs instinctively went around his, drawing him deeper as his movements came stronger, magnifying all those sensations until she wondered how she could bear them without screaming.

She heard her own cry, and his mouth came down on hers, his kiss snatching the sound from her, as he made one last mighty thrust and erupted inside her, sending waves and waves of shuddering warmth through her, shocks of ecstasy that rocked her and then exploded like falling stars, casting a rich, mellow glow in its wake. Her body quaked with tremors as he quieted inside her and held her tightly, as if she were a treasure of inestimable value. She felt safe and loved. She felt . . . so wonderful. So new. Different and yet the same. Richer. So much richer. As if she'd found a vein of gold she didn't know existed, that would change her life forever.

He rolled over on his side, taking her with him, and she felt his body shudder, his hands moved over her as if they had found something wondrous. They were that gentle.

Neither of them said anything. Lori didn't want to prick this beautiful cocoon they were in. She just wanted to feel him inside, his hands touching her. She felt his rough cheek against hers. Then his whisper, "Dear God, Lori." It was like a cry of pain, an animal wounded near death.

She closed her eyes, knowing the wonder of this moment was ending, that they both had to return to a world where they were enemies, where tenderness had no place, where the law had divided them. Where they were forbidden each other by whatever god ruled their lives.

She felt him withdraw from her, move slightly away. His breath was still labored. A tear trickled down her face, and one of his fingers wiped it away. Still, she wouldn't open her eyes. As long as she kept them closed, she didn't have to face what she'd just done.

"Look at me, Lori," he said. She didn't want to. She wanted to curl up in a ball and just hurt.

"Lori," he said again, and she forced herself to look up into a face that was rough and hard and . . . dear. Loved and hated. No, not hated. No longer hated. And that fact hurt as much as the hate had.

He took her hand, held it tightly, his eyes willing her to listen, to believe. "Trust me," he said, his voice rough, rough with feeling. "Trust me about your brother. I *can* help. I *will* help."

If it had been her life, she would have done it. She would have agreed. But it wasn't hers. It was Nick's. She knew Morgan Davis didn't lie. He would do his best for Nick, but what if the best wasn't good enough?

"I . . . can't."

He didn't say anything for a moment, then moved several feet away from her. That blankness fell over his face, that hard impassivity, and he stared out at the stream. "Then what was this all about?"

It was about love. Lori realized she had loved him ever since he'd put that knife to his wound so many days ago. Nearly a lifetime ago. She'd known it from the way she'd felt his hurt. And Morgan . . . he also cared. She knew that something . . . something much greater than lust had driven him to her. He'd been too tender, too gentle for it to be otherwise.

But she couldn't let him know how she felt. They had already done too much damage to each other.

"Need," she said simply. "Just . . . need. Man and woman."

He turned back to face her. "It was one hell of a lot more than that," he said.

She swallowed. She couldn't deny that. She still glowed from his lovemaking, her body still seemed to burn from his touch. She still remembered the wonder on his face as they had collapsed together.

"Nothing's changed," she said in a whisper. "Nothing has really changed."

He just stared at her, but she couldn't read his eyes, not in the dark. "Dammit, why can't you trust me?"

Lori's heart was breaking. She wanted to trust him. She wanted it more than anything. But that kind of trust wasn't hers to give. She tried not to hear that rough plea in his voice, tried not to understand that he was hurting as much as she was, tried not to acknowledge the fact that her denial was destroying something fine and beautiful.

"Let him go," she said. "Let us go." The last words caught in her throat.

"For services rendered?" he said bitterly, his face haggard, his words cutting through her.

"Yes," she said defiantly.

"Sorry," he said coldly, but then he hesitated, his eyes softening as he apparently read something else in her face. "If I thought . . . if I believed that would solve anything, I would. It won't. He can't run forever, and I'm his best chance, whether you and he believe it or not."

"I don't," she said flatly, the old frustration flooding back, more bitter now than ever before. "You just can't give up your man, can you? You don't know how to be a human being. You don't know . . ." Her voice broke, and she turned away.

His voice was haggard when he finally answered. "I think I just proved I'm human," he said wearily. He hesitated. "I'm sorry, Lori. That shouldn't have happened. I . . . had hoped . . ." His voice trailed off.

Lori wished she didn't feel every ounce of the self-disgust she heard in his voice, but she couldn't surrender. Not now. "That we would make it easy for you?"

"No, I didn't think that," he said dryly. "At least, Lori, give me your parole. For now, anyway."

The pain stabbed even deeper than it had a moment ago. "Why?" She was going to make him say it. Damn him, she was going to make him put it into words.

But he was silent, his dark eyes impassive again, watching her, and she felt so vulnerable, particularly in her nakedness. She saw his gaze wash over her, saw the fire blaze in his eyes, and then the resignation.

"So you don't have to chain me, again?" she said in a cold, bright voice. "Why not? That's what you do best. Keep your prisoners on a leash, keep them helpless and hopeless. You're so damn good at it that . . ." She stopped, her voice suddenly breaking again. Her words had meant to hurt, and they had. She saw from the way his head jerked back.

He pulled on his trousers and his boots without comment, then his shirt, buttoning it with a deliberation that was obviously designed to hide something. Anger? Disappointment? He stood and walked over to a tree, silent and alone. As he always was.

Miserably, she dressed. It shouldn't be like this. But she knew she had struck a blow he wouldn't forget. He walked back to where she now stood, his back stiffer than she'd seen it. He hesitated, then tried again. "Lori, don't make it worse than it already is."

Lori stared at the ground. She felt her mouth quivering. "Are you going to chain Nick tonight?"

"He isn't giving me a choice."

"Then you'll have to do the same to me, because I'll try to free him any way I can."

His sigh was audible. Defeated. He turned away from her. "It's time to get back," he said in a weary voice. He took the reins of the three stallions and without looking back headed toward the campsite.

Lori stood there for a moment, wanting to take her words back. Wanting to love him. To trust him.

But she couldn't.

Now she knew what loneliness really was. Loving a man you couldn't trust, who couldn't trust you. She had never thought that possible, but now she knew it was.

Dear Mary and Joseph, she knew it was.

CHAPTER EIGHTEEN

Morgan rose at dawn and checked the back trail again. Beth Andrews was still asleep. So was the child.

Lori hadn't been, he knew. Her eyes had watched his every move. Christ, he would never forget those eyes last night as he'd handcuffed her to Nick Braden. They would always haunt him, that wounded look that was equal parts anguish and defiance. He would never forget the way he had felt, the emptiness and guilt. So much guilt. But he knew he was right. He *knew* they would be safer with him than they would be on their own, running from the law, running from bounty hunters like Whitey Stark.

Wasn't that their decision to make?

They were too damn stubborn to see he was right.

They had reason.

Morgan hadn't treated either of them with much consideration or sympathy. He'd been so damn mad about that poster, he'd automatically assumed Nick Braden was guilty. He didn't believe that anymore. Braden hadn't tried to convince him, not after that first time. But his actions had. Morgan was usually a good judge of character. Someone might fool him for an hour, even a day, but not for weeks, especially under the circumstances they'd been traveling. A man showed his mettle under the intense pressure to which Morgan had subjected Braden.

Braden had shown his. Time and time again. When he had helped Morgan at the cabin. When he had refused to use Lori to help himself. When he had tried to avoid killing the Utes but then had done so with competence. He wasn't a coward who would shoot an unarmed man.

Morgan didn't blame Braden for hating him, for distrusting him. He had given him no reason to do otherwise. In fact, he had given him more than one cause to despise him. Braden's eyes had bored into him last night when he'd returned with Lori. Even in a night lit only by firelight, only a blind person would miss the pine needles in her hair, the flush of her cheeks.

Christ, what a mistake that had been! But he had looked into those golden eyes, and his need for her had wiped away every vestige of decency and good sense he had. He had wanted her as he'd never wanted a woman before. He had needed her as he'd never needed anyone.

He'd also wanted to convince her she could trust him. He'd thought he could . . .

What? Love her into believing . . . after weeks of dragging her and her brother through the woods in irons? *That's what you do best.* He could still hear the bitterness in her voice. And she'd been a virgin! Because he knew she'd played cards in saloons, he'd assumed . . .

He hadn't really listened to her. Bile rose in his throat. He could never convince either of them now to trust him. Braden knew what had happened, Morgan saw it in his eyes, in his bitter expression, and Nick's distaste for killing no longer extended to him. Morgan had no doubt of that.

Which was why he'd had to chain them last night, no matter how hard it was, no matter how Lori had looked at him as his hand had rested on her wrist before locking the bracelet around it. Just as he had been able to do that, she was capable of knocking him unconscious or seizing a gun while he slept. He knew that. She had declared as much.

He *could* help Nick Braden. Goddammit, he would help him, whether he wanted Morgan's aid or not. Morgan had already decided to take Braden to Ranger headquarters and hold him there until Morgan could prove what really happened in Harmony. He would have the backing of his captain and the judge. He always had.

But he knew he couldn't convince the Bradens of that. He didn't even know how. He'd never had to explain his actions or motives or intentions before. He believed in absolutes. Trust was trust. It was there, or it wasn't, and words wouldn't change that. He had hoped to gain Lori's last night, but he had only deepened her distrust. Hers and her brother's.

And Beth Andrews's. She had looked at Morgan in horror last night when he had ironed Nick Braden, and then his sister, to a tree.

"He's sick," she had exclaimed.

But Morgan knew Braden, as he knew himself. A knife wound wouldn't stop him, not if he had an opportunity.

Hellfire, the only creature that looked at him with anything even remotely resembling tolerance was his horse and the damned pig, and the latter, he thought with dry humor, didn't know any better. The horse, he fed.

Lori could have stood anything but the sad, self-accusing look in Nick's eyes. He *knew* what had happened, and he blamed it on himself. She had felt his wrath last night, had seen the tight compression of his lips each time he looked at her. He had glared at the Ranger, with killing rage. She had tried to talk to Nick when she thought the Ranger had gone to sleep, to tell him what Morgan Davis had said about helping.

Nick had just looked at her, and she knew he neither believed the Ranger's words nor was willing to accept his help, even if it had been offered. He thought she had sacrificed herself for him, and that the Ranger had used her. She didn't know how to tell him the truth. That in those moments on the stream bank, she had forgotten that anything existed other than herself and Morgan Davis, and her gnawing hunger for him. The truth was a ball of misery in the pit of her stomach. She felt she had betrayed

Nick even though she still believed that Morgan would try to help. She just didn't believe he could. He was one man, a Ranger sworn to uphold the law, and the law in this case was ugly and twisted.

Nick moved restlessly, and she leaned over and felt his forehead. It was warm, too warm for the chill that had come during the night. She took the blankets from herself and packed them around Nick.

"Is he feverish?"

She looked up. Beth Andrews had approached and was standing there, her pretty face marred with worry. She had spent hours with Nick the night before, spooning broth she had made from the rabbits.

Lori nodded, feeling shame at being locked to her brother as if they were both criminals. But Mrs. Andrews seemed unaware. Or uncaring. She stooped down and put her own hand to Nick's cheek. His eyes fluttered opened and fixed on her face. He tried to smile, but it was more a grimace, and Lori knew then how sick he was. Nick liked women, pure and simple. And she knew he would rather be flayed than show weakness in front of one. He was usually so strong and confident and full of blarney charm.

Mrs. Andrews looked at the handcuffs binding the two of them, then at the leg irons that linked his right leg to a tree, and winced. "Mr. Davis?"

Lori grimaced. "He left at dawn. He built a fire before he left, but it's almost out now. He'll . . . be back soon."

Mrs. Andrews's soft blue eyes clouded as she obviously disapproved of what the Ranger had done, leaving the two of them chained when one was ill. "I'll get some more firewood and heat some more broth," she said. "We need to break the fever."

She gave Nick a lingering, concerned glance, and then she reluctantly turned away, returning in a minute with a full canteen. Nick's eyes had closed again, and she handed it to Lori. "Get him to drink as much as he can."

Lori nodded. "Thank you."

The woman smiled. "Please call me Beth. Maggie and I both think of you as a friend now."

A rush of warm gratitude swept through her. She wondered whether Beth Andrews had noticed what her brother had noticed last night—that she and the Ranger had made love. Her face flushed at the thought.

"Thank you," she said again.

"I wish I could do something about those handcuffs. . . ."

Lori smiled halfheartedly. "I wish you could, too, but he keeps the keys on him."

"Why?"

Lori knew the question wasn't why he kept the keys on him, but why he had felt it necessary to handcuff her in the beginning. "Because I shot him," Lori replied frankly. "He's not sure I wouldn't do it again."

Beth digested that piece of information slowly. Her eyes had a bit of a smile when she asked the obvious question. "Would you?"

Lori looked up. "I don't know."

Beth's smile disappeared. "Because of . . . Nick?"

So it was "Nick," already.

Lori nodded and looked at Nick, whose eyes had closed again. She didn't know whether he was sleeping or feigning sleep.

Beth's expressive eyes softened; then she retreated quickly, as if embarrassed by the conversation. Lori watched as she gathered wood and fed the fire with competence. She was a pretty, slender woman, with a surprisingly determined competence about her despite those gentle blue eyes.

Lori felt Nick's cheek again. It seemed hotter—but, then, that was probably just because she was worried. She tugged at him, and he finally opened his eyes. Lori held the canteen to his mouth with her free hand. "I have orders to make you drink," she said.

Nick's eyes were half-closed, as if he had to fight to

keep them open. His free hand went to the canteen, effectively dismissing her assistance. "Where is . . ."

He obviously hated even to mention his detested nemesis. Lori felt shame wash over her. "He left at dawn. To make sure no one's following, I guess." She had to look away from his steady gaze and tried to change the subject. "It was Beth who said you should drink."

When Morgan Davis returned, the smell of coffee was strong. He tied his horse away from the others. He took the rifle from its scabbard and unloaded it, putting the ammunition into the saddlebags and carrying those over to the tree where the rest of his gear remained. He then went over to Lori and Nick and, his gaze meeting hers with characteristic directness, unlocked the handcuffs holding the Bradens together. She noticed he was very careful not to touch her in doing so. He turned away abruptly, toward Nick, and put his hand to Nick's fever-flushed face. Nick shied away, his eyes filling with anger.

"He's feverish," Lori said. "We can't leave this morning unless you want to kill him."

Morgan merely nodded, watching as she stretched stiffly, rubbing her wrist where the handcuff had created a red circle. "Let me see your wound," he said curtly to Nick.

Nick reluctantly unbuttoned his coat, and then his shirt, leaving the red-stained bandage exposed. The Ranger examined the area around it, obviously looking for signs of infection. His fingers explored and prodded, and he grunted, evidently satisfied.

"We'll stay here today. I'll do some more hunting. I imagine some fresh meat would help." He unlocked the iron band from Nick's ankle, leaving him completely free. As free as the pain and fever allowed. It was a small concession, relatively risk free considering Nick's weakness, but still, for Morgan Davis, a concession just the same.

"Do you need . . ." The Ranger's question was aimed at Nick, but he quickly glanced at Lori and snapped his mouth shut.

Nick's mouth tightened. "I don't need help from you. can manage on my own."

He tried to stand, leaned against a tree, took a few steps, then started to fall. Morgan was there to catch him "A few steps," he said, "just lean on me for a few steps."

Lori realized he was trying to help Nick, to give him few minutes of privacy, and she saw Nick struggling with the decision. It galled him to have to rely on the Range for even that short length of time. She moved away from both of them, knowing her presence merely exacerbate the tension between them.

Nick hated the heaviness of his own body, the struggle it took to move. He'd hated having to lean on Davis, but his own personal needs had been too great to do otherwise He'd somehow summoned the strength to shrug him off but now he was paying the price for that independence. He hurt, and he was as weak as a day-old calf.

Fury coursed through him every time he looked a Morgan, knowing that he had been with Lori last night. If Nick had had the strength, he would have killed him. He had seen the misery in Lori's face, in the eyes that had refused to meet his. So unlike the Lori he knew. The Ranger's face had been set in stone, as usual, when the two had returned last night, the air between them so charged that one would think they were in the midst of an electrical storm. He knew what had happened had been more than a kiss, like the one he'd interrupted before There was new knowledge in Lori's eyes that gave her away, even if the pine straw tucked among her hair and her mussed clothes had not.

Nick didn't blame her. She had been thrust into an emotion-filled situation. She was tired, she was exhausted she was terrified for him. Lori would do anything to help him, she was that loyal, and that was why he had wanted her out of the way days ago. She was vulnerable to someone like Morgan Davis, who evidently had few scruples about taking advantage of the situation. He had even promised to "help," Lori had told him.

Nick almost vomited at the hypocrisy. Help send Nick to a hangman was more like it—so Davis wouldn't have a "look-alike" on the wrong side of the law. If there had been any possibility that Nick might trust him, it had dissipated last night when he realized the man had seduced Lori, if not outright raped her.

Why hadn't he let that Ute kill Morgan?

When he and Davis were out of the others' sight, Nick jerked away from Morgan, then turned on him.

"What do you want to stay away from Lori?" he demanded through gritted teeth. He cursed his weakness. He cursed the fact that it was all he could do to stand. "My word I won't try to escape?"

The Ranger just stood there. A muscle flexed in his cheek. "I don't need it," he said quietly.

Nick felt as if he'd just been kicked in the stomach. "No," he said bitterly. "You don't need it." He turned away and leaned against a tree to relieve himself, knowing if he didn't, he might well fall.

When he had finished, there was utter silence behind him. Nick had never felt so impotent. "What kind of bastard are you, anyway? What kind of man takes advantage of an innocent like Lori, who would do anything . . . God help me, to . . . ?"

Still silence. A painfully long silence. He turned back to face Davis again. The Ranger's face was emotionless. "I don't . . . know," Morgan finally said in a toneless voice.

Nick closed his eyes, still leaning against the tree. He wanted to curse the man several feet away from him, the man with his face. He wanted to beat him to a pulp, but cursing would do no good, and he was too weak to fight anyone. Nick slumped, weakened by the heat in his body as well as by the fierce anger that robbed him of what strength he had left. He had to stay alive, he had to get stronger. By God, he had to. He headed back toward the clearing, every footstep a mammoth effort, as if his feet were still encased in iron. Only too aware of the Ranger's steps immediately behind him, he finally made the clearing and fell back onto his blankets. He expected the Ranger to lock the leg iron back on him, but he didn't. Rather than feeling grateful, Nick only felt more humiliated, more mocked.

I don't need it, the Ranger had said. The only thing Nick had to bargain with, his compliance, had been thrown back in his face as worthless. It had been the most difficult offer he'd ever made—to bargain away all attempts to win his precious freedom to a man who had seduced his sister.

He'd believed for a long time that only one of them would get to Texas—he or the Ranger. Now he didn't care if neither reached its border.

You'll wish you took my offer, he promised the Ranger silently. I'll take you to hell with me.

His enemy stood above him, studying him with that same impassive expression he always wore. Only his eyes showed any kind of feeling, and only for a fraction of a second. Regret? Nick dismissed that notion almost immediately.

But then the impression was gone, and he'd turned, moving over to the fire and returning with a cup of broth, handing it to Nick. Nick took the cup, knowing he needed the warmth, the liquid, to fight the fever, to regain his strength. He needed it to kill Morgan Davis, even if he died with him.

He said as much with his eyes. The Ranger left his side and went to his horse. He took his rifle, then made his way through the woods silently until he was gone from sight.

Nick's horse was fifty feet away. It might as well have been a million. Even if he did manage to reach it, he wouldn't be able to stay on it long.

As usual, the chance the Ranger appeared to be taking was no chance at all.

.   .   .

Beth had been watching from where she was tending the fire, her face twisted with confusion. She was staring at both men, and the intensity of that look drew Lori to look at them too. She had grown so used to the differences between them, that she had ceased to notice the similarity in their features. But now both men had several days' growth of beard on their faces, and except for Morgan's mustache, the resemblance was little more than amazing as they stood so closely together.

"I've never seen two men look so much alike . . . except for some twins I knew once in Kansas City," Beth said.

Lori shook her head. "There is no connection," she said. "There can't be. . . . But that resemblance is one reason the Ranger came after Nick."

Beth checked the coffee on the fire, as well as a pot that had been one of the belongings she'd saved from the wagon. It was filled with water, evidently for Nick. "It's . . . incredible."

Lori sat down on a log Beth had dragged close to the fire. "I know. I think the Ranger is older. He looks older. He said his parents were killed in an Indian attack in Texas at the time he was born. Nick was born in Colorado." She hesitated. "And they're nothing alike in other ways."

"Aren't they?" Beth asked quietly.

Lori stared at her. "What do you mean?"

"Courage," Beth said. "Strength of will. Your brother . . . I can't imagine how or even why he rode so long yesterday without saying anything. And did you notice how they complemented each other when they fought? Their responses when the other was in danger? I thought then they must be . . . close. It was almost as if . . . they had fought together before, that they *knew* what the other would do."

Lori hadn't seen it. She hadn't seen it because she'd been terrified for them both. And she knew how much they disliked and distrusted one another. She stared at the two men, now disappearing among the trees. It couldn't be, she thought. They couldn't be blood related, not unless it was some crazy throwback to a common, long-ago ancestor. There was no way. She and Nick had gone over the possibility a dozen times when the Ranger was out of hearing.

She shook her head of the notion that Beth had planted there. "It's . . . just coincidence," she said. "And they're *not* alike. Nick enjoys life. He likes to laugh and tease, and he takes care of people. Morgan Davis . . . he . . . never smiles. He doesn't know how to laugh. He *hunts* people. He doesn't care about them."

"Doesn't he?" Beth asked in that soft voice of hers, tipping her head to where the two men had vanished into the forest of pines.

"No," Lori said, aware of the emotion behind the word. She couldn't let herself think that he did. She knew these extra days would give her family time to reach Pueblo. And then what? What would happen to Morgan Davis then? And why did she now feel she was betraying him, as she felt she had Nick last night? Dear God, she was being torn apart. Her hand shook as she stuck several pieces of wood into the fire.

Just then Maggie woke with a small cry, and Beth went over to her, leaving Lori alone to consider the other woman's words, the comparisons she hadn't considered before, hadn't seen before. But she had seen others, those rare times when Nick had seemed so withdrawn, so alone, just like . . .

No. It just wasn't possible. Still, she felt spooked, and she knew she would now look for more comparisons. She didn't want to. She didn't want to see any. But the seed had been planted, and now it had to grow.

What if the Ranger hadn't grown up as he did, among hard men in hard country? What if Nick had grown up that way, instead? Would he still have that easy smile, that easygoing nature? What if Nick had suffered through four years of war? Would he too look older?

Don't think that way, she told herself. *Don't equate the two men, or you can't do what must be done.*

Could she, in any event, take up arms against Morgan again? Even for Nick? She had become part of Morgan Davis last night when they'd made love. She could close her eyes and remember every sensation, every second her body and soul had closed around him and they had adventured together, sharing an exquisite journey. Her body quivered just remembering.

Trust me, he'd said. But you couldn't demand trust. Nor could she give it simply because she wanted to.

Lori didn't want to think anymore, couldn't think without going crazy. So she turned her attention to the fire. The coffee was ready, and the broth was hot. She took both off the fire and set them aside, then found the frying pan and started biscuits. Beth had supplemented their supplies with baking soda and flour as well as potatoes and onions, and even some apples.

She looked up. The two men were returning. Nick was managing on his own, holding himself stiffly away from his captor, but Lori saw him gratefully sink down onto the blankets he'd been using. The Ranger came over to the fire and stood there, warming his hands.

"The coffee's ready," she said, hoping that he didn't hear the slight quake in her voice, "and some broth from last night." He merely nodded curtly, poured coffee into one cup, broth into another, and carried the latter to Nick, who took it reluctantly. Morgan then stationed himself against a tree as he so often did and watched her. She was reminded again how much the lone watcher he was.

Her gaze met his. They held, and currents rushed between them, strong and unsettling. She saw his hand tighten around the cup, and then he turned away, disappearing back into the brush, this time alone. Lori felt his loss immediately. Painfully. He had turned away from her, from the sight of her. She felt her eyes begin to mist, and she fought to keep the moisture back where it belonged. But it pounded against her eyes, against her forehead.

"Lori." It was Beth. "Can you keep an eye on Maggie while I check your brother's wound?"

Lori nodded, and Beth picked up the pot as well as the box full of medicines she'd used last night and went over to Nick. He was sitting, leaning against a tree for support, the same tree he'd been chained to last night. The chain still hung from it as a reminder that his current freedom was momentary at best.

Lori turned away from them. She put the biscuits on the fire. When they were done, she would cook some bacon and make gravy. Some food of substance for the first time in several days. Something to occupy her mind. Some small thing to help Nick.

CHAPTER NINETEEN

Lori took Maggie with her to wash clothes while Beth hovered over Nick. Everything she and Nick had was filthy, everything but the dress she still wore out of pure necessity. And Lori desperately needed something to do. Morgan Davis had disappeared early, and Nick had slept much of the morning, taking whatever food and drink offered him. Lori knew, though, that he wasn't really tasting it. He was simply eating because he needed to, because he had renewed purpose. Deadly purpose.

Nick was more bitter than she'd ever seen him. She knew he blamed the Ranger for what had happened last night—because he couldn't, wouldn't, blame her. And she felt so terribly guilty about it. Yet how could she tell her brother that what had happened had been her fault as much as the Ranger's? That she had made love to a man determined to take Nick back to Texas? That—dear God —she thought she loved the man?

How could she tell him any of that when Nick was so weak?

She tried to talk to him, but he'd turned away. Still, there was no blame in his eyes, only a fierce hatred for the Ranger. She knew he was blaming himself, not her, and that made her feel even worse. And the truth, she was afraid, would hurt him even more.

Only when Beth neared did his eyes lose some of their fierceness. He even tried to smile when Maggie sat beside him and asked him if he still hurt. The child hovered around him, perhaps because he had been the one to free her from the Ute's grasp. She seemed oblivious to the anger in him, instead her blue eyes were solemn and worried as she watched her mother change bandages.

Lori was going to take her away, but Beth shook her head. "She's used to seeing me change bandages. She likes to help," Beth said with a slight smile. "She's a good little nurse," she added with a smile so full of pride and love that Lori's own heart twitched.

And the child *was* enchanting. Solemn and well behaved, but curious about everything and quick to learn. Lori had observed that yesterday.

Lori watched as Beth finished bandaging Nick and washing him with the hot water, then covering him with the blankets. There was something about the three of them, Nick, Beth and Maggie, that struck Lori as particularly poignant. A gentleness, a sweetness that was almost painful. Lori had noticed yesterday an immediate attraction between Beth and Nick; she had seen it in the first warmth in Nick's eyes for weeks, in the wry twist of his lips as she nursed him, in the way his eyes followed her, and hers him.

It wasn't that fierce love-hate storm that racked Lori. There had been only a few minutes of gentleness between the Ranger and herself. A few minutes respite in the turbulence that always surrounded them. So little sweetness. So much challenge and anger.

One of those terrible contradictions again. Lori envied what she was seeing, but she didn't think she would exchange it for what she'd felt last night, the violent sea storm of excitement and feelings and emotions. She'd felt each to the core of her being. And alive. So alive. As if every emotion she'd ever had was exploding like fireworks in the sky.

She turned away, giving them privacy as she cleaned the dishes from the morning meal. By then Nick was sleeping, and Lori asked Maggie if she would like to help wash their clothes while her mother watched over Nick.

"Would you like to go with me?" she asked Maggie.

Maggie looked from her to Nick, as if weighing the decision.

"Help me wash his shirts," Lori tempted.

Maggie looked up at her mother, who nodded.

"And we'll take Caroline," Lori further tempted. She was increasingly drawn to the young pig. It had gobbled up grain from a sack Beth had brought along and had stolen several biscuits left from breakfast. The pig was greedy, curious, and affectionate, and Lori, who had never been around one before, was fascinated. She'd never thought of a pig as a pet.

The Ranger had simply disappeared. He had taken all the weapons, all the ammunition, and he was very aware that Nick was too ill to try to escape. Nor would Lori as long as Nick was hurt. He knew them very well by now, she thought dryly. But, then, she was beginning to know him. He wasn't nearly as impassive as he wanted everyone to believe, not just the cold, unfeeling Ranger he tried so hard to be. If only she could believe that he really could do something for Nick . . .

But he had too much trust in the law, so much more than either she or Nick. They had seen their fill of crooked and inept lawman. They'd paid their share of bribes to operate in a town, to have charges dismissed. To her, justice had always been a matter of money, and Wardlaw had money.

She and Maggie gathered her shirt and trousers, then Nick's bloodstained shirt and his spare pair of trousers. She hesitated at the Ranger's bedroll. He was wearing the clothes he had bought in Georgetown, but he'd had no chance to wash the ones he had worn for several days. She scooped them up and put them with the others, not even trying to discern her motives.

The sun was bright and warming, the sky ever so blue. A few wispy clouds drifted slowly overhead, meandering across the heavens at about the same pace she and Maggie were making. She turned left at the stream and went downstream from where she and Morgan had been the night before. She didn't think she could bear returning to that spot.

They found some fine rocks to sit on. Lori wished she had her trousers on, but she tied her skirt up around her knees and started with Nick's shirt. That would be the worst. Bloodstained and knife-ripped. But the way Nick—and Morgan—were using up shirts, they might need it.

"Want to wash one yourself?" Lori asked. Maggie nodded and took a piece of soap Lori offered, and one of the Ranger's shirts. She needed no instruction, and Lori supposed she had helped her mother before. She was a remarkably reliant little girl.

Lori started humming "The Girl I Left Behind Me," and soon Maggie was humming along with her.

"Tell me more stories about the Medicine Show?" she asked when Lori finished the song. So Lori did. She told Maggie about Daniel Webster.

"He's the smallest man you will probably ever see," Lori said, "but he has one of the biggest hearts you'll find."

Maggie's eyes widened. "How tall is he?"

Lori held her hand up to what would be a little more than waist high if she was standing.

"And how big is his heart?"

Lori held her hands out as wide as they would go, and Maggie laughed, but she understood. She didn't have to ask anything else, and Lori's liking for Beth Andrews grew. She had taught her daughter what was important, that a man's character and not his size mattered.

"He practically raised my brother Nick," Lori said, "and he can tell wonderful stories."

"I like Mr. Nick," Maggie said.

"So do I, sweetie," Lori said.

"But the other man doesn't."

Lori squeezed the soap from the shirt before answering, distressed at the dull rusted stain that discolored the blue cotton. She hesitated before answering, wondering how much Maggie really understood about what was going on, or whether she just felt the tension.

"No."

"Why?"

Lori didn't know how to explain. She couldn't explain it herself. The animosity between the two men had festered since the beginning, growing even more malignant after last night. She was part of it, but not all. Another part of it, she suddenly realized, was what Beth had seen. They were too much alike in many ways, and neither liked seeing themselves in the other. But she didn't know how to explain that to Maggie. She didn't know how to explain any of this to a child.

So she took the coward's way out. "I don't know, sweetie," she said. "But I think he's a good man too."

Maggie looked at her doubtfully, and Lori felt a sudden compassion for Morgan. Despite that rigidity of his, he *was* a good man. He had put up with a lot from both her and Nick when he could have easily put a bullet in her brother. Anyone else probably would with far less justification. She remembered what she'd wondered before: if he was a man who ever bent.

He had last night! Her body quaked as she remembered how he had bent.

Trust me. He had meant that, too. He was trying to help as much as his private and stringent code allowed him to help. But the last was the question. How much could he help under that restriction?

If only she could trust him. If only Nick could.

If only she and Nick didn't have to depend on Andy and Jonathon and Daniel.

If only they weren't headed for a showdown in which someone would probably be killed.

She turned back to the Ranger's shirt she'd just picked up, fingering it. It too had stains. Stains from where she had shot him.

So much blood already between them.

So much hate.

So much . . .

Lori felt a tear start down her face, and she rubbed it away before Maggie could see it. She turned away, forcing cheer into her voice. "Let's see if you remember the song from yesterday."

Morgan purposely stayed away from the camp. He set several snares again, before once more scouting the trail behind, looking for signs of either Utes or the bounty hunters.

He was haunted by Braden's words, his fury. By the fact that each charge was justified. He could never earn Braden's trust now, and he knew it. The man had every right to hate him, to distrust him, to want him dead. Morgan had broken every rule he'd ever made for himself, the first and foremost: don't ever let personal feelings get involved with the job.

They had. They were. And not only with Lori, but also, strangely enough, with Nick Braden. And every mile they traveled, those feelings were becoming more complicated. And more dangerous. For one of the few times in his life, he was unsure about what to do. Unsure about right and wrong. The only other time had been the war.

Even the child had stayed away from him, though she'd so easily befriended Lori and his prisoner. That had hurt. Children were said to be good judges of character. Was he such a monster, then? Perhaps he'd seemed so, when he'd snapped the leg irons on the man who had helped save small Maggie. Perhaps he'd seemed so to Lori when he'd handcuffed her again. He hadn't known how to explain that he didn't know what else to do.

He looked up at the sky. It must be near noon. He'd been gone four, five hours now. There was no sign of anyone following. Perhaps he had lost Whitey in Georgetown. And the Utes? Still licking their wounds?

Morgan turned back toward camp, his knees signaling a faster pace. He'd never used spurs. He didn't need them, and he didn't like the way they announced the wearer's presence.

Despite the problems back at camp, he found himself anxious to get there, to see Lori.

To his astonishment he found himself humming.

Christ. It was "Sweet Betsy from Pike."

Beth smiled with quiet pleasure. Her patient was better. Sleep and hot broth had worked miracles. After sleeping all morning he woke, stretched tentatively, then again with a sigh of relief. Beth had already seen the red rings around his wrists and had noticed during the night how restless he'd been, how he'd fought against the irons. She'd hurt for him, for his lack of freedom.

She had been grateful that the Ranger had left him free this morning, though she had noted the simmering anger between the two men hours earlier. Beth couldn't even guess as to the depth of what was going on. She did know that the tensions went way beyond the obvious, that between captor and captive.

"Good afternoon," she said with a smile. "How do you feel?"

Nick looked up at the sky, at the tilting sun. Then back at her. "Better, thanks to you." Then his eyes searched the area.

"He's not here," she said.

He frowned. "Lori?"

"She's looking after Maggie. They washed clothes all morning, and now they've gone after firewood."

His face relaxed. "She's good with children."

"Maggie's already captivated. And she's pretty careful with her affection."

"Your daughter's pretty captivating herself," Nick said, rubbing his hand over his bristled cheek ruefully.

"If I had a razor," she said, "I could help you with that."

His face darkened, a muscle bunching against his jaw. "I'm not trusted with one." He tried to sit, his lips tightening as he struggled to lean against a tree, the blanket falling from his chest, which was bare except for the white bandage wrapped around it. He looked for his shirt, but it was gone.

"Lori got them all," Beth said, indicating the shirts and trousers spread over bushes and branches. "I'm afraid she grabbed everything that wasn't already on."

He smiled weakly and tried to pull up the blanket.

"Don't worry about that," she said softly. "I've seen it several times now. Remember?"

She saw that he did, and he abandoned his efforts at modesty. "My thanks," he said quietly but with obvious gratitude.

She tilted her head. "I'm the one to be thanking you. I could well be living in a wickiup now."

"The danger of being so pretty," Nick said.

Beth felt herself flushing. She couldn't take her gaze from him. She was mesmerized by his eyes. They were so blue, like those of Morgan Davis, but Nick's had humor in them, and charm. Though he was ill and weak, they seemed to gleam with mischief, while the Ranger's were always deadly serious.

She much preferred Nicholas Braden's.

"Can I get you anything?"

"Some food?"

"Ah, that's progress."

"The broth was good, but . . ."

"I'm just glad you're hungry. I'll cook some beans. Caroline . . . ate the leftover biscuits."

Nick chuckled. "Beaten out by a pig. I must be sicker than I thought."

Beth laughed softly. She couldn't remember when last she had laughed, either. "Caroline beats out everyone, sick or not."

A rascally glint came into his eyes, one that was irresistibly charming. "How did she come to be named Caroline? I never met a pig with a name before."

"She was a precocious pig," Beth said with laughter.

"Caroline seemed to know that her existence depended on something other than normal pig behavior. She started following Maggie around. Maggie had never had a pet, and there weren't any children around. She just adopted the pig and named it after a girl in a story book. When time came for slaughter, Joshua didn't have the heart to do it, and gave Caroline to Maggie for her birthday." Some of the smile left her voice when she mentioned her husband's name.

"I'm sorry about your husband," Nick said quietly.

"I am too," she said. "He was a good man, and he adored Maggie. She . . . really misses him. So do I."

She started to get up to leave, but he caught one of her hands with two of his. "Thank you," he said.

Beth smiled. "You already thanked me."

"For doctoring me. Not for"—he hesitated—"for not being afraid of me." The words were obviously difficult, and his gaze went to the leg iron still wrapped around the tree, at the empty band that had been attached to his ankle.

There was something so wistful in those words that they cut to her heart. He was thanking her for something more than just not being afraid. She had handed him a measure of trust, and she realized now how important that was to him. He was wanted for murder, considered so dangerous that a Texas Ranger kept him leashed tighter than a rabid dog. She felt a rising resentment for that.

"I could never be afraid of you," she said. "And I believe you and . . . Lori."

"You *are* very pretty, you know." Despite his light words a shield had suddenly fallen over his eyes, just like that she had seen in the Ranger's. Yet she felt a warmth she hadn't known since her husband died.

"And you are obviously much better," she said, tugging gently away.

Nick reluctantly released her hand, and Beth turned toward the fire. She looked back at him. He was still sitting up, his gaze on her. She felt a hot shiver run down her back. Her blood was suddenly warm in her veins. She bit her lip. It was just . . . that it had been so long since a man had touched her. And she was . . . grateful. She didn't want to think that what she was feeling was stronger —more compelling—than what she'd first felt for Joshua. That had been warm and affectionate. But what she was feeling now was different. She wasn't ready to think how different.

Because he's an outlaw?

She didn't believe that, not for a moment. He'd been gentle with Maggie, protective of his sister. Feelings she didn't, couldn't, equate with a killer.

He was handsome. In a much more dangerous way than Joshua had been, though Joshua had been well favored. Or perhaps it was the dark beard that covered his cheeks, or the animosity that radiated between him and Morgan Davis. Which made her think again about the physical resemblance between the two, and how extraordinary it was.

She wondered if she truly did see it more than the others. Beth remembered the twins she had known. Each seemed to know what the other twin was thinking, almost before the other thought it. They often finished one another's sentences. They didn't wait to catch diseases from one another but seemed to suffer them at the same time, and when one had an accident, the other felt the pain.

And they were perfect images of each other. Nick and Morgan Davis weren't perfect images of each other, but they came close. Take the mustache from Ranger Davis, smooth out some lines, give him a smile . . .

She had noticed that Nick was left-handed and the Ranger was right-handed, and the twins she'd known were both left-handed. Still, it was uncanny. For a fanciful moment she wondered whether the Ranger had felt any pain when Nick was stabbed. Then she dismissed the notion. According to Lori, both men were very sure where they were born and to whom.

Her gaze stole back to Nick. He was trying to stand. She thought about chastising him for doing that, urging him to rest and regain his strength, but she sensed it would do no good. There was a determined glint in his eyes.

She looked down. Her hands were bunched in tight fists as she mentally suffered with him, as she felt the will it took to rise and take several steps. His gaze found hers, and he gave her a conspiratorial smile. It was strained, but a smile just the same, and she found herself responding, so very pleased at his success. Her heart tipped inside as she watched him take several more steps, moving ever so slowly over to his horse and rubbing its neck affectionately. She could feel his desire to mount, to ride away, his chagrin at not having the strength to do so.

Beth wished she could help him, that she could saddle his horse and help him escape. But she knew he wouldn't get far, not with the knife wound. He rubbed the horse once more, whispered something to it, and then returned to where he'd been lying, where his blankets lay strewn around. She saw his gaze go down to the leg irons again, and the look in his face—a mixture of longing and despair, frustration and bitterness—made her want to cry.

Nick sat heavily as if his legs refused to hold him any longer, and he turned away from her and looked toward the mountains to the north. Toward freedom. The heart that had merely twitched before now hammered in her chest. She couldn't believe how much she wanted to give that freedom to him.

When he first woke up, Nick had looked up at those damn cornflower-blue eyes and momentarily thought he had already gone to heaven. Prematurely, but not by much, if everything worked out as Morgan Davis hoped. That's what hurt so damn badly. He'd never been so taken with a woman, and now that his life expectancy was about as great as a steer's at a slaughterhouse, it was his luck to find something rare and . . . wonderful.

He tried to tell himself it was only because Beth Andrews had patched him up, that it was gratitude on his part, and on hers, and that was why those small hands were so gentle. She was a small woman, but her hands had calluses and her fingers had been efficient when they had worked on his wound. Her eyes were soft, but her back was straight and determined, and he thought how much strength there had to be in her to try to keep a farm going in this country.

And those damn Indians. She had stood there, defying them, holding on to her daughter with all her strength. He had felt like Lochinvar rushing to her rescue—not what he was, what Davis had made him. Familiar anger rushed through him. He still wanted to be Lochinvar to Beth Andrews. Instead, he was a man headed for the gallows.

For a few moments he'd forgotten. His hands were free. His ankles were free. She had smiled at him, sharing a moment of laughter as she told him about Caroline. And then the smile had fled at the mention of her husband, and he knew he had no right even to think of trying to make her care. Even then he had held her hand a moment too long, so reluctant to release that contact, that moment of empathy he didn't remember ever sharing with a woman before.

When she'd left, he'd tried to stand, hoping the pain and effort would drive away other more intimate physical reactions. And he wanted to test his strength. Damn, Dickens was only feet away, but Nick doubted he could even saddle the horse. He managed to get to his feet, inwardly cursing the weakness in his legs, in his body. But he felt a glimmer of triumph as he managed the steps to the horse, and he stood there, thinking about jumping bareback on the horse as he used to do so often, grabbing Beth and Maggie, and making off for the sunset.

Hell, he could barely stand. He looked around and saw the compassion in Beth's eyes. Dammit, he didn't want compassion. He didn't want pity. He wanted to feel like a man again, a free man. The ache in his soul was so much greater than that in his body as he barely managed to stumble back to his resting place. He hated it. He hated the dangling leg irons that kept reminding him he was a prisoner, but he knew he needed rest. Rest and food. He couldn't do anything without them.

He turned away from Beth, not wanting understanding. He wanted strength. He wanted freedom. He turned north from where they had come, from his small piece of land in Wyoming, the home he'd hoped to make. Beth would have liked those rolling rich hills. He knew it.

Morgan saw a small antelope on his return and decided to take a chance at shooting it. They all needed fresh meat, Braden most of all.

He'd seen nothing all morning. No sign of life. Mrs. Andrews had said the Ute leader had violated the words of the Ute chief. Perhaps there would be no problem with them; perhaps they would regard the episode as finished, as just punishment for rash young renegades who disregarded their chief.

And Whitey. Morgan knew in his bones he hadn't seen the last of the bounty hunter. Whitey was smart. Cunning smart. Morgan tried to put himself in Whitey's shoes. There would be almost no way of tracking the Ranger out of Georgetown, not with all the tracks leading in and out of town. The bounty hunter might hear about a skirmish with Indians, but the Utes sure as hell wouldn't talk about it, not and bring the army down on their heads for attacking a white woman.

There were three of them now—Whitey and two companions—and Morgan would bet his last dollar that the three would split up, check every possible town along the way, keep in contact through the telegraph. That meant Morgan had to avoid towns, and that meant keeping Beth and her daughter with them for a while longer. It also meant they had to live off the land.

He took his rifle from the saddle scabbard and aimed at the elegant animal. He slowly squeezed off a shot, and the antelope leaped into the air, then collapsed on the ground. Morgan approached it slowly. There was no movement. He thought of the child, little Maggie, and her obvious love for animals, and decided to butcher the animal there.

Morgan took his knife from his belt and knelt beside the dead animal, hoping to hell no one heard that shot.

Curt Nesbitt heard a distant gunshot. He and Ford and Whitey had separated two days earlier. Curt was the best tracker, so he was given the job of trying to pick up the Ranger and his prisoner in the mountains. The other two rode ahead to towns along the Ranger's possible route.

If they failed in these places, there was always Pueblo.

Curt felt a momentary satisfaction, a reward for his skills as he heard the faint echo. The gunshot might not mean his quarry was near, but instinct said otherwise, and he trusted his instinct. Curt had lost the Ranger's trail—hell, he'd never found it—but he knew these mountains. He knew that was why Whitey had recruited him.

He had specific orders from Whitey to do nothing on his own and to contact the other two. But he was so damn close. And he thought about the five-thousand-dollar reward, and about not sharing it. He knew Whitey would take the lion's share even if Curt did all the work. There was only one Ranger. And he was burdened with a prisoner. And a woman. Now that Curt knew what direction to take, he should be able to locate the trail. Perhaps he would try to take the reward himself.

Thinking about the five thousand dollars and all the liquor and women it could buy, Curt Nesbitt headed in the direction of the gunshot.

CHAPTER TWENTY

Lori's heart jumped when she saw Morgan return. Icy fingers poked into that same heart, yet it continued to thump with eager welcome. She wondered whether she would ever understand her extraordinary reactions to him: the fire that roared in the most private places at the very sight of him, the gentler need to erase at least some of that solemnity that indicated he'd had precious little joy in his life.

His expression was unreadable as he dismounted, his hat pulled down low over his eyes. He didn't empty his rifle this time. She imagined he'd already done so—he didn't make mistakes like that. He evidently knew what she was thinking, as he so often seemed to do. His mouth twisted crookedly as he untied two large haunches of meat. He used his rope to hang one from a tree. The other he brought to where Lori and Beth had kept a fire going. He cut several pieces off and threaded them on a spit he'd fashioned earlier with his knife.

Beth had been sitting again with Nick, and she rose and came over, a tentative smile on her lips. She was evidently uncertain exactly what to do or say, but her eyes fastened on the meat.

"How is he?" Morgan asked her.

Lori watched Beth. She seemed to search the Ranger's face, trying to find something there, but his expression was, as usual, undecipherable.

"A little better," she said, then added hurriedly, "but he needs more rest. He lost a lot of blood."

Lori wondered if she detected the smallest softening in his face as he nodded. "We'll stay through tomorrow," he said.

"Can he shave?" Beth asked.

Morgan shifted his weight, then knelt next to the fire, throwing a few more pieces of wood on it. He was avoiding the question, Lori knew that. She didn't know why. He had allowed Nick to shave before—under close scrutiny, but he'd permitted it.

"Let him ask," he finally said abruptly.

"He won't," Beth said.

"I don't think he'd appreciate your asking for him, either," Morgan said, but there was something unexpectedly kind in his voice despite the harshness of the words themselves. The icy fingers in Lori's heart withdrew just a little.

"Why?" Beth asked softly. "Because you wouldn't?"

He gave her a sharp look. Lori looked over to Nick. He was out of hearing range, and both Beth and the Ranger had spoken in low voices, but Nick seemed to know they were talking about him. Frustration was written all over his face.

And Morgan had been right, Lori knew. Nick wouldn't appreciate Beth's interference on his behalf. And Beth had been right. He wouldn't ask for himself. Not now.

They were both so stubborn, the Ranger and her brother. How could she ever make either of them compromise now? How would Nick ever accept his help, even if she thought Morgan could really do something?

Morgan finished stoking the fire and rose. "Can you tend the fire while . . . Miss Braden and I . . ." He stopped suddenly, apparently just then noticing all the clothes spread over bushes, including his own. He turned to Lori, raising one of his dark eyebrows in question.

"You've been in my bedroll, Miss Lori," he said, unexpectedly formal, apparently for Beth's sake.

Lori resented the implication when she'd tried to do a good deed despite her better judgment. "Of course," she said acidly. "I was looking for the weapons you're always so damn careful to take with you."

He suddenly grinned. It was an unexpectedly pleasant expression. The movement was tighter than Nick's. Not as easy, as if Morgan had to work at it. But still . . . it was nice. So nice that her heart started thumping wildly again, so wild she thought he must hear it.

"Then I guess I should thank you."

"Is that so hard?"

The smile disappeared. His face was a mask once more, hard and emotionless, as if the smile had been an aberration. "Yes, I guess it is. I'm not used to . . ."

"Your prisoners doing things for you?"

"You're not my prisoner," he said evenly.

"You're pretty good at playacting, then," she said. "I didn't imagine you'd lock that handcuff on me last night."

"Protecting you from yourself," he said, his mouth crooking up again, this time only slightly.

"Protecting you, you mean," she retorted.

"All right," he conceded. "I needed some rest."

"And tonight?"

"It depends. I'll take your word that you'll behave yourself."

"You said you wouldn't believe me if I sprouted wings," she countered.

"I know you better now."

Lori wondered whether his voice had really softened again, or if it was just wistful thinking on her part. "Do you?" she said. "Do you really?"

"Shouldn't I trust you?"

"I don't know," she said truthfully. "I would do anything . . ."

"To help your brother," he finished flatly.

"Yes."

He turned around toward the horses. "Come help me water the horses," he said.

That had been his excuse yesterday. Still, she knew
they did have to be watered. She also knew he wanted to
talk to her alone, with Beth out of hearing range. Without
Nick glaring at them.

She nodded. "I'm going to talk to Nick first." She didn't
wait for an answer. She turned around and went over to
where Nick sat, clenching his fists together.

"Stay away from him," Nick said.

"I can't," she replied simply.

His jaw worked. "Not for me," he ground out through
clenched teeth.

"It's not for you," she said in a low voice. "Not this. Not
last night." She didn't even try to deny what she realized
he knew. "I . . . care about him."

"You can't," he said. "He's just taking advantage of you,
of his power."

She swallowed. She couldn't let him believe that. It
would only make the tension between the two men worse,
deepen the danger of one killing the other, make it more
difficult for him ever to believe Morgan. And she knew
that Morgan hadn't taken advantage, any more than she
had. He had fought it as much as she.

"No," she said flatly.

"Dammit, Lori. He isn't any good for you. Even if . . ."

It was the "even if" that was so damning. "Even if" the
Ranger wasn't dead set on returning Nick to Texas—the
"even if" that spelled heartbreak. She knew it. She also
knew she couldn't stay away from Morgan Davis. She'd
tried. She'd tried to keep her heart intact. She'd tried to
keep it from flipping, from thumping, from turning cart-
wheels when she looked at him, when he so rarely smiled.

"I know," she said miserably.

His hand took hers. "I wish . . ."

"Me, too," she replied wistfully.

One of Nick's eyebrows raised, just as Morgan's had
moments earlier. It was eerie. "Be careful, Button," he
said, using a name he hadn't used in years. "It might well
come down to him or me. How will you feel then?"

"It can't come to that," she said. "He knows you're not guilty. He said as much. He said . . ."

"What did he say?" Nick asked grimly. "What did he say last night to make you—" He stopped suddenly, unable to go on.

"Nick . . ." She had thought Morgan might have extended his offer to Nick this morning. Obviously, he had not. Obviously, Nick had been too angry to hear it.

"Yes," he said coldly.

"He believes you. He says he thinks he can help you."

"In Texas," Nick said. It wasn't a question.

She nodded.

"Let me understand this," Nick said sarcastically. "He was going to take me to Texas because he believed I killed a man in cold blood. Now he thinks I'm innocent, so he still intends to take me back. Well, I don't give a damn what he thinks. I'm not going back."

"Maybe . . . he *can* help."

"Right to a noose," Nick said dryly.

"He said bounty hunters . . . will eventually catch up with you."

He shrugged. "Maybe. Maybe not. Texas, though, is a sure thing."

Lori knew she wasn't going to change his mind. Maybe she could have before last night, but not now. Not unless there was some kind of assurance. That left only convincing Morgan to let Nick go.

"No," Nick said explosively, obviously reading her thoughts. "I'll not have you bargain for me."

Lori had never felt so miserable in her life. She was so torn between wanting to believe Morgan, and respecting Nick's wishes. She wanted to be on both sides, and she couldn't do that, so she had to be on Nick's.

She nodded. "I'm just going to water the horses."

His eyes showed aching disbelief, but he didn't say anything. That hurt. She knew he felt ineffectual, unable to protect her. But she needed to talk to Morgan, to know more about what he planned. And she couldn't do that with Nick's furious eyes on her, and Beth's inquisitive ones, and Maggie's innocent ones.

She stood and walked over to the horses, taking the same three she had taken before, knowing that Morgan was following her. He was no longer "the Ranger" to her. Last night had destroyed that barrier forever.

He didn't say anything until they reached the stream. Lori had led the way, and she chose a spot other than the one where they had made love.

They both concentrated on watering the horses.

When the animals had slaked their thirst, Morgan led his charges up to the bank and hobbled them, then hobbled Lori's, giving them a chance to graze.

"Did you talk to Nick?" The question was abrupt, without niceties; she'd come to expect directness from him. But she hadn't expected his use of her brother's given name.

"He doesn't believe you. He thinks you said that just to make it easier to take him back and . . ." She stopped.

"And?"

Lori felt her face redden. She couldn't answer. She couldn't bring up last night, and her very brazen behavior.

Morgan turned away from her and slammed his fist against a tree. He cursed, then turned back to her. "I'm sorry, Lori. I'm damned sorry about last night. I didn't mean that to happen. Christ, I can't blame . . . your brother for feeling the way he does. I would probably try to kill him, if the situation were reversed."

"He *will* try that," she said quietly.

"I know," he said. "He said as much this morning."

Lori took a couple steps away. He was too close. She couldn't think when he was so close. "You said you wanted to help. Can you guarantee he won't hang? Or go to prison? He couldn't stand that, you know. He loves the outdoors. He can't stand being inside for long."

Morgan hesitated. "No, I can't guarantee anything. But

I do have friends. In the Rangers. Among the judges. They trust me. And I can get people to talk, now that I know what happened."

"And if you can't?"

"Dammit, Lori. I'm the best chance he has."

She shook her head. "That's not good enough. Let him go, Morgan."

"I can't do that. It would be like tethering a sheep among wolves."

"He's not a sheep. He can take care of himself."

Morgan shook his head. "He's not a killer, either. I've discovered that. And it will take a killer with killer instincts to survive that pack after him."

"He would kill *you*."

"That's different. I . . . hurt someone he loves."

"Are you a killer, Morgan?"

He looked her straight in the eye. "Yes," he said bleakly. "I kill in the name of the law, but I kill. And most of the time, I feel damn little regret."

"And if it comes to Nick? Would you be one of those wolves?"

"Don't ask me that, Lori."

"I have to know."

"I don't have an answer. I'm not going to make promises I can't keep or give you words I don't mean."

Lori felt her eyes fill with tears. It had been happening with dismaying frequency. She wanted to look away from him, but she couldn't. His own gaze held her where she stood. Uncompromising but compelling. And then she heard his voice again. Another curse. Almost under his breath, but not quite. And then his lips were on hers, hard and ruthless and demanding.

And desperate. She felt the desperation. In him and in her. She didn't want to respond to him. Her body stiffened and she tried to back away, but his arms went around her, holding her there, his lips probing hers, seeking a response she was determined not to give him. Not this time.

This time she couldn't, or she could never live with herself again.

Lori broke away. "Don't," she said brokenly. "Please don't."

He dropped his arms and turned away. He didn't say anything but efficiently unhobbled the horses. His back stiff, he started back to the camp. Lori didn't follow. She sat down next to a tree. When she was sure he was out of hearing and sight, she let the tears come, spending them in huge, gasping, life-sucking sobs. When there was nothing left, she stumbled down to the stream and washed her face with the icy water. It wouldn't help her eyes. They were sore, and she knew they would be red for a very long time. She cared for Nick's sake. She didn't want Morgan to see how much she hurt. She couldn't go back, not until it started to get dark.

Lori looked at the horses. They had no saddles, but she and Nick had learned to ride bareback, even stand on their back—another one of their odd skills accumulated over the years with the Medicine Wagon. She wished she could take one now, ride it to Pueblo. She wanted to see her parents, but most of all she wanted to talk to Daniel. Outside of Nick, Daniel was her best friend. Perhaps because of his size and all the misery it had brought him, he never judged. He always just listened and usually was silent, letting Lori figure out things for herself.

If only she hadn't needed Morgan's touch so badly. If only she hadn't ached to press her body against his, to spend her own desperation in his.

Morgan's will was almost broken. When he'd heard the desperation in her voice, he'd almost said he would release Nick. Anything would be worth bringing that sunbright smile back to her face. He cursed himself all the way back to camp. *He* had put that sadness in her eyes, that tremor in her lips. He had made her choose, even when he'd known what that choice had to be. He didn't know what the hell he hoped to achieve by that kiss, unless a certain sick jealousy drove him to make the decision more difficult. Christ, jealous of a girl's brother. How pathetic could he get?

But he *was* jealous. Not of Nick personally, but of that unreserved love and regard he had from Lori. He'd wanted to tell her he wasn't one of the wolves. That he wouldn't shoot Nick, even if he tried to escape now. But, then, that would only make the possibility a likelihood. He would lose any edge he had with the man. He needed time to reason with Nick Braden, even though he feared it would do little good. He had to try, though.

Once back at the campsite, he was met with more suspicious glares, and with the smell of cooking meat, which made him want to retch. He secured the horses, then went over to Nick.

Nick glared at him. "Where's Lori?"

"Watering the horses," Morgan replied. "How's the knife wound?"

"I'll live."

Small talk obviously was not indicated here, not that Morgan was any good at it, in any event. He got to the point. "Did Lori tell you I might be able to help down in Texas?"

Nick stiffened. "And why would you do that? You've already taken my sister to bed. Looking for a second tumble?"

Morgan bristled. "Leave Lori out of this."

"I don't want to leave Lori out of it. You've made her a part of it, damn your arrogant, sorry hide."

Morgan inwardly flinched at the well-placed shot, and his voice was harsh when he finally spoke again. "Braden, goddammit, I want to help."

"Why?"

Morgan stared at him, willing him to believe. "You're no killer. You didn't want to kill those Utes. You could have left me to die outside that cabin."

"Not doing that was the biggest mistake I ever made."

Morgan ignored him. "Dammit, just listen. I'm taking you to Ranger headquarters in El Paso. That will give me time to do some investigating on my own."

"Meanwhile, I'm supposed to sit back obediently while you bed my sister," Nick said bitterly. "And if you can't convince anyone in a scared-stiff town to talk, I'm dead."

"I won't touch her."

"Noble of you."

Morgan bit back his own frustration. "Will you at least think about it? Think about making it easier on yourself as well as Lori," he said impatiently. "What if those bounty hunters had reached you before I did?"

"I can't see how either of us would be worse off." His meaning was only too clear, and Morgan felt his own anger rising again. Damn, but the man knew how to aim his blows.

"Then you don't know Whitey Stark and his friends."

"I don't see the difference, Davis." Nick turned away. "I want some sleep."

Morgan sighed with defeat and went over to the fire. Beth had been watching them, and he gave her a rueful smile. He wished Lori would return, but he had seen the glitter in her eyes, had known she wanted to be alone. He wished he could go to her, tell her everything she wanted to hear, but he couldn't do that, and she wouldn't accept any other comfort. She wouldn't accept it any more than her brother would accept anything from him. He'd made a royal mess of everything.

Maggie had been feeding Caroline some grain, and Morgan smiled slightly at the sight of the little girl and the pig.

"Thank you for letting us bring Caroline," Beth said.

He shrugged. "I'm glad we could." He continued to look toward the child. "I never had a pet," he said.

"Not even a horse?"

"I was raised to take good care of my horses, but never

to forget they're working animals," he said slowly. "It's not wise to get too attached. During the war . . ."

"During the war?" she prompted.

"I lost five horses. I decided then that . . ." He stopped suddenly, as if he'd revealed too much. Christ, what was happening to him?

"You shouldn't get too attached to anything or anyone?"

He stared at her in surprise. "Something like that."

"Doesn't it get lonely?"

He shrugged again, then rose. "I'd better feed the animals."

"Do you ever stop?"

"No, ma'am," he said. "Don't guess I do."

"Do you ever want to?"

He thought about the question for a moment. "I don't know," he said honestly.

"Did you ever think about doing anything other than being a Ranger?"

"No, ma'am."

The answer came so sure and fast, Beth looked startled.

"Even when the man you're hunting is innocent?"

"You, too, ma'am?" he asked, wryly.

"Me, too," she acknowledged gently.

"Then convince him I'm his best hope," Morgan said.

"Are you?"

"Yes."

She looked him straight in the eyes, searching for something there. "Why should he listen to me?"

"I think anyone would listen to you, Mrs. Andrews," he said in a rare compliment. He liked her. He liked the way she accepted hardship and circumstance without complaint. He liked the way she smiled at her daughter and praised her often. He liked the way she cared for Braden's wound with both efficiency and gentleness.

And he hadn't missed the glances between Nick Braden and Beth Andrews, hadn't missed her unmistakable concern, or Braden's clear interest.

"I think that's a compliment, Mr. Davis. Thank you."

Morgan smiled suddenly. "It was, and you're welcome." He started to leave, then turned back. "My shaving gear is in my bedroll, if you want to give it to him." He hesitated a moment, then added, "Tell him I suggested it. Health reasons."

Morgan saw instant understanding in her face. *I don't think he would appreciate your asking for him.* His earlier words.

She nodded. "You two have a lot in common," she said.

He stilled. "I don't think so."

"You know that about him."

He shrugged. "He fights his own battles. I've discovered that."

Beth rose. "So do you, Mr. Davis. No matter how much it hurts, so do you."

Nick rubbed his face. Damn, but it felt good. Sitting while someone shaved him had been even better. Beth Andrews had offered to do it, and he'd accepted after she'd said she often shaved her husband, that it was something she enjoyed doing.

Her hands on his face had been pure heaven. Despite the calluses on them, the fingers had been firm and gentle. And efficient. As one hand carefully skimmed his cheek with Morgan Davis's razor, the other held his chin. He'd been able to look up into those blue eyes, so filled with concentration, and he wondered what it would be like to feel those hands often, to become familiar with that care and tenderness.

And then she would give him that slow, wide smile that transformed her quiet, pretty face into something of real beauty, and he'd wanted to take her in his arms and just hold her, to know whether she was as soft as she looked.

He knew, though, he couldn't do that. His hands and ankles were free temporarily, through the dubious grace of the man who continued to watch him as a hawk watched a rabbit. But he still felt the chains on them, on his future. So he had merely squeezed a handful of dirt with wanting fingers, wanting hands, to keep them from reaching for her.

She tipped her head when she was finished and studied him. He found himself smiling. "Do I pass muster?"

"You have a dimple. Just like Mr. Davis."

He scowled.

She ignored it and sat next to him, one eye still on the meat on the fire. Maggie came over to join them, shyly sitting next to her mother.

"I know a song," Maggie said.

Nick found himself grinning at her. She was a pretty little thing, part shy, part bold, as some little girls were wont to be. Lori had never been shy. She'd always just embraced life, positive that everyone would like her. Probably because everyone had. Until the Ranger. He still wondered if that wasn't part of her fascination with him. He hoped to God it was only that, and nothing deeper.

"Will you sing it for me, Button?" he said, using Lori's pet name.

She started the song about the cat and the pig named Caroline. Nick listened at first, then hunted around and found his harmonica. He leaned against the tree and started to accompany Maggie. He warmed to Beth's delighted smile, and when Maggie finished, he started a new tune, feeling a lightness he hadn't known since he'd been accused of murder.

Maggie snuggled closer to him, her blue eyes wide. "Can you teach me to play?"

The child had almost perfect pitch. She would learn easily. Nick's smile stiffened slightly. "If we have time," he said, not allowing himself to forget that his time with the Andrewses was limited in any event. They would go on their way, and Nick would have his showdown with Davis.

"Can you play 'Betsy'?" Maggie said, losing the last of her shyness.

" 'Sweet Betsy from Pike'?" he said roguishly. "Can I

play that? Ah, can I ever play that." He looked down at Maggie. "I used to play that song for Lori when she was no taller than you."

"I like Miss Lori."

"Everybody likes Miss Lori," he said.

"But me best," Maggie argued. "She likes Caroline."

"I like Caroline too," he complained, his voice teasing.

Maggie squirmed happily next to Beth, who put her arm around the girl and pulled her close while her eyes rolled at the thought of Caroline's admirers.

Nick chuckled.

Beth tipped her head in a gesture that was becoming increasingly dear to Nick. "You should do that more often," she said.

Nick felt that warmth spread into his heart, take root there, and begin to fill it. He found a rock in his throat, so he lifted the harmonica and let it talk for him. The lively sound of "Sweet Betsy" filled the clearing, and when he was finished, he started another, this time a plaintive melody, a lovely, haunting melody that sang through the woods. Before he was finished, he heard the melody put into voice, and saw Lori coming over, her mouth framing the words with such sweet clarity. It was one of the songs that never failed to move an audience: "Red Rosey Bush."

Nick turned his head and saw Davis. He was, as usual, leaning against a tree, watching. His gaze turned hungry as it followed Lori's movements. Hungry and intense and brooding.

The bittersweet melody had always affected Lori's sentimental streak, but Nick noticed her eyes were already red and swollen, though her voice was pure and strong as ever. Something flickered on the Ranger's face, but Nick couldn't tell what it was before he turned away and disappeared into the shadows.

Nick finished, and all of them were silent, a heavy emotion gripping them all. Even Maggie was still, her hand caught in her mother's tight grasp. Nick wished that brief

moment of peace hadn't been swallowed whole by fore-
boding, by a suffocating presentiment.

For the child he tried to shake it off. He started another
tune, one he'd heard Lori sing for Maggie. Lori approached and sat down next to Maggie, her voice losing
the plaintive quality as she matched Nick's forced playfulness.

> *"Froggie went a'courting, he did ride,*
> *Uh-huh"*

Just as Nick moved slightly in rhythm to the music, a
rifle shot rang out, raising a cloud of dirt a fraction of an
inch away from where he'd moved. His reaction was in-
stantaneous. "Take cover," he yelled to the two women as
his own body shielded Maggie, picking her up and following the two women to sparse shelter behind thin aspen
trees.

Nick kept his body over Maggie's as he looked for Beth
and Lori. Both were hugging the ground as another shot
rang out, then a third, the latter coming again within
inches of Nick. Whoever the shooter was, he was good.
Very good.

Nick heard another shot, this time from a six-gun. Davis. The other man, the shooter, had a rifle. Nick knew
enough about guns to recognize the difference.

The rifle sounded again, this time coming nowhere
close, and he knew the gunman was now aiming for Davis.
The Ranger didn't have a chance against a rifle. Nick lifted
himself. "Go to your mother," he told Maggie, and nodded
his head to Lori for the three of them to move back.

If only he was stronger. If only he could get his hands
on the rifle in the Ranger's saddle, now lying about fifty
feet away. And bullets. Davis kept them in his gunbelt or
saddlebags, both with him, while the rifle was a good hundred feet away in clear ground. He prayed his legs would
work, that his body still had enough strength in it to reach
the rifle.

Another shot rang out, then another. How many bullets

from the rifle now? Four? He would wait until he heard the sixth, then make a run for the rifle and try to get bullets from Davis.

If Davis would give them to him.

He found his harmonica and tossed it out, drawing the gunman's attention. A shot threw the harmonica in the air, and the Ranger fired again, but he was too far away to be effective.

Five shots.

He waited impatiently and then realized the gunman didn't have a good shot. He was waiting too. Nick saw a movement to the side. He guessed it was Lori, who had also understood what needed to be done and had shaken some bushes.

Another shot. Six.

Nick got to his feet and dashed toward Davis's saddle, desperation driving a body that felt leaden. He grabbed the rifle, just as another shot barely missed him, and he rolled behind some bushes, crawling toward where he guessed Davis to be. He heard several pistol shots and realized Davis was providing cover for him.

He located the Ranger approximately six feet away. He was on his side, reloading his six-gun as bullets splattered around him. Like Nick, he was only partly covered by the tree trunks. Nick would have sold his soul at that moment for an honest, good-sized rock.

He found his own limited cover. "Bullets?" he asked Davis.

The Ranger hesitated only a moment. "I'll trade you the pistol for the rifle."

Nick was loath to give up the weapon, but he knew Davis was probably better at this than he was. He, like Lori, was damn good at bottles and apples, but the Ranger had more experience at human targets. He threw the rifle to the Ranger and caught the pistol the man threw back at him.

Christ, it felt good to be able to defend himself, though

he knew his role now was to give Davis cover, to distract the gunman while Davis did the real work. Still, the gun felt fine in his hands.

"That hill up there," the Ranger said, and Nick found the glint of late sun on a rifle barrel. He nodded.

"Shoot as close to that as you can," Davis said. "I'll move around and try for a better shot."

Nick aimed at the rocks above, coming damn close to where he'd seen the gleam of metal. The rifle sounded again, dirt spurting up a foot away. Nick crawled in that direction, thinking the gunman would now move his sights a bit to the left. He fired, knowing he was making himself a target, knowing it was necessary if Davis was to get a clean shot.

He didn't care about Davis, but he cared about the child and Lori and Beth, and he realized Davis had been right all along about the bounty hunters. The gunman had come close to hitting Maggie; he obviously didn't care whom he killed, and that meant the women and child were in danger. He'd settle the score with Morgan Davis later. He rolled another couple of feet and shot again. Damn, he had only one more bullet left.

How long had it been? Had Davis had a chance to move upward. Then he heard a rifle shot, and a grunt of pain. Something rolled down the incline where the gunman had lain in wait.

Everything was quiet. Morgan was apparently waiting too, making sure the man had been hit and wasn't just faking. A bird started trilling again, overhead. Nick saw Morgan finally rise and carefully approach the clump of rocks that had hidden the gunman. He went behind them, then came back out, his hands holding a second rifle.

Nick looked down at his pistol. One shot left. That's all he needed. Morgan's hands were at his side, the rifles pointed downward.

One damn shot.

He aimed.

The Ranger saw the gun in his hand, stilled. Waiting.

Nick couldn't pull the trigger. He tried. His finger closed around the trigger, but he couldn't make that final movement. He cursed himself. He'd been able to pull the trigger on Wardlaw, to save Andy. Instinct pure and simple. But it failed him now. Perhaps if Davis had a rifle pointed at him . . . if it were a fair fight . . .

If. Nick felt waves of defeat as the Ranger started moving forward again. He reached Nick, tucked both rifles under his arm, and held out his hand for the pistol. "No bullets left?" he said.

Nick shook his head. "No," he said.

Davis laid the rifles on the ground and checked the pistol. "You don't count so good."

A muscle jerked in Nick's cheek. He felt it, and he damned it. He wanted to be as impassive as the man two feet away from him. He just turned around and headed back to camp, to his bed, to Beth . . . to captivity.

He didn't even care who it was up there.

"Braden?"

He turned around.

"No curiosity about who it was?"

A muscle flexed in Nick's face again. "What difference does it make to me?"

"Then why did you help?"

"He almost hit Beth and Maggie," Nick said tonelessly.

"Well, he's dead now, thanks to you. A bounty hunter named Curt Nesbitt."

Nick stiffened, the area around his mouth tensing.

But Morgan wasn't through. "You were real good back there."

Nick didn't want the Ranger's praise. Especially not now. He shrugged, mindless of the fact that it was the same gesture he had seen Davis use so many times. He felt sick. Now that the urgency was gone, he felt leaden and weak and . . . crushed. He hadn't been able to do what he needed to do. Every step seemed like a mile, but finally he reached his bedroll—and the tree he'd been chained to. The tree that represented every damn failure.

He ignored Beth's anxious question, Maggie's frightened face, Lori's concerned glance. He lowered himself and turned away from all of them.

The Ranger had won!

CHAPTER TWENTY-ONE

Lori realized immediately that the level of tension, already near the boiling point between the Ranger and Nick, had increased even further in the minutes after the shooting.

Nick's knife wound was bleeding again, and Beth tended it, carefully sewing back where the threads had broken. Lori tried to calm Maggie and a disgruntled pig, which had been disturbed from its dinner.

Neither of the men seemed disposed to talk about what had happened. After accompanying Nick back to his blankets, Morgan disappeared again without words. Nick was unusually sullen, bearing the pain of restitching with clenched teeth.

As Lori comforted a still frightened Maggie in her arms, she kept her eyes on her brother. Something vital had drained from Nick, and a twisting pain snaked through her. She wondered what had happened now to plunge him into such despair. She squeezed Maggie affectionately and asked her to help look for Nick's harmonica. They finally found the mouth organ, a bullet stuck halfway through it. There would be no more music from that source, and it had been one of Nick's most treasured possessions, a gift from years back.

She whispered to Maggie, telling her a story until Beth finished doctoring Nick and moved over to Lori to take Maggie in her arms. Lori traded places with her, sitting next to Nick, wanting desperately to know what had taken place.

"What happened?" she asked quietly, keeping her voice too low for Beth and Maggie to hear.

"I had a chance, Lori, I had a chance to take him, and I couldn't."

"The shooter?"

"Hell no—Davis. After he'd shot the man. Bounty hunter, he said. I had Davis in clear sight, a gun in my hand, and I couldn't pull the trigger."

Lori privately thanked God, but she wisely refrained from saying so. And she was surprised. She knew Nick, knew his temper, knew how the anger had been building against Morgan, especially after the past two days. Her hand went to him, locking her fingers in his.

He looked around, saw that Beth was out of hearing distance, calming Maggie. "I'm a coward, Lori," he said with a defeat that almost broke Lori's heart.

"Cowardice had nothing to do with it," she said. "Look how you exposed yourself to help . . ."

"To help the man who's taking me to hang and who's sleeping with my sister." This time Nick's frustration exploded with words he hadn't said to her before, though they had been in his eyes.

Lori swallowed, her face reddening, but she wasn't going to lie to him. "That was as much my doing as his," she said. "I care about him. I didn't want to. I still don't, but I do, and . . . dear God, I'm so glad you couldn't shoot him."

He was silent.

"The family will be waiting in Pueblo," she said. "We can find some way to free you."

"Without killing him?" he asked, disbelieving. "He'll chase me the rest of his life. He's that kind of man." With that comment he turned away from her, closing her out, and Lori's heart cracked into pieces. Her heart was divided against itself, and she wondered whether it could ever be whole again.

She hesitated, then left his side. There was nothing she could say to ease the burden he'd taken upon himself. She knew he felt he had not been up to the task of killing Morgan Davis—not only for himself but for her.

Lori wished there was something she could do. Anything to keep busy. But the meat was almost done on the spit. She'd already washed every piece of clothing she could find. Beth was still soothing Maggie, and her brother didn't want anything to do with her.

And she couldn't go to Morgan. Not now, and do even more injury to Nick. She'd done enough already.

She went over to Clementine and rubbed the mare's neck, taking a tiny satisfaction in the way the horse shivered in delight. She rested her head against the animal's neck. She needed to give affection to someone, something. Holy Mary, but she was burgeoning with the need, and no one wanted any.

The horse wasn't saddled, but it was bridled. In sudden impulse she unbuckled the hobbles and bolted to the horse's back. She had to get away from the unrelieved tension, from the blame and guilt and uncertainty.

Without looking back, she turned toward the mountain to the west and tightened her knees against Clementine's sides. She was a child again, riding in front of an approving crowd, looking down and seeing Nick's proud face. She closed her eyes for a moment, bringing back those days, letting Clementine have her head, trusting her as she had always trusted her.

Lori was still thinking of those days when the side of her head hit the low branch of a tree.

Morgan returned from burying the ambusher. He'd also checked cautiously for other tracks but found none. He finally concluded that the man had acted alone. He didn't understand how he had missed the man's approach this morning. He didn't like the carelessness that error indicated.

But he'd never had a distraction like Lorilee Braden before, either. The thought did not soothe him. He realized how closely he'd come to a bullet today, both from the bounty hunter and then from Nick Braden. He'd been damn lucky the latter had not pulled the trigger, especially considering the circumstances.

Why hadn't he? The question haunted him. Braden had killed Wardlaw in defense of his brother. Why hadn't he been able to kill the man he had every reason to hate?

And then Morgan had turned the question around on himself. Morgan had had two rifles in his hands today when Braden had pointed the gun at him. Morgan was probably fast enough to beat Braden even then. He knew the moves, but he'd never even considered the possibility.

Killing Braden would be like killing himself. No matter how different they were, how much anger was between them, Morgan accepted the fact there was something else too, an odd connection of some kind that always heightened the tension between them, rather than lessened it.

He rode slowly back to camp, his gaze searching for all who should be there.

"Lori?" he asked Beth.

"She took her horse," Beth said.

"Which direction?" Morgan snapped out the words. Dammit, she shouldn't be out by herself. He felt the ambusher had been alone, but he couldn't be sure. He'd made too many mistakes lately. Panic gnawed at his usually calm and deliberate assessment of situations. He mounted his bay and turned in the direction Beth had indicated. The trail was easy to follow. She had not tried to be careful. He knew she wasn't trying to escape—not now, not with Nick as badly wounded as he was.

Apprehension pricked at him. A feeling. He knew she felt torn between him and her brother. He didn't know what Braden had told her about the occurrences of the last hour. And she was reckless. She didn't think about consequences. It was one of the qualities that so attracted him. He always thought of consequences—at least he had until recently. And now . . . well, he supposed he *did* think of them—he just hadn't heeded them.

He heard the neigh of a horse, and he kicked his own bay into a gallop, finding Clementine nudging her fallen rider. Lori lay still on the ground. Morgan jumped to the ground and knelt beside her, his hands ranging over her body, trying to find injuries. His heart was arching against his ribs, his fingers unsteady. There was no blood, but he found a large lump on her head.

He held her close to him for a moment, feeling the lightness of her body, the softness of her skin. "Little fool," he whispered, his voice breaking slightly. His fingers skimmed her face, the area around her closed eyes. She was so pretty, and so much more vulnerable than she wanted anyone to believe. She loved so fiercely.

He swallowed. She had loved him fiercely for that hour last night, when she had been able to forget who and what he was to Nick.

"Lori," he whispered. Her breathing was regular, not labored, but he wouldn't know whether there was any damage other than the head wound until she regained consciousness.

"Lori," he said again, insistently this time. One arm was around her, the other still exploring for injury.

She moaned.

"Lori!"

She opened her eyes slowly, obviously trying to focus. Christ, they were beautiful. The amber appeared even more golden now as her lashes partially shielded them from the dimming light. Her gaze slowly focused on his face, and then she smiled, a smile so beautiful his heart rocked against his rib cage. That smile made her face glow, and he knew, for just this instant, it was for him. Spontaneous and unreserved.

He couldn't help himself. He leaned down and kissed her. Lightly, but with his heart in that kiss, and he saw that she knew it. Her eyes widened.

"Don't ever do that again," he scolded. And then he made his voice matter-of-fact. "Do you hurt anyplace? Other than your head?"

"Only my pride," she said, wincing as one of her hands probed her head. "I haven't fallen from a horse since I was ten years old. And my head hurts enough for the rest of me." She tried to smile, and a tightness squeezed Morgan's chest. "I suppose I felt left out. You and Nick have been taking all the blows. Getting all the attention."

His hand brushed a strand of hair from her forehead, resting there for a moment. "I'm sorry, Lori. So damn sorry for everything."

Her hand took his, and she brought it to her mouth, holding it there for a moment. "I was so worried about you, about you both. If either of you . . ." Her voice trembled.

"Nothing is going to happen to either of us," he promised. He leaned down and picked her up. He wanted to continue holding her. Hell, he wanted to hold her forever, to remove that worry from eyes that could sparkle so. But they weren't sparkling now, and it was because of him. His arms tightened around her for a moment. "Do you feel up to riding back? I think you need something cold for that bump."

She nodded. He carried her over to Clementine, helping her on, then holding her hand a moment longer than necessary. His mouth tightened, a muscle in his cheek flexing under the black stubble of his beard. She could have so easily been killed. The thought was excruciating.

He released her hand and turned back to his horse, wishing with all his soul that he could make things right for all of them. He just wasn't sure he could. And he knew that if anything happened to Nick Braden, Lori would never forgive him.

Nick watched suspiciously as Morgan returned with Lori. She was covered with dirt and pine needles. Morgan helped her down gingerly, and she took a moment in his arms to regain her balance, just standing there. Then Nick saw the bruises beginning to show on her face. He tried to stand, barely making it to his feet as his hand used the tree for support. Lori apparently saw the suspicion and anger suffusing his face, and she walked over to him, followed by Davis.

"I fell," she said before he could make any accusation.

"You never fall," Nick observed acidly.

"I did this time," she said, her lip trembling slightly. She reached out and put her hand on his arm. "I wasn't paying attention. I was upset about you, and I closed my eyes for a moment, I must have hit a branch and fell. Morgan found me."

Nick's mouth tightened at the familiar use of Davis's name, but he didn't say anything. Lori didn't lie to him. But he still didn't like the way the Ranger had held her. He didn't like the fact that Morgan Davis had been the one to find her.

His voice softened, but his mouth was grim. "Are you hurt?"

She shook her head.

"She hit her head," Davis interrupted. "She needs to rest."

Nick hated agreeing with him but saw he was right. "I think that's a good idea, Lori." She hesitated, then nodded. Nick watched as she went to her bedroll several feet away and sat down. His face white with effort to remain standing, he turned back to Davis.

"Any one else out there?" He had concluded that Davis had searched the area, made sure the shooter didn't have any friends with him.

"Not with him, but probably around someplace. I saw three men ride into Georgetown when we were there, including Whitey Stark. I knew him from that white hair, but the other two wore hats, and I couldn't see their faces. I think our friend on the hill was one of them. Probably they split up, and Nesbitt decided to act on his own, thought he could take me alone, what with a wounded prisoner. He might have been right if you hadn't helped."

His gaze met Nick's. "That was good shooting."

Nick glared at him. "Up until the end."

"For God's sake, man," Morgan said, unexpectedly angry. "Killing sure as hell isn't anything to be proud of. It takes more courage not to pull that trigger."

Then Morgan walked away. Nick knew he'd said more than he intended, but he wasn't soothed nor did he feel vindicated. He was angry—no, furious—that he hadn't been able to do what needed to be done. Angry at himself, at the Ranger, even at Lori, who looked at the Ranger with stark yearning in her eyes.

He understood wanting. He knew wanting often had nothing to do with right or wrong, was oblivious to timing or suitability. After all, he wanted Beth now, and that was just as disastrous as Lori falling in love with the Ranger.

Nick closed his eyes. He was weak and hurting and so goddamn tense. He wondered how long the five of them could travel without something blowing up in their faces, something a hell of a lot worse than what had happened today.

Even Maggie was subdued during a silent supper, and then she had curled up next to Caroline, hugging the animal as if her young life depended on holding her tight.

With increasing awareness of the feelings of those around him, Morgan realized how frightening her life must be: her father's death, the Utes, then this shooting. She had sat next to Nick during supper, at one time holding his hand tightly, and Morgan realized he had not helped ease the child's fear by keeping her friend, Nick, prisoner.

But Morgan didn't know how to make music, or charm, or even smile in a nonthreatening way. He cared, but he didn't know how to show he cared, and so he stayed away, watching from a distance, as he'd learned always to watch. He'd thought he'd also learned not to get involved in others' lives, but now he knew the lesson hadn't taken as well as he'd imagined. He felt so very alone, so very inadequate, so damnably empty.

Nick was sleeping on and off, Beth sitting next to him, her hand on his arm. Morgan had not chained him, nor had he asked for his word. They all realized Nick had no more strength in him. But Morgan knew he had to ask for Lori's. He understood her well enough to know she would still try any desperate scheme to help Nick. She wouldn't kill Morgan, he knew that now, but she wasn't beyond trying to steal his guns and horses.

He'd put his offer in a way she couldn't refuse. "Your brother needs all the rest he can get. He can't get much with you attached to him. I want your word you won't try anything, anything at all. Your other alternative is to be attached to me." He knew she wouldn't accept the second choice. And he waited, even as he ached inside at her obvious distaste at being close to him. He could chain her to a tree, but he wasn't going to give her that option. He couldn't lock metal on her again, not any longer. He wanted her word, plain and simple, so he would never have to do that again. And to obtain it, he gave an unacceptable choice—purposely, almost cruelly, bending her to his will.

She had stared at him with disbelief, with eyes full of disappointment in him, and he felt as if she were ripping out his heart. But she finally gave him her word. Bitterly. Reluctantly. He knew she would keep it, even as she remained distant from him during the evening. Beth had already moved Maggie's sleeping body closer to the fire, and her own blankets near Nick, so she could hear if there was any change.

Morgan nearly suffocated in the pall that had descended on their small divided party. Nick was still sullen, Beth anxious, Lori sad. Only Caroline seemed indifferent to the stifling atmosphere. After suffering Maggie's embrace, the pig had nonchalantly scouted around for any remaining scraps, gobbling up every piece of food in sight and some that wasn't. She rooted constantly, often butting those individuals who paid her little mind. She even butted Morgan, whom everyone else was avoiding. He found himself grateful for that small notice. It was, he thought, a pretty demeaning state to find oneself in.

Morgan added more wood to the fire and rolled up in his blankets, his six-shooter still strapped to his body, the rifle immediately at his side. He heard Beth whisper something to Nick, and he envied his prisoner. He wanted to whisper to Lori, to draw her close, to share his blankets and the night, to wipe away the taste of killing.

But he felt stained with blood and wryly realized his whole life had been that way. For the first time in years he wondered how it would feel not to be a Ranger, not to be the hunter.

He couldn't picture it. God help him, he just couldn't imagine it.

They left the clearing two days later. It had taken that long for Nick to regain enough strength to ride any distance at all, and even now the going would be slow.

The delay was agonizing for Morgan. He had left Nick free, knowing he couldn't get far in his condition. He scouted, this time more thoroughly, and set several rabbit snares, but decided not to do any more shooting. He suspected that was what had led the gunman to them. He cursed himself more than once for that lapse in judgment, even though he knew the meat had been essential to Nick's slow but steady recovery.

It was Lori that made the wait so terrible. She avoided him as if he might have the plague, and he suspected she considered him just that to her family. Nick was taciturn, speaking very little to him, keeping what words he had for Beth and Maggie.

Morgan had never thought he would miss the sound of that damned harmonica, but he did. Lori still sang a little, but mostly to Maggie, none of the plaintive melodies that she and Nick seemed to like so much, the melodies that had taunted at first and then had struck at his heart. He had wanted to talk to Nick, to try to convince him again that returning to Texas was the best way to handle this, but he met with a stone face whenever he neared the man. It was as if Braden had closed himself completely off. Morgan understood that. God knew he had done it enough times himself.

And what could Morgan say? *I'll try to prove your innocence, but I won't let you go.* He'd already said that, and he knew they were meaningless words to Nick Braden. Braden didn't trust him, would probably never trust him. Morgan found it odd that, on the other hand, he did trust Braden—had done exactly that, in fact.

Morgan couldn't say the other words pounding unmercifully inside, that he had fallen in love with Lori. He had been alone too long, had been too cautious all his life with feelings and words. He didn't know how to express feelings without making a fool of himself. He could only hold them inside, knowing he was distrusted by the woman from whom he so wanted trust, by a man he was growing to respect by leaps and bounds. So he clung to the stoicism by which he'd lived for so long, expecting little, asking nothing, drawing deeper into himself to keep the new pain at bay.

On the third morning Nick seemed well enough to ride, and it was more than time to get going. Morgan had decided to make one last try with Nick. Lord knew he didn't want to use the irons any longer, he didn't want Nick to make it necessary—but Morgan was afraid he would.

They had both shaved that morning after eating, and Morgan found himself once more comparing their faces. Nick's seemed even more like his own now, the lines in his prisoner's face deepened by the last few days. Nick looked wary as Morgan collected his shaving gear and hesitated next to him. "Have you thought any more about what I said about returning voluntarily to Texas?"

"No," Nick said flatly.

Morgan felt his mouth tighten. Their eyes clashed.

"I don't suppose you'd give me your word not to try to run?"

"No," Nick said again.

"Damn you, Braden, why do you have to make this so difficult? Particularly on yourself?"

Nick shrugged. "I have no intention of making it easy for you, not with me, not with Lori."

Morgan felt his gut clench. "Hold out your hands, then," he said curtly, taking a pair of handcuffs he had placed in his belt. Nick looked at him with loathing but did as he was ordered.

Morgan fastened the handcuffs on him. He motioned toward the horses, which he'd already saddled. "Take mine," he said. "Mrs. Andrews can have yours. I'll take her stallion. And this time let me know if you feel you have to stop. I don't want you bleeding again."

"Because it will slow us up?"

"Right," Morgan said icily. "I don't want any more delays."

Nick smiled at him, but it wasn't friendly, and Morgan was strangely relieved to see the anger back in his eyes, that fractious spirit returning.

Lori rode alongside Beth during the early part of the day. Morgan had not used the second pair of handcuffs to lock Nick to the saddle horn this time, but he had tied his horse's reins to the lead again. Nick had rebuffed any attempt at conversation by anyone, including Beth and Lori. But when they had stopped for a brief break at midday, Maggie had charmed Nick and begged to ride with him, and Nick had taken Maggie on the saddle in front of him, holding her firmly with hands that were still cuffed.

Although Lori had hoped for delay, Nick's wound had not been exactly what she'd had in mind. But these few days were exactly what Nick had needed. Surely, the family had received the message she'd sent from Georgetown.

Now it was essential she reach Pueblo before Morgan and make sure any plan precluded harm to either man. She couldn't bear to think of Morgan dead. Andy would have no such scruples. Neither, she feared, would her father or even Daniel if they thought Nick was in danger.

She didn't want to care, dammit. She'd wanted to hate him for forcing her word, for putting handcuffs on Nick again this morning. But she couldn't. Not after that night. She knew now he really did want to help, but she felt his intentions were misguided. He simply believed in things she didn't, in justice, in the law, in his capacity to go up against a wealthy, powerful man like Wardlaw. It was a case, she feared, of "I'm going to help you if it kills you."

And now she had given him her word, though she considered it temporary. She would have to rescind it before Pueblo, give him fair warning so he could try to stop her, if he had the heart for it. Sometimes she wondered if he had one, and then he would do something so unexpected, like bringing Caroline along with them, or getting the hotel room in Georgetown.

Her heart cracked a little more each time he gave her that tentative, wry half smile, every time she thought of his tenderness, the very sweetness of his touch. Sweeter because she knew he'd shared a bit of the same wonder she'd experienced. And now she looked at that straight, uncompromising back, and she hurt for both of them. The last two days had been pure purgatory, watching his eyes, which had so warmed several days ago, turn icy and watchful again as she so obviously rejected his offer, rejected his help in any way.

Lori leaned over and ran her hand down Clementine's neck, fighting against the lump in her throat, the one that had been there for two days, the one she feared would be there for a very long time.

Nick readjusted his arms around Maggie to shift her away from the still painful wound. Her head, nodding ever so slightly, had fallen against his chest. Lord, but he hated the damn cuffs. Still, he wasn't locked to the saddle horn, and that was something, and his arms went neatly around the child. The irons, though, were a constant reminder of his situation.

He had tried to rebuff Beth during the past few days, feigning a sullenness and hostility that he hoped would frighten her off. Oh, he had enough hostility, all right—all directed toward Morgan Davis, but none toward her.

He knew something was happening to him, something that had never happened before. He was falling in love, and he was desperately afraid Beth Andrews might be doing the same. He sensed as much in the stolen glances, the gentle but almost possessive touch, the way their eyes met and held, exchanging knowledge as old as man.

He relished it, and yet he knew he could only hurt her, and so he'd tried everything he could to turn her away. God knew she'd had enough misery to last a lifetime. He couldn't bring her anymore. Every movement was a reminder that he was headed to the hangman, every jingle of the chain that bound his wrists. The Ranger wasn't going to let go, and Nick's only release was the Ranger's death, and that would only increase the price on his head, the danger he would bring to every one around him.

He'd had an opportunity and hadn't taken it. He tried to tell himself that it was because the Ranger had no chance at that moment. His weapons were pointed to the ground, and it would have been like killing an unarmed man. But the truth, he knew, was more complicated, and even he didn't understand it. He hated Morgan Davis, yet there was some kind of odd feeling that had kept him from pulling the trigger, even from trying to wound him again.

But now, handcuffed again, he realized how very short his life expectancy was, how he had nothing but heartache to offer Beth, with the gentle eyes and warm heart. And Maggie, with the solemn eyes, whom he had already taken to his heart. Another death, Morgan Davis's death, would do nothing to help that. His hands tightened around

Maggie. He'd always liked children, had always thought he would have some of his own once he got the ranch started and had something other than a wandering life to offer. Holding Maggie now was probably as close as he was ever going to get to it, whether he reached Texas or not. He sure as hell wouldn't drag a family around as a wanted man.

Morgan Davis turned around, and their gazes caught. Nick thought he saw pain in the Ranger's eyes too. Maybe he really did love Lori. If he did, that too seemed destined to fail. For a moment understanding flickered between the two men, understanding and even a kind of mutual compassion. Nick's lips thinned. He couldn't afford understanding or compassion. It still came down to him or the Ranger if he was to survive, much less have any kind of life.

Maggie wriggled restlessly in his arms, and his gaze went down to her. "It's all right, Button," he said softly, and he felt her settle down against him once more, felt her childish trust, and a bittersweet longing that he knew would never be fulfilled.

CHAPTER TWENTY-TWO

Lori felt numb. Seven days of endless riding through rugged mountain terrain, particularly without a saddle, took their toll. She was thankful for the numbness, though, for being too tired to think. A few more days and they would be in Pueblo, and then she didn't know what would happen. She sickened every time she thought of it, but her determination never flagged, particularly when she saw Nick in irons again.

The battle of wills continued between Morgan and Nick. She thought that Morgan was making things particularly difficult for her brother, hoping he would give in, that he would decide to give himself up voluntarily. But she knew Nick better than that. The one thing the two men had in common, other than their faces, was dogged stubbornness.

Beth and Maggie and Caroline were still with them, though Morgan could often be heard swearing as the pig sometimes refused to move. Beth, the only one of them Morgan really trusted, would often have to go back and prod the animal forward.

Morgan had diverted them to one town, where he'd hoped to find a stage for Maggie and Beth. But since he had last been there, it had become a ghost town, a mining community still on the maps but consisting only of worn-out buildings ready to collapse. Lori doubted now whether Beth and Maggie would leave them. Beth had already mentioned to her she planned to accompany them to

Texas, to do what she could to help Nick. She hadn't said anything about the Ranger, but Lori knew Beth had more faith in Morgan Davis than either she or Nick had. But, then, Beth had never been in Harmony, Texas.

Neither Nick nor Lori tried to persuade her to help in other ways. Nick, in fact, was adamant about it: he wouldn't use Mrs. Andrews to try to get a gun, or try for the key. He'd hang first, and Lori knew it. She had never seen Nick in love before, but he was surely that now. His eyes glowed with it, for both Beth and little Maggie, even as much as he tried to hide it, even as he forced bad temper to frighten Beth off. Lori hurt for him now as much as she hurt for herself.

Morgan Davis had reverted back to his stoic, unemotional self. Each night now he ordered Nick, rather than Lori, to help him water the horses. He made sure he was never alone with her, and his eyes were cool, his mouth unsmiling.

And so he drove them, day and night, toward Pueblo.

On the seventh day Lori knew it was time to tell him she no longer intended to keep her word. They stopped in late afternoon, after passing what appeared to be another warm spring. Morgan had halted, dismounted, and tried the water. He then led his horse a small distance away where a stream bubbled along a canyon floor.

"This seems a good place to camp tonight. We can take baths at the spring back there."

Maggie had started whining, which was most unusual for the girl. She had been extraordinarily good throughout the trip, particularly when she sat with Nick, but she was obviously exhausted. Morgan reached up for Maggie, who was riding with Nick, and Maggie's whine turned into full-fledged tears. Dismay flickered across the Ranger's face, as it always did when Maggie avoided him. To Maggie, Morgan was still the "bad man" who was doing something unpleasant to her new friend to whom she'd given a big piece of her heart.

Beth dismounted and hurried over to calm Maggie.

Lori watched as Nick dismounted, wincing a bit as he did. Although he was much stronger than he had been, he tired quicker than the rest, and she knew he still felt pain from the knife wound. Morgan had been careful with him the first few days on the trail, but then he'd resorted to driving them again, just as he had driven himself so soon after his own wound.

Lori also dismounted, stretched her legs a bit, and then started gathering firewood as Nick and Morgan took the horses to the stream. She tried to tease Maggie into a song, but Maggie wasn't having any of it today. She just huddled against her mother, who looked apologetic as Lori piled up wood. Morgan had the matches in his saddle-bag, so she couldn't do more.

Beth was tired too. Her face showed it. The traveling was bad enough, but the tension between the four adults was even worse, which was probably, Lori guessed, why Maggie was unusually fussy. It was as if they were all walking on eggs, none of them doing it successfully.

When the two men returned, Morgan unsaddled the horses while Nick went over to Maggie. Her face brightened immediately, and she crawled into his lap as Beth shook her head in amazement.

"I've never seen her take to anyone like she took to Nick," she said quietly to Lori, her voice too low for the others to hear. "No one but her father."

"Nick practically raised me," Lori said. "He's always been the Pied Piper of children. He and that harmonica. I wish I could find him a new one." It was a small thing, she knew, but that harmonica had always been Nick's way of releasing pent-up emotions.

"Perhaps in Pueblo," Beth said. They all knew where they were going now. Morgan was no longer keeping it to himself, now that there seemed no reason for it.

Perhaps in Pueblo. Perhaps in Pueblo Nick would go free. Perhaps in Pueblo Morgan would die. Perhaps in Pueblo . . .

"Perhaps," she murmured.

Beth tipped her head. "You don't believe Morgan Davis, do you?"

"I believe him," Lori said wretchedly. "I just don't think he can do what he thinks he can. At least I don't want to chance it."

"I do," Beth said suddenly, and Lori was surprised. Beth had been very careful about not taking sides. "I think he can accomplish anything he sets out to do, and I don't think he would promise something he can't."

"But he hasn't promised anything," Lori said. "Just that he will *try* to help."

Beth was silent, thinking. "And that's not good enough?"

"Is it for you?" Lori asked Beth. "I think you care about Nick. Would you risk his life?"

Beth looked up, her heart in her eyes. "Oh, I care. I didn't think I ever would again, not after Joshua, but Nick . . ." She stopped. "I loved Joshua, he was such a good man, but with Nick I feel as if my heart's been turned inside out. And I know that as long as he's wanted, there will never be any peace for him. Mr. Davis is right about that."

"It's his job," Lori said, trying not to agree. "That's what he cares about."

"He cares about you, and I think he cares very much about what happens to Nick. There's more between them than their faces, Lori. I don't know exactly what, but something binds them together, which is why they get so angry with each other."

Lori swallowed. Maybe Beth was right. She'd thought the same thing several times, and Beth had a more objective view. But then she saw Morgan approaching with the sack of supplies and his saddlebags, the ever-present saddlebags with Nick's gun and the extra ammunition and the leg irons. The tools of his trade. The rifles, she knew—his and the one he'd picked up from the dead bounty hunter—were still in the saddle scabbards, unloaded now, a precaution that he took when Nick wasn't bound both hand and foot.

He looked toward Beth and Maggie, his grim mouth gentling just a little. "Why don't you ladies take a bath? We can eat the last of that antelope. I'll make some coffee."

Beth accepted gratefully. Water had been freezing every place they'd stopped. She'd heated some and washed herself and Maggie, but not to the extent she would have liked. Washing her hair in a warm spring sounded wonderful.

Lori hesitated. She wanted to talk to him, but she had to do it privately. Later, then. She started to turn.

"Lori."

She turned back to him.

"I still have your word, don't I?"

He did at the moment. She nodded.

He reached into the saddlebags and drew out the pistol she had used to shoot him weeks ago. "I think you know how to use this," he said dryly.

Lori didn't smile. All those conflicting emotions warred again. She appreciated his trust. But it made the next step so very difficult. She hesitated.

"Take it," he said. "I don't want you out there alone . . . after the other day. I think it's safe, but . . ."

She reached out and took it, her fingers touching his, like lightning hitting a tree and running through its length. Her heart beat faster, harder. She swallowed and turned away, reluctantly withdrawing her hand from his.

She waited while Beth retrieved some soap from her saddlebags, then caught up Maggie in her arms. "We're going to wash our hair," Beth said happily, and ignored Maggie's wail of protest.

Lori looked around the clearing. Nick was sitting on a log, his gaze on the pistol in her hand—the gun she'd stolen from the sheriff's office, the one she'd aimed at the man she now knew she loved. The one she'd thought to free Nick with, and still could, if she had the will. It felt heavy now, heavier than before. Weighted with responsibility and guilt.

Morgan had not moved, his own gaze on her. Challenging? Watchful? She didn't know. She didn't know what was real and what was wishful thinking any longer. He kept surprising her, and this most of all. He cared enough about her, about her safety, to risk putting this gun back in her hands.

She turned abruptly and followed Beth and Maggie.

Morgan finished preparing the coffee. The sun was going down, and it would be dark within another hour. He too wished for a bath, but he would probably delay that, for both himself and Braden, until the morning. He didn't relish trying to keep track of his prisoner during a dark night, and it promised to be exactly that. Clouds were skimming across the sky, and he said a brief prayer that bad weather would hold off until they reached Pueblo.

Braden was also looking toward the sky. He looked tired, his face still drawn, the face that looked so much like Morgan's—more so, it seemed, every day. His wrists were still manacled, but Morgan had stopped using the leg irons except when they settled down for sleep, and then he removed the handcuffs. The new arrangements provided some relief for his prisoner, he knew, but it still rankled him that he had to use anything at all. Every time, locking the bands became more distasteful to Morgan.

"We should reach Pueblo in two days," he said. "Those damn bounty hunters will probably pick up our trail there, but I want the women and child safe."

"And then what?" Nick asked.

"El Paso," Morgan said flatly. "My company headquarters. You'll stay there until we can get evidence in Harmony to clear you."

"A jail?"

Morgan nodded reluctantly. "You'll be safer there."

"I can't stand small spaces. I thought I would go crazy in Laramie."

Morgan couldn't tolerate them, either. He used to think the fear went back to when he'd been a newborn in that fruit cellar where Callum had said he found him. It had been the only thing that had ever made sense to him, that sense of choking whenever he was in a small room. Callum had said the cabin had burned, that some smoke must have filtered into the room below.

"It shouldn't be long," Morgan said instead. "A few weeks, no more. I'll need witnesses to the shooting."

"You won't get them there. Not honest ones."

Morgan threw some more wood into the fire, watching the flames dance into the air, concentrating on that rather than on the man several feet away. He didn't want to spook him, not now that he was finally listening. "Now that I have a damn good idea what happened, I can get people to talk."

Nick was silent, his face emotionless. Morgan didn't know whether he believed or not. Nick finally stood. "Mind if I walk around a little?"

"Just keep in sight and away from the horses."

"Of course," Nick said dryly. "I wouldn't consider anything else."

Morgan nearly chuckled openly at the obvious falsehood. He choked it off, but he found himself liking Nick Braden more and more. He knew, though, that the feeling wasn't mutual, probably never would be. He regretted that, but friends didn't go with his occupation. Rangers came and went: died, wounded, transferred, retired. He'd not been close to anyone since Callum died, and even then Callum had been more mentor than friend, more guardian than father.

He shrugged off the unsettling thoughts. They had never bothered him until lately. He'd never realized something was missing.

Or maybe he just hadn't been willing to admit it.

.   .   .

The five of them ate quietly. Maggie crawled into Nick's lap, wanting him to brush her wet hair dry. Beth sensed that Nick had an honest liking for children, an easiness with them, combined with the intelligence to treat Maggie as a small adult. And he had a quick, natural smile that warmed. It came rarely now, usually only for Maggie, and a few more hesitant times for Beth, but it was always worth the wait.

Beth combed out her own hair as she watched Nick brush Maggie's in easy, gentle strokes despite his handcuffs. She hurt every time she saw those cuffs, every time the Ranger used the leg irons to restrain him at night. Nick Braden was a man meant to be free, and she had watched him withdraw from her more and more over the succeeding days as they moved closer to Texas. Only Maggie seemed able to lure that smile from him, that confidence that Beth had glimpsed the day he and Mr. Davis had rescued the two of them. It showed itself only rarely now, hidden in his obvious frustration.

Nick Braden was the last man Beth should want. Maggie had already lost one father. She swallowed deeply. She couldn't bear the thought of Maggie losing someone else she was growing to love.

Nor could Beth. Her feelings for Nick grew stronger each day, despite—or perhaps because of—the way he tried to protect her through gruffness, avoiding her as much as he could, given his limited movement. But his eyes told her what he would not, the sudden deepening of that incredible deep blue, the pleasure so quickly shielded by caution.

Which was why Beth, unlike Lori, was placing so many hopes on Ranger Davis. She had watched him change during the last ten days, had seen his eyes soften when they rested on Lori, had seen the muscles strain in his cheek when he'd locked the leg irons on Nick. She noticed the frustration when he'd tried to persuade both Bradens to trust him, the pain in his eyes when Maggie rebuffed him or Lori avoided him.

There was a strength in him that Beth trusted, just as there was strength in Nick. Although Nick wouldn't accept it, she knew it had taken more courage for him not to kill the Ranger than to fire. And it was taking Morgan Davis more strength to try to vindicate Nick than it would just to release him. The Ranger was risking everything to do that, including Lori.

She wondered why neither Nick nor Lori saw that.

She looked up. The Ranger was gathering the cups and utensils they'd used. He was always moving, a constant restlessness seeming to drive him. He never appeared to rest, to be at ease.

Lori moved next to her. She had been unusually quiet, even at the spring when she had helped wash Maggie's hair. Maggie had begged for a song, and Lori had complied but without her usual zest. She had kept her eyes on the pistol, instead, and Beth had felt the tension in her, and shivers of apprehension in herself. But her new friend had surrendered the gun easily on their return, and Beth had felt a certain relief. She was already caught in the vicious pull of all the eddies of emotion and strained loyalties swirling among them. She didn't know what she would do if a direct confrontation developed. She believed that Morgan Davis was Nick's one hope, but she knew that the two Bradens did not.

Lori stood and walked over to the Ranger. Beth couldn't hear the words between them, but she saw the Ranger nod curtly, then move over to Nick.

"Braden." He didn't have to say more. They'd been through this every night. Nick whispered something to Maggie, and she stirred unhappily but rose and returned to Beth, who held her tightly, averting her gaze while the Ranger used the leg iron to chain Nick to the tree. In the firelight Beth saw Nick's lips tighten, a muscle grind against his throat, and she wondered how long it would be before he exploded with rage. He was so much stronger now, though he couldn't yet match the Ranger's strength. The Ranger hesitated, as if he sensed the sudden menace, then leaned down and unlocked the handcuffs, tucking them into his belt.

Nick's lips tightened even more as Morgan looked at Lori, then walked off in the direction of the spring. Lori hesitated a moment, glanced briefly at Nick, then followed Morgan, disappearing through the woods. Beth could almost hear Nick's indrawn breath, the curse just smothered as he became aware of Maggie nearby.

Beth gave Maggie some grain to feed Caroline before settling her daughter down for the night, singing a small lullaby until Maggie's eyes closed. When she was sure Maggie was asleep, Beth went over to sit with Nick. His eyes didn't leave the place where his sister had disappeared. And then he buried his head in his hands.

"Nick," Beth whispered.

"I almost believed him," he said bitterly. "Damn him."

"I think you can," she said, reaching over and taking his hand, playing with it.

He looked up at her. She couldn't see what was in his eyes, not in the dark, but she felt his desperation. "You'll be safe in Pueblo," he said, "you and Maggie."

"I want to go with you."

His hand suddenly wrapped around hers, tightened for a moment. "That's not possible."

"I'll stay with you. I'll make sure he keeps his promise," she said.

"No." He shook his head. "I want you to stay in Pueblo, head back up to Denver if that's what you want." He let go of her hand and tried to smile. "Make a new life for yourself, for Maggie. Forget about me."

"I . . . don't think I can."

He shook his head. "It's too late for me, Beth. My life isn't worth a plugged nickel. I won't put you and Maggie in danger."

"If you go back . . . ?"

"There are no guarantees, even then," he said. "My face will still be on posters all over the west. And that's if

Davis can prevent my immediate hanging, which I doubt. I won't take that chance."

"You're going to try to escape." She said it softly.

His jaw set. "When we get to Pueblo, go to a hotel. Don't try to . . . see me again. Please. For me, if not for Maggie."

"That's why Lori . . ." Beth said the words almost to herself.

"Lori what?"

"She was . . . very quiet, sad." She hesitated. "She's in love with Mr. Davis."

"She can't be."

"Just like I can't . . . love you? It doesn't happen that way, Nick. Love is something you can't control."

He stared at her, his mouth opening slightly, and Beth suddenly leaned over, her lips touching his, trying to convince him of her words, trying to dissuade him from something that would take him away from her forever.

He didn't move for a moment, and then his mouth closed over hers and his arms went around her, bringing her close to him. She felt him tremble; then his tongue entered her mouth greedily, and his hands pulled her tightly against him.

Beth thought the world was exploding. She'd enjoyed lovemaking with her husband, but it had never been like this, never so painfully wanting.

His mouth moved from hers, traveled down her neck. "Ah Beth, sweet Beth, you taste so good, so sweet, and I . . ." He stopped. "Dear God, Beth, I want . . ." His words were broken, full of denial and pain, and Beth thought her heart would break. Her hand went up to his cheek, stubbled again with new beard, and her fingers ran along it, memorizing the feel of his face, the fine, handsome sculpted lines, the new crevices around his eyes.

She felt his mouth do the same with her, explore. He left fire in his wake, fire and storm and sunrise. The sunrise was the beauty, the tenderness of his mouth, his arms, his hands. An awakening, a bringing to life something she'd thought dead. She glanced over toward Maggie. She appeared to be asleep on her bedroll, Caroline breathing noisily next to her. She swallowed deeply as she remembered the sight of Maggie in Nick's arms, the trust that the child instinctively had for him, the trust she herself instinctively had.

She wouldn't let it go. She turned her head to him again, and his lips came back upon hers, seeking at first, then desperately imploring, and she knew then that he wanted her as much as she wanted him, that he felt the same terrible desperation at losing something just found.

Just found, but so very magnificent she knew it was incredibly rare.

He moved slightly, and she heard his low curse as the chain on his ankle stopped him. His hands dropped from her.

"Don't," she whispered. "Please don't stop."

"I have no right, dammit."

"You have every right," she said. "I gave you that right." Her hand touched his chest, and even through his shirt she felt him shudder, felt the thump of his heart. Her own breathing quickened as familiar yet newly exciting sensations flowed through her. Exciting and poignant and sensual. So very, very sensual. So very yearning. His hands stroked her sides, fondling, caressing as if he were memorizing every detail. Pleasure soared through her. Physical pleasure. But something more. A fine sense of belonging, of rightness.

Nick groaned, both with need and dismay. Dear God, how he had waited a lifetime for this. And now it came too late. He ran his hands through her hair. It was still damp, but it felt like silk against his fingers. Desire pooled in him, stronger than he'd ever felt before, and he knew the reason: he'd never felt anything but physical desire before, and now he felt so much more.

His hands left her hair and cupped her breasts, felt them tightening under his touch, and he knew that Beth's surface tranquility hid a depth of feeling and passion he'd never experienced before. "Beth . . . Beth," he whispered. He had never known there could be so much sweetness with a woman. He was torn between touching her like fragile glass and clutching her to him so tightly he'd never lose her.

And then their lips touched again, and he tasted a tear that had rolled down her cheek. He hurt as he'd never hurt before, and he tasted as he'd never tasted before. This moment, this golden splendor, would have to last him forever, through days and weeks and months in jail, or of running.

Images rushed through his mind. Beth smiling at the door of the ranch in Wyoming, Maggie crawling up on his lap, a small boy who was half Beth, half himself, grinning at his first pony. Too late. Too late for any of it.

"Don't run away," she whispered. "Don't ask me to go."

He felt the breath being squeezed out of him. His hand went to her chin, and he lifted it until her gaze met his. "I can't stand jail, Beth. I can't. And I won't risk hanging for something I didn't do."

She bit the corner of her lip, and he saw something dark well there—blood. "I'll always be waiting for you," she finally said.

He crushed her to him, and she melted against his body, every curve fitting into his, moving so he did not have to. He felt wetness against his cheek. Another tear. And then he wondered whether it had been hers, or his.

CHAPTER TWENTY-THREE

Lori was so aware of Morgan's disturbing presence that she found it nearly impossible to walk. Her legs didn't work right, and she stumbled; only his hand kept her from falling. She had almost blindly led the way through the thicket of pine and wild raspberries. His very touch made her legs even weaker, her blood quicken, creating an ache in the core of her.

She had been able to be strong because she hadn't let him near her. *What are you going to do now?* An inner voice kept asking the question, and she didn't know the answer.

He turned her toward him. "Have we gone far enough?" he asked hoarsely, and she knew he was as affected as she by their closeness. She had asked to speak with him, and his eyes had flared with surprise, then with something else, before they had shuttered again. They had both tried hard to keep away from each other the past week.

No! They hadn't gone far enough. She wasn't ready yet to face him alone. She wondered whether she would ever be ready. Her voice was buried deep inside her heart. She had to say words that would forever divide them, and she didn't know how she could bear that.

"Lori?" The hoarseness was still in his voice, a hoarseness that came, she knew now, from need. But there was also that odd gentleness again. She hadn't heard it in the past few days. He had schooled himself against it, just as she had. She couldn't make herself look at him. If she did, she would reach up and touch him, her lips would want to meet his, her heart to greet his heart.

"Why did you give me the gun?" The words finally exploded from her, even though she didn't want the answer. She didn't want to hear he trusted her, when she had known all the time they were riding into a trap.

"I told you," he said mildly. "I didn't want you to run into varmints." He chuckled, a wonderful, rare sound. "Though I would give the varmints a damn poor chance even if you didn't have a gun. *With* one . . . whew!"

She nearly melted then. He so seldom indulged in humor that it was always surprising, and incredibly endearing. She couldn't bear for him to be endearing now. Dear Mary, her heart was so fragile now, one small jab would send it crashing into a million pieces.

He moved his hand, which had righted her, up to her shoulder. It fell possessively around her, as if she belonged to him. Part of her did. Part of her always would.

"Were you so sure I would hand it back?"

He stilled, as if he knew he wasn't going to like what came next. As he always did, though, he met the challenge directly. "What's on your mind, Lori?"

"I gave you my word, and I kept it," she said stiffly, formally. "I'm now withdrawing it." She knew it sounded ridiculous.

"And what does that mean, exactly?" he said quietly.

She braced herself against the billows of regret already embracing her, choking her. She and Nick had talked today, and he was never going to agree to return to Texas. She'd already set things in motion by telegraphing the family, and she had no choice now but to follow the course she'd charted. She could only try to see that no one was hurt.

Except she knew, heart deep, that they were all going to be hurt. She, Nick, Beth, Morgan. She felt it now in Morgan's quiet tone, in the sudden stiffness of his body. It spoke of emotions he'd tried to hide for so long.

"You're going to have to spell it out for me, Lori," he said. "Sometimes I'm a little slow."

If only that were true. If only she didn't care so much. If only she didn't love him so.

"No more promises," she said.

"Why?" Again that directness was disconcerting.

"I don't think I have to explain that to you," she said stiffly.

"Don't help your brother ruin his life," he said tightly. "Don't ruin yours. Ours."

It was the first time he had ever alluded to a future, and her stomach churned miserably. "I can't go against him," she said.

"Does he really want that kind of help from you?" His voice was contemptuous. "Then he's not the man I thought he was."

She twisted away from his hand, from his nearness. "He doesn't want my help, but I can't sit back and watch you take him in."

"What are you going to do about it, Lori? Shoot me again?" His voice was soft, dangerously so. "Your brother couldn't do it. Can you?"

"He couldn't do it for himself. He could do it for me."

"And you can do it for him."

"I did before," she said, trembling.

"I haven't forgotten," Morgan said grimly.

"Why do you have to be so stubborn? Why won't you just release him? Then . . ."

"Then what, Lori?" Lori heard a warning in his voice. Hurt. Pain. "Are you bargaining again?"

"You don't bargain, do you, Ranger? You don't compromise. You don't care about anything but your damn job, about finishing what you started."

"No, I don't bargain," he said in a dry, flat tone. "But I do care, damn it to hell." His jaw set. "You're right about one thing. I haven't cared about anything in a long time, but now . . ." His lips came down on hers. Hard, like that first kiss in Laramie. Angry. Frustrated. Lori felt the familiar fire rush through her blood, the less familiar but even more compelling sweet lust within her. Her heart hammered against its cage as he pulled her close to him, and she could hear the pounding of his own.

She writhed against him, her insides melting at the feel of his hard body against hers, at the demanding, possessive lips crushing down on her mouth. Her mouth opened to him, and her mind was spinning, soaring with her need for him as his mouth plundered hers with deep, fierce kisses.

She was barely aware of him pulling away, unbuckling his gunbelt, placing it carefully near a tree. He was back in an instant, taking her in his arms and laying her down on the ground. Her arms went around his shoulders as his tongue trailed over her neck, to the opening of her shirt. She wasn't sure whether it was his hands or hers that freed her buttons. Their fingers were entwined, their bodies, as they both desperately sought something the other could give. As if each knew this was the last time . . .

"Ah, Lori," he rasped before his mouth found her breasts, caressing her nipples as she felt them grow taut and hard and so very sensitive, so very responsive to his every touch. Her arms went around him, under his shirt, feeling the hard, moving muscles of his back, her fingers finding a scar and gentling for a moment before grasping him closer to her, feeling his arousal against her. Her body arched, and even through the clothes they still wore, she felt the fierce hunger of them both. She looked up, and though the dark shadowed his eyes, she saw the pain etched into his expression. And uncertainty.

The uncertainty was more sensuous, more irresistible, than confidence would have been. Her hand moved from his back, up to his face, along his mouth. She swallowed words she couldn't allow herself to say. *I love you. I'll always love you.* But she knew her fingers were saying them. She felt it in his mouth, the way his lips twisted into the slightest smile.

His hands became gentle as they slipped down to her

waist, unbuttoning her trousers; then one hand caressed her lower stomach, then slipped down between her legs, working a magic that swept away everything but sensation. And then his own trousers were gone, and he was poised above her, his arousal teasing that part of her which was already on fire from his touch.

"Morgan," she whispered, her own voice hoarse now, as hoarse as his had been. Hoarse with need and want, hoarse with words choked inside her.

His hands went under her, sliding along her hips, pulling her body up to meet his, and she felt his warmth enter, fill her, glide in and out with rhythmic perfection until she heard herself cry out. His mouth covered hers, catching the sound as her body pulsed with his, danced with his, giving and taking in a golden glow that was both electrifying and beautiful. She vibrated with love, with giving the one thing she could give him, with taking the one thing she could take.

And then there was a shattering burst of ecstasy, of pleasure so strong she wanted to remain there forever, in his arms. Her hands dug into him as the pleasure climaxed, then receded slowly, ever so slowly, into something just as wondrous: a warm, lazy contentment of having him next to her, in her, feeling with him those quivering shudders of sensation that continued to dance through them.

She felt suspended in a dreamlike state as he moved, carrying her with him, to his side, his mouth on hers, so gently now, so tenderly. His fingers traced her mouth as she had done to his. They were large, callused, yet so sensitive against her skin. He caught a strand of her hair. "Like honey," he said.

His hand caught her chin and drew it up so she had to stare straight into his eyes. The moon peeked out from behind a cloud then and seemed to shine directly down into those eyes, deepening that dark blue, sharpening even more its intensity. He seemed to look into her soul, into her heart, and she wanted to cry out in protest.

Instead, her hand ran down his chest, fingering the tufts of dark hair that made an arrow down toward his manhood. She felt him stiffen, felt him growing hard inside her again. He pulled her closer to him and rolled over, so she was on top of him. She felt his manhood arch inside, reaching, and instinctively she sat up, taking more of him into her, so much more than she'd ever imagined possible.

She could see his face, the eyes partly covered by those dark lashes. The face was uniquely his now, its expression troubled, and she knew as did he that while they had just finished making love, this was something else. She wanted him. She would always want him. But as she moved on top of him, she knew she couldn't afford sweetness, and love, and the trust it demanded. So this was to be physical pleasure alone.

Lori looked away from his face, from the puzzlement forming in his eyes, from the sudden understanding that was like a knife in her heart, even as their bodies reacted together as if they had been made for each other. She felt the sensations, the fire and the glow, the physical satisfaction and reactions, but she also felt an incredible sadness rather than the soul-felt joy of a few moments earlier.

His movements became almost violent, hard and thrusting as if pursuing devils he knew he couldn't defeat. The explosion of warmth came, and Lori tried to absorb herself into it.

But he moved, his hands firm as he rolled over, then withdrew and silently dressed. After a few stunned moments Lori did the same. Bereft at the loss, her fingers had difficulty with the buttons, and she turned away from his silent appraisal. When she'd finished, she felt his hands on her shoulder. He turned her to face him. "I was a fool to think . . . making love to you would make a difference, make you trust me." He turned away. "It's a mistake I won't repeat." He tried to be coldly indifferent, but she felt the ache in his voice.

"Morgan . . ." Her voice broke.

"I can't compete with him, can I?" he said bitterly.

"You're making me choose between you and someone I've loved all my life."

"I'm not making you do anything." His voice was cold now, angry. "I've never asked you to choose. I just asked you to trust me."

"It's the same thing."

"Only because you want to make it that way." He turned and started back as if she didn't exist, and she knew just then how much she had hurt him. And herself.

Morgan didn't know when he'd ever been so angry, as much at himself as at her. It was as if Lori had deliberately twisted something that had been so good, so fine, into something else altogether. Now he knew why he'd taken so much trouble all these years not to care—hell, even made a damn art of it. It hurt too much.

He'd known, dammit. He'd known how idiotic it had been to come with her tonight. He simply didn't know how to deal with that blind loyalty of hers. He didn't even know how to deal with himself at the moment. He'd never left himself vulnerable like this before.

He wouldn't do it again, by God.

What in the hell was she planning?

Something, that was for sure, or she wouldn't have warned him. That paradox again. That mixture of recklessness and integrity, that fierce passion for whatever and whomever she loved, were part of what he'd learned to love.

But what was she planning? He couldn't even imagine. Despite her words, he didn't think she would try to harm him again. What else could she do on her own? After knowing her for the last month, he didn't even want to think about it.

She couldn't know where they were heading. He hadn't told them until a few days ago. He hadn't even decided himself until after they'd left Laramie, the only place she could have passed on information. Perhaps that was it. Perhaps she planned to head into Pueblo and try to enlist assistance there.

Damn it all. If only he could let Nick Braden go. It would make things so easy. He could court Lori. He could rid himself of Braden's hatred. But he wouldn't be able to live with himself. Neither Braden nor himself could breathe easily again.

How far would she go?

He didn't know. He did know he didn't have the heart to chain her. If she wanted to shoot him, well, she damn well could.

Morgan saw the firelight ahead, and he slipped into the shadows, allowing her to pass and go in alone. Nick, he saw, was holding Mrs. Andrews. The child was apparently sleeping. He watched for another ten minutes or so and then went in. Beth had straightened up, moved away from Braden. Lori was sitting stiffly by herself.

"Get some sleep," he told them all, and placed several pieces of wood on the fire. He then retreated to where he'd folded his own bedroll. He checked the saddlebags, obviously for guns and ammunition. "We'll leave early," he added, ignoring Lori's surprised face as she realized he was not going to handcuff her. He turned away, lying down in his own blankets and closing his eyes.

The pain inside him was excruciating, choking out all the life so new to him. He had lost her completely, and he knew it, and all he felt now was a terrible wrenching loneliness.

Morgan rose before dawn. He'd dozed on and off, the slightest sound snapping him into full wakefulness. He felt weighted with weariness and defeat. He hoped activity would numb him. He went over to Braden and unlocked the leg iron. His prisoner was also awake, and Morgan wondered if he'd spent as poor a night as himself.

A twist of his head indicated the spring they had passed

yesterday, and Braden nodded, understanding the silent message. Morgan had his saddlebags with him as well as his rifle, and he motioned for Braden to go ahead. The other members of their party were apparently still sleeping.

The two men said nothing until they reached the spring, well out of earshot.

"I thought you might like to bathe," Morgan said.

His face carefully controlled, Braden went to the edge of the pool. He tested the temperature, his face gradually relaxing. He sat down and started to take off his boots.

Morgan watched idly from several feet away. He planned to take his own bath after Braden finished. His mind was still occupied, as it had been last night, with Lori.

Braden had finished taking off the right boot and was pulling off the left, then the sock. Morgan stiffened. The bottom of Braden's foot was completely visible, and Morgan was staring at a red mark, the shape of half a heart, just like the one he had on his right foot.

Christ! A clammy shiver crawled up Morgan's back. He stared again at the foot just as Nick Braden moved, and the mark disappeared out of sight as Braden started peeling off his coat and then his shirt. "Soap?" he asked. Morgan found a piece in the saddlebags and threw it to him as Braden continued undressing.

Feeling like a damn voyeur, Morgan studied him intently. The same arrow of black hair that Morgan had grew down Braden's chest. He swallowed as Braden looked up, and something in Morgan's face made him frown. "Something wrong?"

Hell, everything was wrong, everything was spinning wildly out of control. He hesitated. "That mark on your foot . . ."

Nick shrugged. "It's always been there. Lori used to tease me . . ." He stopped abruptly, his jaw tightening.

"Lori used to . . . ?" Morgan prompted.

For a moment Braden's mouth set stubbornly, and then

he seemed to think it wasn't important as he said lightly, "She used to say that since I had only half a heart, part of me must be missing." His dark brows knitted together. "The strange thing was that I . . . used to think that, too." His lips clamped together as if he were puzzled why he'd shared that particularly odd piece of information, but Morgan felt his whole body go rigid.

How many times had he felt that way, that a vital part of him had somehow been left out, like a missing piece of a puzzle?

Braden slipped into the water, and Morgan turned away, his mind whirling with the implications of the birth-mark. Questions and more questions pounded at him. He had always considered Nick Braden one of those odd coincidences, an uncanny look-alike, because there seemed to be no other possibility. What were the odds of a look-alike having the identical birthmark?

How old was Braden? Although he looked younger than Morgan, they had roughly the same body. And Morgan was only too aware of what years of war, and their aftermath, had done to him. All those years of killing, of hunting, of . . . being alone. He knew that his face had the etched lines of a man older than his actual years.

He remembered the time Braden was hit by that Ute knife; he had felt a sharp pain in the same part of his body. And then he recalled another oddity: the image of Braden's face, of agony crossing it, at the same time Morgan had pressed the hot knife to his own wound. It was one of the last things Morgan had seen before he'd lost consciousness.

More impressions flitted through his mind now. The way he'd known what Braden was thinking, almost from the beginning. He'd chalked it up to experience, of knowing what to expect from criminals. But Braden had always been different. The thoughts had always been clearer, more vivid, even when they were unlike the thoughts of Morgan's other prisoners.

How?

Morgan's breath locked up inside him. His heart pounded with discovery. Still, his mind told him it couldn't be so.

Texas. He had been born in Texas. Alone. The only child of parents who had died immediately after his birth. He tried to remember everything Callum had ever told him about the circumstances of his birth.

Callum had been there to warn them, had heard his mother's childbirthing cries, and then had to leave to warn others. When he'd returned hours later with help, the cabin was gone, burned, the charred bodies of his parents next to each other. Morgan had been found in the fruit cellar.

What had happened that day? He tried to dredge up every memory. He used to ask all the Rangers about that day, about his parents. Was there anything he had missed?

A woman. There had been another woman, Callum had said once. A woman helping with the childbirth, but she was never found, and everyone had believed she had been taken by the Comanche. They had looked for her but never found a trace. She had been assumed dead.

What if there had been another baby, that somehow the woman had managed to save it? But, then, why would she not report it?

Hell, he was reaching. He tried to dismiss the thought as preposterous—like the odds that he and Nick Braden had the same birthmark. But the thought kept haunting him.

He looked back to the pool. Braden was washing his hair, the same dark, thick hair Morgan had, the same texture, nearly the same unruliness. All the other Bradens, except for the mother, had honey-colored hair and golden eyes. Braden's eyes were just like his. And the mother. She'd also had light-colored hair, and he remembered the color of her eyes. Brown. Dark brown.

Braden was left-handed. His birthmark was on the left foot. What did that mean?

Morgan had never known any twins. Doubt gnawed at his belly, and yet . . .

Part of me was missing. Braden's words. Morgan's own feelings. He'd thought it was a lack in him of some kind. He'd been accused often enough of not having any heart at all. Only on this trip had he discovered how much of one he had.

Should he show Braden his own birthmark? The half heart?

He chuckled grimly. Braden would not be a bit pleased about the possibility of kinship. No, he needed to wait until he was sure. Questions to ask at the Ranger post, questions to ask Jonathon and Fleur Braden. He had to be sure that this was not just a once-in-a-million coincidence.

And Lori? Braden's sister. Sickness swept through him for a moment until he realized that if Braden was really his full brother, Lori couldn't be any relation to either of them. He thought of the love and loyalty the two had for each other. Sibling love, but would that change if Lori knew Nick wasn't her brother after all?

Of the two, he and Nick Braden, Morgan fully realized which one a woman would be more apt to choose. If Morgan hadn't already lost her.

He heard a ripple as Nick Braden pulled himself up from the warm water and quickly dressed in the cool air. Morgan looked at the sky. Full light now. How long had they been there? He'd been so absorbed in his discovery, in his thoughts, he'd allowed more time to pass than he'd intended. His own bath would have to wait. He looked toward Braden as his prisoner started to pull on his socks, hoping once more to catch sight of the mark. But Braden's movements were too quick.

Braden looked at him curiously, and Morgan knew he must have been staring. He emptied his face of expression and picked up the rifle and saddlebags. Braden ran fingers through his wet hair in a gesture so familiar that Morgan felt his heart pound again. How many times had he done that himself?

"Let's get back," he said, trying to force authority back into his voice.

Braden shrugged as if surprised that Morgan wasn't going to avail himself of the spring.

"It's getting late," Morgan replied to the unasked question. His voice sounded strange, even to himself.

Braden turned and started back through the pines. Morgan matched his wide strides, realizing how good it must feel to the man to be unfettered. *His brother.* The possibility—if there was one—was still astounding.

"Braden?"

Nick stopped and turned around, his face blank.

"When were you born?"

The blankness dropped from Braden's face, replaced by puzzlement, then wariness. "Why?"

"Records," Morgan said, feeling as foolish as he knew the excuse sounded.

"I don't give a damn about your records."

"I could ask Lori." It was a challenge, easily slipped into after the past weeks.

Braden's eyes blazed. "July fifteenth, 1844. Now you can put it on my tombstone." He turned back to the path they were taking and started walking again.

Morgan placed a hand against a tree for support. July fifteen. His birthday. The same year in which he had been born. Nick Braden *was* his brother. He didn't know how or why, but now there were few doubts.

He was wrestling with the idea of telling Braden when he reached the clearing, a minute behind his prisoner. Braden's face was pale. He turned to Morgan.

"Lori's gone," he said, and there was as much fear in his voice as there suddenly was in Morgan's battered heart.

CHAPTER TWENTY-FOUR

Daniel Webster tried to soothe Andy, who was watching the road north of Pueblo. "Patience, Andy."

"Where are they? Could we have missed them?"

Daniel raised his eyebrows, "I don't think so. A Texas Ranger, his prisoner, and a girl as pretty as Lori? That would be big news in Pueblo."

"Maybe they changed direction."

Daniel shook his head. "Lori would have found some way of letting us know."

"It's all my fault," Andy blurted out. "I'm the one they should be after."

They had camped north of town, a mile away from the road and alongside a river where clumps of trees hid the gaily painted wagon. Fleur had stayed with the wagon. Jonathon had ridden into town and taken a room in the cheapest hotel. He was always able to fit in, to extract any news from a barroom crowd. He'd heard nothing of Nick or Lori or the man taking Nick in. He had seen, however, two men reputed to be bounty hunters. One had hair so blond it looked white.

At first Daniel feared they might not have made it in time, though they had driven day and night to reach Pueblo, even selling horses at a loss several times to get fresh ones. Daniel was obviously identifiable, so he'd stayed out of sight, but Jonathon had checked the telegraph office and found nothing.

Three days. They had been waiting three days now.

Daniel tried to keep Andy's spirits high, but his own were sinking. Could something have happened along the way? Had the Ranger killed Nick? Bounty hunters? He felt helpless. None of them were gunmen. None of them had ever killed a man. Their only hope in freeing Nick was an ambush, pure and simple. Surprise. A bluff. Violence only if necessary.

Daniel checked his rifle. He knew how to shoot. All of them did. The knowledge gave them confidence to bluff. They had bluffed more times than Daniel even wanted to consider, including the time they'd escaped raiding Comanches so many years ago, just before they'd found Fleur.

Bluffing had worked then. Bluff and Daniel's size. That had been one time his small stature had been of great benefit. The Comanches had surrounded the Medicine Wagon, and he and Jonathon had taken out the rifles, but then one of the Indians saw Daniel's small legs, and they'd started whispering among themselves. Daniel had gathered he was "bad medicine." The Indians hadn't bothered the Medicine Wagon again.

Daniel heard the sound of approaching riders, and he and Andy peered over the rise at the road below. Two cowhands. Daniel watched as Andy tried to relax, but his hands shook as he rolled some tobacco in a paper and lit it. Daniel knew it wasn't that his young charge was scared. That was just the problem. Daniel wished Andy *were* scared. He was too eager, too bent on righting things. Daniel was very much aware that killing a Texas Ranger would right nothing, but Andy might well do something rash. He and Lori had a lot in common.

"What about a game of poker?" Daniel said, hoping to get Andy to relax.

"You've already won enough to keep me in debt the rest of my life," Andy said, a small grin on his unusually grim face.

"There's always an afterlife," Daniel said. "Keep trying, and someday you might be as good as Lori."

That jab worked, as Daniel knew it would. Andy hated being the youngest. He was always trying to compete with Lori and Nick. Daniel took a worn deck of cards from his pocket and started dealing, though his attention remained fixed on the road.

Lori doubted whether Morgan would come after her. She'd realized last night when he allowed her to remain free that he had made a conscious decision to let her go if that was what she wanted.

It wasn't. She knew he didn't believe she would ambush him again. He didn't know that there were others waiting to do it for her. Tears had burned behind her eyes all day, even the night before. She'd seen the defeat in his eyes, the momentary pain before he shuttered them again. He had offered everything but the one thing she needed most.

She had ridden hard, not caring if she left tracks. Morgan had to look after a woman and a child, as well as a prisoner. And a moseying pig. She smiled at the latter. She'd noted Morgan's frequent impatient looks toward Caroline, but he wasn't going to leave behind a child's pet. So much for the hard-hearted Ranger.

Except where Nick was concerned.

Her smile disappeared, and she pressed Clementine into a gallop. Pueblo couldn't be far now. The trail she had found had widened, looked more traveled. Please God, she prayed, let me find Papa and Daniel before they find Morgan.

Morgan felt as if he were carrying the weight of the world on his back. Maggie kept asking where Lori was. Beth looked pale and stricken, Braden was tight-lipped and grim. They ate silently as Morgan saddled two horses. Lori had taken Clementine and her saddle. That left them one saddle short. Braden would have to ride bareback.

No one had an answer as to where Lori had gone. Morgan had the premonition he'd find out soon enough.

Beth looked distressed. "She left just after you did," she said. "She didn't say where she was going, just to tell Nick that she would be all right."

Morgan had turned to Braden. "Do you know where she's gone?"

Braden didn't answer.

"Dammit, there are bounty hunters out there, not to mention mountain lions, snakes, and . . ."

"She doesn't have a gun," Braden finished. "You made sure of that." Morgan sensed Nick wasn't any happier about Lori's disappearance than he was. He was looking at Nicholas Braden now with different eyes. Trying to see something of himself in the man. Part of him wanted to tell Braden what he suspected, but it was probably the last thing the man wanted to hear now.

The possibility that they were brothers strengthened Morgan's determination to solve Braden's problem, and that still meant taking him back while he was in one piece. Morgan damn well wasn't going to find a brother only to lose him to a bounty hunter. Even though, he acknowledged privately and with some pain, Braden probably preferred a bounty hunter to him.

"Let's go. You can ride bareback. Mrs. Andrews will take your saddle."

"Lori?" Braden asked again, obviously not ready to drop the subject. Beth stood next to him, quietly supportive, her expressive eyes questioning. Morgan knew he was also falling considerably below her expectations. He had damn little choice, though, but to go on. If he chased after Lori, he would have to leave Beth and Maggie unprotected, unless, of course, he let Braden go.

Morgan wondered whether that was what Lori had in mind. She knew exactly what she was doing; her warning last night was evidence of that. He'd been a fool not to handcuff her, but he was so damn tired of being the villain. Morgan had really thought she would stay with Braden, if not with himself.

"As you pointed out before," he said curtly, shielding his own misgivings, "she can take care of herself, and I rather guess you have some idea of where she's gone."

"You really are a bastard, Davis."

"You could have stopped her," Morgan said. "I don't doubt for a moment you knew she was leaving. If anything happens, it will be on your head." His own temper was heating now, worry fanning it to the boiling point, worry and . . . a pain he didn't want to recognize. He felt like a volcano headed toward eruption.

The two men glared at each other.

Caroline started snorting, as if the pig sensed all the antagonism in the air.

Morgan took the handcuffs from his belt and stalked over to Braden.

Braden backed up. "Not this time."

"The longer we delay, the more time Lori has to get in trouble," Morgan warned. "And right now you don't have the strength to best me." He hoped like hell he wouldn't have to test that statement. The last thing he wanted now was another fight with Braden. Despite his recent discovery, he feared he might just do more harm than he intended, if that volcano bubbling inside blew loose.

Braden seemed to read the violence in his eyes. He looked at Beth, his eyes defensive, tired. He finally held out his wrists, and Morgan found himself hesitating. But Lori's very disappearance, the fact that Braden had to know what she was planning, made the cuffs necessary until Morgan got everything sorted out. He snapped the bands shut around Braden's wrists.

"If we don't find Lori along the way, I'll go after her once you and Mrs. Andrews are in Pueblo." Morgan turned toward the horses. "We've delayed enough. Get on the horse. I assume you don't need help."

Braden looked at him disdainfully and went to Beth's stallion, which was already tied to a lead. He mounted the horse's bare back easily despite the handcuffs and sat there waiting as Morgan helped Beth up, then Maggie in front of her.

Morgan was surprised to see the sympathy on Beth Andrews's face. "She really does love you," she said in a low voice.

He didn't pretend not to understand. He just shook his head and turned away, taking the few steps to his horse and mounting. He found Lori's eastbound tracks. She hadn't bothered to hide her trail. She was moving fast—toward Pueblo.

It was almost twilight when Daniel saw Lori and Clementine. Both rider and horse looked exhausted. He tugged at Andy, who was taking a nap as Daniel watched the road.

Daniel whistled, a long birdcall, and Lori glanced up, searching the rise, then turned Clementine toward where Andy now stood, waving frantically at her. Lori slid off the saddle and hugged Andy, then leaned down and hugged Daniel. "Thank God I found you."

"Where's Nick?" Andy demanded.

"The Ranger's bringing him in, probably later today. There's a woman and child with them, and I . . . I want to make sure the Ranger isn't hurt."

Daniel stared at her, at a face that had changed considerably in the past months. Too much of the joy was gone. "Why?" he asked with a very bad feeling in the pit of his stomach.

"He's been . . . well . . . he's been . . . decent," she finally said. "He could have killed Nick, and he . . . might have had cause . . ." Her words were stumbling, her face turning rosy.

Andy interrupted. "Surely you don't suggest we let him take Nick in."

Lori hesitated. "No. He said he would try to help Nick in Texas, but . . . Nick doesn't believe him."

Daniel looked at her closely. "What do you believe, Lori?"

"What difference does it make what she believes?" Andy broke in. "It's Nick's life."

"What do you suggest, Lori?"

She swallowed hard, then looked at Andy. "You have to promise no harm will come to the Ranger. No shooting."

"I can't promise that," Andy said.

"I can," Daniel said quietly, casting Andy a warning glance.

"I think they will be coming down this road, though the Ranger's very careful. But he doesn't know I contacted you," Lori said. "There's no way he can know you might be in Pueblo, so he won't be looking for you."

"What if he was?" Andy said belligerently. "He doesn't know what we look like."

"I think he does," she said. "He knew who I was. He knew a great deal about the family." She looked around. "Where's Papa? And Mama?"

"He's in town, just in case you came in from another direction. Fleur's with the wagon about a mile from here. We didn't want to take it into town. It's pretty difficult to disguise," Daniel said. He chuckled. "So am I."

Lori returned his smile. "I really missed you, Daniel."

Daniel hesitated. "There's something else you should know. There are two men in town. Jonathon thinks they might be bounty hunters."

"Does one have white hair?"

Daniel nodded.

Lori's face paled. "He . . . Morgan . . . mentioned a man named Whitey. . . ."

Daniel raised his eyebrows as he noted that Lori used Morgan's given name. He made his own voice matter-of-fact. "I think you'd probably better go into town and fetch Jonathon. We might need some help."

She hesitated. "Daniel . . . you should know. He . . . the Ranger . . . his name is Davis, Morgan Davis. He looks exactly like Nick. That's one reason he went so far to fetch Nick, to bring him back. It's been his face on the poster as well as Nick's."

Cold apprehension shot through Daniel, almost paralyzing him.

Lori hesitated. "Nick *was* born in Colorado, wasn't he? He is my brother?"

"He is your brother," Daniel said, ignoring the first question. And he'd always believed that Nick was Fleur's child, if not Jonathon's. Why else would she be clutching a child in the middle of the Texas prairie? Still, something nagged at him. Something from far back. Something Fleur had murmured just after they had found her. He couldn't remember the exact words. He would have to try. While they waited, he would try to remember everything that happened that hot summer day more than thirty years ago.

Her frown lifted a little but not the trouble in her eyes.

"You go after your Papa," Daniel said. "I think it's better if Nick doesn't reach Pueblo."

She nodded reluctantly. "You will . . ."

"Nothing will happen to your Ranger," Daniel said softly, his eyes warning Andy again. "I swear."

Lori mounted Clementine. The horse was exhausted. She ran her hand down the beast's neck and looked back to Daniel. "Do you have any money?"

Daniel took several bills from his pocket. "Is that enough?"

Lori nodded. "She deserves some pampering."

He smiled. "I think you do, too."

"No," she said, and Daniel heard pain in her voice. "I don't deserve anything." She turned Clementine's head toward Pueblo. "I am so glad to see you, Daniel, you and Andy."

Daniel only wished she didn't sound so terribly sad as he watched her start back down the road, her slender back drooping slightly, so unlike the explosively joyful Lori he knew.

·   ·   ·

Whitey Stark was growing impatient. So was Curt's brother, Ford. Curt should have turned up by now. So should have Davis and his prisoner. Whitey knew Morgan Davis, knew he didn't waste time. He didn't like the idea he might have been outfoxed, that the telegram could have been a hoax of some kind. Someone in Laramie said the Ranger seemed sweet on the girl, though Whitey couldn't imagine Morgan Davis being sweet on anyone. He had, though, apparently put the girl up in the fancy Georgetown hotel.

Maybe the Ranger had gone so soft, he'd decided to let Braden go. Maybe in exchange for certain services. If what he was told about the girl was right, he could understand. Almost. Whitey never let women get in the way of money. They were too easily bought—the kinds he liked, anyway. Those who were easy and enthusiastic. He wondered what kind of woman might attract Davis. He might have to find out for himself. If he couldn't get Nicholas Braden, he could take Morgan Davis. They looked enough alike, for sure. Whitey liked the idea. Exchanging a dead Ranger for five thousand dollars in cash. It appealed to his sense of humor. Nick Braden might even be grateful and throw in some more cash.

Whitey was lounging outside one of the saloons when he saw the woman riding a palomino mare. Alone. His eyes slid over her. How many young women rode palomino mares? Especially young women who rode astride in a split skirt, and whose hair was somewhere between gold and light brown?

Lorilee Braden!

His gaze followed her as she rode down to the town livery and disappeared inside with her horse. He went into the saloon and fetched Ford with a gesture of his head, knowing he would follow him back out. Ford was afraid of him—Curt wasn't, but his little brother was.

"The girl's in the livery," Whitey said. "Let's get her."

"Why do we want her?" Ford complained.

"Hell, she could lead us to them . . . or we might be

able to make a little trade. She'll be useful, one way or another."

"You think they're around here, then?"

Whitey nodded.

"What about Curt?"

"Maybe he's trailing them. Maybe he was killed by a bear or some damn thing. How should I know?" Whitey said impatiently.

Ford stopped. "You think that Ranger got him?"

"How should I know?" Whitey repeated as they reached the livery. He stopped just outside the door. The girl was inside talking to the livery owner. He heard some of the words: ". . . oats . . . the best, and rub her down. As soon as possible. I might need her again today or . . . do you have a horse I can borrow for a short time? You'll have Clementine."

Whitey didn't hear the answer. He looked down the street. A few people were hurrying along it. A couple of kids were playing with hoops. He looked back into the livery. The owner's back was to him. He put his hand on his pistol and whispered to Ford, "You take the man from the back. Use the butt of your pistol. I'll grab the girl."

The girl's attention was centered on the horse, her hand running along its neck as Whitey and Ford approached. The livery man was just turning around at the sound of their spurs when Ford's pistol hit the back of his head. The girl looked up, her mouth opening in a scream when Whitey clamped his hand over it, and his hand hit the back of her head. He caught her as she started to slump to the floor.

"Get our horses," he ordered Ford, lowering the girl to the floor. As Ford did so, Whitey got his saddle and bridle. In minutes the two horses were saddled.

Whitey tied the girl's hands, then mounted and told Ford to hand her up to him. He placed her in front of him on the saddle. Ford went first, checking out the street. He nodded to Whitey, and they trotted out of the livery stable and away from town.

. . .

Jonathon nursed his beer. He liked drinking, sometimes to the point of excess, but he also knew when to control it. And that time was now. He had been sipping on the same beer for an hour. If he heard nothing soon, he would ride back to where Andy and Daniel were guarding the road. He was also keeping an eye on the two men who had been showing Nick's wanted poster all over town.

He saw them leave, and he wandered out on the porch, lighting a cigarette. When they went into the livery stable, he shrugged. Perhaps they were giving up. He went back into the saloon, wishing he were a younger man. Age was finally catching up with him. He was sixty now, really a few years over sixty, but he'd stopped counting. Nick had been right about settling down, but he'd refused to listen, and now his son was paying for that bit of self-indulgence on his father's part.

He would pay the bill and ride out to where Daniel was watching. Nothing was happening in town, no strangers other than the bounty hunters. He hoped that Lori had been right about Pueblo. He hoped she was all right, but he knew that Nick would make sure she was. They had always been close, those two. He and Fleur had loved their children, but he was the first to admit they hadn't been the best of parents. He'd always been a dreamer more than a practical man, and Fleur sometimes had spells. She'd be often completely divorced from reality, talking about places and times none of them knew.

Jonathon loved Fleur, had from the first moment he'd seen her so desperately clutching that baby when she was near death herself. But whatever happened during the preceding days had affected her. She remembered little about that time and grew distant when he or Daniel questioned her. She would, instead, start singing a lullaby, her eyes looking beyond them into another world. They had learned not to ask, or to mention the past, and Jonathon had accepted Nick as his own.

He reached the stable where his horse was kept and

went inside. He almost immediately saw the man stretched out on the wood floor near a palomino horse. Clementine! His heart pounded, thudded against his chest with abnormal rhythm. He leaned against a wall, then stooped down and shook the man on the floor. There was no effect. He found a pail and filled it with water from a pump, then splashed it on the fallen man.

Eyes fluttered open, stared at him. "What happened?" Jonathon whispered harshly.

The man's eyes were bewildered, trying to make some sense. His hand went to his head, and he groaned with pain.

"What happened?" Jonathon insisted.

"I don't . . . know. I was talking to a young lady, and then . . . I don't remember anything." He tried to sit, then moaned again.

"A pretty girl. Blond hair, amber eyes?"

The man nodded. "Fetch the . . . doc."

Jonathon nodded. He went out the door and hollered at someone in the street to fetch the doctor and sheriff. Then he went back in and saddled one of the two riding horses the Bradens owned. Andy had the other.

Without another word to the livery man, Jonathon raced the horse out of town toward Andy and Daniel.

They made a ridiculous party, Morgan knew, with that infernal pig trailing along behind. Not for the first time he wished there was some way of making pork chops out of it without breaking a child's heart.

But there wasn't, any more than there had been a way of reasoning with Lori or Nick Braden.

He couldn't stop thinking of her, couldn't keep his mind from remembering those tears. Or Beth's words. *She really does love you.*

Morgan didn't know much about love. He'd never had any. He supposed he'd loved Callum, but they'd never exchanged any kind of affection. He questioned whether he expected too much because he'd had so little experience with it. But surely it included some measure of trust.

He wondered, as he had during this whole day, what in the hell she was up to. She'd tried to enlist the aid of a sheriff in Laramie. Might she have done that again? Could he expect a hostile lawman? She didn't have any money, nor a gun, though that hadn't proved an impediment before. He still didn't know where she got the gun that she ambushed him with. She hadn't said, and he hadn't asked, knowing she wouldn't answer. It had been one more battle he had avoided, since he was only too well aware that his prospects of winning were slim.

So he had kept his eyes open, forced himself to stay alert, though he was exhausted from lack of sleep and tension. He'd found himself casting frequent glances at Nick, each time looking for more and more familiarities. He'd tried to talk to Nick, but received only blank, wary stares for his trouble. Morgan looked behind him. Mrs. Andrews was struggling valiantly, but she was obviously tired and straggling behind. He stopped, waiting for her to catch up. The pig with the ridiculous name was trailing right behind, evidently knowing where its bread was buttered or its bacon saved. Morgan wondered for a moment whether the pig wasn't a hell of a lot smarter than he was. Nick was abreast of him now, his hands rising to brush hair that had fallen over his forehead.

"Are you all right, Mrs. Andrews?" Morgan asked.

She smiled wanly, readjusting a fussing Maggie. "I think Maggie's getting restless."

"Can I take her?" Morgan had hesitated before saying the words, afraid Maggie would decline.

Beth Andrews whispered to Maggie, who looked at him suspiciously.

"I don't bite, Maggie," he said awkwardly, inwardly flinching at the reluctance in the girl's face. "I promise," he added with a small, wry smile.

The girl looked at Nick longingly.

"Go with him, Button," Nick said. "You wouldn't be comfortable without a saddle."

Beth Andrews whispered something else, and finally Maggie nodded. Morgan wished he knew what the bribe was, or then again, maybe he didn't.

He reached out and took Maggie, setting her gently in the saddle in front of him, one of his arms going around her to anchor her. She turned around and looked up at him, wide blue eyes that seemed to search his soul. Such innocent eyes. Even trusting eyes now as if he'd passed some kind of test. He smiled back, and he felt as if he had finally broken some kind of lock that had always kept part of him isolated and alone. It had started to break loose with Lori, and then with his complicated feelings toward Nick Braden, and now . . .

He was *feeling*. Pleasure at being touched, at the prospect of being loved. Pain in the uncertainty. But caring all the same. That fierce caring which made him understand why Lori did what she did, that enabled him to accept, even envy, that loyalty between Lori and Nick, the self-sacrificing that was so new to him. It was still uncomfortable, like a pair of new boots, this feeling. He suspected, though, that when he'd adjusted to it, it might become well worth the pain.

He felt a lump forming in his throat as Maggie leaned against him, as he looked toward the man he thought might well be a brother. When exactly had he cut himself off from feeling, from personal contact with other human beings? During the war? When Callum had died? Or had Callum instilled that within him when he was a boy? *Your father would be alive if he hadn't married. Rangers can't afford families. Your father was the best there was until he met . . .*

Morgan had been trained to be the best there was. Like Callum. And Morgan suddenly knew he didn't want to end like Callum. A hard man mourned only by other hard men. He wanted some softness in his life.

He wanted Lori. He wanted children. He wanted a family he'd never had. He wanted them all desperately now—but these were all frightening desires to him. He didn't know whether he could be good at any of that. He'd been good at only two things in his life: hunting and killing.

His arm tightened around Maggie instinctively as he heard a gunshot. Dust on the road just feet ahead spurted up, and he started to move his hand toward his gun, realizing suddenly that if he did, Maggie would fall or might be in the line of fire. He heard Beth scream, Nick curse as his eyes scanned the sides of the road. One man stepped out, a tall, lanky youth with hair the color of honey, his rifle pointed directly at Nick. On the other side Morgan saw another rifle.

And Morgan was helpless. Anything he did would endanger the child and Beth. If he took a chance and spurred his horse, a wild shot might well kill Maggie. He checked his horse, and slowly raised his left hand.

CHAPTER TWENTY-FIVE

"Andy!" Nick greeted his brother as his knees moved his horse abreast of Morgan Davis's mount. He looked around. Daniel Webster was standing now, a rifle in his hands.

Davis had stopped, raising his free hand, his other one balancing Maggie.

Nick grimaced. He didn't want it like this. He saw the fear in Beth's face, terror in Maggie's, resignation in Davis's—understanding, even, as he looked at Andy, then at Nick.

"It's all right," Nick told Beth. "My brother and a friend." He turned to Morgan, holding up his hands. "Hand Maggie to her mother and give me the key to these. Then you can unbuckle that gunbelt real slow. I may not have been able to pull the trigger, but I wouldn't guarantee the same from my friends."

The Ranger handed the child to Beth and took the key to the handcuffs from his pocket, handing it to Nick, watching as Nick unlocked them, then rubbed his wrists for a moment. God, it felt good to be free of them. He wanted to throw them away, but he had use for them now. It was time Davis learned some of the humiliation of being chained like an animal.

"The gunbelt," Nick urged.

"Don't do this, Nick," Davis said. "Don't keep running." There was an urgency in his face Nick hadn't seen before, but, then, the Ranger had been acting strangely all day, casting searching looks toward him. It was almost as if he had been holding a secret to himself. But there were no secrets between them. None Nick could figure.

"Easy for you to say, Ranger," he said, making the last word almost a curse. "Now hand me that gunbelt before my impatient brother does something we might both regret."

Morgan Davis looked toward Andy. Nick saw him taking measure, probably seeing the obvious resemblance to Lori in the blond hair, the golden eyes, the tall, slender grace. Andy tightened his finger around the trigger.

Davis unbuckled the gunbelt and handed it to Nick. Nick, in trade, handed him the handcuffs. "Lock them on," he said. "I think it's past time you knew exactly how they feel."

"What are you going to do?" The question was calm, the tone merely curious. Nick had struggled against his growing respect for Davis, but he had to admit to himself now that he was impressed with the man's integrity. He knew the only reason Morgan Davis had surrendered was because of Maggie and Beth.

"Merely make sure you can't follow me for a couple of days. Unless you make more drastic steps necessary. Now lock them, before Andy's finger starts itching any more."

"Lori?"

The question was aimed at Nick, who looked toward Andy for an answer.

"She went into town to get Papa."

Nick smiled. "They're all here?"

Andy nodded. "Ma's about a mile away with the wagon."

Nick turned back to Davis. "Satisfied?"

The Ranger didn't say anything, but his eyes seemed to bore right into Nick.

"We'd better get off this road," Andy warned.

Nick nodded. "The handcuffs," he reminded his former captor. "I'd hate to patch up another bullet hole in you."

Davis smiled ironically, then closed the bracelets on his wrists.

Nick dismounted and took the reins of Morgan's horse. "I think we'll do a little swapping here," he said. When the two men had changed mounts, Nick was on his own horse, Dickens. He rose in the stirrups, stretching, savoring the feel of leather underneath him again. Pure luxury. *His* horse. *His* hands free. He turned his attention back to Beth.

"Andy, this is Beth Andrews and her daughter, Maggie. Take them to Ma. I'll be there later to say good-bye. Daniel and I will take care of Mr. Davis."

Andy protested. "Why can't I . . . ?"

"Because I would feel better if I knew you were taking care of them," he said. He grinned. "And I want to see how you herd pigs."

For the first time Andy's attention went to Caroline, who had finally waddled up to the rest of them. "Awww, Nick, you don't mean that . . . pig goes with us?"

"Caroline?" Nick said innocently, but a smile lit his eyes. "But of course. She's Maggie's best friend, isn't she, Button?" he said, his voice softening as he leaned over and smoothed back a curl from the child's face. Maggie giggled, and Andy looked from one to the other, astonished.

Nick chuckled. "If my dour companion here tolerated Caroline, I suppose you can, too," he said. The smile disappeared. "And Andy . . . thank you."

A smile of pure pleasure shone across his brother's face. He nodded. "How long should I tell Ma?"

"No more than an hour. We'll just find a nice quiet place for my friend to get some much-needed rest." His voice was ironic.

Andy cradled his rifle in his arms and disappeared over the rise, returning in minutes mounted on a chestnut horse. He grinned at Beth and Maggie, the charming devil-may-care smile that had won him women's hearts all over Colorado—the same smile that had started all this trouble.

He bowed to them. "My pleasure, ladies."

Beth looked toward Nick, her face worried. He rode over to her, leaned over, and kissed her lightly. "I'll see you soon."

Beth hesitated. "Are you . . . sure about this?"

He gave her a slow, lazy grin and nodded. He wished he *were* sure, but he was committed now. Andy and the family had risked everything to free him. And the Ranger would be all right. For now.

But Nick knew Morgan Davis would come after him again. And again. Unless Nick killed him.

Nick reached down and took the rifles from Daniel, putting one in the scabbard and throwing the second the few feet to Andy. He watched Andy ride off with Beth, Maggie, the pack horses, and Caroline before giving Daniel a hand up to sit behind him. Then Nick turned away from the road, toward the hills and trees.

The irony of the situation did not escape Morgan. *Your father was the best there was until he met . . .*

The Braden family was turning out to be his nemesis.

He had expected nearly everything but this. He still didn't understand how the Braden family appeared in Pueblo—but, then, he had underestimated both Nick and Lori before. The fact that he was thinking of Braden as "Nick" now surprised him. Or maybe it shouldn't. He'd been thinking of him as a brother for a day, during the long ride. He threw that thought away for a moment. It was obvious Nick thought of him in a none too brotherly way.

At least Lori was safe. That was his one consolation. He still hoped he could change Nick's mind. He wanted to do that before he shared his suspicions with him. Nick, though, would be even more difficult to convince than before, now that he had the upper hand.

Except for the telltale birthmark. Would that strike Nick Braden as much as it did him? Except Braden was so sure of his past, of his family. Morgan understood why. Lori had been willing to do anything to help Nick, and the others were now. He wondered what it would be like to have that kind of family.

He moved his hands, and he understood Nick's frustration. Handcuffs had always been a tool to him, and he had never given much thought to how they might feel to one of his prisoners. They felt damn cold and hard. He was understanding Nick's frustration, his reluctance to return to Texas, more and more. If he was in Nick's position, he doubted he would have any faith in a man who'd had none in him.

They reached the river. The Arkansas, according to Morgan's map. *The map!* Lori must have seen it, guessed at their destination.

Nick stopped his animal, and now it was Morgan's turn to wait. Nick had the guns now; Morgan wore the handcuffs. The only weapon Morgan had was his knowledge that Nick Braden had no heart for violence. Morgan wasn't so sure about the dwarf who rode with him.

He watched as Nick lowered the small man. There was real affection between the two. Morgan saw it in the glances they exchanged. The man was older. Late forties or early fifties, and he had one of the most intriguing faces Morgan had ever seen. It was full of lively curiosity, and his eyes reflected both pain and acceptance. He held a gun as if he knew how to use it, and he studied Morgan with avid interest.

Morgan was getting used to the looks he received when he was near Nick. He slid down from his horse and stood there, as Nick had stood so many times, waiting to see what would come next.

Nick was a hell of a lot cleaner than Morgan was, mainly because Morgan had been too taken aback that morning by Nick's birthmark to bother to shave or bathe. His stubble was several days old, and he still had a mustache. Yet the man called Daniel couldn't seem to stop looking from man to man.

"My God," he whispered. "Lori said . . . but I didn't . . ."

"Crazy, isn't it?" Nick said cheerfully. "But watch him, Daniel. He doesn't give up easily."

"Takes after you, does he?" Daniel retorted.

Now Morgan knew what it felt like, being talked about as if he weren't present. He shifted his weight to the other foot as if to announce his presence, feeling awkward in the handcuffs. It was goddamn annoying.

Daniel looked at Morgan again, this time directly into his eyes. Morgan knew how alike they were, his eyes and Nick's, and he tolerated the inspection, hoping that something would jar a memory. How long had this man been with the Bradens? Lori had once said all her life. Had he been present at Nick's birth?

Nick was digging into Morgan's saddlebags, and Morgan didn't have to guess twice to know what he was after. He was still stronger than Nick, though the handcuffs were an obstacle. Still, Nick had made a damn good fight with them that night at the cabin.

Morgan looked back at Daniel. "I told him if he would go back, I could help him clear this thing up. Running isn't going to help. He'll be dead inside a year."

Daniel looked worried, thoughtful. "If he doesn't trust you, why should I?"

Look, damn you. Look. Morgan willed the small man to see the similarities, understand why Morgan wanted to help. Nick threw the leg irons at him. "You know what to do," he said with some bitterness.

Morgan looked down at them. "You planning to leave me alone here, chained to a tree?"

"Sounds reasonable to me," Nick said. "But Daniel will check on you frequently enough. Food and water. Blankets. Even conversation if you want some. Daniel's good at that. Forty-eight hours, and you can go."

"What makes you think I'll let Daniel go then?"

"Because I've come to know you, Ranger. You don't punish loyalty."

"We know each other too well," Morgan said. "I don't think you'll use that gun."

"But you don't *really* know, do you? I wouldn't kill you, but after the past few weeks I wouldn't be too sad about putting another bullet in you some place painful, if not fatal."

Morgan understood that. If he'd been Nick, he wouldn't feel too damn sad about it, either.

"Nick," Daniel suddenly said. "Maybe he's right. Jonathon says there's a couple of men in town looking for you. Bounty hunters."

Morgan felt a chill run down his back. Lori had gone into town. His eyes met Nick's suddenly, and he saw the same fear he knew must be in his own. "Did he describe them?" Morgan asked.

"Man with white hair. He was real distinctive, according to Jonathon."

Morgan turned on the little man with intensity. "How did you find out where we would be heading?"

Nick answered instead. "A telegram. She managed to send a telegram from Georgetown."

"That means they checked the telegraph office. It also means they know Lori was traveling with us," Morgan said. "They'll go after her."

Nick closed his eyes for a moment. It was Morgan's chance, but he didn't take it. Something else was more important at the moment.

"Daniel," Nick finally said, "stay here with him. I'll ride to the wagon, see if Lori is there."

Daniel gave him directions, then worried aloud. "She should have been back by now. She said she was coming back to the road." It was obvious he hadn't thought of the possibility of someone going after Lori. Otherwise, Morgan knew, he would probably have wondered about Lori's tardiness before now. The chill grew deeper inside.

"I want to go with you," he said to Nick. He knew it sounded arrogant, but he wasn't any damn good at asking favors.

"No," Nick said. "If she isn't with the wagon, I'll come back for you. Put on that leg iron before we waste more time."

Morgan thought about protesting further, even doing something physical, but he believed Nick's promise to return, and he didn't want to delay things more. He reached over and did what he'd ordered Nick to do so often. He didn't like it, particularly now. He wanted to go after Lori, and he clenched his teeth tightly shut to keep from saying anything, to delay Nick or to change his mind about returning.

Nick didn't show any satisfaction in the turnabout. He mounted his horse and with a slap to its backside galloped toward the road.

As Lori regained consciousness, she became slowly aware of being balanced on a horse by a strange hand. She tried to move her hands, but they were tied. She struggled to remember what had happened. Shadowy figures, then pain. That's all.

Her slight movements apparently alerted the man holding her. His arm tightened painfully just below her breasts.

"Coming awake, are you?" a voice said into her ear. It was an ugly voice, insinuating and taunting. The smell of him wrapped around her unpleasantly, and she tried to move away from him, but he merely tightened his hold, bruising her breasts.

"Don't squirm," he said, "or you might start something a little earlier than I planned."

She stilled.

"An obedient woman. I like that," the man whispered in her ear. "I hope for your sake you continue that way."

A shudder ran through her. "What do you want?"

"Merely to serve the purposes of law and order," he said, his hand going up to her breast and fondling it. He was deliberately trying to frighten her, to threaten her, and he was succeeding.

"Bounty hunter?" she said with contempt.

His hand became more punishing. "Have some respect," he said. "Your brother is a murderer. No need to be so falutin high and mighty."

Lori forced herself to remain silent. This must be the man Morgan warned Nick and her about. The partner of the one killed in the mountains. How had he found them?

Lori had learned from her encounters with Morgan. She had learned to wait and pick her time. She slumped in the saddle as if cowed. It cost her to do that; she wanted to yell and swear and spit. But that would accomplish nothing but make him more alert.

Her family would know now. She should have been back to them by now. They would come looking for her. Nick. Papa. Andy.

Morgan.

Her heart pounded as she thought of him. She had tried to avoid it since she left early this morning. She had tried to quiet the despair at leading him into a trap, tried not to think about the look in his eyes when he realized what had happened. What *had* happened? Had he reached Pueblo? Had Nick been freed? Had either of them been hurt?

She was so consumed with worry about them, she didn't have space in her heart to worry about herself. She was startled then when they came to a stop and she was unceremoniously dumped from the horse. She turned and looked up at her captor. His hair was white, although he was not an old man. His face was cruel, his eyes narrow and pale blue.

He dismounted. "Now," he said, "you're going to tell me where I can find Nicholas Braden."

Morgan stood and leaned against a tree. He couldn't remain sitting. He was too restless. Goddamn chains.

He looked over at Daniel, who was sitting on a log, a rifle nearby. "Nick mentioned conversation," Morgan said.

Daniel's eyebrows furrowed together thoughtfully as he studied Morgan. "Suits me," he said finally.

"How long have you been with the Bradens?"

Daniel smiled wryly. "No threats, no pleas?"

Morgan shrugged. "Wouldn't do any good, would it?"

"No."

"I don't particularly want to talk about the weather."

Daniel chuckled, despite the worry lines deepening around his face. He spread his small legs out. "I've been with Jonathon since I was a boy."

Morgan held his breath. "You were there when Nick was born, then?"

Daniel's eyes were almost black, but Morgan saw something flicker there. Caution?

Instead of answering, Daniel threw a question back at Morgan. "Why?"

"It's important," Morgan said tersely. For one of the few times in his life he wished he were better at . . . being subtle rather than demanding answers. He didn't know how to do anything but attack directly. He'd never felt it important before to skirmish around something he wanted to know.

"Why?" Daniel asked again, and Morgan made a sudden decision. He sat back down on the ground and pulled the boot off his free right foot, then the woolen sock. Without explanation or words he showed Daniel the bottom of his foot and watched the man's face pale.

"Nick has a mark just like it on his left foot," Morgan said. "I saw it this morning. The likeness, a coincidence maybe . . . but the birthmark . . . ?"

"Did you say anything to Nick?" Daniel's face was strained, his voice ragged.

"No . . . I wanted to be sure."

"I can't help you."

Damn this family's loyalty. Daniel knew something. Morgan sensed it. He felt urgency creep into his voice. "I was born in southwest Texas in 1844. July. Near where El Paso is now."

What little color that remained in the man's face left it. He closed his eyes as if trying to remember something, and then awareness passed across his face as his eyes opened again, and he stared at Morgan as if seeing a ghost. He stood and walked away, leaving Morgan to clench his fists in frustration.

Maggie was fascinated with the colorful Medicine Wagon. Beth watched her trail her fingers along the paint. She had already explored the interior. It was like a tiny house inside, incredibly efficient, with a tiny stove and its neatly made up beds. Nick had grown up here, Beth thought, in this small space. Nick and Lori, who had regaled Maggie with her adventures.

Still, Beth couldn't imagine it as home, nor could she imagine Nick being content in such a small place, with such a roving life. He had talked of his ranch, of his plans, with such wistful longing.

Fleur Braden had been gentle and welcoming but appeared rather ethereal, fragile. Everyone seemed to spare her feelings, to assure her that Nick was all right, that Lori was fine. And then she glanced away, her eyes fixed on some distant object that no one else could see.

Although Andy had been charming and scrupulously polite, he was obviously disgruntled that he had been given the job of nursemaiding her and Maggie when more interesting events were taking place elsewhere. He stalked restlessly around the camp, and Beth saw much of Lori in him, in the gold eyes and impatience, in the compulsion to "do something." She saw little of Nick, and she wondered for the hundredth time why Nick and Morgan seemed so much more alike to her than Nick did to his own family.

She also wondered about the Ranger's strange attitude all morning, his quick glances toward Nick, his attempts to start conversations he'd never bothered with before. He'd always seemed intense to her, but never as much as today, and his reaction to the Braden-family ambush had been exceedingly mild. It worried her. For Nick's sake it worried her.

Caroline bumped her for attention. The pig was wandering around looking for food, bringing a smile from Fleur, who was stirring a pot of something that smelled very good. Beth sighed. When Nick returned, decisions would have to be made. She couldn't stay here; there wasn't room, and where would she go with Caroline? A livery stable might keep the animal while she and Maggie took a hotel room. Then what?

Before she'd met Nick, she'd made plans. With the sale of the stallion and what little money she had, she would start a small restaurant in Denver, perhaps build it into a boardinghouse. But now she thought only of Nick. Where would he go? She'd never thought one could fall in love so quickly. It had taken months with Joshua, but now her feelings were just as deep, just as strong, and, she admitted with no little guilt, more exciting, more passionate.

She had such mixed feelings about the Ranger. She believed him but knew Nick didn't, and if there was the slightest chance that Nick might hang, shouldn't he strike for freedom? There must be hundreds of places he could hide. But she knew he would never take her and Maggie with him, would never risk their lives.

She swallowed, biting back the tears.

Andy yelled something, and she looked up. A man was riding in fast, and Beth immediately sensed it was Jonathon Braden. The man pulled up the horse in front of Andy. "There was no one at the road," he said.

"We got him, Papa," Andy said. "We got Nick. He's taking care of that Ranger fellow. They sure as hell look alike. Where's Lori?"

"Those bounty hunters must have her," the older man said. "I found her horse in the stable, the stable owner unconscious. I saw those two heading toward the stable earlier. Dammit. I must have just missed her. I was half-way hoping she might be here."

The two men stared at each other, and Beth felt the depth of their concern. She felt like an onlooker, and yet her heart was involved now, too. She really liked Lori, and Nick . . . Nick would be frantic.

"Where's Nick now?" asked the older man, a much older version of Andy, with gold hair now mixed with white, and a handsome, still youthful face, considering that he must be in his late fifties or early sixties.

"Down at the river. He should be back anytime now."

As if the words had summoned him, Nick appeared, a smile of greeting spreading across his face as he saw his father.

He trotted over to the older man and put out his hand, clasping the other's hand warmly. But the smile quickly disappeared at the expression on Jonathon Braden's face. "What's wrong?"

"Lori's disappeared. Clementine was still saddled in the stable, the owner unconscious. Those bounty hunters . . ."

"We have to go after them," Andy said.

"Where would that be?" Nick asked in a strained voice. "Where would we even start looking?" He ran his hand down his horse's neck as the horse apparently sensed his disquiet and moved nervously. Nick looked back toward the direction from which he'd come. "He warned us," he said almost to himself, then looked at his father. "They want me. Not Lori. I'm going to give them what they want."

Beth heard herself cry out, "No. They'll kill you."

"God knows what they'll do to Lori," Nick said quietly. He laughed bitterly. "I'm going to need Davis."

"The Ranger?" Andy said with disbelief. "You have us."

"I know," Nick said gently, and Beth felt her heart thud with the kindness and affection in his voice. And the strength. "And you were very good, you and Daniel. I don't know whether I thanked you or not, but you've grown up, boy. You've really grown up."

"Then . . ." Andy's voice was hopeful.

Nick shook his head. "For what I have in mind, only one person can help now. If he will." He hesitated. "Will you saddle the Ranger's horse, the one Beth rode in on? And wait here. It's important."

"But . . . ," Andy protested.

"I don't have time to argue with you. It may be the only way to keep Lori alive, Andy. Trust me, please. Maybe later."

Andy nodded reluctantly and immediately lifted the nearby saddle onto the Ranger's bay horse.

"Mr. Davis *will* help," Beth said clearly.

Nick looked around at her, his mouth softening. "You've always liked him, haven't you?"

"I don't know if 'like' is the word," she said slowly. " 'Respect,' maybe."

"I hope you're right." He looked down at her, longing in his eyes, as well as determination. He leaned down from his horse and his hand touched her face and then he kissed her. Softly. Slowly. In front of everyone.

It was good-bye. She knew it. She reached up, grabbed his hand, holding it for a moment. She felt a tear rolling down her cheek. "Be careful," she whispered.

He nodded, then trotted over to where his mother stood. He looked at her for a long time and then leaned down and kissed her cheek. Beth saw tears on her cheeks too, and she went over to her as Nick straightened. Beth clutched the woman's hand as the man who had so completely invaded her heart took the reins of the second horse from Andy and rode away without another word, without looking back.

CHAPTER TWENTY-SIX

Morgan tried to relax, but he couldn't. His orderly world had exploded into chaos. He had no idea how to right it again. He didn't even know whether he wanted to, not back to the way it had been. He knew he damn well couldn't return to the solitary world he'd built these past few years. In these past weeks he'd found a magic he'd never known existed. He loved and had been loved. It was a touch of heaven that he never thought to have, and he yearned for more.

And a brother. Daniel Webster's expression, if not words, had been the final confirmation he needed. It was uncharted, this discovery of family, and he didn't know what to do with it. Part of him wanted to tell everyone, most of all Nick Braden. He still could, by asking Daniel to go after him. But he knew how unwelcome would be the prospect of being related to the man who'd made his life hell. It would be a bitter shock to Nick, who apparently loved the family he already had.

Morgan knew he would be a damn poor substitute.

He stood, wishing the small man would return. Morgan had liked him. Daniel Webster was a man tempered by misfortune and made strong by it. There was a compassion in him, and even humor, where many would have had only bitterness. That Nick and he had so much affection for each other reflected well on both men, and Morgan knew that he would never again prejudge anyone. He had so readily believed the rumors about the Medicine Show, when rumors followed so many of that type of business. He had accepted the worst said about Nick and Lori because he usually accepted the worst about people. No wonder they believed the worst of him now.

The fact was, he had come to believe that Nick was the better man of the two of them. Nick had been friend and protector, while Morgan had been hunter and killer. Killer on the side of the law, but killer all the same. And now, as the leg iron pulled on his left ankle and handcuffs bound his wrists, he knew exactly the hopelessness and the frustration Nick had felt these past weeks, and Morgan wondered whether he could ever tell him they were brothers. Better to let him think that Andy and Lori were his siblings.

He could give him one gift, though. Whether or not Nick went back with him, Morgan intended to clear him. If it took him the rest of his life, he would prove Nick Braden innocent.

The sun was going down in the west when Daniel appeared again, seemingly out of nowhere. He seemed years older than an hour before. He handed Morgan a slender flask, and Morgan tipped it, taking an exploratory sip, then an appreciative one.

"Tell me everything you've heard about your birth," Daniel said, as if he'd suddenly made a decision. Morgan started to do just that when they heard the sound of pounding hoofbeats. They both turned in the direction of the sound.

Nick pulled up on Dickens. He had Morgan's horse, now equipped with Morgan's own saddle, in tow. He slipped down from the saddle and walked over to Morgan, fishing in his pocket for keys. He unlocked the handcuffs, then handed Morgan the key to the leg irons, ignoring Morgan's astonished look as the Ranger leaned down, unlocked his leg, and straightened up again.

Nick had taken his gun from his holster, was handling it as a man does before reluctantly giving it up.

"What in the hell . . . ?"

"I want you to take me into Pueblo."

"Take you . . . ?"

"They have Lori. Those bounty hunters you mentioned," Nick said, his voice nearly strangled. "I want you to trade me for her."

Morgan's heart stopped, then thudded heavily against its cage. "You know what will happen. They don't take back live prisoners."

"Will you do it?"

"Do you know where they are?"

Nick shook his head. "They apparently took her from the stable in Pueblo. That's why you have to take me into town, so they can make contact."

"And just hand you over?"

"That's right," Nick said evenly. "You've told me repeatedly my life expectancy isn't that long, in any event. You've also said you didn't care about the bounty on my head. This way you get Lori and get rid of me, and all the damn trouble that poster cost you."

Morgan wondered whether he deserved that or not. In either case, each word hacked through his heart like a rusty sword. "I have a better idea," he said slowly.

"Hell, I thought you would jump at it."

"Then you don't know me very well."

"I don't want to know you at all. I just want you to do this one thing. For Lori. I thought . . . you might care something about her."

"Will you listen for a moment?"

Nick was nearly shaking with anger. Morgan saw him visibly try to control it. "I'm listening."

"We'll trade places. If I shave off this mustache, no one will know the difference."

"Why?" Nick demanded suspiciously.

"Because I'll have a chance and you won't," Morgan said softly. "Because I won't hesitate to kill when it's necessary."

Nick retorted angrily, "I killed Wardlaw. That's what started this whole goddamn mess."

"Lori said you tried to avoid it, that he moved in front of a bullet."

"I'm no coward," Nick said furiously.

"That's for goddamn sure," Morgan said, one side of his mouth quirking up. "But killing takes practice, and you just don't have it. I'm not all that proud that I have."

Nick hesitated, out of arguments and out of time. "She's *my* sister."

"And I love her," Morgan said softly. "How will she feel if I do what you suggest?"

Nick looked stunned. "Love?"

"Odd, isn't it?" Morgan said. "I wouldn't have believed it myself a few weeks ago." He looked bemused before continuing. "My shaving gear is in the saddlebags." He looked down at the gun. "Can I get it?"

Nick nodded, the stunned look still in his eyes. "That doesn't mean I agree to your proposal."

"I know," Morgan said gently as he looked over at Daniel, who was listening intently. Morgan shook his head, warning the man not to say anything about their previous conversation. He nodded slightly.

Ten minutes later Morgan had finished shaving by the river. He looked up and saw Nick's face. He looked in the small mirror he was using, then up at Nick's. Christ, but they were the same. Without the mustache there were no differences, just those few lines around the eyes, a little more weathering of the skin on Morgan's face.

"Damn," Nick whispered.

Morgan rose. "My gun?"

"In *my* saddlebags," Nick said.

Morgan went over to the saddlebags and took out his gunbelt, the pistol in the holster. He checked it for ammunition and found it loaded. His knife was also in place. He took out the knife, cut the end of the saddle blanket into three thin strips, then tied the gun to the outside of the calf of his leg and pulled his trouser leg over it. He then tied the knife to the other leg. "They probably won't check for weapons, not if they believe I'm your prisoner. I'm usually pretty thorough," he said dryly.

"I know," Nick said. "Too well. But I'm still not sure about this. I'd rather . . ."

Morgan found the handcuffs on the ground where they had been left, picked them up, and locked them back onto his wrists. "Just think of it this way, Braden," he said. "If I don't make it, you're home free. And if I happen to take them with me, you can collect the reward. I hope to hell you take my body back as yours. You should like that piece of irony."

"I don't like it at all," Nick said. "I don't like anything about this."

"But it's Lori's best hope, and you know it," Morgan said quietly, all the mockery gone. "This way we're both armed. They won't be expecting it. All their attention will be on the man they believe is more dangerous, not the man in handcuffs. That gives me an edge."

"Even in handcuffs?"

Morgan nodded. "Even in handcuffs. Tell them you lost the key in a fight with me. I'll have it with me. I can slip out of them anytime I want."

"What if they don't believe it?"

"I have a certain . . . reputation," Morgan said matter-of-factly, without arrogance. "I don't make mistakes." His lips suddenly twitched. "Until I met Lori."

Nick ignored the last comment. "Why should they think you'd give me up, then?"

"Lori. A woman. They think that way. And they'll jump at the chance of taking you without fighting me. They don't like risking their necks. They much prefer bushwhacking and back shooting. They would think it's not all that important to me, anyway." Morgan shrugged. "They just figure you'd end up the same way, anyway, and that that's all I wanted. They wouldn't see the difference."

"I don't think I do, either," Nick said wryly. "Dead is dead. Whether by the law or bounty hunters."

"We always did have a difference of opinion on that," Morgan said.

"That's because you're not on the receiving end."

"No," Morgan allowed with a slight curl to his mouth. He held up his handcuffed wrists. "I'm beginning to see your point of view, though."

Nick stilled. "Does that mean . . . ?"

Morgan shook his head. "If we both get out of this alive, I still want you to go back."

"Want?"

Morgan shrugged. "Do you really want to go through this the rest of your life? Worrying about your back? About Lori? About the others?"

"You have it all figured, don't you?" Nick said bitterly.

"Yeah," Morgan said without humor, "I always have everything figured."

They took a room in town, the same hotel where Jonathon had been staying. The handcuffs were chafing Morgan's wrists, but he didn't dare take them off. The pistol was rubbing against his leg, and the knife wasn't any more comfortable.

Nick had been silent during the ride to town. He had dropped Daniel off near the Medicine Wagon but had stayed out of sight. Morgan knew he didn't want explanations. Neither did he.

Nick signed Morgan's name on the register. Morgan hoped that no one knew he wasn't left-handed. The clerk briefly protested the prisoner's presence, suggesting he be taken to the jail.

"I don't let him out of my sight," Nick said in a harsh voice Morgan recognized as close to his own. Nick was a natural mimic.

Nick then took his arm none too gently and guided him up to the room. "Ever think about being a lawman?" Morgan said, trying hard to keep sardonic humor from his voice. He didn't think Nick would appreciate it. Humor was rare for Morgan, but he felt the need to say something to break the tension.

Nick's glare was withering. He went to the window and looked out. Morgan followed him, leaning against the opposite windowsill. It was full dark now, but lights in the store windows made the streets visible. They heard a train whistle. More people were in the streets now, visiting saloons. Cowboys, train workers, drifters.

Morgan suddenly stiffened as he saw a lone rider stop down the street at a hotel. Nick looked at him curiously.

"Curt Nesbitt," Morgan said. "It was his brother I killed."

"You mean *I* killed," Nick said, his lips twisting in an ironic smile, referring to their changed roles.

"Well, he doesn't know it, and I think it's best he doesn't find out," Morgan said. "I've run into him before. Like Whitey, he's a bounty hunter who prefers to take back dead men."

"What do we do now?"

A current of warmth snaked through Morgan. A small bit of trust was developing between them. Not much on Nick's part, but a beginning.

"Wait for him to find us," he said. "He mustn't know that we already know they have Lori." He went over to the bed and sat down, leaning lazily against the wall.

The knock came approximately fifteen minutes later. Gun in hand, Nick cautiously opened the door as Morgan tried to look suitably sullen. It was the clerk who took one look at the gun, at Nick's dour face, and shoved a note into his hand.

"From a man who says he's a friend of yours," he said, and stepped backward cautiously before scurrying down the steps.

Nick turned to Morgan. "Damn," he said. "I've never frightened anyone like that before. I'd hate to think I've started looking like you."

Morgan started to smile, but his lips thinned into a

hard line as he walked over to read the note over Nick's shoulder.

> *Lori Braden is with us. North road*
> *out of Pueblo at ten tonight.*

"No threats, no evidence," Morgan said. "He's smarter than I thought."

"What time is it?"

Morgan took out his pocket watch. "Eight."

"How did they know we would be here?"

"Same way your family did, I expect. They're hunters, too. They would have checked the telegraph from George-town to see whether any messages were sent. When Lori showed up, they must have known we would be nearby."

Nick's brows furrowed together. "They *would* have found us in Wyoming."

"Yep, and not too long after I did."

Nick crushed the note in his hands and went back to the window. It was going to be a long evening.

Lori cried out as the fist hit her face again. She didn't want to. She didn't want to give him the pleasure. The man called Whitey seemed to enjoy inflicting pain.

But it had been unexpected. He had stopped for a while, then suddenly turned and hit already-bruised skin.

"Where are they?"

"I don't know," she said again. "I escaped from the Ranger two days ago. He was headed straight down to Texas."

"Then why did you send a telegram to your family to meet you here?"

"The . . . Ranger found out that I knew where they were headed. He overheard me talking to Nick. He changed course. I ran away."

"I don't believe you. I heard there was something be-tween you and Morgan."

"That pig! I shot him."

His hand traveled along her cheek. She was hog-tied, her hands bound behind her and then tied by a short rope to her ankles. She shuddered at his touch.

"Did you do that for the Ranger, too?" Whitey said. "Shiver like that?" His finger dug down into her shirt, finding her breast. "You like that? Or do you like being hit?"

"I can't tell you what I don't know."

He backhanded her. "I don't believe you. I want to know where they are."

Her head hit the ground, and she feigned unconsciousness. The other man, Ford, had reluctantly left earlier, ordered to check the hotels once more to see whether their quarry had arrived. She heard the man curse. She had to buy some time. She had to. Buy time for Nick to escape. She hoped he would be free by now. And Morgan?

Dear God, he didn't know what he was walking into, didn't know about the ambush her family had planned for him. She was afraid to try the ropes, afraid to give any indication that she was conscious. It was one of the hardest physical things she'd done, trying to remain so still when she hurt so badly. The rope was cutting into her wrists, her ankles, and her legs were cramping.

As long as possible. Hold out as long as possible, her mind kept repeating. One minute, then another. And another. Remember Morgan, how he seared his own wound. If he could stand that kind of pain, you can stand a lesser one.

Another moment.

Then she heard the horse coming. She would have prayed, but she didn't know what to pray for.

"Ford, did you find out anything?" Whitey asked.

"They're there all right. At the Trader's Post Hotel. I wrote what you told me. The north road at ten."

"A shame," Whitey said. "I was just beginning to like the idea of keeping her."

"You said . . ."

"I know what I said, but no woman is worth five thousand dollars," Whitey said. Lori felt his hand snake along her cheek again, and she couldn't help flinching this time. His flesh was cold and cruel and repulsive. "You hear that? I guess we'll just have to wait for another time. If they come, that is. They may not think you're worth it, trading your brother for you, and then you and I can have a high old time. I've never had no five-thousand-dollar whore before."

She turned around and spit at him, and he slapped her again.

"Do that once more," he said, "and I'll show you who's boss and take my chances with Davis."

"He won't trade my brother," she said with complete confidence. "And he'll kill you."

Whitey smirked. "So you don't hate him, after all. What a good little liar you are. Just how much is there between you?"

"There's nothing! I just know he doesn't release prisoners."

"Ah, but there's never been such a tasty reason before. Now shut up."

He walked away from her, joining his partner out of earshot. She squirmed, trying to ease her discomfort, but every movement only seemed to tighten the ropes. But far more painful than the ropes were the questions in her mind. Morgan wouldn't trade Nick for her. He *wouldn't*.

She couldn't bear that. She tried not to think about it, tried not to even consider the possibility. He never gave up prisoners. He'd said as much several times. Lori strained to hear the conversation between the two men, but they kept their voices too low. This was her fault. All her fault. If she hadn't sent that telegram . . .

If she'd only trusted Morgan.

Morgan and Nick got their horses from the livery, along with Clementine. They had walked past Jonathon Braden on their way out of the hotel. Nick went over to him and told him what had happened. "We'll get Lori," he said. "You go back to the wagon. We'll get her back there."

Jonathon Braden looked long and hard at Morgan, then nodded. "Thank you," he said, and turned away before Morgan could reply.

Morgan and Nick mounted at approximately ten P.M., walking their horses toward the north road. There was only a partial moon, but the stars were bright, and both men's eyes quickly adjusted to the dim light. The road was lonely, particularly when they were both so wary, not knowing if and when they might be ambushed or confronted. But here the land was flat; there were few places to hide.

They rode thirty minutes or more in silence. Morgan was used to this kind of tension, even that quickening speed of the blood that always occurred before action. His senses always became more acute, his mind aware of every sound, every movement.

He didn't like the handcuffs. He didn't like being impeded that way. He didn't like the fact he couldn't make the normal reach for his gun. He also knew he might well be dead before he could reach the hidden weapons. Whitey wouldn't keep him alive long, probably no longer than it took Nick to disappear with Lori, and even then he feared that Whitey would go after Nick. He'd painted an optimistic picture for Nick. He'd known it was the only way he would get his cooperation. Even now, though, he didn't know how long that cooperation would last.

He'd suggested that Nick wear Morgan's own gunbelt. Whitey knew Morgan was right-handed, and he was the kind of man who would note that detail. It put Nick at a disadvantage, but there was no help for it. If all went well, Nick wouldn't need his gun, in any event. And if worst came to worst, Nick also had the rifle in his saddle scabbard.

Morgan saw a figure on horseback ahead. He exchanged a brief look with Nick. Even in the very dim light he saw the tension in Nick's body. "Easy," he whispered.

"It should be me," Nick said.

"Don't be a fool," Morgan said, deliberately angering his companion. "It's too late now to change plans. The man ahead is Ford Nesbitt. We know each other, so acknowledge him with his last name. The other man is Whitey. The less you say . . ."

"I know you're not the most gregarious man I ever met," Nick said stiffly.

"Just take Lori out of here as quickly as possible. I can take care of myself."

"There's no telling what she'll do."

Morgan sighed. "You're going to have to take care of that."

Nick lapsed into brooding silence. They were nearing the man on horseback.

When they reached him, Nick nodded. "Nesbitt," he said.

The man wet his lips, and Morgan saw his nervousness. Even in the slight moonlight he saw sweat glistening on his face.

The man's gaze went to Morgan. "Hell, he's your double."

Nick shrugged. Morgan wondered whether he really looked that arrogant.

Ford Nesbitt looked distinctly uncomfortable. "Give me your guns."

"Hell, no," Nick said curtly. "You have yours. I have mine. Keeps things equal. Where's the girl?"

The man smiled. "Whitey said you'd be hot to get her. Guess he was right."

Nick started to turn his horse, and Morgan silently approved.

"Wait," Nesbitt said.

"Where's Whitey?"

"Right here," said a man's voice from behind them. "Just wanted to make sure you weren't followed." He was coming from behind them. Lori was in front of him, her hands tied, her body pinned against Whitey's by an arm.

In the darkness Morgan wondered whether she yet sensed the deception.

As Whitey and she neared, Morgan saw that her face was swollen, her dress torn. He knew a rage he'd never felt before. If not for the handcuffs, he would have gone after Whitey's throat. He sensed Nick's corresponding anger, heard his curse. Lori did too. Her head snapped in his direction, her eyes widening as she looked from one man to the other and back.

Morgan didn't know how she knew, whether it was the way they sat their horses, or . . . something else. But she knew. And said nothing. Morgan silently blessed her.

"Are you hurt?" Morgan asked softly, playing the role of dutiful brother, and her gaze returned to his. It was too dark to read the expression in her eyes, but she shook her head.

Nick was more forceful, befitting Morgan Davis. "I could kill you for that."

"She's all right," Whitey said. "Just a few bruises where she fell. Didn't touch anything important. Left that for you," he added with an insinuating sneer.

"Untie her and let her down."

"Not until we make a deal."

"What do you want?" Nick's voice was a growl. "Other than Braden."

"Your word you won't follow us."

"What makes you think I'll keep it?"

"Morgan Davis is famous for keeping his word," Whitey said.

Nick hesitated a moment. "Done," he said. "I'll give you Morgan Davis's word."

Morgan bit back a grunt of satisfaction. Whitey was too confident to catch that clever, sardonic bit of wording.

"No!" Lori's agonized protest interrupted the negotiation, and Morgan heard the sound straight through his soul. It hurt, but it also pleasured. She did care.

"Just think, Davis," Whitey was saying now, completely

ignoring her. "I'll be doing your work for you. You should be grateful."

"Untie her," Nick said with the same curt impatience that Morgan had so often used.

"Whatever you say, Ranger," Whitey said. He took out a knife and quickly cut Lori's bonds, whispering something into her ear before lowering her to the ground.

"No," she said again, stopping at Morgan's horse and looking up at him. He saw tears on her cheek, and he leaned down to wipe them away, forcing himself to make it a brotherly caress. He ached that he had caused her so many tears.

"It'll be all right," he whispered. She caught his hand, holding it for a moment until he forced it free and sat back upright as Lori went to Clementine and mounted.

"Real tender," Whitey observed sarcastically. He took Morgan's reins from him. "The key to the handcuffs?" The question was directed toward Nick.

Nick shrugged. "Lost it some time back. I was going to get a blacksmith to cut them loose and borrow another pair from the sheriff."

Whitey stared at him a moment, then took a knife from his belt and cut a piece of rope from a lariat on his saddle. He leaned over and tied Morgan's handcuffed hands to the saddle horn. "Looks like you're slipping, Davis."

Nick stared right back. "The handcuffs were all *I* needed," he said contemptuously.

"I don't take chances," Whitey Stark replied as he started to turn back.

"Stark!"

Whitey turned back to Nick.

"I want him returned alive."

Whitey smiled. "Depends on whether he tries to escape or not."

"I had no trouble," Nick said.

"I heard you were shot."

"That was Miss Braden. She apparently has all the guts in the family."

"That's what she said," Whitey chuckled. "I didn't believe it. A woman besting you. And you still want her?"

"That's why I want her," Nick said. "No one ambushes me and gets away with it." It was a warning, clear and simple, as much as an explanation.

"I'll remember that," Whitey said, then turned to his companion. "You stay and watch them, follow them a way."

Ford nodded.

Whitey spurred his horse into a trot, leading Morgan's horse. Morgan turned around. Nick and Lori were watching, but both soon disappeared as the night closed in around them.

CHAPTER TWENTY-SEVEN

Lori watched the two men disappear and turned on Nick. "How can you . . . ?"

He shook his head in warning, turning his horse back toward Pueblo. Lori had no choice but to follow him. When they had gone a short distance, she leaned over, pulling on his reins. "Nick . . ."

Nick turned around and looked back, then stopped. "Davis planned it this way. He has the key to the handcuffs, hidden weapons." He reached out. "Are you really all right?"

She nodded slowly. She was, physically. Just a few cuts and bruises. But otherwise? She wondered whether she would ever be all right again.

Lori swallowed hard. She still felt Morgan's touch on her cheek. Miserably, she remembered how many times he had asked her to trust him, and she'd refused. And now he was risking his life for her, and for Nick.

"Why?"

Nick was silent for a moment, wondering whether he should tell her what Morgan Davis had told him, and then decided he owed it to both Lori and Davis. "He said he loved you."

"How could he?" Lori whispered brokenly.

"Easily, Button," Nick said. "If I weren't your brother . . ."

But his teasing had no effect. She knew now that Whitey Stark was capable of anything. She remembered

Morgan's words about Whitey never taking in prisoners alive.

She had never quite believed him. She'd always halfway thought he'd used it as a threat, perhaps because she wanted to. It had been easier to believe he was the enemy.

"We can't leave him alone with them."

"I have no intentions of doing that," Nick said. "I gave his word, not mine. I think our father will be down this road a little way. We'll take Nesbitt and then go after Morgan."

"I'm going with you."

"The hell you are," Nick said roughly. "If you hadn't gone off on your own . . ."

He stopped suddenly, but the sickness in Lori's stomach churned viciously. "He wouldn't be in . . . so much danger," she finished for him.

His voice softened. "I know you were trying to help. And, to tell the truth, I was real glad to see Andy and Daniel. We just didn't count on those two."

Lori shivered. "How long do we have before he'll . . . kill Morgan?"

"He's afraid of Davis, or he never would have tried that trade instead of following and trying to ambush us," Nick explained, wondering how he knew this. But he did. "I hope my warning will protect Davis for a while, anyway. But when Nesbitt doesn't return . . ."

Lori shivered again. She was cold, so cold. So afraid for Morgan. So very afraid she would never have the chance to thank him.

Trust me! Even now she could hear that strained, agonized plea. Morgan Davis, she knew, was not a man who begged, who pleaded. And yet he had done exactly that, and she had turned her back on him. And still he was risking his life for them, for Lori and Nick. She knew suddenly he would have done it for anyone in his charge. He was not a man to abdicate responsibility. She'd observed that stubborn integrity from the beginning, but her heart had been too confused to understand it.

Nick stopped his horse and motioned for Lori to do the same. They sat there several seconds, listening for Ford Nesbitt, listening for hoofbeats from the other direction. There was nothing.

"Do you think he went back?"

"Whitey told him to follow us to town. I don't think he'll cross him." Then they heard the soft snort of a horse. "He's there," Nick said. "If only Pa or Andy would come along . . . or if there was some cover."

But there was none on the road, and Lori guessed that was why it had been chosen. They needed a stranger to approach Ford, to pass him, to get behind him and get the drop on him. And they knew Nesbitt had never seen Jonathon Braden. If Nick suddenly turned on Ford, there could be gunfire, and Morgan would surely die. The sound of a bullet carried a long way out here.

Then, seemingly out of nowhere, Jonathon appeared. He nodded to them, then stopped.

"There's a man down the road, following us," Nick said. "If you can get behind him . . . and take his gun."

"Without any noise," Lori said.

Jonathon nodded. "I think I can do that." He took a pouch from his belt and balanced it in his hand. "I'll just get a little clumsy."

His gold pouch. One of his props. Mixture of coins and nuggets. Fool's gold, most of it, but enough of the real thing to lure a greedy mark into a fool's bet. His gaze went to Lori. "Are you all right, Lorilee?" He was always formal with her name.

She nodded, wishing everyone would stop asking her that when she wasn't all right at all. "Thanks to the Ranger," she whispered.

He reached over and touched her. "Never had much use for lawmen, but this one might be different."

"He's very different, Papa," Lori said.

Her father looked as if he wanted to say something else, but there was no time. He raised his voice to carry.

"Sorry to hold you folks up, but maybe someone else

can help me out." He spurred his horse into a canter, and
Nick and Lori forced their horses on, their ears straining
in the darkness, hoping they wouldn't hear a gunshot.

Jonathon made one of his few bargains with the Almighty.
He'd done it twice before, and both times his awkward
prayer had been answered. The first was that Fleur and
the baby would survive so many years earlier; the second
that he and Andy would reach Pueblo in time to save his
oldest son. It didn't seem odd to him at all that now he was
praying to help the man whom he'd been praying against
just a little while earlier.

He had accepted the vagaries of life long ago, even
enjoyed them. He'd made few rules for himself, and for his
family. One of those few was repayment of a debt. He
owed that Texas Ranger now. Just as he would have reluctantly killed him earlier, he was now determined to save
him.

He hadn't believed his eyes when the Ranger took
Nick's place. He hadn't believed that two men could look
so much alike. But it was true, and now he had to do what
little he could to right things.

Jonathon soon encountered the man who was following
his two oldest children, and he drew his horse over so the
man couldn't pass without going around. "I wonder if you
can help me, sir," he said politely.

"Get out of my way," the horseman said rudely.

"Just simple directions, and I'll be on my way. I have an
appointment at a ranch around here . . . I'm a govern-
ment man here to purchase some horses." Just then the
pouch fell from where it had been tied around his wrist.
Several of the pieces rolled out along the ground, catching
what little light the partial moon gave.

Ford Nesbitt was out of his saddle, scooping up one of
the nuggets, eyeing it greedily, when the butt of a gun hit
the back of his head.

.   .   .

Daniel knew his role was to keep Fleur calm, Fleur and now Beth and Maggie. Andy was reluctantly staying, but he wasn't any help; he'd been pacing up and down like a caged bear. Daniel wasn't sure how long he could keep him there. The only way thus far was to convince him this was where Jonathon and Nick would turn if they needed help. If Andy went off on his own, Daniel warned him, he might not be found when needed.

The strategy had worked thus far.

Daniel had brought his chair to the fire and placed it next to Fleur. It had been made especially for him, and he sat around the fire with the others. None of them had eaten much of the stew bubbling in the pot over the fire. He made conversation until Beth disappeared to put Maggie to bed. Daniel then turned to Fleur and tried to choose his words carefully. But now he had to know the truth about Nick.

"The Ranger . . . who was bringing Nick in," he said, "could be his twin. I've never seen such a close likeness."

Fleur just rocked in her chair, her eyes focused on the flames.

"He has a birthmark on his right foot," Daniel continued conversationally. "Just like Nick's on the left foot."

The rocking of Fleur's chair stopped.

"His name is Davis, Morgan Davis, and he was born just about where Jonathon found you all those years ago. The same year as Nick. The same month."

Daniel looked at Fleur's face. She was as still as stone. Her face as white as that same stone washed clean by a fast-running stream. "No," she whispered. "It can't be."

Daniel swallowed hard. "When you were still delirious, I remember you saying 'poor babies.' Was there more than one, Fleur? Did you have more than one?" He knew Fleur had nursed the baby; therefore, she must have been the mother. He also felt, from the conversation he'd had with Morgan Davis and what he'd heard between Davis and Nick, that Morgan Davis was most probably in love with Lori. His half sister.

Emotions flickered across Fleur's face in the firelight. Daniel saw memories trying to surface. There was fear, reluctance.

"Fire," Fleur said in a whisper. "I saw the fire. He couldn't have survived."

"He did," Daniel said softly, not knowing exactly what she was saying, but knowing it was necessary to keep her talking, to keep the memories alive. Fleur had often retreated into a world of her own. Was this why? Because she thought she'd lost a child to fire?

Her hand reached out and clutched his. She swallowed hard.

"What happened?" Daniel questioned gently.

"Nicholas is mine," she said.

"Of course, he is," Daniel soothed her.

A faraway look came into her eyes. "He didn't really die of the fever. Not really. God gave him back to me."

Daniel's blood started to run cold. "How did God give him back?"

Fleur started rocking again.

"Fleur," Daniel insisted, "how *did* He give him back?"

Fleur started singing a lullaby.

Daniel waited patiently until she finished. "Tell me about the first Nicholas," Daniel said.

"He died . . . just like my husband. Cholera," Fleur said.

Daniel closed his eyes. He and Jonathon had always known there was a deep sadness in Fleur. It was one of the reasons Jonathon had always been so protective of her: that vulnerability, that haunting sadness that clouded so much of her life, that often made her retreat into another world.

"Where did you find Nicholas?" he persisted, wondering whether he should or not. Yet this was too important to Nick not to know. To Lori.

If the Ranger lived. If he didn't, perhaps everyone would be better off not knowing. Everyone but Daniel. He had to know.

"The stage . . . I was going home to Kansas after . . . my baby and husband died . . . and the stage stopped to change horses. The woman was having birth pains before she should. I stayed. I didn't want to. I've never been good at that, and I still hurt so . . . from losing my own. But . . . the husband . . . was so frantic, so insistent."

"Then what?" Daniel said, hoping to keep her going before she faded away again.

"She had two babies . . . two boys. We'd been warned about Comanches, and we were getting ready to leave. I was putting one baby in the wagon when . . ." Her eyes clouded with tears.

"When what?" Daniel urged gently.

She blinked, and her hand went over to Daniel's, clutching it. "The horses bolted. I don't know how far they ran, but the wagon turned over, and then I saw . . ."

"What?"

"The cabin. Smoke. Fire. No one could live through that. I knew they all had to be dead. I started walking. I don't know how long I walked. I just knew that God had given me another chance, that I had to save this baby." She looked down at Daniel. "I thought they were all dead. But . . ."

Daniel waited patiently. She was alert now, the fog gone from her eyes.

"They had birthmarks. Half hearts on their feet that would have fit together to make one heart," she whispered. "That's what I thought then. I tried so hard to make Nick not miss that second half." The tears were flowing harder now. "But he did," she said. "I know he did. He used to wander by himself, and I always sensed he was looking for something, for someone." She buried her head in her hands. "What have I done?"

"You saved a baby," Daniel said gently. "And you and Jonathon gave him a fine life with much love. He's a good man, Fleur."

"And . . . the other one?"

Daniel nodded. "Also a good man, I think."

"They . . . don't know?"

"The Ranger suspects. Hell, he knows, I guess. Inside he knows. That's why I suspect he took Nick's place."

"And Nick?"

"He has no idea."

"What if . . . the Ranger is killed?"

"Then I think we should keep this to ourselves," Danie said softly. "But I think he's very capable. Very capable indeed."

Morgan cursed bitterly to himself. The key to the hand-cuffs was in his hat, and there was no way in hell he could get it as long as his hands were tied to the saddle horn. Whitey was shrewder than he'd thought.

But Nick had played his role well. His last admonition about keeping him alive was well placed. Whitey would probably wait at least until he was out of earshot.

He wondered whether Nick would come after him. He doubted it. Even though Nick Braden would probably have to tie Lori to a horse to keep her out of this. He smiled at that. She was a she-cat. But, like Nick, he didn't want her involved. And Nick certainly had no reason to help out the man who had dragged him across Colorado.

No, he was on his own. As he'd always been. As he'd always planned to be. It was what he wanted, what had been drummed into him since he was a boy. Never depend on anyone, other than fellow Rangers.

A brother. And Lori. In just a matter of weeks all that advice had come to naught. He found a heart couldn't be told whom to love, or what to want. He'd also discovered exactly how lonely he had been, how much a part of him had been missing. He had dismissed it as fancy years ago, this idea of something missing. But even when he and Nick had been at loggerheads, they had worked so damned well together. At the cabin. When they were ambushed. And now. Neither of them needed to explain anything. They just knew.

And Lori. Lori with the golden eyes that looked at him with such anger and longing. Lori, who had cried for him. No one had ever cried for him before.

He had never made her laugh. He regretted that. He didn't even know if he could. But he would like the chance to try. He would like to see her smile, not with sadness, but with the pure joy he knew she was capable of. He wanted to learn to share it. Dammit, he wanted so much now. It was as if he'd never really lived.

Finally Whitey came to a stop. "We'll wait here for Ford," he said, untying Morgan from the saddle horn and pushing him from the saddle before Morgan could slip down. He landed on his side, and Whitey was next to him, tying his feet together with a rope. He then tied his elbows behind him, stretching the chain between the handcuffs as tight as possible so Morgan could barely move.

"Davis bought you a little time," he said. "I don't carry irons like he does. Don't need them for dead men, and you're as good as dead anyway. You should be grateful. A bullet's a hell of a lot better than a noose."

He didn't wait for an answer but went over to his horse and took a canteen from the saddle. He took a long pull from it, and Morgan caught the scent of whiskey. He just lay there, hoping that Whitey would accept Nick's word that the prisoner presented no threat.

It was one of the hardest things he'd ever done, but he would have to go into contortions to reach the key to the cuffs now. His hat had dropped to his back, held only by the leather thong around his neck. He would have to twist his neck, work the hat over his head, and reach the lining with hands that had damn little movement.

How long would it take for Ford Nesbitt to return? Once he did, Morgan suspected they would waste little time in ridding themselves of a live man.

Christ, but he hurt. The bonds bit into both his ankles and arms. Think of Lori. Think of that tremulous smile. But all he could think of were her tears. If he ever got out of this, he swore he would never cause her so much as a blink again. Whitey took another long pull from the canteen. That's right, Stark, keep drinking, Morgan thought. Whitey walked impatiently to where he could see the road, giving Morgan a chance to try to twist the damn hat off.

Whitey turned abruptly and Morgan stilled. "That must be one superior piece of goods your sister has," he said, "for Davis to give you up."

Morgan tried to hold his temper. He was Nick Braden. If Whitey figured for a moment he was the Ranger, Morgan knew he would die immediately.

Whitey came over and prodded him in the side. "Nothing to say? I had fun with her myself while we was waiting together."

"Bastard!" Morgan spit out.

"I wondered what it would take to rile you," Whitey said.

Morgan kept his mouth shut. He knew Whitey was baiting him, just like a bully pulling wings from a fly. He wasn't going to give him that satisfaction, nor an excuse to shoot him now.

"Guess Davis was right," Whitey said. "No gumption, none at all." He aimed a kick at Morgan's ribs, then another. "That Ranger didn't happen on one of my partners, did he?"

Morgan moaned. His chest felt as if it had caved in, but the sound was mostly for Whitey's benefit. The foot rammed into him again. "Answer me."

"I don't know what you mean," Morgan managed.

"You didn't happen to see a big man, black hair and beard?"

"Haven't . . . seen anyone since Georgetown."

Whitey turned away, as if bored, and retreated to where he could watch the road.

Morgan didn't know how much time passed. His ribs hurt like hell, and every movement was painful, but still he tried to untangle his hat from around his neck. He had just started twisting his head when his ears picked up the sound of a horse, a sort of snorting sound. The ground

was too soft to hear the hoofbeats. It had to be Nesbitt.
Morgan knew Nick's horse would greet his own once the
familiar scent reached it, so it wasn't he. He felt suddenly
forlorn, disappointed, though he knew he shouldn't be.
Nick Braden had no reason to come back for him, and
every reason not to.

He angled his head sharper as Whitey's attention riv-
eted on the road. Finally the hat fell over his head, dropping to the ground. Ignoring the increasing pain in his
chest, Morgan twisted his body this time, one of the fingers on his right hand managing to reach the key inside
the lining of the hat. Morgan glanced up. He saw a man on
horseback appearing out of the darkness. He was wearing
Nesbitt's duster and hat, and riding Nesbitt's chestnut
horse, but there was something different.

Frantically, Morgan tried to unlock the cuff on his left
wrist, but the bonds pulling his elbows back and stretching the chain taut gave him no leeway. He pulled, feeling
the ropes cut into his skin.

He looked up again. The man, until now shielded and
fogged by darkness, was closer. There was no doubt now.
Nick Braden. And Nick was no match for Whitey. He tried
again, and then there was a hand on his shoulder quieting
him. He glanced around quickly. Jonathon Braden! The
man had a knife in his hand and quickly cut the ropes
behind Morgan, and Morgan unlocked the cuffs. The man
faded off into the darkness as Morgan bent down and retrieved the pistol tied to his ankle and silently got to his
feet.

Just then he heard Whitey curse loudly as he discovered the rider wasn't Nesbitt, and his hand went to the six-
shooter in its holster.

"Whitey!"

At the sound of Morgan's harsh voice, Whitey whirled
around, his gun now out and pointing toward Morgan.
Morgan fired, and Whitey sprawled on the ground, his
body twitching a moment before stilling.

Morgan stooped next to him and felt for the pulse in his

throat. There was none. He stood painfully and walked slowly over to Nick. He was too filled with emotion to say anything. He simply held out his hand, and Nick hesitated a moment, then leaned over and took it.

"Would have been here sooner," Nick said, "but Pa had to circle around on foot. We didn't know what . . . the situation would be, but we figured another hand might be useful."

"Lori?"

"Holding a shotgun on the other one back on the road. That was the only way we could keep her out of this."

Morgan felt himself grin foolishly. He was glad it was too dark for any one to see it. "I owe you," he said finally.

"No, you don't," Nick said. "We . . . Lori and me . . . owed you. You didn't have to change places with me."

Morgan felt strangely awkward and humble. *Humble.* By God, that was a new one. His fellow Rangers would have a hoot over that.

The other man, Jonathon Braden, approached. Morgan remembered him from the bar and from months ago when he'd started tracking Nick. "Sir," he said, "my thanks."

It was too dark to see the expression in the man's face, but Morgan felt himself being studied as though he were some peculiar specimen. This man was Lori's father. Nick thought him his father. Morgan remembered his first impression of Jonathon Braden. A con man, pure and simple, a crook, a charlatan. But a charlatan wouldn't have done what he'd just done, wouldn't have raised Lori and Nick with that fierce loyalty, wouldn't have made a friend out of a man many would consider a freak. Morgan again swore to himself he would never make quick judgments.

"You're the man dead set on taking my son to hang," Jonathon said without friendliness and refusing Morgan's proffered hand.

Morgan's lips quirked up in a half smile. He knew where Lori and Nick had learned stubbornness. "I was," he admitted.

"And now?" Jonathon demanded.

Morgan looked toward Nick, who dismounted from the chestnut. "I still think it's best for him to return to my Ranger post and let me get this straightened out. This is only a taste of what will happen if he doesn't." It was one of Morgan's longest speeches, heartfelt and pleading.

Jonathon looked up at Nick, and Morgan sensed the man who had helped save him would just as quickly kill Morgan to save his son.

"He's right, dammit," Nick said slowly, obviously hating each and every word. "I won't keep putting you all in danger."

"Do you trust him?" Jonathon's words were doubtful, and Morgan wished like hell they wouldn't talk as if he weren't there.

"I guess I just did. We all did," Nick said. He looked down at Morgan. "Lori's going to be crazy if we don't get you back in one piece pretty soon. You all right?"

Morgan didn't know when he'd felt better. His body damned well hurt, but he knew an elation now he'd never felt before. Lori was waiting for him. The man he believed to be a brother had just risked everything for him, including his life and future. He wanted to say something, wanted to say it now. But he had to be sure. He had to talk with Jonathon and Fleur Braden first. He had to be absolutely sure.

Morgan nodded belatedly in answer to Nick's question. "We'll take Whitey and Nesbitt into the sheriff's office, and I'll make sure they hold Nesbitt for kidnapping."

"Always the lawman," Nick said somewhat bitterly, but also with resignation. He rode over to where Jonathon stood and gave him a hand up behind him. "Lori and Pa can go back to camp. They're probably worried sick."

"You go, too," Morgan said. "I expect Mrs. Andrews and a little girl are more than a little anxious."

Nick couldn't hide his astonishment. "You'd trust me?"

Morgan walked over and picked up the handcuffs he'd discarded. When he returned, he saw that Nick had tensed. "I can use them for Nesbitt," he said, tucking them into his belt.

He went over to Whitey and started to lift him when he had to stop for the pain in his ribs. A groan came from deep in his throat, and Nick stared at him a moment. "What . . ."

Morgan tried to shrug it off, but Nick reached down and with Jonathon's help laid Whitey's body over the saddle, tying him there. Morgan watched gratefully, then mounted his horse as Nick mounted Nesbitt's chestnut and helped Jonathon up behind him. Morgan turned to Nick. "You really planned to go up against him yourself?"

"If I had to," Nick said. "But I had confidence in you. You're too damn ornery to die."

Morgan chuckled. "That why you saved my skin?"

Nick grinned back. "Don't remind me."

Morgan nodded, and the three of them started back to Pueblo.

Lori had the rifle aimed directly at Ford Nesbitt, who was tied and gagged when Morgan reached her. He slid off the horse, and she ran into his arms, her own going around his neck and holding him tightly to her.

"Ah, Lori," he whispered. "Dear God, I was worried about you. Are you really all right? He didn't hurt you?"

"No," she whispered. "And you?"

"Your brother says I'm too mean to die." Lori pulled away from him for a moment, studied his face. "We've made peace of sorts," Morgan said gently. "He and your father are going back to your camp. I'm going to take Whitey and . . . Nesbitt into town."

Lori's gaze moved to the man tied to the horse. "Dead?"

Morgan nodded.

"You or Nick?"

"Me, but I couldn't have done it without Nick or your father."

"I . . . when I saw you taking Nick's place . . ."

"Hush," he whispered. And his lips pressed down on hers, tasting their sweetness, delighting in their welcome. He wanted to do more, he wanted to deepen the kiss, to expend all that terror he'd never felt for another person before. But her injuries needed attention. He reluctantly took his mouth from hers, his finger barely touching a swollen, bruised place on her face. "It's good he's dead," Morgan said, "or I would kill him right now in cold blood."

"I really am all right," Lori said, trying to make her voice light, but Morgan saw the dried blood around her wrists, her torn dress. Rage surged through him again.

"I'm going to take you to a doctor," he said.

To his surprise she nodded. "And then what, Morgan?" Her voice was soft.

"We'll stay in town tonight," he said. "You can get some rest and medical attention, and I can take care of our friends here. It might take a while."

"Nick?"

Nick stretched wearily in his saddle, then said somewhat dryly, "I'm going back with him to . . ." He paused. "El Paso, is it?"

Morgan nodded, and Lori stiffened against his body. Morgan knew a moment of resentment. Even jealousy.

"My choice," Nick said simply. "He was right. I can't keep running the rest of my life. I have to trust him. I don't have any alternative."

"I'm going with you," Lori interrupted.

"I thought as much," Morgan said grimly, resignation in his voice. "Nothing I say or do will make any difference, will it?"

She shook her head. "No. I'll just follow you again."

Morgan didn't want to ask the question hammering in his head: because of him, or Nick? He wasn't sure he wanted to know. It would be both heaven and hell to have her with them. He helped her mount Clementine and then mounted his own horse. Nick had also changed mounts, helping a bound Ford Nesbitt up on his chestnut while he took his own Dickens.

As they reached the outskirts of Pueblo, Nick and Jonathon took one trail, Lori and Morgan the other with their prisoner and Whitey Stark's corpse. There were no words this time. They had been said, and they all knew what lay ahead. Suspicion lingered. Morgan could feel it in the other two men if not Lori. He told himself it was natural; it would take a long time to earn Nick's confidence completely.

And in a matter of hours, perhaps he would learn whether his own suspicions were true, that Nick was his brother.

CHAPTER TWENTY-EIGHT

Nick guessed it was early in the morning by the time he and his father reached the Braden camp. They had ridden mostly in silence, except for a few words about Lori, a few questions about Morgan Davis.

"He sure as hell looks like you," Jonathon said.

Nick was getting increasingly irritated at hearing the obvious. He nodded.

"He seems sweet on Lori."

Nick nodded again. He didn't know how he felt about that now. He'd been furious when he'd believed the Ranger had been trifling with Lori. He didn't think that anymore. But he damn well wasn't sure fun-loving, exuberant Lori would be happy with a dour lawman.

"And Lori on him," his father probed further.

Nick nodded again.

"Dammit, boy. You aren't saying much."

"Nope," Nick said, realizing that he sounded just like Morgan Davis. There was something to be said for few words.

Despite the lateness of the hour, a fire was crackling merrily, and Nick made out four figures around it. His mother. Beth. Andy. Daniel. Andy bounded up to meet them.

"What happened?"

Nick waited until he dismounted and neared the fire to answer. He smiled at Beth and saw the sudden glory of her smile. "Both Lori and Morgan Davis are fine," he said.

"I think they both needed a little doctoring, and Morgan needed to talk to the law about a dead body." Nick suddenly realized he'd used Davis's first name.

"Lori?" Fleur said. "Why a doctor?"

"Just some bruises and cuts." He grinned at Beth. "I really think she wanted to stay with Morgan."

" 'Morgan'?" Beth's eyebrows raised.

"He saved my life, and I . . . helped save his. I guess that puts us on a first-name basis."

"Does that mean he's letting you go?"

Beth was standing now, and he took her into his arms. "It would, if I wanted it." His arms pulled her to him. "I decided to go back with him, get this settled once and for all. I can't even think about the ranch, or a . . . family until then. I've discovered recently that's very important to me." His eyes met Beth's in the firelight. Hopes, even promises, flashed between them. He swallowed hard. She felt so right in his arms, her body leaning trustingly against his.

He lifted his gaze from her serious face and settled on his mother. She'd been crying. Daniel was next to her, his solemn face looking years older, graver than Nick had ever seen it.

"Don't worry," Nick said. "I've developed a certain confidence in Davis, despite . . ."

Daniel stood up, looking somehow regal in his earnestness, in the somber look on his face. As long as Nick had known him, he'd never seen anything quite like it.

"I'll help you with the horses," Daniel said.

The offer was more than that, and very odd coming from Daniel, who rarely interfered. He had something to say, and Nick wasn't sure he wanted to hear it. He wasn't going to change his mind now about going back to Texas. He wasn't going to risk Lori or Andy again, and he wasn't going to surrender every hope and dream he'd had. Davis held out his one hope. It might be one in ten, but it was a hell of a lot better than his odds during the last months.

Nick reluctantly let go of Beth's hand. Andy started to

get up and help, but Daniel shook his head, and Andy sat back down, a heavy scowl on his face.

"There's a stream just over to the left," Daniel said. "The horses look tired."

"They are," Nick said. "They've been going since dawn this morning, and every day between dawn and sunset before that."

"He drives real hard, does he?" Daniel asked.

Nick chuckled. "You could say that."

They reached the stream, and both men allowed the horses to drink, silent as they did so. Nick was waiting. Daniel had something on his mind, something very important.

"What do you think of Davis?" Daniel finally asked.

"I don't know," Nick said simply. "Christ, I hated him for a long time, but lately . . . well, we won't ever be friends, but I've learned to respect him." A raised eyebrow asked Daniel why the question.

Daniel dug a heel into the dirt. "Fleur asked me to talk to you. She . . . couldn't."

Nick was thoroughly confused now. "Talk to me about what?"

"Maybe you'd better sit down."

Nick was growing more and more confused. "I don't think I want to sit down. Spit it out, Daniel. Like you usually do."

"Fleur . . . I . . . well, we think that Ranger is . . . could be . . . your twin brother."

Nick felt as if he'd been felled by an oak tree. Or stabbed in the gut. The ground seemed to fall away from him. "I don't understand."

"She told me tonight, Nick. I didn't know myself. I knew that Jonathon wasn't your real father. I was . . . there in Texas, near where El Paso is now when he found her in the desert, a newborn baby in her arms. She was nursing the child, so we assumed it was hers. When Jonathon and Fleur married, they just both claimed you."

Nick wished he had sat. He did so now, reins trailing through his hands. "But . . . how . . ."

"I just found out tonight. The Ranger . . . Davis . . . suspected. He showed me his right foot this afternoon. Nick, he has a birthmark identical to yours. So I asked Fleur." Daniel looked down at the ground. "She told me she had just lost a boy, a boy named Nicholas, when she stopped to help a woman giving birth. Twins. They were attacked by Comanches. Fleur was putting one of the babies in a wagon, and the horses ran off while she was in it. When she looked back, she saw the cabin burning. She didn't think anyone survived. You became her Nicholas."

"Oh, my God," Nick said, burying his head in his hands.

"Her husband and baby died of cholera. I think she thought of you as a gift from God. She didn't mean to do anything wrong."

"I . . . understand," Nick whispered, remembering so many things, so many times he'd felt that something was missing, that part of him was somehow misplaced. He remembered how he had hurt when the Ranger had seared his wound. How uncanny the resemblance. And then that odd connection, as if they could read each other's minds at times.

"Why didn't he say anything?"

"I think he wanted to be sure. You were so sure about your birth. He knew you didn't like him much; he . . . didn't want . . . hell, I don't know." Daniel never swore. That he did now only demonstrated his agitation. "You have a right to know. So does he."

Nick didn't know how he felt. Numb, for one thing. Completely numb. How could he not be the person he'd been all these years? But that was what Daniel was telling him. He wasn't Nick Braden at all. His name was Davis.

"Lori? Andy?"

Daniel looked down at the ground. "No relation, Nick, other than . . ."

"Other than . . ."

"Your heart."

Nick felt raw inside. Naked. His family stripped away from him.

And so alone.

Sure, there was the heart connection, but . . . somehow that wasn't enough. Not now. Not when his whole life had been a lie. He felt swift anger toward his mother and Jonathon, for lying to him. And it spread to include Morgan Davis.

"How long has . . . Davis suspected?"

"Not long, I think. He apparently saw the birthmark this morning."

This morning. A lifetime ago.

His brother. Dear God, his brother! Not only brother, but twin.

Pain billowed through him, settling deep in his gut. He'd come close to killing Davis several times. God knew he'd wanted to. He recalled how Morgan had stuck out his hand several hours ago, knowing it would probably be rejected, almost was. Now he understood the puzzled looks earlier today, the searching glances. He wondered whether the relationship was as hard for Morgan to accept as it was for him.

A Ranger and an outlaw.

His hand had been digging into the earth, seeking some kind of ballast. Daniel was still standing there, waiting.

"I want to be alone," Nick said.

Daniel nodded. "Fleur . . . is sick with worry. Afraid you wouldn't understand. Can I tell her . . . ?"

"Tell her she'll always be my mother," Nick said softly.

Daniel went over to him, touched his shoulder. Nick looked up and saw tears in his eyes. He had never seen Daniel shed tears before, not even after he endured brutal attacks and vicious taunts because of his size. Before Nick could say anything, though, the small man took the reins of the horses and started back to camp.

"Leave Dickens here," Nick said.

Daniel hesitated, then tied the reins of Nick's horse to a tree and disappeared through the woods.

Lori couldn't take her eyes away from Morgan's face. She had come too close to losing him. Not only a few hours ago but several times. She was still dreadfully afraid of losing him.

She wondered how it was possible to love this much, especially someone she'd once thought she hated. Part of her understood. Hate and love were both strong, passionate emotions, each causing earthquake tremors in a soul.

And her heart and soul had been torn asunder by those quakes, ripped by her loyalty to Nick and her blossoming love for a man who didn't know the meaning of compromise. He probably never would, she thought wistfully. Morgan Davis was a man of black and white. A loner by nature. A lawman by choice. If anyone had told her months ago that she would fall so completely in love with such a man, she would have laughed aloud.

There was no laughter in her now as she looked at him. Both she and Nick rode well, better than well. They had both been able to leap to the bare back of a pony, landing on their feet. But neither of them had the affinity that Morgan had with a horse. It was as if the two were one, Morgan and his Damien.

But now he sat stiffly, and Lori wondered whether he hadn't been hurt more than he'd indicated. She knew from her own experience with Whitey Stark that he enjoyed inflicting pain. She knew enough about Morgan to realize he would never give in to it.

As if he sensed her perusal, he turned and gave her a slow tentative smile. It came as close to a real smile as any she'd seen on his face. And, surprise of surprise, he winked at her. He was astonishingly good at it. Delightedly, she sensed a playfulness that must have had been lurking deep inside him for years. It wasn't very experienced, but it would do, she thought, as a start.

"Do I look as bad as you do?" she asked suddenly.

Not only was his face covered by several days' beard, but his skin was bruised, his clothes filthy, and he sat as if a couple of ribs had been cracked. He studied her carefully before answering. As always, his stare was painfully honest and direct. His jaw set, and the smile disappeared.

"I don't know how bad that is, Miss Lori, but as a guess I'd say we're pretty equal. You're going to have a shiner for a few days." Lori barely detected a glint of humor in the words, in the "Miss Lori" he used to bait her with. He needed practice with humor. Lots of it.

She winced, but the corners of her mouth turned up.

He leaned over, and his hand gently picked pine straw from her hair. "I like the way this straw got there the last time better," he said quietly.

Lori's heart thumped. Memories flooded back. His body on hers, his hand doing the same thing then, brushing away a piece of pine straw as he gazed at her with such . . . surprised wonder.

"Thank you," she said softly. "Thank you for coming after me, for helping Nick."

Something in his face changed, hardened suddenly, and he looked away. Lori didn't understand it. He and Nick had made peace. He'd said as much and then proved it by letting Nick go.

"Morgan?" she said tentatively.

He didn't look toward her as he increased their pace.

"Morgan? What's wrong?"

She saw a muscle flex in his cheek. "If Nick wasn't your brother . . . ?" he began.

She didn't understand. She tipped her head in question.

He didn't say anything for a few seconds, then plowed on, obviously at a loss. It was endearing for a man who prided himself in always being in control. Endearing until she started listening to his words.

"You and I . . . is it just because I look like Nick?"

Lori was stunned. The two men were so completely different that she didn't even think of the resemblance anymore except as a curiosity. Yet she sensed how troubled he was by the thought.

"Of course not. Nick's my brother."

"But if he wasn't?" Morgan persisted.

"Why?" she asked suddenly. "Why do you ask that?"

Morgan wanted to tell her, though he feared the answer. He wanted to tell her there was a very good chance that Nick Braden was really Nick Davis, and no relation to her. Who would she want then? He had little doubt. There was such an easy camaraderie between Lori and Nick, and though he'd seen damned little of it himself, he knew Nick was legendary for charm. He, Morgan, was legendary for something that had absolutely nothing to do with charm.

He had caused them enough pain, Nick and Lori. He wouldn't inflict any more. He would clear Nick and wish them well, though it would destroy his newly discovered heart to do so.

Morgan owed them that at the very least.

"Morgan?" Her usually lilting voice was full of question. The minute she'd mentioned Nick, something dark had fallen over his eyes, something secretive. And his question had been so odd, so unexpected.

The first storefronts came into view now, and he used them to avoid the question. "I'll take our friends here to the sheriff. You go on to the hotel and get a room. I'll ask the sheriff about a doctor." He saw familiar rebellion in her face. "Please," he said in a tone she couldn't refuse. "Then we can both get some badly needed rest."

Lori felt herself melting. She always did when he disarmed her this way. She nodded. "But if you aren't there in thirty minutes, I'll send a bounty hunter after you." It was a poor joke at best, even tasteless, but it brought a small smile to his solemn face.

"Yes, ma'am," he said altogether too courteously.

Beth waited a long time for Nick to return. Daniel had returned without Nick, had spoken in whispers to Fleur, and then they both had disappeared into the wagon, along with Jonathon. Andy had spread out his bedroll under the Medicine Wagon.

Beth had checked on Maggie earlier. She was happily asleep on a feather mattress in the amazing wagon, which hadn't ceased to fascinate her. There was room there for Beth, too, and curtains that separated the sleepers from one another. Then she went back out and waited for Nick's return. She'd heard from Jonathon what had happened with Whitey. She knew that Nick had agreed to return to Texas with the Ranger. But something else had happened, too.

A new tension radiated in the air, like the prelude to a vicious storm. She felt as if her newfound friends were all walking on tiptoe between shards of glass.

She had no idea what time it might be. She knew how tired Nick must be, and she couldn't understand what kept him away. She couldn't quiet the feeling that Nick needed her. She knew she needed him, after this day. She needed him just to hold her. Finally, throwing caution and discretion to the cold wind now blowing through the camp, she went in search of him, drawing a shawl around her.

Beth knew he and Daniel had taken the horses for water, so she started toward the stream where she'd washed clothes earlier while nervously waiting Nick's return. He wasn't there. She didn't dare go farther for fear of missing him altogether. She sat down next to the stream, shivered in the cold, and waited.

Minutes passed. Maybe an hour. She didn't know. She felt the cold, but the outside cold wasn't nearly as painful as that inside her. She hadn't realized exactly how much she cared about Nick until today, until he had kissed her with such wistfulness, such incredible tenderness. She hadn't wanted to let go, and she'd known then she never wanted to let go.

She heard the clopping of hoofbeats. Slow. Tired. She stood as he drew into sight, his shoulders slumped, almost defeated. So unlike the proud, defiant man who had fought the Ranger with every breath he took.

"Nick?"

His head lifted then, and she knew he saw her. His broad shoulders straightened, and he dismounted, leading his horse over to where she stood.

He looked down at her, his eyes veiled in the darkness. "You shouldn't be here alone," he said.

"Neither should you, I think," she replied. "I . . . was worried. Mr. Webster looked upset."

He put his left arm around her and drew her up close. She shivered, and he released her, taking his coat from his shoulders and putting it around hers. Then he stood apart from her, his body taut, nearly rigid.

"What's wrong?" she said softly. "What did Daniel say?"

"That my life is a lie," he said bitterly.

She didn't know how to respond. The bitterness was deep, deeper than she'd ever heard in his voice, even deeper than when he'd been so angry at Morgan Davis. He swallowed hard, as if trying to down a particularly unpalatable meal. "Daniel just told me my family isn't my family at all. That . . . Morgan Davis is my brother. Twin brother."

Beth winced at the bitterness. She took his hand. It was cold. She brought it to her mouth and touched it with her lips, her hand trying to rub warmth into it.

Suddenly she was in his arms, held so tightly she could barely breathe, and now she knew the extent of his desperation, of the loss he felt, the confusion, the need to understand. She wanted to say something. She wanted to ask if it was really so bad. He wouldn't lose what he already had, he wouldn't lose their love, that was obvious, and he could gain something very important. But he had to come to that conclusion on his own.

"*He* knew," Nick said brokenly. "Davis knows. Why didn't I? Why couldn't I have known my own brother?"

"Tell me what Daniel said," she said softly.

He did. In short, painful sentences, each obvious an

effort. Beth realized he was still trying to grasp the reality of what he'd been told. She wondered how she would feel if someone told her she was not the daughter of James and Elizabeth Carroll, but someone else altogether, that she was related to someone she had come to think of as an enemy.

She couldn't even imagine.

"Mr. Davis didn't know until just recently, and then because of the birthmark," she finally said. "So how could you possibly know?"

"I should have . . . felt something."

"You did," Beth said gently. "You just wouldn't recognize it because . . . of the anger between you. Lori told me how you helped him during that snowstorm, and then . . . you were so good together when you rescued me and later when you were attacked by the bounty hunter." She hesitated, then continued carefully. "You didn't have to go back for him tonight. From the beginning I saw something similar, natural, between the two of you. I always wondered about a kinship, but Lori told me it was impossible."

"Hell, I don't even like him."

She smiled. "Did you ever think about the fact that you both have bay horses, which are very much alike? His is Damien. Yours is Dickens."

"Bays are common."

"Or the same quirk of the lips." She put her hand up to where his lips did that. "Not quite a smile . . . more like acknowledgment."

He looked at her suspiciously. "I've never seen him . . ."

But she interrupted. "Or dimple?" Her hands roamed to the dimple in his chin, deep like a cleft.

He tried to catch her finger in his mouth, but she was too quick. "Even your eyebrow lifts in the same way."

He lifted it now. Her hand moved up to it, her fingers massaging the area around his eyes.

"You've been paying too much attention to him," he said suspiciously.

"Only because he resembles you," she said. "In some ways."

She earned a slight grin. "Thank you for that, at least," he said.

She leaned against him and snuggled inside his arms. "Is it so bad, finding a brother?"

"Hell, anyone but him."

"Whitey Stark?" she asked innocently.

"Almost anyone," he amended.

His arms went around her, gathering her close to him. She snuggled deeper. "He might have been your brother in any event," she said. "He and Lori are in love."

"That's an indecent thought."

She looked up at him, trying to gauge his expression. Lori, after all, was apparently no blood relation to either man.

"My . . . brother marrying my sister," he explained. He'd realized tonight the depth of Morgan's feeling for his sister, in that farewell kiss, in the sacrificial act itself. Nick ran his fingers down Beth's hair. "She'll always be my sister. Since she was little more than a babe, she always came to me with her hurts. So did Andy."

"Nothing daunts her, does it?"

"Sometimes I wish it would," Nick said. "She always just plunges into life. Into trouble, more likely. Trouble like Morgan," he grumbled.

Beth smiled to herself. Just talking seemed to have sapped some of the tension from Nick. He seemed almost reconciled to the fact now, if not pleased by it.

She twisted her head until her mouth was just inches away from his. "I wish I was more like her," she said wistfully.

"Ah," Nick said, "this from a lady who tried to run a ranch herself in the midst of Indians, who struck out at night all on her own. You have your own share of grit." His voice ended in a whisper, or more of a sigh, just before his lips met hers.

And then there was no more Morgan and Lori.

There was only Beth and Nick, and the night.

The sheriff in Pueblo was anything but a happy man when wakened from a deep sleep in one of the jail's empty cells. He eyed Morgan's stubbled face, his dusty clothes, and his obviously well-used six-shooter with dislike. Even the Ranger's badge made little impact. Then his gaze moved to Ford Nesbitt, who was standing next to Morgan, hand-cuffed. His frown deepened.

"Why in the hell didn't you come here when you first came into town?" he asked Morgan. "That's usual courtesy."

"I wanted as little attention as possible," Morgan said. "I knew these two were looking for us."

"Well, apparently they found you," the sheriff said dryly. He was a tall, lean man with hard eyes. Morgan instantly judged him as one of the good lawmen. He'd seen his share of bad ones.

Morgan nodded and related the recent events, starting with the kidnapping of Lori.

"Where's your prisoner now?"

"With his family outside of town."

The sheriff's brows furrowed together. "Trusting sort, are you?"

No one had ever called Morgan that before. He grinned suddenly. "No, but this is rather an unusual case. He quite possibly saved my life."

"Well, it's your business, I guess, but I don't want any more trouble in my town."

"There won't be. I want to prefer kidnapping charges against Nesbitt here. Lori Braden will be here in the morning to sign anything you need."

"Where is she now?"

"The Trader's Post Hotel. I need to find a doctor for her."

The sheriff looked at his face, the stiff way he stood. "I'd say you need one, too."

Morgan shrugged.

"Your business," the sheriff said. "Doc Simpson is in the building across the street. I'll take care of Nesbitt here and send someone after the undertaker for the other one."

"Thanks," Morgan said.

"Next time come to me first," the sheriff said, "and have the lady in here in the morning."

The doctor spent about thirty minutes with them at the hotel, bandaging several cuts on Lori and taping Morgan's ribs, one of which the doctor suspected was cracked. He took one look at the battle-scarred body, including the new scar on his left shoulder, and shook his head. "How and why you're still alive must be one of God's wonders."

"You're not the first to think that, Doc. Thanks." He gave the man a five-dollar piece and closed the door behind him. They were in Lori's room, Morgan having taken a second room next door. He'd brought the doctor directly to Lori, and then stayed to have his own wounds attended.

It was time to go. He knew it. Lori was grateful to him now, and he didn't want gratitude. She was vulnerable. Hell, he was vulnerable. For the first time he could remember, he was vulnerable to a woman, to another human being. Dammit, though, he couldn't turn the knob in the door. Those great golden eyes of hers were asking him so many questions, and he didn't know how to answer them. Not until he got things settled with Nick.

Go! His mind screamed the order, but the rest of him paid it no mind. His heart, his body was obeying another call, a more elemental one.

"Don't go," Lori said. "I really need . . . you tonight." He saw her tremble and thought of what she'd gone through in the past few hours. God knew what Whitey had said and done, and then she'd spent hours worrying about him, and about Nick.

"Just hold me," she said. "Just hold me for a little while."

He drew his arms around her, feeling her tremble. "You've had a hell of a day, haven't you?"

Her hand traced his chest, the new burn scar, the bandages around his chest, old wounds. "It looks as if you've had a lot of hell of a days. You don't take very good care of yourself."

"No," he agreed, liking the feel of her hand on his skin, as if it were trying to soak up old pain. But now there was a new piercing pain that had nothing to do with physical wounds. He wanted her. Cracked ribs and all, he wanted her. He had come so close to death again tonight, and now he wanted everything he'd had so little of in his life. He wanted to touch and be touched. He wanted to know that someone cared whether he lived or died.

Christ, when had that need become so strong, so compelling, that he would forget everything else? And then he wondered how he had so barricaded his soul all these years that it hadn't mattered before. Now the barricades were down, and he felt raw and exposed inside. And needy. So incredibly needy. It scared the hell out of him.

The urge to sweep her up, to take the life and love she offered was so strong, he felt himself shake with the power of it. But that innate honesty in him wouldn't permit it. She had to know what he suspected. But when she looked up at him with those damn glowing eyes, as if he were ten feet tall and three times a hero, the words stuck in his throat.

"Thank you," she whispered.

What was soaring inside him dropped to the ground, like a shot bird. He didn't want goddamn gratitude.

He forced himself away, forced harsh words, directed his eyes at the first glimmers of dawn filtering through the window. "I didn't do anything I wouldn't do to protect any prisoner in my custody. No one takes a prisoner from me. No one," he said with added emphasis.

He heard a small sigh, and his gaze was unwillingly

drawn back to her. Her face was earnest, her eyes thoughtful. "I think I was thanking you for just being you," she said slowly. "Not for any other reason. I *know* you would have done it for someone else. Perhaps that's one reason I love you."

Love. The word crept into his consciousness, warm and beguiling and invasive. But foreign. New. Difficult, no, impossible, to accept, to believe. He started to say something, but she put her fingers to his lips and stopped him. "I never met anyone like you before," she said. "That rock-hard integrity that won't give an inch, no matter what. I couldn't believe it for a long time, that it was real."

Morgan tried to say something, to deny the sense of her words. He was stubborn, pure and simple, nothing more. But her lips stopped his words. Convincing, willing him to believe the unbelievable. He knew he was unlovable. No one had ever loved him.

She must have seen the disbelief, the doubt, in his eyes. "You asked me to trust you, and I was . . . foolish not to," she said slowly. "Now I'm asking you to trust me, Morgan. I know I don't have any right . . . not after everything that . . ." Her voice broke off. Morgan heard the guilt in it, the regret.

"Don't," he said. "You had no reason . . ."

"I had my heart. I just wouldn't listen to it."

"I've never believed in thinking from the heart," he said gently.

She shook her head. "That's not true. You told me that once . . ." She was remembering his tale about that prisoner, the one he released to tend his wife and who had almost killed him.

"I learned better that one time," he said.

"And now?" she asked.

"I don't know if I can," he said, but he knew differently. He'd been thinking with his heart for the last few days—one reason he had got them all into so much danger.

Your father died because of a woman. A Ranger can't have attachments. Callum's words haunted him. A Ranger was what Morgan was. What he had always been. He never even questioned it before, never thought of anything else.

"Try," Lori said. "I want some of that heart. I think it's a lot bigger than you want to believe."

Christ, she already had it, had the whole blasted thing. That was the hell of it.

"Morgan?"

He focused.

"Stay with me now. Don't . . . leave."

He brushed back a curl from her face, the lovely face that was so bruised. And he knew he couldn't let her go. Not tonight. Not with the fear still in her eyes. Not with the love there. Not with the hope.

There was still the question of Nick. But he quieted even that thought now.

He drew her to the bed, lying down with her, his hands running over her arms, then her face, lightly. He felt her flinch once and knew that her body was as bruised as his own. Still, passion flared as they kissed, that passion that had been between them since that first kiss in Laramie. Neither of them were in any kind of condition to make love, though his manhood didn't seem to understand that. He felt it swell with hunger, but he was determined to control it. She needed safety now. Caring. Not more confusion.

He gentled his kiss, fighting himself as he did so, fighting his need for her, knowing her body was fragile and her emotions even more so after the last few days. "Sleep," he whispered.

"Don't go away," she said again, sleepily, and he realized how tired she must be, how close to the edge.

"I won't."

"Ever," she demanded.

But he was spared an answer as her eyes closed and she sighed contentedly. He watched for a long time, the golden eyelashes over those fine eyes, the honey-blond hair tumbling across his chest, the softness of her cheek against his skin.

And then he too went to sleep, wondering about the miracle in his arms.

Or a dream to disappear in the bright light and reality of day.

CHAPTER TWENTY-NINE

Lori woke up in Morgan's arms. Light was streaming through the window, and she wondered what time it was. Her body was stiff and sore, and she started to move, then stopped. He needed all the rest he could get. So she concentrated on watching his face.

She had never seen it at rest before. The severity was gone. The harshness. Long dark lashes covered those dark-blue eyes, which were always so watchful. She longed to touch that face. He'd been so gentle last night, so careful not to hurt her.

But he'd not said anything about love. And why should he? She had shot him, run from him, mistrusted him, and finally nearly gotten him killed.

His eyes flickered open, and he smiled at her lazily. "Hummm, you feel good," he said.

"So do you," she said.

He smiled wryly and stretched, groaning a little as his bruises made themselves known. "I might feel good to you, but not to myself. I don't think . . ." He stopped suddenly.

Lori did what she'd been wanting to do since she woke. She touched his mouth, traced the hollow of his cheek, feeling the rough beard stubble. "Don't think . . . ?" she prompted.

But he set his jaw stubbornly as his hand felt his own cheek, and he winced. "I must look like the devil."

She grinned. "You do."

His eyes were still sleepy, lids half covering a deep, rich, amused blue. He shook his head. "It's unfair. You're still so damn pretty."

Lori felt anything but. She knew her face must still be swollen. Her hair was a mass of uncombed curls, and her clothes . . . well, less considered the better. She stretched out against him, not wanting to lose that contact, that intimacy.

He moved away quickly, but not before she felt his response to her body. He sat and pulled on the shirt he'd been wearing. She barely remembered he'd taken his bedroll into another room last night.

"I'm going to get a shave and a bath," he said. "I'll have some water sent up for you. And then we'd better get you back to your family before your brother appears with a shotgun."

Stunned by his abruptness, she just nodded, swallowing hard against disappointment, emptiness. He stood there a moment, his eyes shadowed, dark, wary again, and then he opened the door and left.

It was one of the hardest things he had ever done, leaving her this morning, and he wasn't sure whom he was doing it for—Lori or himself.

He looked over at her. She was silent as she rode next to him. She had been silent since he'd returned to the hotel room, bringing coffee with him from downstairs. He'd also managed to scavenge some bread and meat.

Morgan had found a barber and a bathhouse and had indulged in both, letting the heat drain some of the soreness from his body. But it couldn't drain the other pain. The pain of wanting something so much he couldn't think around it. He had wanted her so damn bad this morning, but the specter of Nick kept interfering. And his badge. He had caused her enough grief and injury already. Even if she still cared for him after knowing about Nick, could she ever be happy as a Ranger's wife? He was gone three quarters of the year, sometimes more. And she'd made it clear more than once she had little use for lawmen.

Morgan kept trying to tell himself it was only the extraordinary circumstances that had her believing she loved him. He had to give her time to discover that. No matter how damn much it hurt now.

He tried to shake the thought from his mind, to discipline his thoughts as he had so many times before. His hand reached into his pocket and found the object he'd just purchased at the general store. It probably wouldn't even be appreciated, and it had taken a goodly portion of what little money he had left. They still had a long way to go to El Paso, though once in Texas he could stop at a Ranger station and wrangle some additional funds.

Lori glanced at him. She had directions to the camp. "I think we turn here," she said, and Morgan saw her biting her lip as if to keep from saying more. He wanted to reassure her, God, how he wanted to do that. He wanted to reach out and just touch her, damn it. But he knew if he did that, he would do more. He would say things he had no right to say. Not now.

So he just nodded, turning Damien along with her mare. Christ, it was going to be a long trip to Texas if she went with them. Even now, he throbbed with an all-too familiar need for her. If there was some way to . . . prevent it, but after the last few weeks he doubted any effort on his part would keep her from accompanying them. He'd never met a woman with so much damn determination, so much grit. Any other woman would be swooning in bed for weeks after what she'd suffered last night with Whitey.

A brightly painted wagon soon became visible through some trees. Lori prompted her mare into a gallop, and Morgan followed behind, watching as she came to a stop and dismounted, taking quick steps to a striking looking woman standing next to a fire with Jonathon Braden. Morgan stopped, watching as she hugged the woman and then Jonathon, and feeling like the outsider he'd always been.

Suddenly, Nick appeared on foot next to him, his face inscrutable as it had been the first days of his capture, before the simmering anger and hostility had taken over. But something was different about him, perhaps in the very controlled rigidity of his features.

"We need to talk," he said, and his voice was strained. Tense.

Morgan nodded and dismounted, tying Damien to a sturdy scrub. He found himself falling in step with Nick, allowing him to lead them away from the camp to the banks of a river. Cottonwoods and pines crowded the bank, and Nick found one, leaning against it as Morgan had so many times as he'd watched Nick and Lori. Now Nick studied him with an intensity that told him Nick knew, or suspected, they might be brothers.

Daniel!

Nick suddenly turned away, picked up a stone, and skipped it across the water, watching the circle form and then fade away. "I feel like that circle," he said suddenly. "There and then not there." He turned to Morgan, and his eyes were no longer inscrutable. They were filled with a kind of pain Morgan knew he couldn't understand. But he felt it. Just as he had felt so many other things with Nick. A stabbing loneliness, bewilderment that the world Nick knew had been turned inside out.

Morgan didn't know what to do, except try to absorb part of the agony, the confusion Nick felt. He'd had time over the past several days to adapt to the idea that he might have a brother. But he'd had no identity to lose, no family he'd spent a lifetime believing his.

"You're sure?" Morgan finally said, not having to explain more.

"Daniel told me last night. He'd talked to . . . my mother after his conversation with you."

Morgan listened as Nick haltingly repeated Daniel's story and looked directly into Morgan's eyes. "Why didn't you say anything to me?"

"I wasn't certain," Morgan said.

"And you always have to be certain of everything, don't you?" Nick asked bitterly. "You seemed certain enough that I'd murdered a boy."

Morgan realized his hands were clenched into fists. He tried to straighten them, but he couldn't seem to do it. So much was at stake now. He wanted to reach out to Nick, but he didn't know how. His brother. His twin brother. And so much pain in him at the moment.

Nick whirled on him. "Dammit, say something."

"What?" Morgan said quietly. "That I've gained something, and you feel you've lost a lot? That I have the best of the bargain?"

Nick stared at him, the confusion in his eyes deepening as the words seeped into his consciousness. "You're . . ."

"Damn . . . happy," Morgan said. He hesitated, not knowing whether Nick wanted to hear what Morgan needed to say. "And proud."

"Of an outlaw? A man with a price on his head?" The words were flung out, a bitter challenge after weeks of frustration.

Morgan heard his own sigh, and he wished he had the gift of words to say what was in his heart, that he'd learned days, even weeks, ago that Nick was a good man. Loyal. Decent. Courageous. A man anyone would be proud to call brother.

And in the past weeks he had treated Nick little better than a vicious animal. Perhaps because of his own bewildering responses to the man, he'd given him even less consideration than most prisoners. And now Morgan didn't know how to right things, to explain. Hell, there was no explanation. But he felt compelled to try. "I think . . . that from the beginning I sensed, maybe even knew, there was something so familiar about you . . . that, Christ, I don't know," Morgan said, and turned away. "What you said yesterday . . . at the spring. About missing something. I've always felt the same. I thought maybe it was because I never had any kind of family, but now I realize that it was you. . . ."

He stopped. "God help me, I know you hate the whole damn idea. I . . . don't blame you. I put you through hell and I understand . . ."

He started to walk away.

"Morgan." Nick's voice stopped him.

It was the first time Nick had ever called him by his given name. Morgan turned around, waiting. He expected a blow, not the question that came.

"When you . . . said you wanted to help, days ago, did you suspect anything then?"

"No," Morgan said. "I just knew then you'd never shoot an unarmed man, much less a boy. I didn't see that birthmark until yesterday."

Nick was silent for a long time, then said with a wry quirk of his lips, "It'll take some getting used to, this idea of having a . . . twin who's a lawman."

Morgan stood absolutely still, wondering whether he had heard correctly.

"It will probably take you longer," Nick continued, his smile spreading, "to get used to having a somewhat lawless family. You get all of us, you know." Mischief shaded his words.

Morgan's gaze met Nick's. He wondered if his own eyes were clouded, even a little wet, with the same emotions as Nick's. He felt almost overcome by them, by wonder and discovery and something he couldn't name. He held out his hand, and Nick took it, clasping it firmly, needing no words as differences drained away.

Morgan was the first to let go, and he hunted in his pocket, bringing out the object he'd purchased in Pueblo. He tossed it to Nick, who caught it easily and grinned as he fingered the harmonica in his hands.

"I thought you hated that harmonica."

"I did," Morgan said. "You enjoyed taunting me with that damn thing."

"My one weapon," Nick said soberly, remembering those first bitter days, but then he tried a couple of notes and smiled his thanks. Morgan realized his . . . brother, his . . . twin was also having difficulty in saying much. But then Nick's smile disappeared. "Lori? Does she have any idea?"

Morgan shook his head.

"Damn," Nick said. "I don't know now whether to be indignant about my sister or . . . give you brotherly advice." He looked at Morgan speculatively. "I wonder which of us is the elder."

Morgan found himself chuckling. It had a rusty sound to it. "I think it's probably better if we don't know."

Nick nodded his agreement, then his brows furrowed together. "*What* about Lori?"

Morgan had never shared his thoughts with anyone before. He didn't know if he could, even now. "Are my intentions honorable?"

"Something like that."

"I . . . wonder if maybe something of what she thinks she feels is just because of . . . my resemblance to you."

Nick stared at him, then smiled. "That cursed nobility again, huh? That's going to be hard to stomach on a regular basis. Lori and I will always be brother and sister, Morgan, no matter what. And you and I, for whatever reasons, are different enough that she sure as hell couldn't mistake you for me, or vice versa. For some indecipherable reason, she fell in love with you, not your face." His smile widened into a grin. "And I have a girl of my own as soon as you get my name cleared. *Our* name cleared."

Morgan felt as if he had just been given the moon, and a shot at the stars, in one gift. It was the first gift he remembered, but it made up for all the ones he'd missed. Christ, it was all too much. A brother. And . . . perhaps Lori. Words stuck in his throat, crowded his heart.

He could merely nod and turn away, feeling the presence of Nick next to him, hearing his low voice. "We'll work it out, Morgan. Some way. It sure isn't going to be easy, not after all these years, not after the past month, not for either of us, but last night was one hell of a beginning."

"You'd make a damn good Ranger," Morgan said.

"Oh, no," Nick replied. "All I've ever wanted was a home, a ranch to work." He hesitated. "Have you ever thought about . . . giving up rangering?"

Morgan shook his head. "It's all I know, all I've ever known. My . . . our father . . ."

Pain suddenly reflected in Nick's eyes, and Morgan understood the uncertainty and confusion roiling around in him. To learn you're not who you thought you were had to be painful. And he felt that hurting, just as he'd felt that knife that had penetrated Nick days ago. He experienced Nick's bewilderment, loss, even as a quiet exultation flowed through Morgan.

Nick sighed. "Sometime I would like to hear everything you know. But . . . not now. I'm still trying to make sense of . . ." He stopped. "I think we'd better get back. Lori . . . I'm sure she knows now and is probably going crazy. I'm surprised she's not here, trying to protect one or the other of us." He shook his head. "She's had a rough time lately with her loyalties."

Morgan stopped, stared at him.

Nick shook his head. "Didn't you know? She begged me to trust you, but I was just too damn angry. I knew she was in love with you, I knew it since I saw you two kissing at the cabin. Lori's . . . well, Lori's never been interested in a man before, not seriously. I'd never seen that look in her eyes, the way they followed your every damn step. It practically killed her to take my side against yours, but she felt . . . she had to. I didn't make things easier," he said wryly, "even when I saw how it was tearing her apart."

Morgan took a deep breath. So she had trusted him, after all. It had been Nick who'd hesitated.

He nodded.

"Morgan?" Nick's voice was hesitant. "Don't blame my mother. She didn't know you were alive."

"I won't. I'm just grateful she saved your life. And it had to take . . . a great deal of courage to tell what happened after all these years."

Nick gave him a lazy, grateful smile. "Maybe you won't be too hard to get used to, after all."

Lori sat there, disbelieving, as Daniel told her and Andrew about Nick and Morgan.

Her mother sat quietly listening, great weariness and sadness in her eyes. Lori kept looking at her, as if seeking reassurance that what she was hearing was truth. Her mother looked years older, but she nodded occasionally as she listened to words she'd said earlier.

When Daniel mentioned that Morgan had seen the birthmark a day earlier and had suspected that he and Nick might be brothers, Lori felt betrayed, hurt, angry. Morgan had mentioned none of it to her last night. He'd been so quiet, so withdrawn, even when he had held her, just as he had been during so much of the first part of their journey.

She hurt for Nick. She hurt for her mother. She hurt for herself, though she knew Nick would always be her brother, no matter what. Yet it had to be devastating for him to learn after all these years that he'd been born to someone else, that he had a living brother. Especially a man he'd hated so fiercely.

And Morgan. Dear God. She remembered his telling her about growing up. No family. No one to love, or to love him. Now to learn that all this time he had a brother—not only a brother, but a twin. It must have been excruciatingly painful, but he had not told her. He'd never told her much of anything. He had never asked her for much, either, only trust, and she had thrown that in his face by running away and setting up another ambush for him. And yet he had come after her, had risked his life for her and for Nick.

Why didn't you say anything? she wondered. But she knew. She'd given him no reason to trust her, no reason to confide in her. So he'd been silent last night, even as he'd tried to comfort her in that quiet, even way he had.

Andy was asking a dozen questions, but Lori had none. Her eyes met Beth's, and she saw the sympathy in them. She rose and walked over to her, and Beth took her cold hands in her own.

"Nick told me last night," Beth said. "I think he's come to terms with it."

"Morgan didn't say anything," Lori said stiffly.

"Nick was sure. Morgan wasn't," Beth said softly, casting a possessive look down at Maggie, who was playing quietly with a doll in the grass.

Lori looked down at her dress, chosen with such care an hour ago. She had changed clothes quickly after Morgan had left with Nick, putting on a clean dress from the trunk she'd left in the wagon when she'd gone north with Nick. She'd brushed her hair until it shone and had come out to wait for Morgan, when Jonathon and Daniel said there was something she and Andy should know.

Now she felt awkward and foolish. She had told Morgan last night she loved him, and he hadn't replied. And he'd been almost curt this morning, in a hurry to leave the bed they'd shared, in a hurry to leave her. And he'd not said anything to her about Nick. That hurt worst of all. Something that important to Morgan, that important to all three of them, and he hadn't even mentioned it.

"They're coming," Beth said.

Lori looked up and drew a long breath. They had both shaved this morning—Morgan and Nick—and, as they stood together, the resemblance between them seemed more incredible than ever. Even she had to look twice to tell which was which. Nick's hair was longer, and he wore his holster on the left. Morgan's smile was more guarded, his face more weathered. Until now their antipathy toward each other had somehow separated them; now it was gone.

Lori went over to Nick first. He gave her that familiar mischievous smile, the fun-loving glint back in his blue eyes. "You know?"

She nodded her head.

"Hell of a thing, isn't it?" he asked.

Lori nodded again.

He leaned down and hugged her tight. "You'll always be my Button, you know."

She winced at the child's nickname. "You'll always be my big brother."

"Damn right," he said. His gaze wandered over to his double and back to Lori, and the smile disappeared as he evidently saw her unhappiness. "Ah, hell," Nick said, "I don't know who to be brotherly to." He glared at Morgan. "Do you always have to be so damn uncompromising?"

Morgan regarded him warily.

"Then tell her you love her, for God's sake," Nick said in an irritated voice. "I'm not much good at wielding shotguns, especially at a newfound twin."

Lori felt her face flush, but she managed to meet Morgan's gaze directly. His was searching. She answered in the only way she knew, with her heart. She was handing it to him. It was all there in her face.

He smiled suddenly, and Lori felt as if a stormy sky had just opened up and revealed a glorious sun. "I think I'd better do what I'm told, Miss Lori," he said, then looked at Nick. "But in private."

He took Lori's hand, leading her first to Fleur Braden. Jonathon and Daniel immediately moved over to her as if to protect. But Morgan merely reached out his free hand and took Fleur's. "Thank you for helping my mother. Thank you for taking care of Nick so well, and thank you for being courageous enough to give him back to me. I know it must have been . . . very difficult after all these years."

Her eyes glittered with tears. Jonathon cleared his throat, but his voice was somewhat raspy when he finally spoke. "Nick's family is our family. You belong here now, too."

"Thank you," Morgan said simply. He turned back to Lori and smiled. A heartbreakingly open smile. And Lori knew she would follow him anywhere. She no longer doubted he had a heart, and she knew now it was the stubbornly forever kind.

"I love you." Morgan said the words as if they were precious gems, each to be handled very, very carefully.

It had taken him nearly the whole day to say them, because it had taken that long for him to do it privately. But they had finally broken away after dinner, and he had taken her for a walk along the riverbank. The moon was a little larger, a little brighter, and it reflected in the swift, running water of the river. He had suddenly stopped and rubbed his fingers along the contours of her face. And then he'd said the words he'd promised to say.

"I'm sorry about this morning," he said. "It was so damned hard to leave you, but . . . I had to know about Nick first. I kept thinking that maybe you . . . if he wasn't your brother . . ." Morgan was stammering like a schoolboy who didn't know his lesson. "Christ, I don't know what I thought. I don't think I've had a logical thought since I met you."

Lori laughed ruefully. "You didn't show it. I've never met anyone so deliberately careful."

"Self-defense," he said with a wry smile.

"Why didn't you tell me what you suspected about Nick?"

"You were gone, and then . . . all hell broke loose."

"But . . . last night . . . ?"

"I wasn't sure. And I thought he should know first."

She stretched up on her tiptoes, kissing him slowly, lingeringly, feeling his lips hard against hers. She felt his arms go around her, clasp her tightly as if he were afraid she would disappear.

Her hands went up to his neck, playing with the thick hair. He still smelled of soap from this morning, and some seductively masculine scent that the barber had apparently used. The kiss changed from light and loving to greedy, each seeking more and more of the other, his tongue invading her mouth and hers responding to its sensuous wanderings. She needed him so badly, and that aching, yearning hunger stirred inside her again.

He finally pulled away. "I have so damn little to offer you, Lori."

"I don't care."

"I do," he said. He pulled far enough away so that he could look at her. "I'm a Ranger, Lori. The pay's poor. It's sufficient for a single man, and I have some money saved, but it's barely adequate for two. I'm gone most of the year. The life is hell on wives." The last words were ragged, and Lori realized he had thought of this before. "Dammit, Rangers have no business marrying. Love, contentment takes away the edge. It gets them killed. It makes widows. I don't want that for you."

Lori's happiness seeped away, and a chill started to replace the warmth inside. She knew she would accept any life with him. But could she endanger him? You can leave the Rangers, she wanted to say, but she couldn't. She knew him well now, knew how much the Texas Rangers were steeped in him. It wasn't just a job to him, it was who he was. She couldn't change such an elemental part of him. He would eventually hate her if she tried.

"We'll work it out," she said fiercely. "Someway we will."

Nick's words. *We'll work it out.* Morgan wondered whether he would ever have the same optimism the Braden clan had. He wanted to. God, how he wanted to. He wanted to think he and Lori had a future. Children. He closed his eyes as the image rambled around his mind with unexpected impact. A longing, deeper even than any he'd ever felt, stabbed through him like a jagged knife. Children with Lori. Children to raise as they should be. With love. Could he ever offer that? Love? Security? Safety?

Or would he leave orphans?

He felt the cry of pain deep in his throat. He wasn't aware, however, that it reached the air until he saw Lori's face, the mixture of compassion and grief and fear on it. Desperately, he reached for her, clasping her as a choking man struggling for air. She was that important to him now. As essential to him as breathing.

"I love you," she whispered. "I'll never love anyone else like this. No matter what, I'll always love you."

The words, instead of a balm, only deepened his agony. He felt ripped apart. He knew he should leave, leave now, but he couldn't, not when she was so near, not when she offered everything she had. He'd never known that kind of giving. He'd never been presented with a heart before, had never felt loved, wanted, and it was irresistible. He had been empty so long. So . . . alone. All his life.

Knowing he was doing the worst thing he'd ever done, the most despicable, he lowered his head and his lips met hers in mindless desperation. Her response was equally as desperate, as needy, and yet there was a sweetness in it he'd never felt before, in the way her lips gentled and her hands, her fingers, touched him. Physical need was there, it had always been there between them, but this was something so new and miraculous, so compelling, that he felt as if she had somehow reached inside and embraced his soul, wrapping his heart in tenderness and understanding. She loved him for what he was, what she knew him to be, and she told him that by not asking him to be something else.

We'll work it out. For the first time he felt her optimism, shaded only by the residue of caution he feared would always be with him. How could anything this fine not be right, not be *meant*?

And then her body was next to his, and even through their clothes, there was communion. He stopped thinking altogether. He was lost in those splendid eyes of hers, lost in the silkiness of her hair, the smoothness of her skin. He felt her fingers touch his face as if they were memorizing each plane, etching every part of him into her being. And then the two of them were sliding downward, to their knees, kneeling together as their lips met again, exchanging wonders.

He felt her hands against his skin as his shirt came off, then her dress, and his hands went under her chemise, touching the already erect, hard nipples. He went slowly this time, his hands loving, seducing until she cried out to him, and when he entered her, he knew a depth of feeling, of love, that he never knew existed.

It was exquisitely painful, so powerful were their reactions to each other, so tender as to make him weep inside. As they climbed to fulfillment, the physical sensations became so much more, a sharing of self and joy that magnified every tremor of pleasure until Morgan wondered how anyone could withstand such magnificence.

And then he understood exactly how much magnificence one could tolerate as the world he knew exploded and was replaced by a totally new shining one.

CHAPTER THIRTY

Thirty minutes after arriving at the El Paso headquarters of Morgan's Ranger company, Lori knew she would never underestimate Morgan again. She should have known he never would have suggested he could help Nick if he had not been sure in his mind that he could.

Ira Langford, captain of Morgan's company, was a laconic man whose eyes studied, weighed, and judged before he spoke, and even then his words were sparse. Like Morgan's. Lori wondered whether all Rangers were like that, and it was a sobering thought if she was ever to live among them.

It had been a long, fast, wearying journey from Pueblo, but unmarked by the hostility of the one through Colorado. There was, instead, a cautious companionship between Morgan and Nick, a growing trust that still had a long way to go to be complete. But where there had been dread before, there was hope waiting at the end of this trip.

They had left Pueblo two days after Lori's kidnapping and rescue. They had all needed rest, and Morgan had said Lori and Nick also needed time with their family, to accept and even heal from whatever wounds Fleur's revelation had caused.

Lori was no longer surprised by Morgan's sensitivity. He had always understood far more than either she or Nick had credited him; he'd just been very good at disguising it under that rough, protected exterior.

When Nick had told her about the harmonica, she'd wanted to cry. Morgan had not mentioned it to her, had just tried in his own singular way to give something to a man who might or might not accept him. It had been no peace offering, no bribe, just a simple act of caring.

She loved him so, and she ached for him. Since that night when he'd told her he loved her, he'd taken great pains to never be alone with her again. It wasn't fair, he said, not until everything was settled.

Beth was still in Pueblo. She would wait there with the other Bradens until Nick returned. She couldn't leave Maggie, and the Texas journey would be long, hot, and dangerous. Their new measure of faith in Morgan was reflected by the fact that both Nick and Beth said *when* he was free, they would marry. Not if.

There had been no question whether Lori would go. She had expected Nick to protest, and he had. She had expected Morgan to forbid it, and he hadn't. She didn't know whether it was because he knew she would follow anyway, or whether he had a reason of his own to take her. He still apparently found it difficult to explain his actions. But at night, after they ate the usual beans and bacon, he would hold her, and that was enough for the moment. Nick would play his new harmonica and watch them with apparent disinterest, still not entirely sure whether he should approve or not.

On the sixth day they reached a scattering of buildings. Both Morgan and Nick had shaved that morning, and their clothes were dusty. Their tastes ran in the same vein: dark-blue shirts, dark trousers, though as usual Morgan wore a hat pulled down low, and Nick scorned his. They were both wearing gunbelts, Morgan suggesting they were wise to do so while traveling this part of Texas, with the bounty hanging over them both.

Lori's heart couldn't help but sink within her as she looked around. This was Morgan's life, and it seemed terribly barren and lonely. The largest building was a barn. A corral outside held a number of horses, and a boy was pumping water into a trough. The boy turned, and he gave Morgan a wide smile; Morgan returned the smile, tipping his hat slightly in acknowledgment. Lori remembered Morgan telling her about taking care of horses as a boy, and she wondered why he wished to stay here, why this life was so ingrained in him.

She saw two men come out the door of a long building, stop and stare at Morgan and Nick, their eyes darting from one to another. "Morgan?" one said.

A gleam of devilment glowed in Morgan's eyes. "Yep," he said. "And this is my brother, Nick."

"Hell you say," one of the men said, and then noticed Lori. "Beggin' your pardon, ma'am." But then his gaze moved again between Nick and Morgan curiously. "Didn't know you had one."

"Long story, Tommy. I'll tell you later. The captain in?"

"Yep, and he's in a right foul mood."

"I think it might be a little more foul before I finish," Morgan said.

"Dammit, Morgan, you're smiling." The tone was pure astonishment.

"Am I?" Morgan asked. "I guess it's that damn fool expression on your face."

The man chuckled. "Can't wait to see the captain's face when he sees you . . . the two of you. He hasn't stopped complaining since you left."

"Trouble?"

"When ain't there?"

"Well, I brought him a little bit more."

"Think I'll go for a nice long ride. Good seeing you, Morgan." He tipped the edge of his hat to Lori. "Ma'am," he acknowledged, and walked on.

Morgan chuckled as he turned to Nick. "I think we're in for a lot more of that." He reached out. "Better give me your gun."

Nick raised an eyebrow in question.

"Captain Ira's rather a stickler on some matters. You're still wanted at the moment."

Nick shrugged. "I've trusted you this long, I guess." He took out his gun and handed it to Morgan, who stuck it into his saddlebags. The three dismounted, Lori not waiting for Morgan's help. Anxiety was beginning to eat at her.

Morgan knocked once on the door of an adobe building.

"Come in, dammit," a voice roared out, and Lori was beginning to understand where all Morgan's cussing came from. Morgan gave her a reassuring wink and opened the door, allowing Nick to go in first, his hand holding Lori back with him.

"Davis, goddammit. Where in the thunderation have you been? Should have been back weeks ago." There was a stream of curses. "Lose my damn lieutenant when all hell is breaking loose." Then a quieter, "Morgan?"

Morgan opened the door wider and sauntered in, letting Lori follow. "Nope, Captain, that's Nick. The man you know as Nicholas Braden."

Lori saw the man lean over a desk, glaring at Morgan, then at Nick. "The man you went after? Damn." Then, "I never would have believed it. He's the spitting image of you."

"There's a reason, Ira." Morgan's tone was soothing now, all the mischief gone. "He's my brother. My twin brother."

The Ranger captain slowly sat down as he studied one man, then the other. Then his eyes saw Lori. "And who, if I can be so bold as to ask, is this?"

Morgan grinned, and the Ranger looked as astonished as the other man had. "She's his sister. Captain, Lorilee Braden. Lori, this is Captain Ira Langford."

The captain ignored the introduction. "You want to explain this to me, Lieutenant? Slowly."

Lori bit her lip. Morgan had never said he was a lieutenant in the Rangers. She realized again how little she knew about him, how much she still had to learn. Morgan motioned for Nick and her to sit, and they did as he prowled behind them like a restless jungle cat. "You know the story of how I was found."

"Hell, everyone does. It's a damn legend around here, how you survived."

"There was another woman, helping, when the Comanches attacked. She was never found."

The Ranger captain nodded as Morgan continued. "She wasn't taken. There were twins, and she had taken one to a wagon when the attack started. The horses bolted, and she and the baby were thrown to the bottom of the wagon. The wagon broke up some distance away, and she was injured. But she saw flame and smoke rise from the cabin and thought everyone had died. She apparently walked and crawled, trying to keep away from the Comanches, and a medicine wagon picked her up two days later. She'd lost her own baby not long before, still had milk and believed the baby was, well, fated to be hers."

The Ranger's eyes moved over to Nick, studying every feature.

"We have the same birthmark, Ira. A half heart on the bottom of our feet. My right, his left."

The Ranger captain nodded. "Even if you didn't . . . I don't think there would be much doubt. Yet you brought him back." His eyes were questioning.

"He came back. Willingly." Morgan stopped pacing and leaned over Ira's desk, placing both hands there. "He saved my life, Ira. Not once, but several times, even before he knew . . . that I was his brother, even when he had every reason to want me dead. He's not a killer, Ira, and I need your help to prove it."

An odd smile wrinkled the captain's stern face. "I've known you twenty years, Morgan, and this is the first time you've ever asked for help." He looked back down at his desk through a pile of posters and papers and drew out one. He read it slowly, and Lori knew it must be the one with Nick's face on it. Morgan's face, too.

He turned to Nick. "What happened?"

Nick told him. The captain's gaze never left Nick's face as he haltingly told the events of that night.

"This has been a hell of a nuisance," Ira Langford said. "You know Morgan was ambushed twice before he went after you."

Nick smiled dryly. "He reminded me several times while he was dragging me across Colorado."

The Ranger captain looked bemused. "Must have been an interesting trip. But what in the hell took you so long?"

"I was shot," Morgan said.

Ira Langford looked quickly back at Nick. "I thought you said . . ."

Morgan hesitated, his eyes quickly warning Lori. "Bounty hunters. Whitey Stark and some friends. Made it real interesting for a while."

"Dead?"

Morgan nodded.

"What do you want me to do?"

"Let me take some men to Harmony. Lori saw the whole thing. She knows who witnessed the shooting. I can get someone to talk."

The Ranger captain leaned back in his chair. "If they don't . . . ?"

"Lori says everyone there is scared to death of Wardlaw. He has gunhands. An honest rancher doesn't have hired guns," Morgan said. "When I went sniffing down there after I saw the poster months ago, there was plenty of talk about rustled cattle, and the fact that some folks have been selling out real cheap. My mind was on something else then, but I sorta filed the information to tell you later. It wasn't until Lori and Nick told me more about Harmony that I started putting it together. I think an invasion of Rangers is exactly what Harmony needs for some witnesses to get a little brave."

Both Nick and Lori stared at him, questions in their eyes. Lori knew suddenly that she had been allowed to come for a reason, not because Morgan particularly wanted her with them. She wished she didn't feel so intolerably disappointed . . . even betrayed in some way.

Morgan straightened, looking uncomfortable. "I didn't . . . want to get your hopes up," he said to the two of them.

Ira released a long-suffering sigh. "I've been putting up with this for years. Morgan's the most closemouthed bast —Ranger in the company." He stood. "When do you want to leave?"

Morgan relaxed. "Tomorrow morning. How many men?"

"Ten. And myself. With that face you're going to need some backing. I don't want to hear of your hanging by mistake. I won't risk losing you."

"You won't get in trouble?"

"There's been a mandate from the governor to stop rustling with whatever means we have," Ira said complacently. "That's why I've been so damned impatient for your return. You're being named captain of a new special force."

Morgan's gaze moved to Lori, and it was suddenly dark and brooding. A muscle flexed in his cheek for a moment.

"Morgan?" Captain Langford's voice was sharp.

Morgan looked back. "Leave at sunrise?"

The captain turned to Lori. "Ma'am?"

She nodded, her eyes still locked with Morgan's.

Nick was on his feet. "I'm going too."

"No, you're not," Morgan said curtly. "I don't want you in their jurisdiction."

"It's my neck, dammit."

"Not yours alone. You're staying here if I have to lock you up again."

"You'll have to do that, then." They were toe to toe, their eyes furious, the old tension vibrating between them.

"Morgan." Again the Ranger captain's voice was sharp. Morgan reluctantly turned back to him.

"Can he handle a gun?"

Morgan nodded, again reluctantly.

"Does Wardlaw know about you?"

Morgan shook his head. "I don't think so. When I was there, I had the mustache and wore the hat and eye patch."

Ira Langford smiled slowly. "I think it would be mighty interesting for Mr. Wardlaw to meet up with two Nicholas Bradens. Might confuse him enough to make a mistake."

Morgan started to say something, but Ira held up his hand. "No one will take him out of my custody, I promise you that."

Lori saw the struggle on Morgan's face. She thought she understood it. He'd just found Nick. He didn't want to lose him, even if he destroyed something else trying to protect him. Morgan was far more like Nick than he'd ever admitted.

He finally nodded, and Nick smiled grimly, still angry at Morgan's attempt to control him.

"Your . . . brother can sleep in the bunkhouse to-night. Miss Braden can stay with Mary Jo Williams," Ira said. "She'll be glad for the company. I'll send someone over to tell Mary Jo."

"How are she and the boy?" Morgan's voice had softened. "I saw Jeffry in the corral."

"She's still fending off half the Rangers here. Swears she'll never marry another one, but the money's on Ty Smith."

"How long has it been now? Two years since Jeff died?"

"Closer to three."

Lori listened with fascination, especially after Morgan's voice softened. It didn't do that often. It had with Beth, with her. She felt a stab of jealousy as the Ranger captain went outside and said a few words to a man out there.

"Mary Jo?" Lori couldn't keep herself from asking.

"Her husband was a Ranger. He was killed two years ago. Mary Jo didn't have anyplace to go, so she became the cook here. She and her son have a small house. You'll like her." His voice was suddenly rough, almost harsh.

They were alone; the Ranger captain had gone outside, and Nick had followed him.

Morgan's arms went around her and held her tight for a moment. "I hate to drag you and Nick along tomorrow, but . . ."

"I think I'll feel safe with a company of Rangers," she said. "I feel safe with just you."

He rested his head against her hair in a gesture she was growing to love. "I . . . I didn't know you were a lieutenant," she said hesitantly. "This . . . job he mentioned. It's a promotion, isn't it?"

He shrugged, and she knew there was something he wasn't saying. He just held her a little tighter, and then someone cleared his throat behind Morgan. Morgan moved, but not quickly, and held on to her waist as he turned around and faced Ira.

"We need to talk later, Morgan," he said. "After supper, here." It wasn't a request but an order, and Morgan nodded. Lori felt her face flame as Ira looked at her more intently than he had before.

"Ma'am," he said in dismissal, and Lori was guided out the door by Morgan. Nick was standing by his horse, waiting.

By then news apparently had circulated, and a growing crowd of men gathered around, greeting Morgan. Most of them, Lori noted, were lean men with cold eyes and with about as much to say as Morgan usually did. Whatever curiosity they had about Nick was tamped, whether because he and Lori were around or because they respected Morgan's privacy. They all nodded politely to her and to Nick, welcoming Morgan back with few words but a hearty handshake, and Lori again understood more about Morgan.

These were the kind of men who raised him. She felt lost and lonely around them, felt as if she were losing Morgan to something she didn't know how to fight.

Just then a pretty woman stepped from a small adobe building and hurried over to her. "I'm Mary Jo. Ira said you needed a place to stay, and I'm mighty glad to see another woman." She glared at the men, particularly at Morgan. "Making her stand out here in this heat. Thought you had better manners than that. On second thought . . ."

Morgan winked at Lori. "She's a lot tougher than she looks. In fact . . ."

Lori was enchanted, just as she had been before when he exercised that rare, mischievous humor. Spontaneously, she reached out for his hand, just wanting to touch him, and his gaze met hers . . . warm and loving. It surprised her, here in the middle of men he worked with, but, then, he'd always been direct. He wouldn't hide her any more than he would hide his relationship with Nick. Even if he could.

Mary Jo looked thunderstruck. "Well, Morgan Davis," she said. Then obviously stuck for words, she repeated, "Well . . . well. Well."

Morgan chuckled. "I don't think I've ever seen you speechless before, but you're right, Mary Jo. I think Lori would like to clean up a little. Nick and I could use a bath, too."

The woman nodded, scooping up a strand of auburn hair and tucking it back in a knot at her neck. She wore an apron over a blue gingham dress, and Lori felt suddenly awkward in the shirt and divided skirt she'd worn the past several days. She had one dress with her, and the shirt and trousers she'd worn the first few days. Mary Jo Williams was very pretty, very much a lady, and yet so at ease with these hard, laconic men. Lori had always been at ease with men before, but these were a different breed from the townsmen and cowboys who'd gathered around the Medicine Show Wagon, wanting to be entertained. And she so badly wanted them to like her.

She followed Mary Jo to the small house she shared with her son. "Aren't there any other women here?" she asked.

Mary Jo shook her head in the negative, and some of

the laughter left her eyes. "There's Carolyn Talbot. She and George have a ranch about ten miles away where she goes when he's out on a job. That's all of us. Rangers don't marry much. They usually leave if they do."

Lori saw a picture on a table, a handsome man standing next to Mary Jo.

"That's Jeff. He kept saying he would leave the Rangers, start a little spread someplace, but he never could quite bring himself to do it."

"Why don't you leave?"

"No place to go. No family but Jeffry. And I don't know how to do anything but cook and sew. Seemed easier to stay, but now I don't know. I don't want Jeffry growing up this way . . . thinking rangering is the only thing to do." She hesitated, then added quietly, "Like Morgan."

"You like him, don't you?"

"He was Jeff's friend, and Jeffry idolizes him. When Morgan's here, he spends a lot of time with my son. I appreciate that." She smiled. "How I do run on. There's a pump in the kitchen, along with a bathtub. I'll start a fire and you can heat some water. I'll get Jeffry to help me in the cookhouse, so you just take your time."

Just then the door swung open, and a freckle-faced boy dashed inside with Lori's bedroll and saddlebag. "Morgan told me to bring this to you," he said. He was ten, maybe eleven, with brown eyes filled with excitement. "You sure are pretty," he said.

Lori suddenly felt at ease. "Thank you, sir," she said. "And thank you for bringing my things."

He ducked his head slightly. "Gotta go see Morgan," he said, and whirled back out the door.

Mary Jo chuckled. "As I said, Morgan's his hero."

And mine, Lori thought, even as her eyes went back to the picture on the table and a shiver ran down her back.

Harmony hadn't changed since the last time Morgan saw it. Dusty, dirty. A cow town thrown up ten years ago to

serve the growing number of ranches that bloomed after
the war.

He looked toward Lori, who was on Clementine. They'd
eaten dinner together, and then he had to leave her to see
Ira. It hadn't been a pleasant experience. . . .

Ira had known instantly that Morgan was thinking of
leaving the Rangers.

"What's happened to you, Morgan?"

Morgan sighed. "I wish I knew. Ira, I love Lori Braden.
I never really believed in love before, but now . . ." He
hesitated. "And then there's Nick. Even if we succeed in
Harmony, those damn posters have a life of their own. You
know that. Both Nick and I will be targets until the word
gets out. Even then, a year from now, two . . . some new
bounty hunter will see an old poster and it starts all over
again."

"You're going to turn down that promotion, aren't you?
You've already made up your mind."

"I appreciate the offer of a special-forces company, but
you know what that means as well as I. Always on the
move. It's bad enough having a wife and being stationed in
one place.

"You're really going to marry her?"

"If she'll have me after talking to Mary Jo," he said,
then stared at Ira. "You did that on purpose, didn't you?"

"She needs to know." Ira paced. "I don't want to lose
you, Morgan. You're the best there is."

"I was," Morgan corrected. "I was, because I didn't feel
anything. Now I do. I may not be so fast next time."

"Think about it, Morgan. Think real carefully."

"I will," Morgan said.

"No decision until we get back," Ira countered, and
Morgan knew his boss was betting that the action, the
teamwork . . . the excitement that always came with a
job like this would win in the end. He'd nodded and had a
drink with Ira. They'd been friends a long time, had suffered through cold nights and long watches, and harrow-

ing battles together. They'd served in the same company during the war. "To the Rangers," Ira had toasted.

"The Rangers," Morgan had replied, feeling torn apart once more. . . .

But now he concentrated on the streets of Harmony. Men watched in amazement as the twelve men in duster coats and well-used pistols rode through town as if they owned it. Only Wardlaw had done that before. Morgan wore his hat pulled down, as he usually did, shading part of his face. Nick, as usual, was riding hatless, almost in open defiance. Two men on the street stared at Nick's face, then dived for their horses and rode away as if the devil were after them.

Ira stopped at the sheriff's office. Morgan and Nick dismounted along with two other men carrying rifles, and then Morgan helped Lori dismount. The remaining Rangers stayed mounted, their eyes scouring every window, every doorway.

The sheriff, a fat, unkempt man, stood at the invasion of his office and started blustering until he saw the Ranger badges. "What the hell . . ." And then his eyes fastened on Morgan, who'd pushed his hat up now and moved over to Nick.

The sheriff's brows furrowed. "What the hell is going on? Which is Braden?"

Ira looked toward Morgan. "This is Ranger Morgan Davis. You've put him at considerable inconvenience. He and his brother, the man you know as Braden."

The sheriff's face paled. "But he . . . Braden's wanted for murder."

"Murder isn't exactly the way I heard it," the Ranger captain said, "nor the way this young lady tells it. I want to hear from every witness myself."

"This is a local . . . matter," the sheriff blustered.

"Not any longer," Ira said. "We have a new mandate from the governor. To stop rustling. I've heard you've had quite a bit of rustling in this area."

"That has nothing to do with . . ."

"But I say it does. Maybe this man knew too much."

"No . . . no, it was . . . Mr. Wardlaw's daughter. She was attacked. . . ."

"This might take us quite a while to settle, Sheriff . . ."

"Sayers," the sheriff answered, his face even paler than moments before.

"I want to see all your arrest records, all the witnesses to . . . this shooting. Privately. Very privately. Which means without you or any of your men. And then I want to see all recent property sales."

"You can't do this."

Ira smiled, and Morgan winked at Nick. It was one of the coldest smiles imaginable. "I have eight Rangers outside that say I can."

"Mr. Wardlaw . . ."

"I'm not talking to Mr. Wardlaw," Ira said softly. "But I will. I understand his cattle herd is growing a little faster than most. But a good sheriff like yourself wouldn't know anything about that, would you?" Ira turned away from the sheriff. "Now, Miss Lori, if you can give me the names of the people you saw here that afternoon, I'll have someone fetch them. No one else will leave town until we're finished."

Throughout the late afternoon Lori increasingly understood Morgan's commitment to the Rangers. She had begun to, in fact, since arriving the day before. There was a camaraderie, a commitment to each other apparent in the captain's immediate support of Morgan. And she'd seldom seen a more impressive sight than the six Rangers outside, their bodies alert as Morgan's always had been, their rifles resting easily, deceptively so, in their hands. Two others guarded the roads in and out of town, preventing anyone from leaving.

How could she ask him to leave them? And how could she bear what Mary Jo had borne? Waiting, always waiting, to see whether her man survived the latest battle with Indians, rustlers, renegades.

They were uncommonly · effective, these men. She

watched as they interviewed witnesses, first Ira, then Morgan, his likeness to Nick obviously unsettling to many of them. By dawn four men had changed their stories and had charged Wardlaw with threatening them with death if they didn't say Wardlaw's son had been unarmed. A swamper in the saloon had been beaten as an example.

All four were locked in the jail for their own protection. Ira planned to arrest Wardlaw in the morning and take him into another jurisdiction for trial. Not only would he be charged with tampering with witnesses and assault but with attempted murder by authorizing the five-thousand-dollar reward money. Once Wardlaw was in custody, the witnesses should be safe.

The town was quiet when they finished. Ira nodded at Morgan. "Why don't you take Miss Braden to the hotel? Take three men with you. The rest stay here. I don't want any surprises."

"Nick?"

"He stays here," Ira said, making them all aware of who exactly was still in charge. Nick was technically still charged with murder by the sheriff.

Morgan and Nick exchanged quick glances, Nick's resigned, but there was renewed life in his eyes. They were sparking with hope.

Lori went over to the Ranger captain, stood on her tiptoes, and kissed his cheek before he could respond. "Thank you," she said simply. He flushed to his roots, turned back to another man, and barked a few orders.

Morgan chuckled and took Lori's arm. "I think that's the first time in his life he's been . . . surprised," he whispered loud enough for Ira to hear.

Ira turned around. "Get the hell out of here, Davis."

"Yes, sir." Morgan feigned meekness, and Lori once more noted the respect between the two.

Morgan led the way, nodding to three of his fellow Rangers as he went, and Lori felt rather than saw them fall into place behind them. They had almost reached the hotel when someone yelled, "Riders coming."

Morgan pushed Lori down, and she had the impression of speed as the other Rangers went to their knees, their rifles suddenly exploding into noise, with spurts of earth flying everywhere. Morgan shoved her behind a trough, and then his six-gun too was out, so fast she could barely follow the movement.

"Braden!" She heard the shout from a distance as the firing continued and horses' hooves pounded against the hard-packed earth of the street. One of the Rangers was lying in the street, blood pouring from his chest. The other two had found scant cover on the porch. Down the street at the sheriff's office, rifles were spitting out their own reports, and three men on horseback went down.

"Braden," she heard again, and she recognized Lew Wardlaw's voice. Morgan raised his hand to signal a cease-fire. The street quickly became quiet.

An older man suddenly stood out in the twenty or more riders in the street. "Braden, this is between you and me. No need for more men to die. "

Morgan looked around. One Ranger was dead, another wounded. Others would die. This was his battle, the one he had chosen. He stood.

"No," Lori whispered.

"He won't give up, Lori," Morgan said. "I've seen others like him. He knows it's over, and he damn well is going to take others with him."

"Ira?"

"He'll leave it to me," Morgan said, then leaned down and kissed her softly. "Haven't you learned yet I can take care of myself, except maybe when it comes to honey-haired hellions?"

He stood suddenly and Lori started to follow, but one of the Rangers behind them held her back. "He don't need any distractions, ma'am."

Lori heard Morgan's voice, now directed to Wardlaw. "Get the others out of the way."

She heard Wardlaw's triumphant voice. "I don't need anyone else."

She ceased struggling and felt the Ranger's hands leave her as he, like the others, aimed his rifle toward the milling horsemen. Lori sat up, watching, not wanting to watch, but helpless to do anything else. She saw Morgan moving toward the center of the street, his gun back in his holster, and her gaze moved to the mounted man facing him.

"You killed my son," Wardlaw said, slowly dismounting, his eyes never leaving Morgan.

Something pulled Lori's attention away, the glint of a rifle from a window. She started to turn to the Ranger next to her, but he had moved away to where he could see the mounted men better. If she yelled, she knew she might distract Morgan.

She moved swiftly from the cover of the trough toward the nearest Ranger when she heard the exchange of gunfire from several feet away, from where Morgan had been standing. She saw the rifle in the window aim toward him. Instinctively, she stepped in front of it, between it and Morgan. Fire ripped through her and she felt herself falling. She tried to catch herself, but she was suddenly without substance, without bone.

Someone was picking her up. She tried to focus, but the fire inside her was becoming all encompassing.

"Morgan?" she whispered, but she didn't hear a reply before she slipped into nothingness.

Morgan stood, watching her sleep. He hadn't left her side in two days, and in those two days he'd lived through hell.

She'd regained consciousness several times, the first time opening her eyes and calling his name. He'd knelt beside her bed, holding her hand, trying to keep from clasping it so tightly he would crush it. She'd smiled through obvious pain, satisfied that he was all right, and then her eyes had closed again, and he'd felt so humble that he wasn't aware of the tears trekking down his face. She hadn't asked about herself, only about him.

Lori was sleeping quietly now, her breathing regular

with the laudanum given by the doctor. The pain had been excruciating, he knew. The bullet had gone in at an angle below her breast, exiting her body at the side. She had bled profusely, but the bullet had missed any vital organs, according to the doctor. She was, he said, a very lucky young woman.

But as Morgan watched her struggle against the pain, he didn't think she was lucky at all. He'd wanted to keep her from harm, and yet he'd been responsible for almost causing her death. He'd never put her in harm's way again, nor could he put her through the agony he was now going through. He was learning that waiting, fearing, was even worse than being wounded oneself. He knew he could never ask Lori to spend her life waiting, fearing.

He looked over at Nick, who was sitting across from him. He wore a bump the size of a large rock. One of the Rangers had hit him in the head when he'd tried to go out into the street after Morgan had answered the challenge meant for him.

They had become closer these last two days as they had waited, feared, and suffered together. They had even talked about the future. Nick had suggested Morgan come with him to Wyoming, help establish the ranch Nick had always dreamed of. Morgan had listened but had not answered. Yet he knew he had made a decision. Nick still needed him. The posters would still be out for a while, and Lori . . . dammit, he would never leave Lori again.

And Ira knew, had known from the time he saw Morgan's face as he'd picked up Lori. He'd even wished Morgan well, telling him there was always a place for him if he changed his mind.

Lori's eyes flickered open, and Morgan moved closer to her. There was a slight whimper before she could catch it, and Morgan thought his heart would break with the sound. "I love you," she said clearly.

He leaned down and gathered her against him gently, putting his face next to hers, his rough face he hadn't taken time to shave. "I love you, hellion," he said brokenly.

He hesitated, wondering if this was the time, but then, looking at her face, he knew it was.

"Would you, by any chance, consider marrying a broken-down ex-Ranger?"

Those golden eyes lit with a majesty that would brighten a kingdom, then searched his face. "Would you be . . . I don't want . . ." She stopped, then started again. "I know how much it means . . ."

And suddenly, the last doubt faded from his mind and heart. Lori had been willing to give not only her life for his, but also so much more. He still couldn't believe there was love like that, not for him. He wasn't fool enough to lose it.

"I hear there's a fine ranch in the making in Wyoming," he said, his voice still cracking. "Even a partner." He looked over at Nick, and Lori's eyes followed his gaze, saw Nick's sudden grin.

She took Morgan's hand, then Nick's, pressing them together. She didn't need to answer Morgan's question. The tears in her eyes, the smile tugging at her mouth, the glorious joy in her eyes did it for her.

EPILOGUE

Morgan sat on Damien, holding young Nick firmly in front of him as he looked down at the ranch house below. This was the same place he'd waited three years ago to this day. Waited and watched. But the scene below had changed, just as he had.

He had added to the cabin, and added again, and now it was a sprawling ranch house, two wings jutting out like welcoming arms.

His hands tightened around his son. Three years. It seemed impossible. He was a husband now, and a father twice over. The reality still astounded him.

A family man and a rancher. A very contented rancher. He hadn't believed it possible, that he could so completely put his rangering days behind him. But Lori had given him a future, one he gave thanks for every day of his life.

And he had discovered, in his own time and his own way, that he had made rangering his life simply because he knew nothing else, because it had been the only family he had ever known. He had made himself the "perfect" Ranger because it was the only identity he had.

He'd told Lori once that being a Ranger was what he was, nothing more. He knew now there was so much more to him. And he also knew he could never be a Ranger again. He could never again act without caring, without hesitating, without being sure he wasn't making a mistake. He no longer had the instincts of a hunter. The sharp edges had been blunted by contentment, by a love that grew rather than diminished with time. He relished every touch, every smile, every laugh from Lori. Even the arguments, sometimes especially the arguments, because they always ended in passion.

And he cherished his children, two-year-old Nick and eight-month-old Joy, who was a bundle of plump sweetness. He never tired of watching them, fascinated with every new step they took, elated at the smiles that lit their faces when they saw him. He wanted them to have everything he hadn't had, all the love and family and security.

Smoke came from the cabin below. Just as it had three years ago when he was a predator rather than protector. Three years. He wiped the mist from his eyes as he viewed his world now: the warm, inviting home, horses in the corral, the bull in the paddock. Hundreds of beeves were grazing in the open range he shared with Nick.

And inside, Lori. Lori with the glowing eyes and spontaneous smile and zest for life. Lori, who had given him so much love, whose lilting voice so often filled the house with music, whose fierce loyalty to those she loved never dimmed. Lori, who had filled every nook and cranny in him, in what had once been little more than a shell.

He watched as a horse approached the cabin and smiled slowly as Nick dismounted. He was a regular visitor, he and Beth and their children, Maggie and new twin sons, just as he and Lori were to Nick's home. They had grown close these years, Morgan and Nick, each finding in the other strengths that complemented his own.

With Morgan and Andy's help Nick had built a new home for himself and Beth, Maggie and the boys. Several months after sharing the same, but enlarged, cabin, they'd decided one of them needed a new home. Nick had insisted they toss a coin for the cabin, and Morgan had won. He still suspected that Nick had cheated, that his brother had known that the cabin held a special significance to Morgan and Lori.

There had been no more trouble from the posters. The Rangers had sent notices to every sheriff in four states hat the reward had been rescinded, and Nick and Morgan had stayed in Wyoming these past three years, quietly building the ranch. The lawmen in the surrounding areas were all aware of the circumstances and ready to quash the expectations of any would-be bounty hunter.

Andy was Nick's top hand, turning into a first-class wrangler. Old enough, and steady enough now, to be charged with returning to Texas in a few weeks to bring up additional longhorns.

Nick and Lori's family had wintered with them. Jonathon and Fleur and Daniel, and this time an out-of-luck magician who had charmed Maggie and astounded them all with his sleight of hand. If a few items had disappeared with him, Morgan had merely chalked it down to payment for services. He no longer believed in black and white; he'd discovered that life was never that exact, that living life, really living it, meant compromise and accepting weaknesses as well as strengths, in himself as well as others.

He'd learned that Jonathon's inherent decency, his compassion toward other people, more than compensated for his rather loose interpretation of honesty. Daniel had taught Morgan that, and Morgan found himself looking forward to Jonathon's visits, to that blind optimism and sense of adventure that was so much a part of him. And to long philosophical discussions with Daniel, who was god-father to young Nick.

How easily Morgan had once dismissed them as charlatans and crooks.

Nick wriggled in his arms. "Go home," he demanded.

Morgan looked up at the endless blue sky above, the valley below that held his heart. He leaned down and rumpled Nick's tawny hair. "All right, Button," he said, hearing the elation in his own voice, a happiness that still astounded him at times. "We're going home."

About the Author

PATRICIA POTTER has become one of the most highly praised writers of historical romance since her impressive debut in 1988, when she won the Maggie Award and a Reviewer's Choice Award from *Romantic Times* for her first novel. She received the *Romantic Times* Career Achievement Award for Storyteller of the Year for 1992 and a Reviewer's Choice nomination for her novel RENE-GADE (Best Historical Romance of 1993). She has worked as a newspaper reporter in Atlanta and was president of the Georgia Romance Writers Association.